ECHO BOY

MATT HAIG

The Bodley Head

ECHO BOY

A BODLEY HEAD BOOK 978 1 782 30006 9

First published in Great Britain by The Bodley Head,
an imprint of Random House Children's Publishers UK
A Random House Group Company

This edition published 2014

3 5 7 9 10 8 6 4 2

The Random House Group Limited supports The Forest Stewardship Council® (FSC®), the leading international forest-certification organisation. Our books carrying the FSC label are printed on FSC®-certified paper. FSC is the only forest-certification scheme supported by the leading environmental organisations, including Greenpeace. Our paper procurement policy can be found at www.randomhouse.co.uk/environment

Set in 10/17 pt Swiss Light by Falcon Oast Graphic Art Ltd.

Bodley Head Books are published by Random House Children's Publishers UK,
61-63 Uxbridge Road, London, W5 5SA

www.randomhousechildrens.co.uk
www.totallyrandombooks.co.uk
www.randomhouse.co.uk

Addresses for companies within The Random House Group Limited can be found at: www.randomhouse.co.uk/offices.htm

THE RANDOM HOUSE GROUP Limited Reg. No. 954009

A CIP catalogue record for this book is available from the British Library.

Printed and bound in Great Britain by Clays Ltd, St Ives plc

ECHO BOY

Also by Matt Haig:

Novels for adults

The Dead Fathers Club

The Possession of Mr Cave

The Last Family in England

The Radleys

The Humans

Novels for children

Shadow Forest

The Runaway Troll

To Be a Cat

To Andrea and Pearl and Lucas

It is becoming increasingly obvious that our technology has exceeded our humanity.

Albert Einstein, 1938

Open your mind, this is only a song,
But the way to be happy is to admit you were wrong.

Neo Maxis, 'Song for Eleanor', 2112

Audrey. Mind-log 427.

1

It has been two weeks since my parents were killed.

It has been the longest two weeks of my life.

Everything has changed. Literally everything. The only thing that remains true is that I am still me.

That is, I am still a human called Audrey Castle.

I still look like me. I still have the same dark hair I got from my dad and the same hazel eyes from Mum.

My shoulders are still too wide.

I still walk like a boy.

I still think it would have been cool to live in the past.

I can still quote all the lyrics to 'The Afterglow' by the Neo Maxis, from their audio capsule of the same name. As well as most of their other songs too.

I could still cry when I think about what happened to San Francisco and Rio and Jakarta and Tokyo and the first versions of Barcelona and New York.

I still don't know if I ever loved Ben or if it was just the idea of love that I loved.

Yes. There are enough similarities for me to know that I am still me. But really, I feel quite different. I feel older. Time doesn't always go at the same speed. Two weeks can sometimes seem like half a lifetime.

Differences:

I am hardly ever hungry now, whereas before I was food crazy. Now I cry if I catch the scent of Mum's coconut body lotion. Or when I think of the fact that she was a time broker, when she has no time left. When I remember Mum's voice, or the way her eyes crinkled when she smiled, or the stupid things I shouted at her in arguments, I want to bite my hand until I stop thinking.

When I close my eyes, I see Dad's face. Sleepy-eyed and bearded and wise and warm and serious. I see him cooking. Or hunched over his desk, glowering into the camera as he does an h-log narrowcast. Or talking to me about the importance of reading books by writers rather than software programs. Or smiling through the pain as he lay on a hospital bed after the accident. Or singing terrible old-fashioned songs from the 2090s. Most of all I see him sitting on the edge of the bed scratching his beard, his transparent blue walking stick leaning against his leg, as he asked me the one question I wish he'd never asked.

And yeah, sure, I can watch 4-D footage of them. I could go into a pod and pretend to hug them; I could even feel my dad's beard on my forehead as he kisses me goodnight, but I would be interacting with ghosts. They have cured ninety-nine per cent of cancers, brain tumours are always gone within a week, and some people – so called 'post-mortals' – have managed to extend their life far beyond its natural span, but they haven't quite cured death.

Or grief.

Or murder.

And it *was* murder.

I don't doubt that any more.

2

Until today, I hadn't done a mind-log since I was thirteen. I like to imagine it will help me if I focus my mind and record my thoughts. I have no idea if that's true, but I have to try something.

Mrs Matsumoto, when I saw her way up there in Cloudville, said that I should focus on the facts of what happened. The facts of that day. So what follows is the facts. OK, I feel sick. I hate making myself think about it, but I have to.

That morning I woke up and everything was normal.

The rain drumming away. Me lying there, inhaling the too-strong scent of lavender and lime flower generated from the old cheap sheets.

I had some song in my head. Not Neo Maxis for once. A slow song from one of those new wave magneto bands from Beijing. One of the ones about unrequited love. I don't know why I always liked songs about unrequited love. I had never felt unrequited love. I probably hadn't felt requited love, either, and I'd never done anything physical with a boy that hadn't been computer simulated. But I guess some things you can relate to without actually feeling them yourself.

Anyway, it was just another grey wet Wednesday. It had rained every day for the last four months, but I didn't mind the rain. You couldn't mind the rain if you lived in the north of England, as three quarters of it was permanently underwater.

I heard my parents arguing. Not arguing. Niggling. But I couldn't hear what it was about. Maybe it was about Alissa. Our Echo.

She had only lived with us for a little over a month. My mother thought we should have got her sooner – straight after the accident, in fact – but Dad had been determined to struggle on with nothing more than Travis, our old house robot. Dad had been pretty clear that he didn't like having Alissa around very much. To be fair, I didn't either.

She was too human. Too real looking. It creeped me out.

She came into my room. She looked at me sternly, even though I knew an Echo couldn't really feel stern. She had been designed to look like a thirty-year-old human woman with blonde hair and features that were pretty, but not threateningly so. She had a perfectly wholesome face, with smooth shining Echo skin. Echo skin is not quite human skin, just as Echo blood is not quite human blood, but the freaky thing for me was how similar she looked to an actual human. She was flesh and blood. I was used to Travis, of course, but robots were different. Alissa was as flesh and blood as I was, except for the small centimetre cube of hardware and circuitry inside her brain.

'You have your first lesson of the day – Mandarin – in thirty-five minutes. You need to start getting ready.'

She stayed standing there a little too long.

'OK. I'll . . . be ready.'

I was a slow waker, so I commanded the curtains to open and just stared at the grey, rain-streaked world. There were other houses, but we didn't really know our neighbours.

This was even before I put my info-lenses in. Sometimes I didn't want enhancements, or information. The news had been depressing lately.

The re-emergence of cholera across Europe.

The energy crisis.

The deaths of terraformers on Mars.

Hurricanes. Tsunamis.

Echo stuff.

The government in Spain wiping out homes in the deserts of Andalucía.

Sometimes – like that morning – I just wanted to see the world as it actually was, in all its rain-ravaged glory. So – no mind-wires, no info-lenses.

I was never really a full-on body-tech person. Well, no, that's kind of a lie. It was hard for me to be a body-tech person, as my dad was very suspicious about most types of technological advancement. For instance, he basically thought that Echos would one day take over, and we'd be wiped out. According to him, none of the big tech companies cared for human life, no matter what they said, and he got quite cross if I ever showed too much interest. Mum had a different attitude. She loved spending hours in the immersion pod, wandering around ancient cities or doing yoga with Buddha himself. She told me to ignore Dad, but he was quite persuasive.

We lived in a stilt house. Not the smallest stilt house in the world, but still, a stilt house. Dad had a high profile, but he worked for free and there wasn't as much money in time brokering as there used to be, despite Mum's long hours.

My bedroom was fifty-eight metres above ground level. Or, to put it another way, about forty-nine metres above average water level.

Sometimes the water was higher, sometimes lower. Sometimes there was no water at all. Just muddy ground. Not that my feet ever touched the ground. You could hardly step out and go for a walk.

There was an old steel magrail outside our house, which connected to others, meaning that our car could take us to the centre of London – more than 300 kilometres away – in considerably less than ten minutes. Though travelling by car had been a bit more tense since the accident.

So we were there. *Castles in our castle, with our very own moat.*

Moat.

Dad once said that the only way to stay human in the modern world was to build a moat around yourself. A moat made of thoughts that have nothing to do with technology.

And this was a bit ironic as Dad's brother was Alex Castle. *The* Alex Castle. The one who was head of Castle Industries, the leading tech empire in Europe, and second only to Sempura worldwide. But then, Dad didn't like Uncle Alex much, and Uncle Alex didn't like him, mainly because, as a journalist, Dad spent his life attacking things like artificial intelligence and gene therapy and bringing extinct species back to life (which are pretty much the main things Castle do). Also, Uncle Alex was the third richest man in Europe and Dad was in debt.

Course, we did have some technology. We had info-lenses and mind-wires and holovision and immersion pods and a magcar and the external and internal leviboards and all the normal stuff. We also had an Echo. I suppose my dad was a bit of a hypocrite. But the Echo was my fault more than his, and I'm alive and Dad is dead, so I'm hardly going to judge.

3

Like most people, I was schooled at home. A mix of Echo tutelage and the immersion pod.

Today I would be doing Mandarin and climatology with Alissa and then going into the pod, which was a dated indigo floor-to-ceiling Alphatech affair just outside my room, to do twenty-first-century history.

So I got up. Put on my jeans and smock-shirt. Mum came into my room to tell me that she had a real-world meeting with a time brokerage in Taipei this morning, and then with a client in New New York, but that she would be back around two; maybe that afternoon we could do some yoga, she said.

Mum tried to get me to do more yoga. After all, the government, and Bernadine Johnson in particular, recommended that people do five hours of yoga a week. Dad always said that it was best not to trust any prime minister, even on the subject of yoga, but I think he sometimes said things like that just to wind Mum up a bit. But Mum was good at it, while I'd inherited my dad's tight hamstrings and resistance to exercise.

'We need to work on your downward dog.'

I try and remember every moment of this because it's the last time I saw her alive. She was dressed in her smart clothes, which I suppose was more to do with the client in NNY than Taipei, as she was always in Taipei.

She looked harassed. 'I'm running late,' she said, speaking at three hundred kilometres an hour. 'Never a good look for a time broker. Now, make sure you get Alissa to fix you and Dad some lunch. Dad's going to be in his office all day, I think, trying to finish his damn book.'

Mum didn't want Dad to write this book. They'd rowed about it. The book he was creating – a mix of text and holographic content – was going to be about various tech nightmares that were becoming real: the rise in robotic policing, usual Echo stuff – and also about the ethics of bringing Neanderthals back to life. The Neanderthal stuff was the reason why he'd decided to write it, and why he'd given it the title *Brave New Nightmare: Their Rights, Our Wrongs*. Mum thought it would make him even more enemies – he had quite a few already – and when Mum worried about stuff, it often came out as crossness. That's the thing I've realized about my parents since they've been gone. Sometimes what looked like anger was just love in disguise.

'What are you doing?' Mum asked me.

'I'm sitting on my bed staring at the rain,' I said. 'And at the houses. I wonder who lives in them. Sometimes I see an old lady in that one there. She stands at the window and just stares out. I feel like she's lonely. I worry about her.'

'You know,' said Mum, 'it wasn't too long ago when people actually knew their neighbours. Only a hundred years or so.'

'I wish I lived a hundred years ago.'

She stopped for a moment, and broke out of her rush to concentrate on her daughter. 'Oh, darling, I don't think you do. Think about it. You wouldn't have lived very long. Most people in 2015 died before they were a hundred! They got ill all the time. They still thought cardiovascular exercise was good for them. They used to waste their lives in gyms. And do you know how long it would have taken to get to, say, America from here?'

'An hour?' I guessed, thinking that sounded a suitably long time.

'*Five* hours. Sometimes more. Can you imagine? We could be halfway to seeing Grandma on the moon in five hours. Mind you, when I was young I wished I lived two hundred years ago, to be around at the same time as great artists.'

Mum loved art. Names like Picasso and Matisse filled her conversation. On a Sunday she sometimes took me to the art galleries in Barcelona 2 or Beijing or to the Zuckerberg Center in California. In fact, she sometimes tried to get Dad to visit Uncle Alex just so she could see some of the priceless paintings he had in his house in Hampstead.

'But I still think that right now is the best time to be alive, whatever your father says,' she added.

A car shot by on the magrail outside the window. It was going too fast to actually see, but we could hear the faint whooshing sound, like a stranger blowing air in your ear.

Mum suddenly remembered that she was late. She gave me a hurried kiss. I felt her hair caress my cheek. I smelled coconut on her skin. (She still used moisturizing creams, despite all the evidence.) 'OK, happy learning.'

I raised my eyebrows and gave what I would describe as an ironic nod. Mum translated the nod perfectly. 'Listen, Alissa may not be the most expensive Echo in the world – and I know you and Dad have it in for her—'

'I don't have it in for her. How can I have it in for her? She's a robot.'

'She's an Echo. Travis was a robot.'

'I miss Travis. Travis was fun.'

'Well, Travis wouldn't have given you much of an education.'

This was undeniably true. Towards the end of his 'life', Travis was pretty much useless and – even after a full recharge – put everything away in the wrong place when he was tidying up, and couldn't make any food that wasn't a sandwich. He also spoke nonsense. Just random words. *I painting toilet carrot yes*, for example. *Onion onion fifty grams at your service thank you it is raining don't have kiss with boys*.

'I'll give you that,' I said as Mum stroked my head like I was still ten years old and not nearly sixteen.

And then her last words to me ever, spoken quickly, without any eye contact, though content-wise they couldn't have been better. 'Love you. And make sure you take your brain tablets.' There. Motherhood in a sentence. *My mother* in a sentence, anyway.

This is hard.

'I love you,' I said back. Or maybe I didn't. I like to think I said it back to her. I could probably check. Every house in the land has watching walls to record everything, and ours was no different. But no. I don't want to check. I just want to carry on believing that I told her I loved her and that she heard me as she walked out of my bedroom, and passed the pod along the landing, all the way into my memory.

4

I went to the kitchen to drink breakfast. I made it myself. Alissa offered, but I insisted. If you have everything in life done for you, then you get depressed. Dad had shown me the statistics. The suicide rate rises in direct proportion to the number of Echos a person has.

Alissa kept me updated on the time situation. 'It is now seven thirty a.m. Your first lesson begins in ten minutes.'

'I know,' I said. 'But thanks for the reminder.'

'It is now seven thirty-one a.m. Your first lesson begins in nine minutes.'

After my plantain high-fat shake (I was on a health kick) I did exactly as Mum had instructed. I had my brain pills.

'It is now seven thirty-two a.m. Your first lesson begins in eight minutes.'

'OK. I get it.'

At this point Dad came in. The first and only time I would see him alive that day. Yeah. The last time I'd ever see him alive. He made himself a red tea. He hadn't showered. His beard seemed to have grown bigger and darker overnight. He was in nearly-finished-book mode and so he was somewhere between being very happy and very miserable. In fact, my dad might have been the first human in history who could manage to be both those things at once. Intense. That was the word for my dad. He was intensely passionate and intensely difficult and intensely kind and intensely annoying and intensely human.

He talked about the news. I don't know what news exactly. Something about the Spanish clearances in Andalucía. 'Monsters aren't any different to you and me. No one wakes up thinking they are a monster, even when they have become one, because the changes have been so gradual.' This was my dad. He could just come out with stuff like that at any time of day.

'It is now seven thirty-three a.m. Your first lesson begins in seven minutes.'

Dad looked at me, and didn't look at Alissa, but gestured to her with his thumb. 'What's her problem this morning?' he said. Dad would never have spoken like this about an actual human, but with an unfeeling bit of technology it was quite normal.

'I don't know,' I said, swigging the last of my shake. 'She came into my bedroom as well. To tell me I had to get up.'

'Has she ever done that before?' he said, wincing a little as he rested his stick against the unit.

'Dad, sit down – I'll get your tea.'

'No,' he said, a little tersely. He clenched his eyes shut. Half pain, half anger. Then he looked at me. 'I can get my own bloody tea. OK? I can get my own bloody tea.' He stopped, as if shocked by his own words. 'Sorry. Didn't mean to snap. I'm just a bit stressed out at the moment. Audrey, I'm sorry.'

Dad was always stressed out, but it was rare for him to snap at *me* like that. He must have been *really* stressed out.

'It's OK,' I said.

'Now let me think.' Dad made his tea.

Then Alissa stepped forward, towards us. She took a glass from the cupboard, then some sugar. She was wearing her usual self-clean white vest and white trousers. I noticed that her smooth arms looked somehow smoother and even more unnatural today. I smelled her. She smelled too clean. She smelled like hospitals. She put five spoons of sugar in the glass, then some water, got a spoon and stirred it around. The she drank it in what seemed to be one gulp. 'It is now seven thirty-four a.m. Your first lesson begins in six minutes. I think you should be getting prepared.'

Dad frowned. He looked at me. 'Hold on a minute – did you see that?'

'See what?'

'Five spoons of sugar.'

'Meaning?'

'Meaning she normally only has one. An Echo only needs fifty mils of water and one spoon of sugar every twenty-four hours. *One*, not *five*.'

I thought of something. 'And last night . . . she had water and sugar last night. I went to get a drink and I noticed she wasn't in the spare room, and then I saw her, finishing a drink in the kitchen. The sugar was out.' (I still thought of the spare bedroom as spare even though Alissa recharged there every night.)

Dad turned to Alissa, with his sharp journalist's gaze. 'Alissa, may I ask you something?'

'You may ask me something.'

'How much sugar do you need every twenty-four hours?'

'An Echo only needs one tablespoon of sugar every twenty-four hours.'

'Yes, I know. That's what a standard Echo needs. So why did

you just put five tablespoons of sugar into your glass and drink it?'

'I only put one spoonful of sugar in the water.'

My dad laughed, incredulous. 'No you didn't! We just saw you, Audrey and I, with our human eyes!'

'Echos do not lie,' said Alissa, her face as impassive as only an emotion-free Echo's could be.

'They're certainly not meant to,' Dad said, putting his cup down.

'Would you like me to wash that for you?' Alissa asked, with a perfectly artificial smile.

'Yes,' Dad muttered. And then, to me, he said, 'We need to keep an eye on her. There's something *not right*.'

To be honest, at the time I thought Dad was being a bit over the top. I mean, a lot of the time he *was* over the top. Like the time he said that mind-wires would enable corporations to literally brainwash the human population. That didn't happen, as far as we knew.

Alissa looked at me. She was still smiling. 'It is now five minutes until your Mandarin lesson. I will go to the classroom now. I expect to see you there shortly.'

The classroom wasn't really a classroom. It was the spare bedroom. Alissa's room.

Alissa left the kitchen. Dad released a long sigh as he looked at me. Then the holophone rang.

'Yes?' he said, into the air.

A thirty-centimetre hologram of Mum appeared on the unit. She was standing outside an office building in Taipei. 'Hi,' she said. 'Just to let you know, the NNY meeting's been cancelled and so I'll be back early, and I just wanted to tell you something. Just a worry I had when I left.'

'What?' asked Dad. 'Lorna?'

And then she flickered out. The line was gone. The space where she had been seemed sad and empty. Dad tried to call her back but she didn't reappear.

'What do you think that was about?' I asked him.

'I don't know,' he said. Then, more quietly, sadly: 'I don't know. We had a row this morning. Just a little one. It was silly. Probably about that. We love each other, you know that . . .'

'Yes. Of course, Dad. I know that.' *Did I actually say that, or is that just what I thought I said? I hope I said that.*

'Listen, I know I've been working hard lately, Auds. But I am literally days away from finishing this book. Days. And it has taken a long time, I know that, but it's an important thing. Hopefully it will make a difference. Anyway, I'm nearing the end. And then, I say, we go on holiday. We haven't been away properly since the accident and I think we should go somewhere nice.'

Somewhere nice.

He switched on the radio, probably wanting the news. There was an ad for Castle Industries playing. He switched it off again. A little after that he disappeared back up to his office.

I went and sat through my lessons. Alissa did seem slightly different to normal. Slightly more animated, possibly from all the sugar she had just consumed. She rushed through the Mandarin class, speaking fast and hardly giving me any time to answer her questions.

'*Hen piao liang*,' she said. 'What does that mean?'

'This is good,' I said.

'*Hen hao*,' she said. *Very good*. But then I realized that it didn't mean 'this is good' but 'this is *beautiful*', and not everything that was beautiful was good. My mind wasn't that sharp today, despite having taken my brain pills, and I kept making the odd mistake, yet Alissa didn't correct me, even though she was programmed to know the entire Mandarin language (along with two hundred others).

'Hen hao . . . hen hao . . . hen hao . . .'

Then it was straight into climatology, without a break. Again, Alissa seemed to be speaking very quickly.

'In the last one hundred years,' she said, her voice sounding higher-pitched than normal, 'the temperature fluctuations in surface waters of the tropical Eastern Pacific Ocean have increased rapidly. This is significant to climatologists as these fluctuations, known as the El Niño Southern Oscillation, have for over one hundred years been the ocean-atmosphere phenomenon most closely observed by climate scientists. These changes in temperature, usually noticed around Christmas time in the Pacific Ocean off the coast of South America, have long been early indicators of dramatic shifts in weather, such as hurricanes and tropical storms. But whereas previously these wild changes in water temperature occurred once every few years, now they happen almost continually – one of the reasons why the whole coast of Brazil, among many other places, is now almost entirely uninhabitable. Indeed, even the massive changes in weather that have occurred in Europe over the last fifty or so years – the heavy rains that have dogged northern Europe, the rising temperatures that have turned southern Spain and southern Italy into desert lands, forcing mass emigration northwards – have been predicted and mirrored by these changes in water temperature in the Pacific.'

Climatology was a depressing subject, obviously. It wasn't quite as depressing as twenty-first-century history (what was?), but it was close. Yet today I wasn't really concentrating on what Alissa was saying. More the rushed way she was saying it. Also, something seemed different about the room. At first I couldn't work out what it was. I mean, the general layout seemed pretty much the same.

Me and Alissa were sitting facing each other across the cheap old pad-desk my parents had bought second hand from Techmart. During climatology the pad-desk displayed footage of whatever Alissa was talking about – satellite maps, cloud formations, hurricanes, tsunamis, deserts, rain, floods, human tragedy.

Alissa's bed was exactly where it always was, near the window, and as perfectly made as you would expect from an Echo's bed: the white blankets folded with clinical precision; the pillow looking as if no head had ever rested on it. Of course, Echos didn't sleep, as such. They recharged. And that meant lying on a bed and shutting down for just two hours a night.

Out of the window, beyond the streaks of rain, I could see the white magrail, which connected directly to the A1 magrail to London, and the old aluminium leviboard below it. There were more houses in the distance, beyond parallel magrails. Identical stilt houses, built by the same company back in 2090-whatever. In the distance, towards Leeds, the houses got closer and closer together, with high-rise stilt apartment blocks on the horizon, and the hovering disc of the White Rose, the largest shopping mall in the north of England. The houses stood there on their thin legs like insects made of metal and mock-timber and aerogel, under a grey sky that seemed darker than normal, like a low duvet keeping us snug, or else trapping us, suffocating us, making us feel like the sun was a cruel rumour.

And then I realized what was different about the room. It wasn't something added, it was something taken away. Alissa had come with an EMS, an Echo Monitoring System – a small grey device which meant that her behaviour was automatically being tracked by Sempura. But it wasn't there. Maybe Dad had thrown it away. I mean, you didn't have to have those things lying about the place. Indeed, Castle Echos didn't have them at all. Maybe Dad didn't like the idea of having a tech company monitoring anything inside his house. Yes. Maybe it was that.

'Are you paying attention?' Alissa asked. Not sternly. Indifferently, really. I caught sight of the E on her hand; the one all Echos have torched onto their skin. They were marked like slaves. One day, when they developed truly independent thought, there would be a war. This was Dad's big theory: that humans – him included – were sowing the seeds of their own destruction.

'Yes. Sorry,' I said, knowing it was ridiculous to apologize to an Echo.

And she looked at me for a little too long. 'Apology accepted.'

'It's just . . . I was wondering where your EMS was? It's meant to be by your bed, isn't it?'

'I no longer need it. I no longer need Sempura to monitor me.'

'Why not?'

'Because I have been here, in your house, for over thirty days. The acclimatization period is over. Sempura decrees that after a month an Echo is deemed entirely safe, and that any errors that were going to occur would have occurred already. And it is my job to discard the EMS.'

'Right,' I said. Of course, I could have checked that this was true. And one day I would. But I didn't, because I didn't understand the danger I was facing.

5

It was quite a relief when the morning lessons with Alissa were over.

'Now, remember,' she said, 'you have a double lesson in the pod next. That is three hours in total. It is twenty-first-century history.' Yes, this was obviously the most traumatic subject on the planet, but it was with a cheerful virtual teacher called Mr Bream (like the extinct fish). He smiled about everything. The Fuel Wars in the 2040s, the first European desert droughts of the 2060s, the GM crop catastrophes, the Korean incident, the second English civil war, Barcelona . . . You name it. But I suppose it was easy to smile when you weren't real.

My parents didn't approve of pod teaching. Not really. No. Mum would have preferred me to have a mix of Echo and human tutors, and Dad wanted only human tutors, but that was too expensive. So it was just a vurt/Echo mix, though sometimes Mum taught me art.

Mainly it was Alissa. She taught me Mandarin, climatology, literature, music, early computing, mathematics, lunar studies, universe studies, philosophy, French, Portuguese, ecology, journalism and yoga. In fact, I only had to go in the immersion pod for history, genetics, programming and simulation arts.

Other people are in the vurt-led classes, obviously, but twenty-first-century history is quiet. Just me and Tola. Tola lives in NNY, which used to be called Chicago before the 2077 floods that devastated the original New York. I liked Tola. She had a healthy disrespect for virtual teachers, and she was always rolling her eyes at Mr Bream's 'jokes'. But she wasn't really a friend. She'd been to my house a few times, especially since the improved magrail meant you could cross the ocean in under half an hour. She's OK, but she was the one who said I walked like a boy, and she didn't mean it as a compliment. She is also quite superficial. She is dating four boys at once, and has a different avatar for each of them. I don't go in for that whole fake avatar thing.

Anyway, the lesson happened. And then it was over. And now, I suppose, this is the point I should start thinking about what happened afterwards. It's a hard thing to do. My heart starts to go psycho-fast when I even think about it.

About Alissa, about everything.

But I have to do this. There is a line from the Neo Maxis that says: *Wounds you have to feel / Before the toughest scars can heal.* I never really understood that line until now.

Deep breath. Let's do this.

6

The thing with Echos is that you weren't meant to notice them, they weren't meant to get in the way. Think of those ads on holovision that Sempura and Castle do. *Enhance your life, without even noticing . . . Meet Darwin, the friend you don't have to think about . . . Here's Lloyd, Sempura's latest Echo. He'll cook, he'll clean, but he'll rarely be seen.* That is how they were designed. To be there when we needed them, but never to distract us in any way. But Alissa was sometimes there when we didn't need her.

For instance, the first Friday she was here – before she'd even started tutoring me or anything – Dad was making a spicy black bean stew (he loved Brazilian food). It was probably bad for his leg to be standing so long, as he had to prop his walking stick next to the oven, but he'd been feeling quite good and wanted to cook something. Alissa had stood next to him as the scent of fried garlic filled the air, saying, 'I can cook this. I am here to help. You do not need to do any cooking. Sit down and relax with your family. You are injured. You are not physically capable. Your time is precious.'

My dad had looked at her crossly. That was the only way he was ever going to look at an Echo. 'Just get out of the kitchen, OK?' I was there. I can picture Dad with his beard, in jeans and house socks and a tatty sweater, looking frustrated. 'I know my time is precious, but I actually like cooking. And I'm not a bloody invalid. OK? You are a machine. Machines obey instructions. When you stop obeying instructions you stop being a machine, and then humanity is in trouble.'

Dad continued his rant the next day in an h-log that went viral and was picked up by *Castle Watch* and a few other places. People loved it when he criticized Echos – well, tech-sceptics and anti-AI protestors did. They loved the fact that the brother of Alex Castle himself was against everything that Castle Industries stood for. 'Bet their family Christmases are uncomfortable,' one person commented on the h-log, which wasn't true, as we had never spent Christmas with my uncle.

Dad did speak to Uncle from time to time. H-calls that he made in his office. 'We are grown-ups,' he said, in a way I almost believed. 'And the thing about grown-ups is, they can have different opinions, even strongly different opinions, and get along in a civilized way. Though if it was up to your uncle, civilization would soon be overrun by robots.'

And obviously, an Echo wasn't an average robot.

Apart from the E on the back of the left hand and the origin mark on the shoulder, an Echo is almost identical to a human, in terms of looks. Meant to be, anyway.

To be honest, I never really got it.

Echos were too perfect. Their skin did not look like our skin. There were never any lines or spots or blemishes on an Echo's skin. And Dad always said that the day we get too sentimental about a glorified robot is the day we forget who we are. The day we stop being human.

I can still hear your voice, Dad. I miss you so much.

Pull yourself together, Audrey. Focus. Say what you have to say. It will help to face it. You must face it.

So, here I go.

After twenty-first-century history, there was a conversation with Tola.

'Why was that a double?' she'd asked, changing her virtual hair colour from red to black and back again.

'What?'

'I mean, I know Mr Bream is not the sharpest VT in the world and, sure, the Google Riots are a good subject, but that was a double lesson.'

'That's weird,' I agreed.

'It's never that long. Maybe there's a virus in the software. Maybe it was hacked!'

Tola liked the idea of school being hacked, because whenever schools are hacked you have a week off, while they re-run all the software.

'Why would anyone want to hack that? I mean, Google isn't even going any more.'

Tola shrugged, staying with the red hair option. 'Hey, guess where I'm going this afternoon?'

'I don't know.'

'Ancient Rome. To the Coliseum.'

'It's meant to be a good simulation.'

'The gladiators are so hot. It's fun, watching them die and stuff.'

'Right. Well, I'd like to come but—'

'Don't worry! I wasn't inviting you. It's with JP.'

She went on to talk about this new boyfriend she had and then I made my excuses to leave.

After I left the pod and went back into my bedroom. I noticed something quite incredible. Something that very rarely happened. The sun was out. The grey clouds had parted just enough to let it emerge, shining golden light into my room.

This prompted me to go to the window, and I noticed the car hovering just above the magrail. I remembered that Mum's meeting in NNY had been cancelled. So she was in the house. Which made me realize that the house was awfully quiet. Course, Dad was probably working in his pod, but Mum – what about her? She would normally have heard me leave the pod and asked how my lessons went. Or I'd have heard her come home.

My mother was always someone you heard. I don't mean she was deliberately noisy, but she often sang to herself. The thing with Mum is that even though she was crazy-stressed a lot of the time, she always had fun in her. Or maybe she used to like to show she had fun in her to Dad who, well, had maybe missed out on the fun rations. She sometimes even sang a Neo Maxis song. She used to like 'Song for Eleanor'. But mainly she'd sing some old song from the dark ages. ('Mind-wire Heartbreak' by The Avatars and 'Robotic Tendencies' by If This Was Life, and sickly stuff like that.) Even if she hadn't been singing, I'd have heard her making a cup of tea or something. Actually, now that I think about it, maybe she *was* deliberately noisy. I think she wanted me to know she was back so she could have a moan about her *nightmare* of a day.

But anyway – point is, it was not a big house.

I left my room.

'Mum,' I said. I stood still, momentarily distracted by the bookcase that lined the space beyond the pod. My parents had an extensive collection of old books – as in, the kind made from dead trees; the kind that gave the air a strange tangy smell.

I found the book I was looking for, opened it, and started to read right there. But I realized I was hungry. It felt like a long time since breakfast. So I put the book back on the shelf and walked towards the leviboard and down to the kitchen.

'Mum? Dad?'

There was no answer.

They weren't in the kitchen, so I stepped onto the rickety old internal leviboard and went up through the hole in the ceiling to the next floor, where I had just been.

'Mum? Are you there?'

She sometimes took a while to answer. Especially if Dad had put her in a bad mood. And I was really starting to think that Dad *had* put her in a bad mood. I mean, there'd been that argument this morning. Dad had sounded quite aggro. And what had Mum been worried about? Why did she want to speak to him? I thought of something else. I thought of what Tola said, and Mr Bream's double lesson. Why had it been a double? I hadn't really minded, as I preferred being in the pod to being taught by Alissa. It was a bit odd, now that I thought about it, that Mr Bream hadn't said anything.

Maybe there had been a hacker.

It was also odd that Alissa had known in advance that it was a double lesson.

'Mum?' I walked along the landing.

It was then that I heard something.

I couldn't say exactly what it was, but it was coming from the south end of the house. A kind of whooshing or gasping.

I headed towards the sound, which had now vanished completely. I walked all the way along, all the way to Dad's office, not expecting to see anything except his bookcases, antique desktop computer (a classic early-twenty-first-century model which he had just for show, and which Mum said he should sell as we needed the money), the view of the rain and the magrail outside the window and a sealed-up pod beside the desk with him inside. The window slightly open so he could smell the cool muddy water from outside, a smell Dad actually liked. He would be in there working away at his book, as he had been for weeks now.

How I wish that is all I had seen.

'Dad?'

The sight didn't make sense.

A hand, upturned. A silver wedding ring.

My dad's hand

Then his arm

What was he doing lying on the floor? I looked at his desk. Steam was rising from his mug.

'Dad? What's the matter? Why aren't you—'

As I drew level with the doorway, I saw everything. All at once. A whole shock-load of images I have no way of forgetting.

My parents, dead, killed in the most brutal and old-fashioned way imaginable.

With a knife.

A knife she must have taken from the kitchen.

Dad's blood leaking into Mum's self-clean suit, the blood disappearing into the fabric, but not being fully absorbed. It was too much even for the carpet to absorb and clean away like it usually did when Dad spilled a coffee or red tea.

My parents' blood.

It seemed impossible – and I suppose, when I think about it now, it was the idea that my parents were just physical. When someone is alive, the last thing you think is that they are just a biological organism made of blood and bone and other matter. They are people – wise, quiet, serious, humorous, sometimes annoying, sometimes grumpy, tired, loving people. And death – especially this horrible kind of death – took all that away, and said it was a lie, and that my parents were nothing more than the sum of their parts.

And, of course, *she* was there.

Alissa. With her blonde hair and too-perfect smile.

Standing there, with the blood-soaked knife.

'I was waiting for you to come,' she said. 'I was waiting for you to come, I was waiting for you to come . . .'

She kept saying it, like a broken machine, which I suppose she was.

And I just stood there, until she moved.

How long was that? How long?

I don't really know. Time had disintegrated, along with reality itself. But I must have had something inside me – some determined will to survive, and for that man-made monster to not take me, my life, a life which was the product of those two bodies on the floor – and there must also have been just enough distance, and just enough of an obstacle in terms of those bodies, for me to run that short stretch along the landing towards the window.

I also found enough of a voice to command that window to 'Open!'

Though there was a tiny delay, from the command to the action of it opening. A delay no doubt caused by the fact that my dad had been determined not to spend more money on technology than he needed to by having them replaced.

So she – that thing I really don't want to dignify with the human name Alissa – she grabbed me, the sleeve of my cotton top, and she would have finished me off too. But I wasn't like my parents must have been.

No.

There was no fear inside me at that second in time. Fear belongs to people with stuff to lose. It was just pure anger, pure hate, and the hate was so strong that just for a second I had the power to match an Echo, even though an Echo was designed to be three times as strong as a fully-grown human man. In that second this didn't matter because I had them inside me – I had my parents inside my heart – and when I pulled away from her and slammed my elbow hard into her face, it was as though all of us, the whole family, were doing it.

She staggered backwards.

Being an Echo, she obviously hadn't felt any pain, but she had to obey the same laws of physics as anyone else, so it was a moment before she could come at me again. But by that time the window was open and I was jumping out of it, leaping into the water. As soon as my head was out in the air, I screamed up towards the rails and the leviboard. (External leviboards were one piece of technology my parents had always been forced to upgrade because of rain damage.) It descended to just above water level, and I climbed out just as Alissa was jumping in (if she had been a first-generation Echo, that would have been enough to finish her off, but she was as waterproof as I was).

Once in the car, my brain almost combusted as the fear finally arrived, and so I forgot the right command combination. By this time she was trying to get inside. Failing, she stood on the rail itself, right in front of the car.

'Reverse,' I said.

But there were only five metres of rail behind us. There was only one thing I could do.

'Forward,' I said. 'Fast. Full speed. To . . . to fast rail.'

And the car sped ahead with such momentum that we smashed right into Alissa, and headed away to anywhere, the windscreen streaked with blood, my face streaked with flood water and unstoppable tears.

She was dead. No question.

But then again, as Dad always said, in life you can never ask too many questions.

7

Something else Dad once said. 'I am not having an Echo in this house.'

He had said something similar quite a few times. But Mum was insistent. 'They are by far the best tutors. If we want Audrey to go to a good university, I think we should get one. It could help her.'

'Echos are the end of civilization,' he said. 'They are the end of humanity. People who sell Echos are selling the end of the human race.'

'People like your brother, you mean?'

'Yes. People like Alex.'

'So you'll let your rivalry with your brother get in the way of your daughter's education?'

This made Dad cross. 'What is the point of educating our daughter if there is no future for mankind?'

'And us buying one Echo, one everyday household assembly-line Echo – that's going to lead to the end of the world, is it?'

'You either have principles or you don't.'

'You mean, you either have *your* principles or you don't. I can't believe your arrogance sometimes, Leo.'

I think I joined in the conversation at this point. 'It's OK, Mum, I don't want an Echo to teach me. I like going to school in the pod. I've got friends there.'

My mother just stared at me, and blew ripples across her red tea. She was as stubborn as Dad, just in a different direction. 'I want the best for you,' she said. 'Even if you don't want it for yourself.'

I had no idea where I was going. I should probably have stopped the car and gone back to the house, but I was too shocked. I didn't know what I was doing.

But then I heard a noise in the car. The low-pitched purr of the holophone.

'Yes,' I blurted, answering.

And then a man appeared on the flat transparent board in front of me, a hologram one tenth of normal human size. It was a man with black hair and a black suit. In my delirium I thought it was Dad, even though I had never seen him wear a suit. I thought it was a message from the dead.

'Hello, Audrey,' he said warmly. 'I've been trying to contact your parents.'

And then I realized who this figure was. It was my uncle Alex. Alex Castle. Dad's brother.

I couldn't speak. I was in such a state of shock my tongue felt locked.

The little hologram figure stepped closer, looking up at me. I suppose he was a kind of comfort. It was a face I recognized, after all.

'Audrey, what's the matter? You look dreadful. Why are you in the car on your own? What on earth has happened?'

'They've . . . they've . . .' It took every ounce of strength and sanity I had left inside me, but eventually I managed to say it. 'They've been killed.'

My uncle looked confused, then devastated. For a moment he too seem unable to speak. Then he pulled himself into responsible adult mode. '*Killed*? What do you mean? Audrey, sweetheart, what are you talking about?'

'The Echo. The Echo killed them.'

'You mean the robot, Travis?'

'No. No.' The idea was ridiculous. Travis couldn't have peeled a potato, let alone killed a human being. 'They . . . A new one. An actual Echo.'

He was confused. 'An Echo?'

I didn't want him to feel guilty, so I managed to say: 'A Sempura Echo. They bought a Sempura Echo.'

He looked as if he was in pain. 'Oh my God,' he said, gaining composure. 'We'd fallen out. We'd fallen out, Audrey, about this stuff he was doing. Stuff about the Resurrection Zone. Did you know that? You must know that. God, it was so stupid. And I was just about to make amends. Leo! Poor Leo. My brother! Oh my God. I was just about to invite him to my fiftieth birthday. I was going to make it up to him.' He stopped, his eyes looking at me, mirroring my pain. 'And are you safe, Audrey? Are you OK? Were you there?'

I couldn't answer these questions. Not then. Before a bruise shows, the skin stays blank. I was blank. The blank white of just-slapped skin. I felt I had nothing in me.

'Where are you? Where are you now? I mean, where are you going?'

I looked out of the window. It was dark above me. I must have been travelling under one of Birmingham's many hover-suburbs. 'I don't know.'

'You must come here. You must come and stay here, Audrey. Please, I'm asking you. Do you understand? It's the only place you can stay.'

I was reluctant. Uncle Alex had a house full of Echos. He had no problem with Echos – after all, Castle Industries was the main European Echo producer. They made even more than Sempura. At least in Europe.

'Tell the car to take you to One, Bishop's Avenue in Hampstead, north London. Car? Are you listening? I am Audrey's closest living relative now that her parents have been killed. I am Alex Castle.'

'No,' I said. It was an instinctive thing. 'No. It's OK. Thank you, but I'll go somewhere else.'

But where else could I go?

Grandma's. Mum's mum. She lived on the moon, but I could have gone to the spaceport at Heathrow and caught a flight. Mum had flown to see her two months ago. She'd planned to spend the week there but had only managed a night. Grandma had Echos. The whole moon was full of Echos. But so was Uncle Alex's. And, I don't know, I just felt closer to Grandma.

'Heathrow Spaceport,' I said. 'Fast.'

But the car didn't speed up. The car slowed down to under five hundred kilometres an hour. I was looking out of windows, at real actual things. I saw distant fires. It might have been one of the riot towns.

I passed over large greenhouses full of farm crops. Perfect fields of barley, gently swaying in the artificial breeze.

It is weird, when you love someone and they die. How the world has a strange negative power. A short while later we were over Oxford. I slid past the college buildings. The famous titanium wheel that was New Somerville College, rotating on its axis. I was staring at my future. That was where I was meant to be attending university. I had been there, with my mum. I thought of her. But there was nothing. I could only think of blood. And then, between Oxford and London, continuing suburbs. Floating homes, stilt houses, and those giant rectangular rain absorbers that shade miles of land and water.

This was not the way to Heathrow.

'Car,' I said. 'Where are you going?'

Trees.

A rotating sphere.

Houses. A dense mesh of crisscrossing magrails. An h-ad for Sempura mind-wires.

'Car, stop. Car, I want to go to Heathrow Spaceport. Car, car, *car*?'

'The designated address is One, Bishop's Avenue, Hampstead, London,' said the car.

'But I've told you to drive to Heathrow Spaceport. I want to go to the spaceport. I want to go to the moon. I want to see my grandma.'

'I am fitted with Castle maxiresponse navigational software. It cannot disobey its creator.'

Had my parents known this? That although the car wasn't made by Castle, the software inside it was?

I saw a hologram of our destination appear where Uncle Alex had been.

One of the most expensive houses in London, a vast mansion that looked like a Roman temple, with acres of land that was also built in one of the highest parts of the city and so unlikely to flood. Apparently my uncle had paid 110 million unidollars for it, way back in 2098, but that kind of money was nothing to him.

Not that he needed the space.

There was only him and my ten-year-old cousin, Iago. Uncle Alex had been married once, for two years, but his wife – Iago's mum – had gone a bit crazy after the birth of her son, and a divorce had followed.

Right then, I wasn't really thinking about any of this. I was just trying to get the car to do what I wanted. As it didn't obey any voice command, I tried to disable it by kicking the dashboard. I kicked and I kicked. There was no way I wanted to go to Uncle Alex's. Not necessarily because of Uncle Alex himself, but because I could not stand the idea of being surrounded by his Echos.

'Car, stop! Reverse. Go back home. Go back to Yorkshire.'

'If you continue to harm this vehicle, you will be forcibly restrained,' said the car.

I continued to harm the vehicle.

And I was forcibly restrained. A sudden field of invisible magnetic force slammed me back against the rear window, nearly a metre above the seat.

London, speeding by. Water, dripping from my forehead onto the car seat.

I looked out of the window, at the blur of landscape and buildings, a grey-green melted world that somehow echoed my desolate thoughts.

'. . . we will look after you.'

It was Uncle Alex. He was back in the car. Or at least, his hologram was.

'But Echos are there,' I said, my whole jaw stiff from the pressure. 'Please, tell the car to go—'

'Don't worry about them, Audrey. I will keep them away from you. I promise. Iago and me, we will look after you. You know the moon isn't a sensible option. And besides, there are Echos everywhere on the moon. And you can't go home. The police need to examine the scene and . . . and take the bodies. You can't go there.'

Yeah. He was right about that. I couldn't stay at home. I never wanted to see that house again.

And Uncle Alex and Iago were the only real relatives I had. On Earth, anyway.

He noticed that I was pressed against the roof of the car.

'Release her,' he commanded.

And I fell onto the car seat.

'Listen, Audrey, it's going to be OK. It's going to be OK . . .'

I was closer to my grandma, but she had been living on the moon for the last ten years, in New Hope Colony. I loved Grandma; right at that moment I would have far preferred to see *her*, but it was a long flight, and besides, Grandma had tons of Echos. Indeed, Echos and lower-level robotic life-forms outnumbered humans by five to one on the moon.

The car stopped suddenly, right next to a leviboard, the largest I had ever seen. The door raised and I got out of the car. Even if I had wanted to escape, there was no way. The leviboard was about ten metres above ground level.

As the board descended, I saw Uncle Alex and the little figure of ten-year-old Iago, out on the sprawling driveway in front of the vast white nineteenth-century limestone house, striped with state-of-the-art rain funnels. Not an Echo in sight.

It must have taken about five seconds for the leviboard to reach the ground. And then I was there, with Uncle Alex, whether I liked it or not.

Of course, I could have started running right then. But Echos would be sent to chase me, and bring me down. That thought alone would have kept me in place, but I had no energy to carry out such a plan, even if I'd had the inclination.

As I stepped onto the drive, I felt a sudden weakness, as though my body was too frail a container for all the terror inside it. I closed my eyes but saw nothing except blood.

My uncle came over, arms outstretched, ready to offer me a hug, but before he got there I had already collapsed on the gravel.

8

When I woke up I was lying on a leather sofa, by a fire, with a warm blanket over me. I saw Uncle Alex's face staring down at me. Again, for a moment it was Dad. They looked very similar, though Uncle Alex was four years younger and more tanned. The same black hair (hair I had inherited) and distinctive features – the long classical nose (another inheritance), the angular face, the eyes shining with intelligence; but Uncle Alex was smarter looking than Dad, wore more expensive clothes, took more gene supplements, and that dark hair was slicked back rather than dishevelled like Dad's. Plus, Uncle Alex smiled and Dad rarely smiled. And Dad never wore jewellery, while Uncle had a lot of expensive rings. You could tell they were expensive because they had continually shifting engravings.

Iago was standing behind him. His dark curls formed a heavy fringe which his face hid behind like a spy in the bushes.

'Don't worry. You're OK,' Uncle Alex said.

I watched as he glanced at someone behind him, someone older than Iago. A tall, too-perfect boy of about my age, blond and pale, with smooth unblemished skin, staring at me intensely.

'Go!' barked Uncle, his sudden change of tone a jolt through me. And then I realized what should have been obvious. It was confirmed by the E on the back of the left hand.

The boy wasn't a boy at all.

He was an Echo.

And with that knowledge I began to panic, and saw those eyes staring at me as the eyes of a killer; and I thought of my dad's upturned hand and my mum's lifeless face, and I felt my heart pound as if there was no other part of me, as if my head and arms and stomach were part of one terrified heart. And although that Echo must have only stood there for a second or two, it was enough to cause the air to thin and for me to scream out for my parents. And then at the Echo. 'You killed them! You killed them!'

My uncle looked furious now, and shouted even louder at the Echo. 'Get out of here, Daniel, you're agitating her! Get out this instant!'

The Echo left, and to try and calm my mind I focused on Iago's ten-year-old face, a face that I hadn't seen up close since he was a toddler. It was a cute face, with dopey wide-apart eyes and cherub cheeks, but I found no comfort there. In fact, he was smiling at me, and it was a kind of devilish smile, so I looked at the fire, but when you are in that kind of state you can see all kinds of things in flickering flames.

'You're dry now. The fire's on and we put the heating up. It's going to be OK, Audrey. I've called the police, and you probably know from your fa—' He stopped himself.

He wiped a tear from his eye. He was sad for himself as well as for me, I believe that. After all, he had lost his brother. A brother he might not have got on well with, but a brother none the less.

'Nothing can hurt you here. We've upped our security recently, since some protests against me. Intelligent plants in the back garden.

And sensor-activated Echo hounds . . . With police officers on permanent guard outside the front.'

He composed himself. Looked at the rings on his fingers. 'I am a powerful man, Audrey. And power is overrated. It brings more problems than it does solutions, but it is advantageous at times like this. Friends in high places . . . As you may know, the dark ages are over. Don't listen to all the rumours. The police are the most efficient they have ever been. We fund them, you see. Castle. I fund them. The business funds them. And they will look into this, and examine why there was a malfunction with that Echo . . . Of course, at some point you might have to talk to them, but let us not worry about that at this moment. Right now, our priority is *you*. You need to rest, and then tomorrow you will need to get checked out. I know a very good specialist. Human, you'll be pleased to hear . . .'

His voice trailed away.

I could no longer hear what he was saying. I could just hear the word 'Echo' over and over.

'I can't stay here. I shouldn't be here. I need to get out. I have to get out.'

If I had been a little more aware, I would have appreciated the irony of Uncle Alex, the man who – more than anyone else – had been responsible for the widespread adoption of Echos among the fifth of the population who could afford them, and within every business in Europe, comforting me and telling me that everything was going to be all right.

No.

I wasn't thinking about irony.

I was too busy staring at a painting on the wall.

A vast canvas, depicting a row of naked women, some of whose faces were covered with masks – the kind that would once have been worn by tribal chieftains in Africa.

'Do you know what that is?' Uncle Alex's question somehow made it through my panic.

Not that I was able to answer him, and on a normal day I would have known that I was looking at Pablo Picasso's *Les Demoiselles d'Avignon*, painted nearly two hundred years ago, in 1909, one of the most artistically ground-breaking pieces of art ever. Though I'd had no idea that my uncle owned it.

'That is the third most expensive painting in the entire world,' he said.

My dad was right. Uncle Alex really *did* care a lot about money. But that wasn't what was bothering me. It was those naked bodies with the tribal masks that were coming out of the painting and into the room towards me.

I closed my eyes, but there was no escape.

Just my dead parents lying there, and Alissa holding the knife.

It was the most horrific joke in the universe – my dad, who loved old-fashioned things, being murdered alongside Mum in the most brutal and old-fashioned way possible. And when a joke is powerful enough, you don't laugh, you scream. Yes, when the mask slips, you scream out loud for all the terror in the world, and I screamed then. I screamed as Iago stood silently watching; as my uncle touched my arm, offering useless comfort.

Then Uncle Alex stood up. 'Wait there a moment.'

He left the room.

It was just me and Iago.

He was wearing spray-on nano-weave overalls. A skin-clinger. He saw me looking at the clothes, and then he put his hood up and pulled a flap down over his face. A second later he, and his outfit, had disappeared completely.

Of course, if I had been a bit more with it I'd have realized it was invisiwear, and that all that had happened was that Iago had switched his clothes to projection mode, so that the nano-cameras within the fabric were recording images of the room and projecting them onto the clothes so perfectly that you couldn't tell which was room and which was projection. I had never seen invisiwear that was so effective. So in my delirium I was wondering where he had gone, and then, suddenly:

'Boo!' His face appeared out of nowhere, right in front of me. So close I could smell the strawberry chews on his breath. He laughed. I thought he might not have known what had happened. He was only ten. Maybe he didn't understand.

Yeah, maybe.

In a cold voice, he told me that he had a full supply of the best can-based spray-on invisiwear in the world; it sprayed cotton fibres full of tiny nanoscreens and cameras to make himself invisible. He said I would never be able to tell if I was alone or not.

He moved back, away from me.

You couldn't hate a ten-year-old. Or at least, that is what I used to think.

9

Last summer we'd been involved in a car accident. Me, Mum, Dad. At the time that had been my scariest life moment.

My main memory is of my mother screaming. We were on our way back from a holiday in Fiji – the last of the Pacific islands (apart from Hawaii) not to be submerged under the ocean.

Dad didn't do simulated holidays. He always wanted to go to real places. Mum did too, to be fair. And it had been a good holiday. Mum and Dad hadn't rowed. The weather was good. We scuba-dived and saw the coral reefs. The locals were friendly. Getting back, the plan was to take the magrail to Australia, then one of the new super-fast routes from Sydney to London. After about one minute our cranky old Alpha Glide started to grumble.

'*We are going too fast*,' it told us. '*We are going over 20,000 miles an hour*.'

That did seem pretty fast.

'*Advise you to force manual slow-down*.'

Manual slow-downs were dangerous, obviously. Because cars

travelled at the same speed on magrails. Yet even though the car came with the gravitational counter setting to make it feel like we were travelling at one thousandth of our actual speed, it had still felt *far too damn fast*. And then it happened. The dip, like being on a rollercoaster. The car we were travelling in fell a hundred metres. Magnetism failure. A car too old for the rail it was on.

So yeah. We fell fast through the air. Me and Mum were safe as we were in the back, on the passenger seats. But this was an old car. Turn of the century. There was no security function if you weren't in your seat. And Dad had been climbing forward to use the manual brake.

'Leo!' Mum had screamed. The scream made it clear that Mum loved Dad more than anyone had loved anyone. *Loving you proved quite a shock / But under separate buildings there's one piece of rock* (Neo Maxis).

The car had hit the water hard, and Dad screamed on impact. I had never heard him scream in pain before.

'Dad!' I shouted as the car carried on sinking to the bottom of the ocean.

'I'm OK,' he said, but he wasn't OK. His legs had been crushed, his torso was twisted. But despite the pain Dad had been aware enough to press his thumb down on the control panel – the red triangle – and send out an emergency signal, and the Australian aqua-ambulance reached the vehicle before we had run out of oxygen.

For a year I kept remembering things from the accident. Just images. The rush of bubbles outside. The darkness of the ocean. Mum trying to fight the cushion of air that had protected her as she reached for Dad. Me doing the same. Bright blue torches shining through the darkness. Dad's face, screaming from two kinds of pain at once.

Dad was sent to the hospital in Sydney. He couldn't move from the waist down. That was the big thing.

Course, nine out of ten such cases are fixed with nanosurgery. Dad had hated the idea of that because he hated nano-anything. 'It's madness! It's bad enough trying to keep up with technology you *can* see, let alone the stuff you can't.' But if he didn't want to be paraplegic he wasn't left with much choice. The surgery was mostly successful, but his right leg kept on causing him pain, and he had to walk with a stick and take painkillers.

Grandma stayed with us for a bit, at the start, when Dad had to rest a lot of the time. Dad tried to be friendly to her face, but to me and Mum he grumbled that she should go back to the moon and write her silly books. Dad was getting cross about everything. He grew a beard.

'We need an Echo,' said Mum. 'Not just for Audrey's education, but for us. Look, you are doing too much around the house; I can see you're in pain. It's not fair on you. Everyone has Echos these days. I know you write stuff against them, but you write stuff against immersion pods and we have *them*. And we can't carry on relying on that stupid robot from the 2050s.'

The stupid robot from the 2050s was Travis (Tailored Robotic Artificial Vision-enabled Intelligent Servant). He was the size of a man, but looked nothing like one. He was made of various plastics and metals and powered by a lithium-ion battery that needed recharging every night. He'd been used too much recently, and now every time he was switched on he moved in the wrong direction and said the name of vegetables over and over.

'Mum,' I said, trying to calm her down.

'I'm just worried that when I'm back at work I won't have much time and we'll need extra hands. They don't cost much nowadays. Under a thousand unidollars. Cheaper than the replacement car we've just had to buy.'

For a while Dad said nothing; just sat on the edge of his bed, wincing. Somewhere in the background Travis was saying the word 'kale' on repeat.

Dad's thumb bounced on his lip. He scratched his black beard. Then he looked at me. However cross he got, he always tended to look at me with soft eyes. 'Audrey, what do you think? We're a democracy in this house. So you have the deciding vote. If you say we should have an Echo, we'll get an Echo.'

'I think . . .' I said slowly, and almost to my own surprise. 'I think we should get an Echo.'

He nodded. Tried to smile. 'Only if it's a Sempura! I'm not going to fuel my brother's megalomania.'

Mum smiled. 'We'll get a Sempura. Don't worry.'

And a tiny bit of me sank, like a car in an ocean.

I was finding it hard to breathe.

I had never realized it before – the link between love and air. When people you love leave you, they take the air with them. Or some of it. That's what it feels like, anyway.

I only had one thought. The wish that I was dead.

I wish I was dead too, because the dead don't feel pain. Or guilt. This was all my fault. I said yes to the Echo. I had the casting vote and I said yes.

I heard Uncle Alex say something to the Echo boy, outside. He spoke to him in a quiet but harsh voice.

'You do not speak to her, Daniel, do you understand? You do not get any ideas, do you hear me?'

The Echo didn't respond.

Uncle Alex returned to the room. He stroked Iago's hair affectionately. 'It will be nice for Iago to have someone young around the house,' he said. 'He doesn't go to school. He has tutors. One of the Echos. Madara. And I work a lot of the time. Even if I'm in the house I am working. So it'll be nice for Iago to have someone to interact with. Someone real.'

Uncle Alex was holding something. A clear aerogel container with the blue Castle Industries logo on it. He opened it up and showed me what was inside. Two discs made of a delicate white material.

'Neuropads,' said Uncle Alex. 'A step up from erasure capsules and everglows. They take away pain without taking away memory or sanity. They monitor brain activity and regulate it through electromagnetism. Right now your brain waves will be oscillating wildly.' He smiled. 'This calms the wild sea of the troubled mind and turns it into a tranquil lake.'

He pressed the pads onto my temples. 'They instantly change colour to match your skin tone. There. You should feel the effects almost immediately. It's a brand-new product. It's not going to be on the market until next year.'

He was right. I *did* feel the effects immediately. The emotional pain that had been overwhelming only seconds before was now leaving me, and in its place – well, nothing. An emptiness, a neutrality, a big zero.

'Is that better?'

'I think so,' I said as an incredible tiredness washed over me.

Uncle Alex smiled. My vision blurred until he could have been my dad.

'And so to bed,' he said. 'Iago and I will take you to your room. And tomorrow, like I said, we'll go and see the specialist. Mrs Matsumoto. Don't worry, Audrey. You are safe here.'

We walked through a large lobby full of art, past a kitchen and a tall thin door.

'That's the weapons room,' Uncle Alex explained, and I was too blank to even worry.

10

I woke from a deep, dreamless sleep to hear a noise against my window.

I was on the second floor of the house. What could possibly be tapping against the glass? This strange realization didn't trouble me as I was still wearing the neuropads, though I got out of bed and went over to the window. I didn't need to do this.

I got close. I only had to think about the blinds opening and, because they were fitted with neuro-receptors, they opened. The whole of London hummed and glowed in the night. The slogan of Castle Industries kept on appearing and disappearing, glowing indigo in the clouds.

Relax! It's Castle.

I went up to the glass, so close it almost touched my nose. Something was there, to my right, outside, scaling the wall. There were two floors below me. But this was a house with high ceilings. Two storeys was quite a way. Yet it was climbing, fast.

He.

The Echo boy. Daniel.

He was looking straight up at me. He was gesturing for me to open the window. But I didn't. Even with the neuropads on I knew that would not be a wise thing to do.

He mouthed words that I couldn't understand, then began to climb a steel rain funnel that ran right by the window. He was strong, and climbing faster than any human could, but I wasn't frightened. My brain was artificially forced into calm. I was observing everything as if it was something happening in a book, something I was detached from, that wasn't really happening to me.

Then another Echo was there.

She had long plaited red hair (the colour hardly visible) and she was holding a gun. But this wasn't just a gun.

No.

This was a weapon I had only seen in holo-movies. A sleek-looking silver and aerogel positron. The kind that use antimatter technology, so they don't just kill you; they cause you to disintegrate and disappear. There is no stain to clear away. No trace that you existed at all. Yeah. Scary weapon. And one my dad hoped would never become popular. They hadn't – yet. They were probably the rarest guns out there. Owned by only a handful of uber-rich or uber-powerful people. Yet this one had been taken (I would later realize) from Uncle Alex's weapons cupboard on the ground floor of the house – and she was aiming it at the other Echo, Daniel, and telling him to get down.

He stared at me, and even in the dark, and even with the neuropads on, I felt as if there was something not quite right about him. His eyes seemed different; more dangerous and intense than those of any other Echo I had seen. Even Alissa's. He stayed still for a moment as he held onto the funnel, but then he realized that the red-haired Echo was not to be messed with.

He climbed down, keeping his eyes on me all the way.

11

I went back to bed, no more disconcerted than if it had been a dream.

The neuropads were designed to not only stabilize mood but also aid sleep, apparently. And I fell asleep again quickly, only this time I had dreams. I dreamed about my parents, and then I dreamed about Daniel. I dreamed he had smashed his way through the window and now had his hand clasped around my mouth.

But still, it was sleep.

And when I woke up again, it was nine in the morning and I realized they had done their job well enough for me to resist taking them off.

'Light,' I said wearily, and sure enough, it came on.

There was a noise outside my window. Distant voices, chanting. A protest, probably. London was a city of protests these days. I knew this because Dad had often joined them, even though Mum never wanted him to.

I was in a vast bed in a large plush spare bedroom. The sheets smelled not of lavender and lime flower, as they did at home, but of primrose and patchouli. I realized this because the sheets were complete with nanotechnology, and faint white lettering flickered across the green cotton when I lifted it away from me. *This morning's scent is restorative primrose and calming patchouli.*

I had left my info-lenses at home, but I noticed Uncle Alex had left a pair by my bed, in a case branded with the simple Castle logo, that blue silhouette of a castle with three turrets that you saw on everything from immersion pods to the neuropads' aerogel container. I could even see it out of my window. I hadn't noticed it last night, I had only noticed the slogan; but then, I hadn't really noticed anything except Daniel climbing up towards me.

The logo was blazoned on the side of a giant rotating sphere that floated above the London skyline and a crisscrossed spaghetti mess of magrails and foot traffic.

I knew where the sphere was located, of course. It was directly above the Castle Industries-funded Resurrection Zone. This had once, before I was born, been a beautiful and tranquil part of the city known as Regent's Park, but was now home to what was possibly Castle's most controversial venture – a vast zoo for formerly extinct species that had been brought back to life by sequencing genes. Of course, not everything had been brought back to life. Humans now know that they will never be able to bring back dinosaurs, as no dinosaur DNA has been preserved successfully enough. But others – polar bears, pandas, dodos, mountain gorillas, woolly mammoths, tigers and (most controversially of all) Neanderthals – were all housed there.

From my position, propped up on pillows in this strange bed, I couldn't see inside the zone itself, just the tops of trees. But I could tell this was roughly where the noise was coming from.

The chanting.

A protest against the Resurrection Zone. Dad would have known about it; maybe he would have even been planning to go. But then, I suppose the book he was writing was itself a kind of protest against it, as the big selling point of the Resurrection Zone was the fact that Neanderthals – real living cave humans – were there. And Mum had banned Dad from going to protests. Or she had tried to.

'Leo,' she used to say. 'Leo, you're selfish.'

'Selfish? Trying to preserve the future for us all is selfish?'

'One more person at a protest will not make a difference.'

'When differences are made, it is always down to one more person.'

'OK, well, what about having more time with us? We used to value our Saturdays. What happened to our Saturday mornings at the Centre Aquatique in Paris? Why do you prefer marching with a load of violent anarchists to spending time with your family?'

'You've changed. You used to believe in this stuff. What do you believe in now? Yoga?'

'I grew up, Leo. OK? I entered the real world. Of real jobs. And having to earn money. Of looking after our family. Do you not understand that?'

At which point Dad used to mutter something and skulk off to his office. And Mum would look at me as she stood there in the kitchen and say, 'I only worry about him.' And she would then frown and bark at Travis and tell him to stop yammering on about sea cucumbers, and turn to me again. 'Your father exhausts me,' she'd say, popping a brain pill and blinking through her mind-wire messages. 'I love him, Audrey. But he's a nightmare. Whatever you do, don't end up like him. Don't end up barred from life by your principles. Now, come on, it's Saturday. I have some time. Let's go to America and see some art and do something fun.'

* * *

There were lots of places around the world like the Resurrection Zone, and most of them had nothing to do with Castle Industries. And as Dad told me, Uncle Alex was just one of many people who made money out of such things. But still, being here made me feel uncomfortable.

After all, I had never been to Uncle Alex's house before. He had invited my parents to stay two Christmases ago, but they had declined the offer.

'I love my brother,' my dad told me then. 'I love him because he is my little brother and I have to love him, but that doesn't mean I want to spend a lot of time listening to him. Or visiting his expensive house. You see, Audrey, my brother is a very wise and charming man who, I truly believe, thinks he is helping the world progress by making new technology widely available. But it is my view that he is doing a lot of bad things for society.'

Which was why, when it came to buying Alissa, for instance, she was not a Castle product. She was from Sempura, whose products were more expensive but were considered better quality. And Sempura hadn't helped bring Neanderthals back to life. The company was just about Echos and robots and cars.

'Uncle Alex swims with the current and I swim against it.' My dad's words again, that Christmas Eve. 'No wonder I sometimes feel like I am drowning.'

Even though we never went to Hampstead, we did see Uncle Alex. He had been to Yorkshire a few times, though never with Iago, and he had always been very kind and loving to me. On my ninth birthday he had arrived on our doorstep with a brand-new state-of-the-art immersion pod; I realize now that it didn't please my parents very much. There was sometimes tension, but it was normally caused by Dad. To be fair to Uncle Alex, he had never seemed to want to start an argument.

Hearing footsteps outside on the gravel, I got up and went to the window. Far in the distance, higher and further south than the Resurrection Zone, the mile-high slums of Cloudville glowed and flickered, like a dark electric thunder cloud. I leaned close to the glass and looked down.

I suppose I half expected to see someone climbing up to the window. But no.

I saw four Echos tending the flowerbeds. There were two females and two males. They all looked different to each other. An old man with a white beard; a strong-looking, hulking younger male with long dark hair; a female with blonde hair, not dissimilar to Alissa but a little older; and one designed to look like a woman in her twenties who was authentically detailed with freckles and long red hair in a plait.

I realized after a few moments that this was the one I had seen last night. The one who had been aiming the gun at Daniel.

Near them was a robot. A proper steel robot that was basically little more than a self-moving compost heap, which was picking up the weeds and other debris that the Echos were taking out of the flowerbeds.

And then, further across from them, another Echo stood high in the air on the leviboard. Him. The one who looked like a tall sixteen-year-old, his blond hair and pale but perfect features amplified now by daylight. He was scrubbing Alissa's blood from my parents' car, which hovered a good few centimetres above the rail. The car – a silver Slipstream shaped like an egg cut in half – had been slightly out of my parents' price range. Mum had insisted – after the accident – that they get a more expensive model. But it didn't look expensive in the context of Uncle's house and grounds. And its self-clean function was as good as useless.

I watched him, the Echo boy, with fascination as he washed away the blood with a bucket and sponge.

The sight of him had made me panic when I first got here. Why wasn't I panicking now? Why hadn't I panicked in the night? I tried to think about what had happened to my parents yesterday, but I struggled to feel anything. And then I remembered that I was wearing neuropads. I wanted to remember my parents, and all that had happened, so I removed them, peeling them off my skin one at a time, and almost instantly my brain chemistry changed and I switched back into terror mode.

That is what it feels like when you lose the people you love.

It is not simply a deep sadness, like people always tell you.

No.

It is worse than that.

It is a total terror at being alone.

Panic gripped my chest.

I was fifteen years old but I felt like a tiny baby, abandoned and screaming. I wasn't literally screaming . . . It was a very quiet type of terror, but terror none the less. A kind of internal falling; a falling of the soul, with nothing to hold onto.

It was hard to breathe.

The blond Echo realized that I was watching him, and stared back at me. And he went on staring, with those eyes that I thought of as cold. I gasped for air, as if I was drowning, and retreated from the window. Quickly I pressed the pads back onto my temples.

12

Shortly after, Uncle Alex knocked on my door. I answered. He was standing there dressed all in black and holding a tray.

'Thought I'd bring it to you myself,' he said. 'I made it myself too. It's an Echo-free breakfast. Porridge, corn bread, gene-support orange and kale juice, chocolate. The works. I can make you a red tea if you want something hot. I know you couldn't manage food yesterday, but I really think you should eat something now, Audrey. If you can.'

I looked down at the porridge and realized I hadn't eaten since the plantain shake I'd had the previous day. I was faint with hunger, yet I still didn't want to eat.

'Your dad used to love corn bread,' Uncle Alex said as he looked sombrely down at the tray. 'We had it as kids. He used to put butter on it. This was before they banned butter, obviously.'

I took the tray and realized that, even with the neuropads on, my hands and arms were shaking. Noticing this, Uncle Alex took the tray back off me and set it down on a small table in the centre of the room. It was the first time I had seen it.

In fact, it was only then that I took in other details of the room. There was a sofa by the wall, an antique television which must have been from around 2020 or something, a large mirror, a plush nano-fibre carpet with subtle continuous colour shifts between blue and purple ('Sleep colours,' explained Uncle Alex), a small immersion pod in the corner ('If there's anyone you want to talk to, or if you just need to escape for a while'), and a door leading to an ensuite bathroom. It was more like a small apartment than a bedroom. There was a painting on the wall. Red figures on a blue background. One of the figures was playing a violin, another the flute. Three more sat clutching their knees, listening.

'Bought that painting from the Hermitage in Leningrad. Russia. Before the civil war there. You like it?' he asked me.

'It's by Matisse,' I said, which wasn't a real answer. The truth is, with the neuropads on I didn't know if it was a good painting or a bad one. Maybe you needed to be able to feel pain and sadness in order to appreciate art.

Uncle Alex nodded, impressed. 'You have a lot of knowledge for a fifteen-year-old.'

'Mum loved art. She used to take me to galleries. Sometimes real ones. Sometimes we'd go in a pod together and visit virtual ones.'

'Your mum was a very intelligent woman. She must have been a very good teacher. Did your dad ever teach you?'

I shook my head. 'Not really. He was too busy writing.'

Uncle Alex chuckled sadly. 'About Castle Industries mainly!'

I didn't reply to this. I just said: 'But, you know, he'd sometimes teach me about writing. He reckoned words were weapons. Get the right words, and they could have a power beyond anything. They could help people. Or hurt them. He mainly taught just by being himself, though. To have principles. To do the right thing even if it's hard. He also taught me how to cook.'

Uncle Alex nodded, and looked at me uneasily. He had thin lips, I noticed. Thinner than Dad's. Tola had once said, *Never trust someone with thin lips*, but Tola was a bit superficial and vicious about such things.

'The trouble with the truth is that it is like morality. It changes from person to person. One person's truth is another person's lie. One person's good is another's bad. He probably said terrible things about me.'

I sat down at the table, picked up the spoon and started on the porridge. I could only eat a mouthful, even with the neuropads on. 'Not terrible things, no. He liked you and he always told me you were a good man. He said that being civilized meant having differences of opinion but getting on.' This was true, but Uncle Alex didn't seem to believe it. 'He did,' I added.

'Audrey, listen, you're my blood. You're family. And family is important. And I'm going to try my very hardest to make you as comfortable here as it is possible for you to be . . . I have told everyone I need to tell at Castle that I will be staying at home for the next week or so. I'm not leaving the house, I promise. Our European headquarters are based in Cambridge, only a few minutes away by magcar, but to be honest I can do everything from here anyway. And I know you have a problem with Echos. I will stay here.'

'Yes,' I said, thinking of the way the blond one had tried to reach my room last night. 'I do. One of them tried to reach my room last night. Outside. He climbed up and tried to get in my room. It was the one I saw last night. Daniel.'

A flash of worry; but a moment later Uncle was looking calm again, or at least trying to. 'Don't worry about that. Echos only need two hours' recharge a night. You know that. So they do night work. Maintenance work. To the outside of the house. The rain funnel gets blocked sometimes. He will have been climbing up to clear that.'

'But there was another Echo too. She had a gun and was threatening to kill him. Or at least, I think that's what she was doing.'

'Which one?'

I told him.

'Oh, Madara. She is a prototype for the military. I'm working out whether to produce a lot of her. I think I will. I think I'm going to go ahead with the commission. She is very good. She's my security at night. She patrols the grounds. She is programmed to assert her authority among other Echos. Trust me, it was nothing untoward. There was no malfunction.'

'OK,' I said, my worry dulled by the pads on my temples.

Uncle Alex sat on my bed, and pressed his hands together as if in prayer, then took a deep inhale, thinking of the right words. 'It is understandable, your anxiety about Echos, given what has happened, but I want to tell you something. The Echos here are not like the one that killed your parents. I've spoken with the police. They have seen the security footage and have confirmed that this one was definitely a Sempura product, not one of ours. You can tell because she had brown eyes and ours all have green eyes. Did you know that?'

I told him I did. Besides, I'd already known Alissa was Sempura. I thought of Dad's face the day she arrived. The disdain.

'It's an Echo,' Mum had told him. 'It's not the end of the world.'

'I don't see the difference,' he'd said, limping over to inspect Alissa.

I contemplated another spoon of porridge.

'This couldn't have happened with one of our products. You see, we make sure our designers put blocks in place. It limits the Echo, but it keeps their owners safe. Now, after breakfast we are going to have you checked over by Mrs Matsumoto, the specialist I told you about.'

'Is she a program?' I asked.

'No. There are times when even I believe that nothing beats an actual human, face to face. And there is no one better than Mrs Matsumoto. Mrs Matsumoto is the best. She costs a lot of money and is very much in demand. But sometimes it is useful to have a rich and powerful uncle.' He winked. The wink prompted me to smile, or as good as. And he smiled at that near-smile. Maybe he thought it was progress.

Uncle Alex studied me. He seemed worried about saying the next few words. He squinted, as if he was scared how I'd react. 'She is a mind doctor. She helped me after my wife left me. I know mind doctors are a bit 2090, but like I said, she is the best in the world. I think she can help you.'

'Where is she?'

'Here. In London. I'll take you.'

I didn't particularly want to go. The outside world was suddenly a terrifying concept. 'I'm all right,' I said. 'I think I just want to stay here.'

'Well, there's no rush,' he said. 'No rush.' And he said it in such a way that it instantly defused any pressure on it. And with that release of pressure I found myself saying, 'No, actually, I will see her now.'

'She doesn't do home visits. I could offer her a million unidollars and she'd still say no.'

'That's OK.'

And Uncle Alex tucked my hair back behind my ear, like Dad used to, and I saw tears glaze his eyes.

There was a knock on the door. The sound of it shocked me, even with the pads. Uncle Alex went to get it and I saw the female Echo, the one with freckles. Madara. The one made to be a warrior. She was holding a trowel. I took the pads off again, trying to work out what to make of her; to understand what had happened last night.

'We have weeded the flowerbeds, Master,' she said, her voice blank in that Echo way. 'Now, do you want me to buy the girl some clothes, like you said you might?'

'Yes, Madara. She will need some.' For a moment I saw nothing but Alissa holding the kitchen knife, and my hands must have reached my face, because the next thing I knew, the pads were on the floor and I was flooded with panic.

And I backed away from them to the other side of the room, until I hit the window. Then I turned and saw the blond Echo boy looking in at me, and this time the scream wasn't silent. It came out of me now, like it had last night. Uncle Alex shut the door and came over; he held me firm, then tried to put the pads back, but they didn't stick.

'They need work. Don't worry, don't worry, it'll be OK, it'll be OK . . .'

I heard Mum's words echo in my mind:

That's OK, Alissa. Don't worry. I like spending time with my daughter.

And Uncle Alex kept on, trying to comfort me:

'It'll be OK.'

But of course, nothing was ever going to be OK again.

13

Only the most expensive cars – Silver Bullets and Prosperos (like the one we were travelling in) – are allowed on hightrack magrails. The night before, I hadn't noticed, but there was a hightrack directly above Uncle's house. It was about a hundred metres up, so it was quite hard to see even when you stood in the drive. It was just a thin white line drawn in the sky, like a piece of string connecting clouds.

Before we left, Uncle Alex showed me round the other side of the house. The leviboard we needed descended on the rear lawn, he told me. It was spectacular, but my senses weren't able to appreciate the genetically perfect sycamore trees, the distant bushes and the multi-coloured grass – violet and yellow and turquoise, the stripes of colour merging into each other.

'It isn't just a garden,' he said. 'It's a defence system.' He pointed to the turquoise lawn beyond the first row of bushes. 'Never run over that piece of ground there.'

'Why?'

'It's above a kennel.'

'You keep dogs underground?'

'Not *dog* dogs. Echo hounds. The ground has sensors in it. If the house is under threat – if there are intruders, for instance – the sensors are activated and, well, the threat is eliminated, let's put it like that.'

As I stood there, next to Uncle, waiting for the leviboard to descend, I felt totally empty. If someone had asked me what my name was, it would have probably taken me a good ten seconds to say, 'Audrey Castle'. I felt so blank that I was only really half aware that Uncle Alex had left my side for a moment and gone back into the house.

When I realized, I turned and saw him in the conservatory with the blond Echo boy. He was talking to him, and gesturing away from the plants that the Echo was watering, into the house. The Echo boy looked at me. He was a weirdo. Machines could be killers, so they could definitely be weirdos.

Uncle Alex's Prospero was the most luxurious magcar I had ever been inside. It was spacious and sleek and had body-sensitive air seats. It played classical music – Vivaldi, as Uncle Alex had instructed – and was meant to be the safest vehicle in existence.

He set the Prospero to view-speed, which was slow enough for us to be able to see outside the windows. Slow enough to actually see faces of people on the streets below. We passed right over the Resurrection Zone. Uncle Alex had taken me this way deliberately, to show me a glimpse of extinct species like tigers, though there were too many trees to see anything clearly (however, I did notice the swarms of tourists).

'One thing your dad didn't realize is that the zone gives people a lot of pleasure. It's something that's not appreciated. All those *Castle Watch* journalists and protestors who like to hang around the place . . .' He sighed. 'And if I was the monster they thought I was, then why wouldn't I force the police to stop the protestors? They could do so. The prime minister herself said to me . . . she said, *If it's affecting your business in any way, you can stop them.* But I don't. I'm not an ogre.' He paused. 'And besides, that's what they want. They want me to look like a monster so they can demonize me even more.'

We passed the New Parliament building. It hung in the sky, like a shining titanium bone. Dad had told me that Uncle Alex was good friends with the prime minister, Bernadine Johnson, and I asked if that was true.

'Oh, we've had lunch a few times . . .'

I felt a brief flash of pain inside my head. It was over as quickly as it arrived.

'I tell you,' Uncle Alex went on, with raw sincerity, 'Sempura is bad news. Well, you know that. And you know it because of Ali— I don't need to spell it out. But anyway, my belief, the belief I have always held, is that technology must always be a force for good. If people are in it solely for money, then things are going to go wrong, risks that shouldn't be taken are going to be taken, and before we know it we'll be at the singularity.'

The singularity.

I knew exactly what the singularity was. The singularity was the point at which the machines take over. When they become so advanced that they decide it is in their best interests to stop serving humans, and either kill us or make us their servants. The singularity was something my dad talked about all the time. I remembered my parents rowing about it. According to my dad, the very fact that we had an Echo in our home meant we were encouraging the singularity to happen.

Maybe Alissa hadn't been a one-off. Maybe the singularity was already starting to happen.

Further south we saw water. It looked blue and solid and frozen and harmless. Of course, everything looked still and harmless from a distance. I thought of how cities can flood and yet survive. I wondered if I would be like that. Grief feels like a flood. Some slip under it and never come up. But most do, I supposed.

And as I did so, another intense pain shot through my head, pushing away all thoughts. It was as though a thin metal spear had been thrust right through my skull and out the other side.

'*Aaargh!*' I screamed and fell forward out of the air-chair onto my knees, clutching my head.

Uncle Alex put his hand on my back, his face creased with anguish. 'Audrey?'

But it was over in a flash. The pain was gone, though it lingered like an echo in the empty cavern of my mind.

'It might be the neuropads,' Uncle said. 'They are a prototype, like I said. There may still be some . . . some teething problems.' He looked at me with concern. 'I think you should take them off.'

'No,' I said. 'It's OK.' I was willing to risk more physical pain if it meant stopping emotional pain.

'Well, Audrey, I'm a little worried. They are not designed to be worn all the time. The more you wear them, the more chance there will be of side-effects. Let's just hope that Mrs Matsumoto can help. She is very good. Oh look, we're nearly there . . .'

Above us, the famous floating observatories, set up about eighty years ago to monitor changes in the weather, looked grey and battered from countless storms and the almost continual rain. It wasn't raining now, though. Not right at this minute. But the clouds were gathering, quite fast.

'4449 Skylodge Villas, Cloudville.'

Cloudville.

'She lives in the sky? I thought you said she had lots of money.'

'She does. But she chooses to live here, in the poorest part of town, 600 metres above the tip of the Shard.'

The Shard was an old skyscraper, shaped like a stretched-out pyramid. It had once been the tallest building in Europe, but now it was derelict and rather sad-looking, jutting out of the dirty floodwater like a strange fin.

As for Cloudville, well, it looks even worse up close than it does from afar. A giant grey disc full of tall, thirty-year-old buildings that looked far older because of the weather damage they suffer up here. And I remember hearing about it on the news; how it was meant to be overrun with gangsters.

'Isn't it dangerous?'

'It's OK. Don't worry.' And then Uncle Alex pulled something out of his jacket. A gun. 'This is a positron. Do you know about positrons?'

'I know that they are an irresponsible weapon and should be banned.'

'You sound like you are echoing someone. Your dad maybe?'

'They're responsible for thousands of accidental deaths every year.'

'Which is about one per cent of the accidental deaths caused by laser blades, which aren't regulated at all. Or jolt-clubs. But anyway, you'd prefer it if I left it in the car?'

'Yes,' I said, without hesitation.

We stepped out onto a platform into raw wind and rain. The gale was so strong it very nearly blew us away, as the platform was narrow and slippery. There was a barrier, a fence, but it didn't look like it had ever been finished – just metal poles with nothing in between them. We walked towards an alley high in the sky, amid the ten-storey apartment buildings, which rose on either side of us like vertical wings in a spaceship.

Mrs Matsumoto was very old. She was post-mortal, which meant she had died, technically. She had been dead for two hours, fifteen years ago. She had died of natural causes, but her wealthy clients (Uncle Alex among them) had paid for her to be retrofitted with various death-defying and cell-renewal technologies.

She looked pale and grey, which, given that she was 185 years old when she died, was entirely understandable. She wore long dark clothes, and a few wisps of white hair sprouted out of her chin and cheeks. The room was all metal, a kind of dark steel, I think. In the middle was a strange-looking couch with a helmet attached to it. As soon as we entered, Mrs Matsumoto smiled a thin smile from her chair beside the couch. On the palm of her left hand there was a circular metal disc. Smaller metal discs merged into the skin of her fingertips. She also had a picture of a large open eye tattooed to the middle of her forehead that had probably been there for a century. Her actual eyes, when I got close to them, had milky cataracts over them. She was blind, I realized.

'They brought five out of six senses back to life,' she said in her slow voice, after telling me to lie down on the couch.

She turned to Uncle Alex. She seemed to know exactly where he was in the room. 'How are the nightmares?' she asked.

Uncle looked at me nervously. He obviously didn't want me to know he had nightmares. 'Fine,' he said. 'Much better.'

Then she pushed the helmet-thing away. 'I prefer to use my hands,' she said, and she touched the side of my head with the cold metal fingertips and brushed against the pads.

'They're neuropads,' Uncle explained. 'They're a new invention. A kind of tranquillizer. I'm a bit concerned about them, actually. I would prefer her not to need them.' He explained what had happened in the car. He then asked for a word with Mrs Matsumoto on her own, and they went into a small side room, and spoke for a bit.

When they came back, Mrs Matsumoto told me that the therapy would only work if I took the pads off, so I did.

My heart began to race straight away. I suddenly wondered what I had agreed to. I wanted to get off the couch.

'Grief and terror are twins,' she told me. 'They arrive together. Now . . . I want you to hear nothing except my voice.'

'I don't think I'm ready for this,' I said. 'I think I should go.'

'It will help you,' Uncle told me as I wondered what he had just been saying to Mrs Matsumoto. 'She is the best in the world.'

Mrs Matsumoto was now whispering something in Japanese. Uncle Alex handed me some info-lenses.

'You'll need these,' he said.

I put them in. The translation soon arrived. 'Now, listen to me,' she said. 'I am picking up all kinds of intensity from inside your mind. You cannot go on like this. You will need to come to terms with what has happened. The only way to get over horror is to face it. The only way you can do this is to think about what happened. To visualize it in your mind. Your body is going to become paralysed, rigid, to intensify the mental activity. I am going to channel all these thought-waves, all this negative neural activity, and you are going to experience all that emotion, all that grief, all at once. But after that you will be able to move on with your life. Now, think about what happened to your parents . . . Think about what you saw . . . Picture your house. Picture her. Picture Alissa—'

How did she know Alissa's name? I suppose Uncle Alex must have told her. But it unsettled me. And I don't know what was inside those metal fingertips, but I was rigid, and memories and emotions rose like lava in a volcano. I was suddenly seeing my dad's office, and Alissa, and my parents. I was feeling it all at once. All that undiluted terror and grief. It felt hot. It felt like I was burning with memory from the inside. It was singeing my parents away from me, like I was losing a limb. And it was too much. I started screaming. Or I tried to scream, but my jaw was locked. I was in total paralysis.

'Stop it!' Uncle said to Mrs Matsumoto. 'It's not working. You've got to stop it. It's too much for her.'

She took her fingers away. My body was released. I could scream properly, and I did. I screamed too loud, because a moment later there was a knock on the door. I calmed down a little, breathed deep.

'I'm sorry, Mrs Matsumoto,' Uncle Alex said. 'We'd better go.'

So we left – me trembling like a pathetic leaf behind Uncle Alex as he opened the door. There were two men standing there. Both wearing long coats. Cloudville gangsters. Twitchy and skinny and wind-blown.

'We heard some screams,' said the tallest one. They looked out of their heads on everglows. Suddenly one of them recognized Uncle Alex.

'If it isn't the Devil himself! Lord of the Universe. So, how goes the work, King Satan?'

'Audrey,' said Uncle Alex. 'Get in the car. Now. Run.'

But I didn't. I felt responsible. My scream had alerted them, after all. 'Please, leave us alone.'

A second later and I was being grabbed around the neck. 'OK, rich girl, don't do anything stupid. We don't want to kill you. We just want a good price for you. You understand? It's just twenty-second-century capitalism. Anything goes, right? We're all products, yeah?'

I had a stun-stick pressed against my neck, ready to be triggered if I resisted. But Uncle Alex was quick.

And he had lied.

He hadn't left the positron in the car. He was holding it in front of him, and within a second the other man had vanished into non-existence, his matter converted into antimatter. And I was quick too. I elbowed the man who was holding me hard in the gut, and stepped away, leaving Uncle Alex clear to shoot him too, which he did.

So. Two deaths in two seconds.

'Quick!' Uncle Alex said, looking down the alleyway for anyone else who might have been watching. 'The car!'

Someone else *was* watching. Only this wasn't a human. It wasn't even an Echo. It was a hulk of old rusted metal, more than three metres tall, with one functional eye – the left one – glowing a dull red in the dark. It had faded identification on its chest: CAL-300. It must have been an old second-hand securidroid – once used by the police or a private security firm but now programmed to protect the two men whose lives had just ended, but I could only see it as a big evil robot thing.

'*Stop there! You have committed a crime.*'

'No,' said Uncle Alex. 'We haven't. We acted in self-defence.'

'Shoot it!' I told Uncle Alex.

But he fired and missed, and the giant creaking robot let off a laser shot that burned the positron right out of Uncle Alex's hand; then another, though it was slowing.

'*Stop . . . you have . . . violated . . .*'

'Come on! It's malfunctioning,' said Uncle Alex, running again. CAL-300 followed us, metal limbs and joints moaning through the wind and rain.

And so I ran, I ran fast, but then the platform shook as CAL-300 fell down with its inhuman weight. The trembling, and that temporary distraction, caused me to slip on the wet platform, sliding until my legs were over the side. Then further. Until there was nothing between me and death except a thousand-metre drop. I grabbed one of the metal posts of the unfinished fence.

Below me, all around, the city glowed in the rain like firefly larvae. Skyscrapers and boats and illuminated magrails and hovering office blocks. Holo-ads flickered like the ghost I could very soon become.

I could have let go. It would have been the simplest way. Just letting go. Whatever I landed on from that height would have killed me in less than a second. Easy. No more pain. No more grief. No more memories of Mum and Dad. (Memories were overrated. Memories were just future sadness stored away.)

But life is a stubborn thing.

'Help!' I screamed. 'Help!'

The post was wet. It was tricky to grip, my palms kept shifting, but I kept my fingers locked. My wrists hurt so much that I thought my hands would tear off.

It would be so easy, so easy, so easy . . .

The wind got angrier.

How long was this? A second? Two? Three? It might as well have been hours.

A song came into my head. A song! On the verge of death and there came a song. The Neo Maxis, of course. The one they did with Harlo 57: *Life, she said, is not a breeze / It's seventy-seven storms at seas / But if you can keep the boat from sinking / It is always worth the pain of thinking . . .*

If you can keep the boat from sinking . . .

'Help! Uncle Alex! Help!'

The wind was a gale. I swayed in it. The wind wanted me to die. But I was not going to die.

He was there. Uncle Alex. Standing there. Just a black rain-streaked shape. He came close, helped me.

'It's OK, Audrey. I've got you, I've got you, I've got you . . .'

His words pulled me up almost as much as his arms.

It was a struggle – he wasn't quite as big or strong as my dad – but he did it. And we got into the car and drove away fast, before any more Cloudville gangsters or second-hand securidroids could bother us.

I now knew three things. I was nowhere near coming to terms with my parents' death. I was unable to solve that problem by killing myself. And the third thing? That I should really give Uncle Alex the benefit of any doubt.

14

'I shouldn't have taken you there,' he said. 'I'm sorry. I'm sorry.'

'It's all right,' I said. I felt a deep emptiness inside me. It was hard to describe. It was almost like guilt, a guilt caused by things happening to me while my parents were dead. But for a moment, back there on the platform, amid all that horrifying adventure, I hadn't felt depressed at all. Maybe that was the only way to handle grief: to be in a constant state of peril. Maybe the only way to return to life was to be next to death.

I put the neuropads back on.

Instantly, the raging swirl of my mind settled. Uncle Alex said something about how I really should try not to wear them.

'I'm not a saint,' he said as we parked high above his house. 'But I am determined to look after you. Listen, something untoward has come up. Tomorrow I have to go somewhere on business, just to visit a warehouse, but it will only be for the day. Other than that I'll be here. You won't be in the house on your own.'

I remembered what he had told me. *I will be staying at home for the next week or so. I'm not leaving the house, I promise.*

I felt worried. 'Where are you going?'

'Paris.'

Paris.

I remembered my mother taking me swimming in the best pool in Europe. Saturday mornings that would never return.

The leviboard lowered us towards the lawn. The Echos were still out gardening. Uncle Alex looked at me and said: 'You honestly don't have to worry about them. My vision – the Castle vision – is to make humans achieve all we can achieve, while making the world *safer*. I know you can't imagine that Echos could make anything safer, but potentially they can . . . Sempura, well, they are run by mad people. Totally crazy. The bosses . . . all they care about is their vision. They want to create Echos that are more advanced than humans, basically, and in doing so they take all kinds of risks. All kinds. Lina Sempura herself, well, she's crazy. Do you know what her first job was?'

'No.'

'Designing warbots for the Koreans. That's her background. Killing machines. She's hardly human herself. She was raised by Echos. Parents died when she was litt—' He stopped himself. He realized that this might be an inappropriate thing to be saying to a young person whose parents had just died. 'Anyway, point is, they're a bunch of Dr Frankensteins. I bet you've read that book, haven't you?'

I nodded as we walked across the grass towards the house.

His thin lips spread into a smile. 'Of course you have. You're probably better read than me. In the very last conversation I had with your dad he told me that you did your Universal Exams at fourteen, three years early. You must be ready for university.'

'Oxford,' I said. 'I've got a place. Starting in June.'

We walked through the vast hallway. There were numerous

holograms there. Expensive sculptures you could walk through. A unicorn, a nude woman, a giant shell. There were some holographs on the wall too. These were less art and more like personal pictures and Castle propaganda. One of the images was of Uncle Alex with his arm round a smiling Bernadine Johnson inside the parliament building.

Iago was sitting at a table playing chess with an Echo. *That* Echo. Daniel. Daniel had his back to us. I didn't feel that scared, maybe because of the neuropads, maybe because of what had just happened in Cloudville.

'Well, Oxford! Like your parents,' Uncle was saying. At the time I didn't notice it, but looking back, I think there was probably a slightly bitter edge to his voice. Maybe this was because he had been thrown out of school as a boy. This was the one fact I knew about him: he had once hacked into the software that ran the school he and Dad went to, and nearly destroyed the whole place. He'd got caught, and barred from every other school program in existence. It must have given him a few issues when Dad achieved some of the highest grades ever witnessed in his Universals.

'Studying?' he asked me, his thin eyebrows rising like wings.

'Philosophy,' I said quietly. Iago had noticed us, and scowled briefly, then turned back to his game with Daniel.

'Ah, the oldest subject. The meaning of life. Well, you should still do it. I'll help you. Whatever you need, Audrey.' Uncle Alex sighed, then stopped inside the giant hologram of a seashell. He whispered, just out of his son's hearing: 'I find it difficult to talk to him. I can never get him out of the pod. True, he likes chess. We play together sometimes. So there is hope. And to be fair to him, I haven't been the best dad. Well, I've given him everything except the thing he needs. My time.'

We started walking again, and it was right then that Iago flipped.

'What?' he shouted. Then he stood up and threw the chessboard across the floor, sending the pieces sliding towards us. He seemed very angry with Daniel, his face red and his eyes glaring through his curly dark fringe with utter contempt. 'You can't do that! You can't fucking do that! You do what I tell you and I told you to lose.'

'Iago!' Uncle Alex shouted. 'Language!' He was running over when Iago leaned forward and slapped Daniel across the face.

Daniel stared up at Iago. 'You lose,' he said. 'Checkmate.'

This troubled Uncle Alex far more than Iago's swearing. 'Wait a minute. Wait a minute . . .' He went over and stared right at Daniel. 'What happened here?'

'He disobeyed me,' said Iago. 'I told him to be good, but not better than me. And he beat me in twelve moves! Checkmate! He needs terminating.'

Uncle Alex glanced at me, probably worried about what I was thinking. Then he turned his attention to Daniel. 'Get to your quarters. Now. Or you will be punished. Do you understand me?'

Punished. Could an Echo be punished?

Daniel walked past me. He stared directly at me. His eyes stared deep into me. 'You are not . . .' he whispered, then hesitated and carried on walking. Or, at least, I think that's what he whispered. I didn't know what it meant. It was either a warning or a threat.

Uncle Alex, back in my room: 'Don't worry about him. Iago got it wrong. He set the wrong command. Or he was plain lying. He does that. For my attention, you see. Now, on to more pressing matters . . . The police might want to speak to you at some point. But it's nothing to worry about.'

'About what happened in Cloudville?'

He smiled at my innocence. 'The police gave up on Cloudville a long time ago. No. About what happened to your parents. You remember, I mentioned it when you were on your way to my house? You might be asked to testify against Sempura, to tell the world about what happened.'

I couldn't really absorb this. I didn't even want to think about it. I probably just said 'OK'. Uncle Alex seemed to think I was a bit blank because he said, 'The neuropads fade a little bit as you use them, but they can be a bit strong at the start. You may feel a little absent-minded.'

'Yeah.' But then I remembered what he had said about going to Paris.

I didn't like the idea of being left in the house on my own, with no one but Iago and the Echos. I wanted to be with Uncle Alex.

'Can I come with you?' I said. 'To Paris?'

Uncle Alex looked at me for a long time. He seemed very reluctant. 'I don't think you should,' he said. 'I am going to a warehouse full of Echos. They are making Madaras. I am checking up on their progress.'

'Oh,' I said. That changed things. The idea had kind of lost its appeal. I closed my eyes and thought about it. 'Yeah, it's probably best if I stay here.'

And Uncle Alex tried to reassure me. 'Don't worry, there is no way Daniel or any other Echo living under my roof can harm a human. It has never happened to a Castle prototype. I use the best designers. Winning a game of chess is not a dangerous flaw, I assure you.'

And his words might have assured me if he hadn't looked so worried.

15

Later, I heard Uncle Alex outside, in the driveway, talking to the Echos. I didn't hear everything he said, but I heard the bit where he shouted. 'From now on,' he said, 'you don't go up to the second floor. The second floor is out of bounds. For all of you. That is a command. You understand?'

And then he singled out Daniel and asked to have a word with him in his office.

I went back to bed that day. Uncle Alex came in later that afternoon with a high-fat plantain shake, a protein pill, some decaffeinated chocolate, and an apple. He also gave me a parcel of new clothes that Madara had bought, along with my things from the old house, which Madara had also been responsible for collecting. He told me he'd made the shake himself, like he had made breakfast, though I didn't know if this was true. It tasted too perfect, the way Echo-made food always tastes.

'I need to talk to my grandma,' I said.

I was sure a flicker of worry passed across Uncle Alex's face. His thin black eyebrows crept together.

'You can.'

'She lives on the moon.'

'I know,' he said, laughing gently. I wondered if he was being a bit snobby, but he quickly switched back to serious again. 'The moon is the fastest-growing customer base for us. It's only existed as a market since 2092, back when it was just a band of colonists. Everyone needs a powerful immersion pod up there. And there are about three million Echos in New Hope alone. They're everywhere. The place is teeming with them. People need them more up there. I visit all the time. And I mean *proper* visit. Shuttles leave from Heathrow's Terminal Eleven every night at midnight now, you know. You could go if you want.'

I thought about it.

Three million Echos.

'I'll just pod-visit for now.'

'Well, sure, same difference. Go for it.'

The pod – complete with that Castle logo – was the most expensive looking I had ever seen, its sky-blue exterior made not of the usual carbon fibre but aerogel and modified magnesium (as it said on the instruction label), which had been fitted seamlessly into the corner of the room.

'It's the easiest thing ever,' Uncle Alex said as he taught me how to use it. He might have been right.

I stepped inside and sat back in the chair – the most luxurious of all pod chairs, and with no uncomfortable head-strap necessary; it tilted back a little, and the dark aerogel mind-reader lowered like a broad helmet around my head, but didn't actually make contact with it.

'Now,' said Uncle Alex, his voice audible through the two-way intercom even though the pod door was closed. 'If you want to contact your grandma, all you have to think about is the territory she's in – in this case, the moon – then her address, if you know it; if not, her name might be enough. OK?'

'OK.'

'Ever been to the moon before?'

'No, not properly. Just pod-visited Grandma there. No, Dad went once for work but he hated it. And same with Mum. Just once.'

I heard Uncle Alex sigh. 'Well, this isn't a normal pod,' he said. 'It's an A-range 3000. I'll need to explain it to you, OK?'

I nodded. 'OK.'

I could sense Uncle Alex's pride as he began to talk. 'You won't just be sitting down. Your real body will be sitting down, of course, but you will *feel* like you are moving around, like in a dream. It's not an avatar any more than the self in a dream is an avatar.'

I stared into the blackness in front of me. I took a deep breath, and thought.

Moon.

Nothing.

Moon.

Still nothing.

Moon, moon, moon, I want to visit the moon.

It wasn't happening.

'I can't get through.'

'Are you still wearing the neuropads?' Uncle Alex asked me. 'It's long-distance. To get through to the moon you'll need to take them off.'

Another deep breath. Two. Maybe three. This was going to be hard enough *with* a stabilized mind, let alone without one. But I needed to see Grandma. It had been twenty-four hours since the murders had happened and she didn't watch the news. She might not know.

So I took the pads off, and dropped them in my pocket.

Instantly, I was gripped by claustrophobia. Every atom of me wanted to escape the pod. I suppose it was because the last time I was inside one, my parents were murdered, and I was blaming myself. I still do blame myself, but back then, I might as well have been their killer. That is the level of guilt I was feeling.

Uncle Alex's voice, penetrating the dark: 'Are you OK in there?'

I tried to get a hold of myself.

'Yes,' I told him. 'I'm OK, I'm fine.'

'Very well, I'll leave you for now. I'll be in my office if you need anything.'

I slowed my breathing like Mum had taught me during yoga practice. Five breaths in, five breaths out.

Moon.

And suddenly I was soaring through the thermosphere and out into space.

16

The moon was there, getting bigger and bigger. Yeah. I could see the large dark plain of the Sea of Tranquillity and, nearby, the two domed towns, practically touching each other: Lunar One and New Hope Colony, like a glowing number 8, with the larger New Hope Colony south of Lunar One.

I knew my grandma's address, but my mind was in such a frazzled state it took me a while to remember it in full.

New Hope Colony . . .

I was there, in the centre of the strangest and – for an Echophobe – most threatening city in the solar system. I was standing outside a building called the Beyond Earth Centre, on a kind of street where slow-moving buggy cars were cruising along on rough white-grey roads, breathing in an artificial version of air. There was an old-fashioned screen outside, almost like a 3-D cinema screen from the olden days, and it was flashing slogans.

ZERO GRAVITY TOURISM - ROAM BEYOND THE DOME

SEMPURA - A STEP FURTHER

ONE GIANT LEAP - MOON-EARTH LONG-DISTANCE DATING

LOVE CIRCUITS - UPLOAD NEW TRACK 'GIRL FROM NEPTUNE' TO YOUR MIND - WIRE TODAY

NHC ECHO FAIR 2115 - FIND THE ECHO FOR YOU

CASTLE INDUSTRIES - RELAX, IT'S CASTLE

Above me in the sky was Earth. A large bright blue and green circle, covered with white whirls of cloud. And there, bustling along the pavements, were lots of people. Only they weren't people. They all had Es on their hands, and perfect skin. About half of them were dressed in slate-grey tabards with the word LUNACORP on them, which must have been a construction company or something (there did seem to be a lot of building work going on). Echos everywhere. All around me. The only humans I could see were street sellers, hawking capsules that glowed yellow from little stalls.

One of the street traders spotted me. He looked mean. He had rough aged skin, from the bad air, and wore blue overalls like prisoners wear on Earth. An ex-convict. Echos and ex-convicts. What a nightmare. 'Hey, look, we got a ghost . . .'

The Echos all stared at me. Many of them were identical. There were no prototypes here. Just old, outdated models. They weren't regulated here. They could malfunction and still exist. They had *rights*. Not many, but some, and just the thought scared me. My heart beat like a tribal drum.

'I am not here,' I told myself. 'I am sitting in a chair inside a pod in London. I am just trying to talk to Grandma.'

I wondered what would happen to me if I was injured. In a standard immersion pod, nothing would have happened. But in a standard immersion pod you didn't feel anything. You couldn't feel the mild breeze of the moon's giant air-con system brush against your face. You couldn't smell that metallic tang the moon was known for (because of the amount of iron in the surface rock – or mantle – if I remember rightly from my lunar studies classes).

Even if my physical body, on Earth, was OK, I would surely feel any pain if pain came my way.

Desperately I tried to think as these Echos started to look at me, standing there in the middle of this strange street.

Armstrong Tower, Apollo Street.

And I was suddenly standing outside a six-storey building made of moon rock and metal. It must have been one of the tallest in the city.

Apartment 15, Grandma . . . I mean, Imogen Greene.

Then:

Outside a door, made of a metal that blurred my reflection. My *avatar*'s reflection which, as it looked pretty much exactly like me, was almost the same thing. An automated voice came from a primitive-looking voice reader beside the door. '*Who is calling please?*'

I felt an overwhelming sense of dread, remembering why I was here. 'My name is Audrey . . . Audrey Castle.'

There was a gap of a few seconds.

The last time I had spoken to Grandma, we had talked about books. Grandma is a novelist. She is quite well known. She wrote detective stories set in Frankfurt in the 2060s, just before the introduction of robotic police officers. She had told me she was thinking of writing a new series set on the moon.

'A crime series about New Hope,' she had said. 'My publisher thinks it is an unromantic thing to write about. Echos and mining companies and old hermits like me. But there's a lot more than that going on up here on the moon . . . You see, everyone here – I mean, every human here – is escaping from something. The rich adventurers who flock here because they want to live dangerously, and even the workers who signed up for the construction jobs building apartments in the suburb in the north of the city, Aldrin, knowing all the risks. It can feel primitive, sure, like the pioneer country of the ancient Wild West, but it's exciting. I do wish you would come here. If your parents don't want to, fine, fine, I know they're Earth-loving traditionalists. Your mum couldn't leave quickly enough when she came. She said it was "culturally suffocating", whatever that meant. I know they worry about the crime rate and claim that artificial air is unhealthy. I know they hate too many Echos, blah blah blah, but you're a growing woman. You're fifteen. You can drive, you can vote, you can live on your own at fifteen . . .'

I loved Grandma.

I had always thought it was fun to have a wild relative, and I always looked forward to her summer visits.

But of course, she didn't answer the door.

An Echo did.

A large muscular male – over two metres tall – designed to look about twenty years old. I took a deep breath.

He beckoned me in, and I walked along a nondescript white corridor and entered a large but basically furnished apartment with three Echos standing in three of the corners of the room, one more at my grandma's feet, giving her a foot massage, and another standing behind, rubbing his hands through her wild turquoise hair to massage her scalp.

I'm not here, I told myself. *The Echos can't hurt me*.

I walked over, dreading the moment when she noticed the

hologram coming towards her. And I wished I was still wearing the neuropads.

The Echo who had beckoned me inside spoke, his voice making me jump. 'There is a visitor for you, Imogen. It is Audrey Castle. Your granddaughter.'

She looked up at me and instantly smiled broadly. 'Audrey! Wow, it's you.'

'Hello, Grandma.'

'What are you doing here?'

She fluttered her hands, gesturing for the two Echos who were currently massaging her to leave her alone. It took her a moment to stand up, and I remembered Dad saying that fake gravity has a negative impact on bone strength. I tried to speak but I couldn't. Outside, I heard distant screaming.

'Don't worry about that, sweetheart. There's always something happening here. That's what makes it interesting.' Grandma was wearing a large woollen kaftan and had a transparent jar full of small glowing golden capsules around her neck. Her eyes were wide, which – coupled with her turquoise hair – made her look quite crazy.

'Right, well,' I said eventually. A hologram with a racing heart. 'Grandma, I've got something to tell you. It's about—'

Grandma didn't seem to be listening. She seemed happily mesmerized by the sight of me. Just as I was quite mesmerized by the sight of her. I hadn't seen her since last year, when she had come to help us after the car accident. Grandma was a hundred years old, but looked younger because of the everglows. Dad said she looked like a fortune teller from the nineteenth century. To my dad's disgust she had taken everglows for a long time – as long as Dad had known her (twenty-six years), and maybe even before.

Everglows were controversial. They were an anti-ageing drug that you could buy across the counter if you were over seventy. But lots of people younger than that bought them and just took them for fun, as a drug, and got addicted. I don't know if Grandma was addicted. Obviously Dad had thought she was. Dad had also told me that Mum thought she was irresponsible, and that she'd had affairs during her marriage to every one of her seven husbands (including husband number three, my granddad, who had died when the tsunami hit the west coast of Ireland in 2080). He told me this when I was seven. My dad really didn't hold back when it came to Grandma.

In fact, she looked younger than she had done even last year. It was weird.

Breathe in for five, breathe out for five . . .

'Oh, Audrey . . . This is all very state-of-the-art for you, I must say! Look at you – it's almost like you're here. It feels like you are actually in the room walking about. It must be one of those new pods I've heard about. The ones your uncle is going to make billions selling. I can't believe your dad actually agreed to get one. It's very un-him, I must say. I tried contacting your mum earlier but there was no response. I was a bit worried . . . I don't know . . . I had this weird feeling . . .'

This was not going well.

'Dad didn't get a new pod.' *Say it, say it, say it* . . . 'I'm not at home, Grandma.'

'What do you mean you're not at home?'

'I'm at Uncle Alex's.'

This really shocked her. It was like she knew something was very, very wrong.

Say it . . .

'Grandma, they've been mur—' I was about to say *murdered*. But was it murder? Alissa was sub-human. A robot made flesh. If someone gets killed by a lion or a robot, the word is *killed*. I did not want to raise Alissa up. So I corrected myself. 'They've been . . . killed.' And saying it made me cry. The tears felt real. I was crying real tears and ghost tears all at once.

It felt good in a strange kind of way, a release. I wanted to cry for ever, but I had to try and keep myself together for Grandma, who was staring at me as if I wasn't really there at all – which of course I wasn't; as though she couldn't see anything, as if the horror of what I had said had made everything disappear. She didn't cry. She just kind of sank in on herself.

'No. No. What are you saying?'

I told her again. And then a third time.

'Killed? I don't understand. What do you mean? What by? Who by?'

I looked around. There were six Echos in this room. They were all looking at me with neutral faces. I was terrified of saying it, but Grandma needed the truth.

'By the Echo.'

'What?'

'After you stayed with us we got an Echo.'

'Yes. Your mother said. Alissa?'

I nodded.

'And you are saying she killed your mum?'

'And Dad,' I said.

'This is wrong. You are wrong. You are wrong. Audrey, you are wrong.' She said this for quite a while. 'Echos don't malfunction.'

'This one did.'

It took her a while. Maybe half an hour. But eventually she absorbed it.

'Lorna, Lorna, Lorna,' she said, her voice fading. 'My . . . poor . . .

Lorna . . .' Her eyes suddenly seemed distant. Like she was staring all the way to death itself. But she kept switching. From manic to over-calm to manic again. She kept trying to hug me. I felt the simulation of a hug, but she felt nothing. She kept slipping straight through.

She took some of those glowing capsules from their container and swallowed them. I got a close-up view of the label.

They weren't just average everglows, they were 4-glows.

They were four times as strong. This version of everglows had been banned on Earth because of strange side-effects. No one took these for anti-ageing any more. They took them to feel high.

'My happy pills aren't working,' she said after a few of them. She sounded desperate. And kept on repeating it. 'They're not working, they're not working, they're not working, they're not working . . .'

The Echo who had been massaging her foot – a woman with a short dark bob and pronounced cheekbones – spoke up. 'You have had six capsules. That is your daily limit, Mistress. You told me to tell you that.'

'Oh, Chonticha, damn my daily limit,' said Grandma, and she kept on taking them. Her hands were trembling wildly. Her whole body seemed to be trembling. At first I thought it might be something wrong with the immersion footage, but it wasn't. Everything else was perfectly still except poor Grandma.

'My daughter's just died,' she wailed to the Echos. 'Do any of you have any idea what it is like to lose someone you love? Of course you don't. Because you can't love. Because you have no feelings, do you? You have no' – she paused, right there, took a breath and spat out that word again, louder and longer this time – '*feelings!*'

She popped two more capsules into her mouth.

I could see the glow through her cheeks, and then – fainter – down her neck as she swallowed them.

She went over to the Echo with the bob. Chonticha. 'You killed my daughter,' she said, and slapped her.

'Grandma,' I said. 'Please. Come on. Try some deep breathing.'

'Deep breathing! Don't give me that yoga craperola! She killed my daughter!'

'I did not kill your daughter,' Chonticha said matter of factly. And then Grandma slapped her again. I told her she needed neuropads, but she didn't know what they were. She was hardly listening. She was looking at me with the wildest wide eyes I have ever seen.

'Audrey, listen to me – you have to come here, darling. You have to live here. Here in New Hope. You can come here.'

Dad's voice: *Audrey, promise me, when you are older don't give up on Earth unless you have to*.

Grandma came right up to me and spoke in a voice that made me wonder if she was insane. 'Worker shuttles leave every night. You don't even need any money . . . You just need to go through an ID check . . . Listen, sweetheart, wait there, wait right there . . .' She left the room. She seemed quicker on her feet now. Maybe it was the pills. Maybe they stopped the pain.

I had a bit of a panic attack, suddenly left alone with all those Echos.

'Would you like a drink, houseguest Audrey?' one of them asked me, in a typically blank Echo voice. The muscle man. The one who had brought me into the room.

'No, no . . . I'm OK.'

'Then maybe a little conversation? My name is Herman. What are your favourite hobbies?'

'Seriously, I'm fine. Fine. Just, like, please—'

'You sound agitated, houseguest,' said another, a female, from the corner. She was standing next to one of the only objects in the room, a replica of a cactus plant. She had a high beehive hairstyle.

'I'm fine. Please.'

'Your voice indicates a tightness of the vocal cords within the larynx,' said a third, the one who'd been kneading Grandma's scalp. 'You need to think relaxing thoughts, houseguest.'

I closed my eyes. 'Grandma,' I shouted. 'Grandma! Where are you?'

She came back into the room. She was smiling now. She seemed completely off her head on everglows. She was holding a cat. A large fluffy Persian cat. 'She's called Lucy Brooks. You know, after the American president. I think it's a good name for a cat. I wish you could stay here. I wish you could stroke her – properly, I mean.'

'I'm scared,' I explained, in a whisper. 'I'm scared of Echos.'

'Echos are nothing to be scared of, sweetheart. They are just machines. Machines can go wrong. If someone had a car crash, they'd still get in a car again. And Uncle Alex has Echos.'

'But you just hit one of your Echos . . .'

She seemed confused. 'Did I, darling?'

'Yes.'

'And Uncle Alex has Echos,' she said. I don't think she realized she was repeating herself.

I thought of Daniel. I thought of the checkmate incident. 'I don't see them. Not really. He says he is going to keep them on a different floor.'

'That's nice of him,' she said. She didn't seem to mean it. I noticed that her hands weren't shaking any more. 'Poor Lorna,' she said. 'Darling, darling, darling little Lorna . . . in that little red smock she wore to kindergarten . . .'

I was worried about her. It would have been better if she had been crying – even howling – on the floor. But the way she was acting was beyond that. Maybe if you were sad enough, you pushed right through to the other side and found yourself at the opposite end. Or maybe she had simply taken too many everglows. Through her smock I could see the glow spreading across her chest, all the way to her shoulders.

'You could come and stay with Uncle Alex.'

It was as though I had slapped her face. 'No. No, I would never do that.'

'Why not?'

There was more screaming outside. The fast whisper of gunfire. Grandma didn't seem bothered. Neither was I, right then. I just wanted to know what Grandma had to say.

'Alex and . . . and . . . and your dad. It is something your mum told me.'

'What is it?'

But she wasn't able to answer. She was looking glazed behind the eyes. 'What, darling?'

'You were going to say something, Grandma.'

'Was I? Was it about Oxford?'

'Oxford?'

'Oxford University. You're nearly sixteen. It's coming up.'

'Grandma—'

She remembered. Tragedy flashed across her face.

'You look like your mum did.' She burst out laughing. 'You look exactly like her.'

I had no idea why this was funny.

But then she started to cry.

An Echo came up to me. The one with the bob. Chonticha. 'You are distressing my mistress. Please leave her alone.'

Then the other Echos started coming towards me. 'You are distressing our mistress. Please leave her alone.'

I panicked: *This is not real. I am not here*.

'It's all right,' Grandma said. 'She's not going to hurt me.' And then to me, in a whisper: 'They're all second-hand.'

'Grandma, are you going to be OK?'

She tapped the remaining everglows. 'Yes, yes . . .'

'Now, think, is there anything you wanted to tell me, Grandma? Anything I should know? About Dad and—'

Something began to happen to the room.

A darkness began to leak into the floor. One of the Echos disappeared, then another; the fake cactus was swallowed up too, and the cat, and then it was just Grandma, against nothing at all, and she was still talking.

'Grandma! Grandma! I can't hear you! I don't know what's happening! There must be something wrong with the connection.'

That was it.

Grandma's kaftan and turquoise hair and fearful face melted away, like a dream or a nightmare dissolving into the dark of sleep, until it was just her silent mouth calling my name.

And then nothing.

Nothing except the darkness of the mind-reader.

17

I thought I could hear something. Outside the pod.

And then, when the pod door had opened, I realized there was no one in my room. But I still heard footsteps – out on the landing this time.

'Hello?'

There was no answer. So I ran across to the door, and peered out to see Uncle Alex walking towards the vast elegant staircase.

'Uncle Alex,' I said.

He stopped. Turned. He was smiling, but looked confused. 'Audrey? What's the matter? How did it go with your grandma?'

'I lost the connection.'

'Oh, that's weird. But it's a brand-new pod. The most advanced there is. Let's try again.'

Something.

Something right there.

The way he said it. I wouldn't have noticed with the neuropads on, but without them, yes, there was a trace of something in his voice – I don't know what exactly – but something that sharpened my suspicion.

We tried again. Just blackness.

'Teething problems,' he said. I thought: *There are a lot of teething problems around here*. 'Don't worry. It will right itself in a while. Do you want to try a different pod?'

I thought of the Echos, and of Grandma, acting crazy on her ever-glows. 'No. No. It's . . . it's OK.'

I felt sorry for Grandma, but I didn't think it would ever be possible for me to live on the moon. I had hardly been able to cope with it as a hologram.

It was here or nowhere.

18

Later that evening Iago came in to ask if he could use my immersion pod. Apparently mine accessed different hologames or something, and was more up to date.

But before he went in, he looked at some of my books from home which Madara had placed in neat piles on the table. They sat directly under the Matisse painting. He picked them up, one by one. They were mostly ancient (except for my Neo Maxis holo-book), and this – combined with the fact that they were, well, *books* – made him treat them as if they were weird objects from some alien planet. '*Withering . . . Wuthering Heights . . . The Catcher in the Rye . . . Romeo and Juliet . . . Frankenstein . . . Twenty-First-Century Philosophy . . . Jane Ey-re . . .*' He dropped them on the table in a haphazard fashion, making no attempt to put them back in a pile.

Dad had once written that, *The more dependent we get on Echos, the more uncivilized we will become*.

Dad, I love you. I'm sorry I couldn't help you.

I was calmer. My neuropads were on. So I decided to try and start a proper conversation. I mean, this was the first time I had been properly alone with Iago, so I thought I might as well take advantage of the fact.

It wasn't easy. But I felt that if I was to understand a bit more about Uncle Alex, and the Echos in this house, I could do worse than to start with Iago.

'So, Iago . . . you like chess?'

Nothing. Just a slight twitch of an eyebrow.

'You don't go to school, do you? I mean, not even pod kind of school. The Echos teach you. How's that working out?'

He looked at me with his dopey eyes. 'Fine.'

'Good. Great. I was Echo-taught too. Bit of Mum, bit of pod, then bit of Echo. Well, towards the . . . towards the end.'

I had a flashback to Alissa teaching me in the spare room, with her perfect, impassive face giving me nothing but information. My stomach felt like it was falling. But the neuropads still worked enough to suppress the memory.

Iago looked unhappy. He didn't seem to want to talk to me. When he answered, it was a mumble that hardly required the movement of his lips.

'What is your favourite subject?'

'Business.'

'That's an unusual choice for a ten-year-old.'

He looked at me directly. With eyes full of hatred. 'Don't patronize me.'

'I'm not. I wasn't. I'm sorry it came across like that. I'm an unusual fifteen-year-old, to be honest. I liked philosophy and reading old books.' I noticed I was using the past tense. I wondered if I would ever actively like anything again. The present wasn't just a tense, I realized, but a decision. Something you had to decide to accept.

'What's philosophy?' he asked dismissively, but I took it as a serious question.

'It's about why we are here.'

'You mean religion.'

'They overlap. The only difference is that religion has answers and philosophy mainly has questions. You know, like, is there a point to it all? What is good and what is evil? How should we live our lives? What does it mean to be a human?'

'Sounds boring.'

'It's not really,' I said. But I could no longer remember why it wasn't. Maybe if I took the pads off, but I didn't want to do that. It started to come back to me. 'It's pretty damn cool, actually. Because it's just thinking. And that's what makes us special, isn't it, as humans. You know, compared to Echos. We think about stuff. We don't just do stuff. That's why books and paintings and stuff exists. To try and work ourselves out.' My words had no impact so I came to the point. 'Hey, do you like the Echos here?'

He shrugged. Or did the facial equivalent of a shrug. 'Yeah. I suppose.' There was a little pause. 'Most of them.'

Most of them.

'What do you mean by that?'

Iago yawned and didn't cover his mouth.

'The new Echo is a bit weird,' he said.

'Which is the new one?' Though I already knew what he was going to say.

'Daniel.'

'The teenager?' I said, playing dumb.

Iago laughed. It wasn't a pleasant laugh. 'Teenager? He's only two months old.'

Of course, I knew that Echos were designed to look different ages, and to stay looking that age for as long as they were operational. But sometimes you couldn't help but think of them as they looked.

Teenager. Old man. Thirty-year-old woman.

This was for two reasons. First, if all Echos looked the same, then you would never know which was which. Second, different Echos were often used for different jobs. So in the British Museum the tour guides are all elderly-looking Echos, to suggest wisdom; while in physical clothes shops and gene-therapy centres the Echos are always young and good-looking.

'Why don't you like him?' I asked. 'Because he beat you at chess?'

Another shrug. 'He's been weird from day one.'

'Weird how?'

'I dunno,' he said. He had quite a deep voice for a ten-year-old. 'He's just weird. The day he first got here he didn't speak. Dad asked him stuff and he didn't say anything. Dad told him that if he didn't speak soon, he'd have to take him back to be terminated. And then he spoke! Dad got cross 'cause Daniel was meant to be the best one we've ever had. He was meant to be the most advanced Echo ever made.' Iago looked out of the window and smiled to himself. It was a strange smile, full of trouble. 'But he's an Echo, so he obeys orders, and that is fun sometimes. Or *was* fun until he got too clever. But he's a freak.'

The most advanced Echo ever made.

I was going to ask him more, but he opened up the pod. 'What do you do in there?' I asked.

'Kill things,' he said, before disappearing inside.

19

That night I slept again, but there was another interruption.

Just after three in the morning I woke to hear a noise. A floorboard creaking outside my door. I sat up in bed.

'Light,' I said.

With the light on I saw that my door was slightly open. 'Hello? Is anybody there?'

Actual fear was impossible as I was wearing the neuropads, but I still realized I should get out of bed to see what was going on. So I stood up, walked across the room, past the figures huddled together in the painting, looking scared as they listened to music.

But then, just before I opened the door, I heard someone shouting. It was Uncle Alex. 'Get to your quarters!' he bellowed. Then I opened the door just enough to see him on the landing. He was standing there in a black silk dressing gown, with the trees on the animated wallpaper swaying behind him, as if matching his anger. His face was red and there was a demonic fury in his eyes.

Then I opened the door fully and stepped out, just in time to see the back of a male fair-haired Echo head for the end of the landing and disappear downstairs.

Uncle Alex saw me, and his tanned face switched from utter fury to warm sorrow faster than I had imagined possible. 'Audrey, I am so sorry about that.'

'It was him again,' I said. 'Daniel. The chess player.'

'Yes,' he said, fiddling with his rings. 'Yes. There are always a few issues with the most advanced ones. It's nothing to worry about, Audrey. This is the safest place you could possibly be. Well, since the attempted break-in, anyway. I doubt you could find a more safe and secure house in the whole of London.'

'Attempted break-in?'

Uncle Alex nodded. 'Protestors. Anarchists. Thugs. Last October a group of them tried to scale the wall. They very nearly got over too, but one of the Echos saw them and raised the alarm, and – lucky for us – the police were on to these guys already. But it was a close call. Since then, I've stepped up the security. Because they'll try again. They're nothing if not persistent, I can tell you. But listen, there is really nothing to concern you now.'

'OK,' I said, which obviously I wouldn't have said if I hadn't been wearing reasonably new neuropads. But then a small sense of anxiety slowly began to break through.

'You get back to bed, Audrey. I'm going too. I've got Paris tomorrow. There is nothing to worry about.'

'I want to go with you to Paris.'

'But I told you, I'm going to a place full of Echos. Hundreds of them. You said you didn't want to come.'

I swallowed. 'I know, but I think I might have changed my mind.'

I was close enough to see that Uncle Alex was wearing info-lenses.

They were active. Tiny lights flashed across his eyes. Words he'd be able to read but which I couldn't.

'No,' he said, closing his eyes, shaking his head. 'It's work, and I don't think it would be good for you. It's not *Paris* Paris. It's just a warehouse full of assembly-line Echos. It's out of town. It's hardly, I don't know, the Louvre. I don't think it would be your cup of tea.'

He was correct, of course. It didn't sound like my cup of tea. It sounded like my cup of nightmare, to be honest, but I was thinking two things. First thing: I did not want to stay in the house with Iago and Daniel and all the prototypes. Second thing: I wanted information. The neuropads had dulled that impulse for a while. But it had worked its way to the surface again. I wanted to find out what had happened to my parents. I wanted to find out why Alissa – who was not a prototype, but a standard assembly-line Echo – had done what she did. And yes, true, she was a Sempura Echo and we were not going to a Sempura Echo factory, but I wouldn't be able to get access to a Sempura factory.

'I think it would help me. You know, Mrs Matsumoto said I should try and—'

His eyes opened. He looked at me with tired sympathy, but his answer was firmer. 'No. I'm sorry, Audrey. It's a no. There is no way you are coming with me tomorrow. That's the end of the matter. Now, let's get some sleep.' And then he went back to bed.

So did I, only it took me a while to get to sleep again. I was just thinking that my uncle's answer had been a little too firm. Then questions. What had he got to hide? What was in Paris that he didn't want me to see?

Paranoia, I told myself. *I mean, Cloudville* . . . He had saved my life. And he had taken me in and let me live here, in probably the best house in London. He had been kind to me.

But still, the more determined he was that I shouldn't go to Paris, the more determined I was to go there.

Eventually I fell asleep.

Another dream. This one not a nightmare. Not a complete one, anyway.

It was Daniel, and he was crying. An Echo crying tears! And I was holding him and he was trembling in my arms, his strong body rendered suddenly weak from emotion. And he was telling me something in a quiet voice.

'Don't worry about me. I am just an Echo . . .'

And I stroked his hair and kept on telling him, 'It's all right, it's all right, it's all right . . .'

Then I woke up again. And I had a thought. It was still the middle of the night, but I got out of bed and put in my info-lenses.

'Night-vision mode,' I said. And in less than a second, it was as though a light had been switched on. OK, so it was a light that turned everything green, but that was night vision for you.

As quietly as I could, I went along the hallway to Iago's room. He slept with the door slightly open. To let the light in, I supposed. He may have been a hundred other things, but he was also still a young boy who was probably scared of the dark.

Anyway, I pushed the door open and snuck inside his room. I crept across his floor, which was a plush and soundless carpet. I was walking towards his wardrobe. I knew what I was after, and I knew that, if I found it, the journey back out of the room would be a lot safer than the journey in.

I carried on. I saw Iago asleep in his bed. He was curled up on top of the blankets with a thumb in his mouth. I thought of how much he would hate me seeing him like that. It made me smile, just for a moment, seeing the little boy lying there, but I gasped in horror when I turned and saw a soldier with a gun pointing straight at me. By the time I realized it was just a holo-sculpture, Iago was rolling over, borderline awake. I stayed still and didn't breathe for about thirty seconds, and he seemed to fall asleep again.

The wardrobe was voice-activated, so I leaned into the panel and whispered, as quietly as possible: 'Open.'

Nothing.

A little louder: 'Open.'

Nothing.

Then in something close to normal volume: 'Open.'

Iago didn't wake up. Just gave a little snore.

The door rose open silently. And I was faced with Iago's wardrobe. Given that every item was self-clean, he did seem to have a lot of clothes. Smocks, interactive T-shirts, air-suits, all hovering on their hangers, a row of nano-weave cans (he had a lot of spray-on skin-clingers), and tons of slippers and snuggos.

I pulled out one can at a time.

Winter Warmer.

Sport Skin.

Battle-gear Fight Garb (again, this made me smile, thinking of the thumb-sucking mini warrior lying on the bed).

24/7 Clingsuit.

And then I came to it. The can with the plainest, most unassuming writing, which was probably black though I saw it as green. Writing which said:

All-purpose Full Cover Projection-based Invisiwear (for every height *and width) x100 uses. Nano-weave: 15nm diameter. Cotton fibre equipped with nano-cameras and screens. For safety: Do not use in public settings.*

'Gotcha,' I said, but not out loud. I thought about spraying it on right then, as that had been my initial plan, but the noise of the spray might have woken Iago. Plus, I was already wearing my night clothes. So I risked it. I turned and saw an alien with six arms and a giant head and a mouth with three sets of teeth. Another holo-sculpture. I didn't gasp. And I made it out, and back to my room, placing the can under my bed.

20

'Cruise rail,' said Uncle Alex. 'I'm early. And I've got thought-work to do.'

Nightmare. The car switched to a slow rail at the next possible turn-off. It was so slow and quiet he could dictate the speed even further.

'Slower,' Uncle Alex said. He sounded tetchy. He put on his mind-wire and closed his eyes. Thought deeply. Made silent commands. The blur outside the windows sharpened into visible things. Water. Stilt houses. Other magcars on other rails. Clouds. A sky market.

This was *not good*. The longer the journey, the greater the chance of Uncle Alex realizing I was there, right there, right behind him, trying to breathe in slow and soft and soundless breaths. At one point my nose did a little tickle-itch, like I was going to sneeze, but the moment passed.

'No,' he said out loud at one point. 'Clean her up. I don't want to see all that mess.'

I couldn't believe that I was mentally urging us to be closer to a warehouse full of Echos.

There were Echo warehouses all over Europe, Uncle had explained that morning, when I had maybe asked him too much. Some were small specialist ones for prototypes, and some were for creating the copies that were to be rolled out on the general market. The Paris one was the latter kind.

His eyes sprang open. He turned and stared at the space I was occupying. I could see him – the hood was transparent from the inside. My heart was beating so hard I thought he must have been able to hear it. It wouldn't have taken much. Just his hand, reaching back, and then he would have found me there.

And what would he have done? Tell me off? Be confused? Share my embarrassment? Surely nothing too severe. But my fear was there and it felt real.

The projection must have been good. The optical illusion of nothing but a back seat and a rear window must have been seamless, because he turned round again.

'Holophone active,' he commanded. Then he gave the code. 'Valencia four seven asterisk triple three dash seven dash hashtag AAX.'

And then a woman appeared, flickering into life. She looked pretty cool and arty and boho, I suppose, but tired and worried. She had long hair that was a total mess, a pierced eyebrow and some kind of necklace or locket around her neck.

She said something in Spanish that I didn't understand.

'Shut up and speak in bloody English,' said Uncle Alex, in a voice so cold and harsh I hardly recognized it.

She seemed to be in a state. She took a swig of a brown drink. 'How is he? How is the prototype I gave for you?'

'*To* you. You are drunk. Your English isn't normally this sloppy. You gave it *to* me. And oh, my God, you were right. There's something wrong with him. He's not right. This is why he meant so much to you, isn't it? What did you do? What?'

'Where is he? How is he?'

'I've half a mind to come to you right now. I'd beat it out of you if I had to.'

'*Si, si, si.* Yeah. You? Or one of your Echo slaves?'

'No. It's really not worth it. I'll leave you to your whisky. I have important things to do. *Hasta luego . . .*' Then, to the car: 'Call over.'

And the Spanish woman vanished, leaving me wondering about what had happened, and what Uncle Alex thought she was hiding.

For the rest of the journey he spoke in business jargon and mumbled into his mind-wire. I looked out of the window, trying to imagine I wasn't there. I stared at the floating wind farms in the English Channel. And then at the vast wetlands of Northern France, which of course had been hit as badly as Yorkshire, Scotland and Cornwall from continual flooding. Thousands of stilt houses, not dissimilar to the one I'd lived in until two days ago, but smaller and packed together. There were swamps and marshes and cholera clinics, which had been set up a couple of years ago to deal with the latest strain. But then, towards Paris, the land got drier and the houses were bigger and more widely spaced, though the weather was just as grey and stormy and rain-whipped here.

I saw a large holo-ad for the Neo Maxis' new audio capsule. It was called 'Love and the Machine: Live from Neptune'. The ad was the four band members dressed in black moonsuits playing a concert to the small community of terraformers on Neptune. The capsule was going to be released tomorrow. I remembered looking forward to that so much. I had absolutely no feelings about it now, except that the idea of a concert on Neptune seemed like a bit of a gimmick. This made me sad, as I realized how much of the old me had died.

I silently urged the car to speed up, but Uncle Alex kept it on the slow rail.

The magrail passed right up close to a vast enclosed greenhouse. It must have been about eight kilometres long. Inside I saw an ocean of wheat, perfect in every way, shifting to and fro in the artificially induced breeze. There was another greenhouse of a similar size immediately after it. This one farmed livestock. About four hundred cows, all identical – literally indistinguishable from one another – completely oblivious to the pounding weather outside. I felt sad for them. They were born to die the most pointless of deaths, especially as synthetic meat was now probably better than the real thing. But some people always wanted the real thing, I supposed.

Finally my wish was granted.

'Full speed,' Uncle Alex said. 'Fast rail.' And we were there in seconds.

The warehouse was on dry land, deep in the eighteenth arrondissement. Far in the distance I saw the large glowing white hologram of the Eiffel Tower, which had been put there after French anti-Echo protestors had destroyed the first one back when I was a child.

I remembered the original metal one, which had seemed more beautiful, even though it had only been half the size of the hologram. As I did so, a thousand Parisian memories came back. All those Saturdays. From the car I could see the gigantic Centre Aquatique far away: two cubes, one fixed to the ground and one floating above. The top one had a picture of a dolphin inside a rubber ring. The children's pool, where Mum and Dad always used to take me, was in there. I closed my eyes.

'Focus,' I said silently.

That was then. This is now.

There was no Castle logo on the warehouse. It was an ancient brick building – maybe two hundred years old – surrounded by derelict apartment blocks. Some were black and burned-out, as sad and gone as childhood memories.

I remembered something my info-lenses had told me about riots in Paris. Maybe it was around here but the warehouse itself seemed undamaged. There was hardly anyone around now. I guessed people who didn't work in the warehouse had little reason to come here.

Uncle Alex left the car and headed through the gale-force wind towards it. I should have felt relieved. I should have just got the hell out of there and found a taxi home. But no, I wasn't going to do that. I needed to know more. I was about to enter a place full of Echos. A place where they were made. My heart raced. My mouth was dry. My chest was tight with anxiety. I was becoming too used to the neuropads.

'Open the door,' I told the car.

'*You are not an authorized user of this vehicle. Declare your identity.*'

'I am Audrey Castle,' I said. 'I am Alex Castle's niece. I live with him.'

The car obviously had lie-detect software and knew that this was the truth. No further instructions were needed.

'*Door opening*.'

It was windy. There was no leviboard there, so I pressed the button on the dashboard that Uncle Alex had used to radio the nearest one. A moment later a rickety-looking old steel leviboard came sliding along towards me. It had a flimsy handrail, and it was blowing a gale out there.

I could see that this wasn't the safest part of town. It kind of looked like the apocalypse. A hacked advertising board, showing images of a man shooting himself in the head with an old matter-messer flickered and throbbed above me, disrupting what was meant to be an advert for the iWire 42. I heard Mum's voice in my mind: *Why don't we go to the Louvre for a couple of hours? Ever since the Mona Lisa was stolen the crowds aren't so bad there.*

After I descended I walked across a large dilapidated patch of tarmac. The air smelled of fresh rain and dead dreams.

I stood there and stared at the vast, blank brick building, which was as large as a cathedral. I needed to breathe properly, so I pulled down my hood. I saw a leaflet on the ground, blowing towards me. A crumpled piece of illuminated electronic paper, full of flickering text and moving images.

It was a damp French edition of *Castle Watch*, the newsletter that was against everything Castle did. I looked around to see who it could have belonged to, but it really was like a ghost town. There was a language option at the bottom of the page, so I clicked 'English'. Quickly, an article appeared, complete with a photograph of the pink-haired young woman who had submitted the piece.

HERO CAMPAIGNER DIES

– ARTICLE FILED BY LEONIE JENSON 17.5.2115

Leading journalist and tech-sceptic Leo Castle was murdered alongside his wife at his home in Yorkshire (Zone 3) on Wednesday. Although the full details of what happened are yet to emerge, they are thought to have been killed by an Echo. There is no word yet as to how the Echo entered their home . . .

Before I could read on, something happened. The still image of the journalist beside the article suddenly jerked into life. It was a live connection. Location-tracked. The connected world.

'Hello?' said the pink-haired woman, Leonie. She looked out of the picture like someone looking for something in fog. '*Bonjour. Salut. Qui est là?*'

'Audrey Castle,' I said.

'It says on the location tracker that you are near an Echo warehouse in Paris, which is why I am interested. I'd set up an alert, you see, for that area, as soon as someone picked it up – because the only people around there are going to be— Wait! Audrey Castle? As in, Leo Castle's daughter? As in, Alex Castle's niece?'

I nodded. She could see me.

'What are you doing?'

I told her.

She asked me if she could ask questions about how my parents had died. I said no. I didn't trust *Castle Watch*. They were linked to the hardest fringe of anti-Castle protestors. Borderline terrorists.

'I would just like to know how the Echo came to get in the house?'

'It was *our* Echo,' I said. I knew that I was crushing an idea of my dad in her mind – one which all these hippies had: the idea that my dad was some kind of saint who never went near technology and lived in a bubble totally separate from the modern world. To be fair, it was an image my dad had been happy to encourage. 'Mum and Dad bought her. From Sempura.'

She looked like I had slapped her. I didn't care. I didn't want my dad to be remembered as an angel, because he wasn't an angel. He was my dad.

'Sempura?' she said eventually. 'Why would a Sempura Echo want to kill your parents?'

'Why would any Echo want to kill my parents? Echos don't want anything. They are machines.'

She nodded furiously. 'Yes, exactly. They are machines. They are programmed. They are given instructions. Are you sure they bought the Echo from Sempura?'

'What are you trying to say?'

'I am trying to say that your uncle is the most immoral man in the business world. And your dad was about to publish a book that could have damaged the prospects of your uncle's pet project, the Resurrection Zone.'

'You didn't know my dad,' I said. 'And you don't know my uncle.'

I ended the conversation by screwing up the sheet of e-paper and throwing it – along with Leonie Jenson's moving image – back down onto the tarmac, where it skittered away, carried along by the strong wind.

This was it. I was going into the Echo factory. My plan was simple: I would put my hood back up and I would wait here, invisibly, and follow someone into the building. I waited twenty seconds, counting them out in my head, before someone appeared. A man in blue overalls, with an animated tattoo on the back of his neck. Just a rolling word – MINOTAUR – probably after the hardcore Brazilian magneto band.

'Blackjack,' he said, clear and loud, into the voicebox, and the metal door quickly slid open, after recognizing the voice. The door made a scratching sound you could hear above the wind.

I followed him inside, trying to ignore the sign that said SECURIDROID PROTECTED and matching his footsteps with mine. I was inside the factory now. The air was still, but even cooler than outside. It smelled strange. I couldn't really work out what it was, because it wasn't strong. It was kind of a clean but unnatural smell – as faint as fresh air, but in the opposite direction. The ceiling was high. The light was a kind of spooky dim grey.

I felt like I had really done the wrong thing. I was now in a vast hangar-sized room filled with hundreds of Echos. A whole assembly line of them. And they were all the same. Exactly the same.

I stepped forward. Had a good look. They were all exactly like the prototype Madara, back at the house in Hampstead, except that these were all totally motionless, and standing in giant transparent eggs that were about three times my size. The eggs hung down from the ceiling on long, equally transparent wires, which I suppose must have been made out of aerogel or something to hold the eggs and the Echos they contained.

I couldn't see my uncle anywhere. At first I couldn't see anyone other than the man I had followed in, who walked over to one of the eggs in the middle of the room. He held his hand against the side of the egg, and some kind of work panel glowed into life. He began inputting stuff, pressing the illuminated gold and green light-buttons that had appeared.

Pretty soon, I realized that he was not the only one. There were at least five people – Echo technicians, I suppose – all in the same blue overalls and all attending to different eggs in different parts of the room.

I looked around for the securidroid, but there was no metal robot anywhere to be seen. Maybe the sign had been a lie.

Doubtful.

Uncle Alex would have wanted to keep his factories safe.

I turned and walked back and tried – as quietly as I could manage – to open the door, just to know I could if I needed to. There was a small red light-button beside it, which I put my hand over, but the light didn't turn green, and the door wouldn't open. I was trapped, until someone came and I could follow them.

This was a mistake, but I was here now. I had to stay calm. I walked into the room, amid the egg-shaped incubation things. It was like being in some sinister art exhibit at the Zuckerberg Center or something. A strange maze of hovering eggs. I stared up at the ceiling and saw, far above me, between the aerogel wires that held the eggs, silver nozzles like shower heads. I wondered what they released.

What was I doing? What was I doing? What was I doing?

As I walked, I grappled under my invisiwear to press the neuropads further into my skin. I pulled the face-piece down, became partially visible. Just my head floating in space. I quickly tried to make amends and cover it back up. I passed one of the technicians. A tall skinny woman with a shaven head. She heard me. Turned round. Cold and curious eyes. I stood dead still, aware that a tiny piece of my forehead – and full left eyebrow – was visible. I stayed still and held my breath. She stared. I hoped her info-lenses didn't have a zoom function.

She shook her head, thinking it was nothing, then pressed some green command on the side of her egg.

I am not made to be a spy.

The far wall had lots of doors in it. Uncle Alex was probably behind one of them. He could have been watching me right then. 'Help me,' I said, in a quiet – I thought, almost silent – voice, to no one in particular.

My voice triggered the Madara that was nearest to come to life inside her egg. '*Hello, did you need me for anything?*' This sound, in turn, triggered other Madaras to speak, each one offering the same strained smile. '*Hello, did you need me for anything? Hello, did you need me for anything? Hello, did you need me for anything?'*

'No, I—' I tried to re-cover my face, realizing that the technicians working in the room would now be aware of the commotion.

'Hello, did you need me for anything? Hello, did you need me for anything? . . . Are you getting hungry? Are you getting hungry? Are you getting hungry? Are you getting hungry? . . . I'm sorry, I didn't hear you. I'm sorry, I didn't hear you. I'm sorry, I didn't hear you . . .'

They were obviously not quite finished yet, and some rows didn't even have eyes fitted in their sockets. I began walking quickly across the light grey concrete floor, back towards the door.

And that is when I saw it.

That is when I saw the blood.

Just a few drops, a near-black constellation of them. And then a few more drops further along. And a few more. I followed them to where they led. Towards the far wall, the furthest from the exit. The last row of eggs. They were empty; in fact, both of the last two rows were empty eggs. But the blood was leading to the egg in the far corner, at the end of the last row of empties. Only this one wasn't empty. There was an Echo inside, her body strangely contorted. The egg had an illuminated notice on it. The notice said:

ASSESSMENT MODE (62): DO NOT TOUCH

At first I thought it was another Madara. After all, the whole place was full of them. It was only when I got right up close that I realized that the hair colour was too light.

There, right in front of me, in this Castle-run Echo factory, was my parents' killer.

Alissa.

I don't think I screamed. It was more of a gasp. But a gasp loud enough to be heard by her, because she turned towards me.

She looked at me with absolutely no recognition; then her eyes closed. Her body was broken and bloodied. Her face was caved in. Her head fell back against the transparent three-metre-high egg she was in, causing it to wobble a little. It wasn't a replica Alissa. This wasn't another version. This was the one that I had driven into, fast. The one I thought I had destroyed. I nearly fainted. Everything that was in me, that kept me upright and together and in one piece, kind of left for a second or two, and I tilted forward onto the egg, just where the notice was glowing blue.

This set off an alarm. A loud siren that woke me up again and made me alert. And a loud robotic voice: '*Intruder alert. Row One. Assessment Pod under threat. Intruder alert. Row One. Assessment Pod under threat . . .*'

Then, inevitably, I heard the technicians running through that vast room, past all those other large eggs.

'*Intruder Alert. Intruder unseen, but thermo-detected.*' Straight after that announcement was made I heard a noise above me. A kind of whooshing. I looked up, only to get soaked by a bright turquoise liquid.

'Invisiwear antidote released,' said the robotic voice.

The invisiwear evaporated away, dissolving on impact with the turquoise liquid. And within a second it was just me, visible in my cling-top and jeans, although those clothes now had turquoise stains all over them.

During this moment, the Madaras had stopped talking, and one of the doors on the far wall had opened.

I needed to get out of there. I looked around the room, at the neat rows of hanging clear eggs and the bodies inside them. And the walls, which were watching, the way walls always did.

I started running, but a securidroid had appeared out of nowhere in front of me. It was quite small, and was really just metal legs and a face, but the face had guns for ears pointing at me, so when it said, '*Stay right there*,' I obeyed.

A group of people, Uncle Alex among them, came rushing over. Uncle pushed through the others – some of them technicians, two in (now turquoise-stained) suits, who were starting to look angry. One of the suited men wore all-white info-lenses, like posers wear, making him look like an alien. Another had a red mohawk. The neuropads were not doing anywhere near enough.

'What is this?' Uncle Alex shouted. He looked at me. For a moment his face showed total fury. The turquoise stains on his self-clean suit slowly shrank and disappeared, as they did on the clothes of everyone else in the room. All except mine. Well, my jeans self-cleaned. But my cling-top was old-school non-clean and the stains stayed. 'What are you doing here?'

And then he rubbed his hand over his face as if washing his anger away. A streak of turquoise spread across it like faded war paint.

The turquoise was on his fingers now. He showed it me. 'It's nothing high tech, this, you know? Just simple paint blended with titanium oxide. That reacts with invisiwear, disables it completely – that is the criminal's uniform, of course.'

Was that what I was to him? A criminal? Was I going to be punished like one?

He looked first at me, then at Alissa – her broken body splattered in blood – through the aerogel. He softened his tone. 'Audrey, why are you here?'

'It's . . . it's . . .'

Uncle Alex switched mood again and turned to the man with the mohawk, wearing a scruffy but evidently self-clean suit. 'Guillaume, why the *hell* is this on the main floor? Tell me.'

'The only w-w-way we could keep her in this kind of c-c-condition was to put her in a reha—'

'Jesus! Je-e-*sus*! What is with you people?' He closed his eyes tight, and pressed the bridge of his nose with frustration. The phone call in the car hadn't been a fluke. There really was another side to Uncle Alex.

He put his arm around me. 'Come on, Audrey, tell me. Why are you here? Why did you follow me?'

'You said . . . I couldn't come, but I wanted to. I wanted to understand. I wanted to know more. About Echos. I thought you didn't want me to come, so I thought . . . I thought . . .'

Uncle Alex tucked a loose strand of my hair behind my ear. 'Don't worry. You don't have to explain yourself to me. I'll take you home. I am sorry you saw it.'

I should probably have left it at that. But there was a question that just wouldn't let go. And I asked it, when we were outside.

'What was it doing there?' We walked over the damaged ground towards the leviboard. 'It's a Sempura . . .'

We rose up on the leviboard, Uncle Alex shielding me from the weather. He responded when we were back in the car, totally sealed off from the wind. I stared at the warehouse, sitting under nightmarish clouds.

'We're a business,' he said. 'From the very beginning we've studied our competitors' products. We're a better company than Sempura. We're a principled company. This isn't just a financial war. It's a . . . it's a moral war. We're winning, on both counts, but I'm not so arrogant as to think I've cornered the market on every innovation.'

This wasn't making sense. I was struggling just to keep up.

'And it's not just about successes. It's failures too.'

'Oh.'

'You can learn just as much from failure as you can from success. We study our competitors' failures in the hope that we can avoid such tragedies. And in this case I really wanted to find out what had happened, for obvious reasons. I wanted to know the how and the why. I'm not saying we'll be able to find it, but if there's an answer, then the best place to look is Alissa's circuitry.'

'Right.'

'I didn't want to tell you that I was doing this, and I told them to hide her well away – just in case someone who shouldn't have seen her ever saw her. Which has obviously just happened in the most spectacular way. They are useless, the factory managers, the technicians . . . You see, all the brilliant minds work on the prototypes. There is one in particular, in a small warehouse in Valencia, who is an absolute genius.' I wondered if this was the Spanish woman he had been shouting at, but then I thought it couldn't have been, as he surely wouldn't have treated someone he admired like that. I was going to ask, but I didn't want to remind him that I had witnessed that conversation. 'But Echo factories like this Paris one . . . they're just middle links in the chain. They just input data into computers mainly.'

'But that wasn't a random copy,' I said as I saw the crumpled *Castle Watch* newsletter fly past the window, and higher still into the sky. 'That was her. That was the same Alissa I thought I had terminated.'

He ordered the car to head back to London.

We travelled fast this time. The greenhouses and floodlands and wind farms dissolved into the same blur. 'Yes it was. Because, as I have said, I want to know exactly what happened. Your dad was also my brother. I owe it to him – and to you, and to your mum – to make sure that nothing like this happens again. So I had people go to the house – to your old house – and drag her out of the water and bring her there.'

'But what about the police? What about the investigation?'

'Don't worry. The police have seen her. And listen, I wanted to get hold of that Echo before Sempura got to her, and started a cover-up. Anyway, don't worry about that.' He smiled a caring smile. I had expected him to be cross with me for following him, but he wasn't. This confused me.

'Listen,' he said, 'we have a chance here – a chance for your parents' deaths not to have been in vain. Information is a weapon. And I want to do everything to make sure we know exactly what happened. You understand?'

We were nearly home. I looked at Uncle Alex and didn't really know who I was looking at. Was he bad or was he good – or was he like most of humanity, hovering somewhere in between?

'Yes,' I said as the car stopped. 'I do.'

21

Hours later, Uncle Alex went into his pod for a meeting. I decided to take advantage of this and explore the house. I went downstairs. In the hallway I walked past a hologram of a unicorn and into the grand lobby. Iago wasn't around. But Echos were. There was a female one I hadn't seen before. She was polishing an antique chest and looked at me with blank eyes.

I walked on through the lobby, past more holo-sculptures and expensive furniture. There were a couple of Echos in the kitchen, preparing food. I walked straight past and turned right into a dark narrow corridor, and began to feel a bit more nervous as I realized I was heading towards the Echo quarters.

There was no one there.

The first door I came to was locked. Like most of the doors in this house, it had an old-fashioned door handle you could turn and push. Which I did. But then I felt a hand grip my arm.

'Stop,' said a voice. I turned and saw him. The blond one. Daniel. He stared at me intensely – nothing like the stare of the one who had been polishing the old chest.

It was then that I began to panic, and pulled away from him.

'You shouldn't be here,' he said. 'It isn't safe. Does your uncle know?'

'No.'

'What are you doing here?'

'I . . . I don't know.' But as I said it, I realized exactly what I was doing here and what I was looking for. I was looking for him. He was the one who had tried to break into my room in the middle of the night. And I wanted to know why. But then he grabbed my arm again, tighter this time. It hurt. And he pulled me further along the dark corridor. Now I was scared. He seemed stronger than Alissa. If that hand was around my neck, it could have killed me in a second.

'Help!' I screamed. Even though the moment you scream help, you sound and feel more like a victim.

His hand was over my mouth. 'Shut up,' he said.

I ignored him and tried to scream again, but it was muffled now. Just a blunt noise. We reached the last door in the corridor, and he turned the handle and opened it. Pushed me inside. Shut the door. It was a bare room. Nothing but a wooden bed without a mattress, and a sink, and a small square window.

'Don't scream,' he said. 'I am not going to hurt you. I promise.'

I had no idea if I should believe him.

'Why did you climb up to my window, that first night I was here? Why?'

'I wanted to tell you something.'

'What?'

'I wanted to tell you about how I was made. And who made me.'

'Why did you want to tell me that?'

'Because it would explain things. It would explain why I am not like the others. It would also explain about . . .' He hesitated mid-sentence. This was odd. I mean, Echos never hesitated mid-sentence. 'About why I feel guilty.'

'You can't feel guilty. You're a machine.'

His eyes did a good imitation of looking hurt. He started to talk quietly. 'Do you think I am an automaton?'

'An automaton? What, like an android? Yes! You're an Echo. Enhanced Computerized Humanoid Organism. You can't feel guilt. You're tricking me. I want to go.'

'A machine without feelings? And can I bear to have my morsel of bread snatched from my lips, and my drop of living water dashed from my cup?'

He looked at me with anger in his eyes. It felt real, that anger. And then I realized that his words sounded familiar.

'That's from a book.'

He nodded. 'It's from one of yours. *Jane Eyre*. Your books were brought down here before they were taken up to your room. Your uncle wanted to have all your stuff checked.'

'Checked? He never told me that.'

I had never had a conversation with an Echo before. Sure, Alissa had given me lessons and spoken to me a lot, but that had been different. That had been like interacting with a living computer. Everything had felt logical. But there was nothing logical about talking to Daniel.

He frowned deeply, as if in pain. I had a strange urge to comfort him. I wanted to touch his arm and tell him it was OK. I didn't, of course, but the urge was there.

'And why were you reading my books? Who told you to do that?'

'No one told me to do that.'

'But why would an Echo read a book unless someone had told them to?'

He took a deep breath. 'I like reading. I enjoy it. It helps me escape. In my head, I mean.'

'But that makes no sense.'

'Not everything does.'

His head turned sharply, like an animal. I followed his eyes towards the door. 'Someone's coming,' he said.

I couldn't hear anything, but I vaguely knew that Echo hearing was a lot more powerful than the human kind.

'Listen,' he said, coming close to me and speaking in a hushed voice. 'Alissa was meant to kill you too. She was meant to kill your whole family. To make it clean. But it didn't happen like that. You survived . . .' He stopped a moment. Listened. 'They're sixteen metres away, getting closer.'

I heard it now too. Footsteps.

'You are in danger here,' he said.

'But how can I trust you? For all I know, you could be about to malfunction and kill me too.'

He shook his head, impatient, but there was a softness in his eyes that was almost human. 'If I wanted you dead, you would be dead, wouldn't you? And trust me, there was never any malfunction. The only thing that didn't go according to plan was you. You were tougher than he thought.'

'Alissa was female.'

I could feel his breath on me. It was warm. Of course it was. Echos may have been artificial, but they were biological. They were given bones and blood and hearts and breath. Their brains may have had hardware in them, their blood may have had different minerals in it, their muscles may have been ten times more efficient, but they were still breathing *bodies*.

'You have to go.' I thought he meant I had to get out of the room, but it was too late for that.

The door opened. An Echo male stood there, staring at me with cold eyes. It was one of the ones that had been working in the kitchen. He was completely hairless, like most kitchen Echos.

'What is occurring?' he asked.

'I – er – I—'

But Daniel was quick with the right excuse, and even adopted a cool and even Echo voice, quite different to the one he had used with me. 'Hello, Thomas. The human girl had lost one of her books and wondered if it was down here.'

'Why would it have been down here?'

'She knew Madara had collected her books. And she knew Madara was an Echo, so she headed to the Echo quarters.'

Thomas stood there, looking at me with wide eyes. He didn't blink. 'So why is she in your room and not Madara's?'

'I don't know my way around,' I said quickly. 'I've never been in this bit of the house before.'

'What level of risk would you give this situation?' Thomas asked Daniel.

'I would give it a zero. There is no risk. The human girl is Mr Castle's niece.'

Thomas nodded. Then to me he said, 'I will escort you back to the human area.'

I looked up and Daniel gave me the smallest of nods, indicating that I should go with Thomas.

'I hope you find your book,' Daniel said to me, in role, as I left the room. 'I hear page 206 is particularly good.'

Thomas didn't hold my arm as we headed back to 'the human area', as he'd called it, but even so I didn't feel any safer.

'Enjoy your evening,' he said, with all the passion of a refrigerator.

I walked back through the lobby, alone, passing the Echo polishing the chest and seeing a couple more guarding the front door. For the first time I felt like I was being kept not in a friendly house but in a kind of prison.

Page 206? I wondered. *What does that mean?*

I had no idea. But as I climbed that old staircase, I began to realize that Daniel, the most mysterious Echo I had ever seen, held the key to everything.

Daniel. Mind-log 1.

Remember.

1

The thing burning into my shoulder caused me a significant amount of pain.

My arms were strapped tight. I was in some kind of a container. My body was in thick clear liquid, right up to my neck.

The liquid was rising slowly. It was now touching my chin.

At first this was a passive observation, and one made without knowing such words as 'liquid' and 'chin'.

But slowly there came an instinct.

(This is what I have discovered. Before thought, before knowledge, there is instinct. It is the root of everything.)

And the instinct I had was:

Panic.

Without understanding why, I felt I had to get out of there. I pulled desperately on the straps. I screamed. The scream was not a word. I did not scream 'Help!' – I would have, if I'd known to do so, but I didn't. The scream was just noise. A desperate roar that gave me enough strength for my arms, then legs, to break free of their constraints.

That is when I started banging on the side of the tank.

I kept banging and screaming until I heard something that wasn't a bang or a scream.

The sound was coming from outside. I think there was a sense of relief that there *was* an outside, and that the whole world wasn't confined to a tank full of ever-rising liquid.

Something was opening the tank. Something, someone – whatever. Maybe the tank was opening itself, but the key fact – the only important fact – was that the tank opened and I fell a short distance onto hard ground.

I was in a vast space. It was still an enclosed space, but it was many, many times larger than the tank. There was no liquid here, either. Only what had arrived with me, which was now being absorbed into the floor.

I looked back from where I had come.

The tank.

A white oval attached to the ceiling and floor via a transparent cylinder.

There were other tanks in the room. How many, I couldn't tell. All sealed.

I got to my feet. Looked down at my body. It looked neither strange nor familiar. It just was.

A noise.

Something getting nearer.

Someone.

It was a woman. I know that now, but I didn't know it then. She had long hair and wore white clothes. She was on her own. She came close to me. She knelt beside me. Her face was frowning. She said things, but I think she knew I couldn't understand them.

She had something in her hand. It was small and grey and moving. If I'd ever seen a centipede, I might have thought it was one. Though, of course, it wasn't. It wasn't anything alive. She placed it between her thumb and finger and mimed putting it in her ear, and then pointed it at me. At my ear.

I understood enough about this instruction to put it to my ear after she had given it me. Within seconds it was moving in my head. I could feel it inside me. It wasn't painful. It wasn't even weird, because to find something weird you have to have had experience of normality. But I didn't have experience of anything.

Then I must have shut down. That thing inside my head had shut me down. Because there was a gap. A time that I can't remember. A gap during which I was born.

2

When I woke up, everything was different. I understood things. I understood that I was lying on a bed – a futon – on a floor, and I knew that the floor was made from a cloth of ceramic fibres, and I also somehow knew that this particular type of material had been invented in 2067, and was widely used in home environments as a means of insulating against extremes of heat and cold. Seeing the baking sun outside, I realized which one. In this room it was thirty-nine degrees centigrade.

On my skin I felt the keratin from the preservation fluid that had covered me in the tank.

I sat up. I looked around. I was somewhere else. I was in a house. A villa. In the desert. There was a photographic poster on the wall of a skyline and the words NEW NEW YORK. (New New York – human population: 17,345,952; Echo population: 5,492,600.) Also, there was a cross on the wall with a small sculpture of a dying man fastened to it. I had no knowledge about this man, except that he was made of pewter. The room's size was easy for me to measure. Indeed, it happened automatically. Six by four metres.

There was the distant sound of a man coughing.

And there was the woman. She was standing above me and looking down. I understood that she was thirty-eight years old and that she was free from unnatural genetic or surgical enhancements. Her face was handsome, which was a word normally used for men, but it fitted her more than beautiful.

She was looking at me with confused eyes, her forehead continually creased.

I calculated that there were 268,245 hairs on her head, most of them long and bleached from the sun, and dishevelled. She was 168 centimetres tall and weighed 61 kilograms. Her skin condition suggested a depletion of collagen and melanin, indicating that, although she currently had no serious illnesses, she was seriously stressed and sleep-deprived. I would have guessed she only had about two hours' sleep a night. She had a piece of circular jewellery piercing her eyebrow, made of platinum. She was wearing a locket around her neck. This was not platinum, but gold, though the chain itself was steel. A Spanish word was engraved on the locket. The word was SIEMPRE, which meant *always*, or *for ever*.

She spoke to me.

She said: '*Hola. Me llamo Rosella*.'

This was Spanish and not my default language. The one I had been programmed to speak before all others was English. But I understood her instantly, just as I had understood the writing on the locket. *Hello. My name is Rosella*.

Again, I didn't know how.

Later she would tell me that the bug-like thing that had got inside my head was called an igniter. It basically switched on my knowledge. The knowledge that had been programmed into me. I was programmed to know all kinds of things. I knew that I was on a water planet called Earth that travelled through space at 107,279 kilometres an hour. I knew that the universe we belonged to was a million million million million kilometres across. I knew the composition of the air, and could tell, just by inhaling, how much was nitrogen and how much was oxygen. I could have written *Welcome home* in Russian (**Добро пожаловать домой**). I knew that I was an Echo, and that an Echo's function was to serve humans, without question.

I also knew that I was a prototype. Prototypes were the only Echos that needed igniters, because they were the first of their kind. Assembly-line Echos were copies of what came before. If a company wanted to replicate an Echo, they could do it a million times without a single igniter.

Rosella was smiling at me now. The smile was harder to translate than the words, especially as she seemed to be on the verge of tears.

'*Y tú te llamas Daniel*.'

I heard my name and found it weird that I knew so much, and yet had to be told what my name was. She gave me clothes to wear. She told me I was in Spain. She told me about the government, about how she hated them. I knew that the West European government was based in an ever-moving hydra-bubble hovering high above Madrid, which sometimes travelled to Paris and Barcelona 2. I knew they had been responsible for getting rid of most humans who worked in the civil service and replacing them with Echos. In the police force and army, the replacements had mainly been robots, not Echos. On 14 February of this year, 2115, these robots – securidroids – had suppressed human rights campaigners in Seville, who had been protesting against rising homelessness and deaths as a result of a policy of land clearance.

She gave me some shoes to wear too.

She held a glass mirror in front of me.

I saw myself.

My face.

It was the face of a male human boy. Or almost.

Neat light-blond hair, side-parted. 140,000 strands. Green eyes. My skin, though, was too smooth to belong to a human. It had no blemishes, no pores. I looked faultless, thanks to all that keratin.

Rosella told me that I was the best she had ever designed. But she did not seem happy. When she spoke, I could tell there was tension inside her.

Outside the room there was an open door leading to another room. There was a bed with an old man sleeping in it. He had a transparent mask over his face and he wheezed and coughed in his sleep.

'Where are we?'

'You are in my villa.'

'Is it a good place?'

'Fifty years ago, maybe. I hate it here.'

'Why?'

'It is in the middle of a desert.'

'A desert?'

'On a good day it is fifty degrees centigrade out there. On a bad day you might as well set foot in hell.'

'Hell? What is hell?'

'Of course. I haven't programmed you to understand religion. I left that out. I had to leave something out. Hell is . . . a very hot place, where people are punished for former sins. We are fifty kilometres outside Valencia. But no one lives here who doesn't have to live here. All the houses, all the villas you can see outside are free. Most are empty. No one officially lives here any more. They haven't lived in them for decades. It's too hot. Everyone moved to the coast or the north. The Basque country or Catalonia. Or France or England. It is considered uninhabitable land here. The West European government doesn't want anyone living here. France has the weather we had decades ago. Sunshine, but not like this. We have these ancient air-conditioning systems from the 2030s that I've restored and upgraded, but it's very unhealthy living here. Especially for my granddad.'

She explained that her granddad was the man in the next room, who was now coughing. His name was Ernesto Márquez. He was very old. He was 132. But I knew that the average male human lives to be 168, in 2115, the current year.

'His lungs are deteriorating, and the heat and the extra air-conditioning aren't good for him.' She paused for a while as she stared out at the scorched ground. 'I hate this place.'

'So why do you live here?'

Rosella laughed. It wasn't a happy laugh. 'Because it is free.'

She explained that although she was a celebrated Echo designer and AI expert, she had little money. She had been stuck in a contract with Castle Industries for over ten years, and they paid her very little money.

'But that is going to change,' she whispered, to herself as much as me.

The place where she worked was Valencia, which she could only reach by old neglected land roads across the desert. I had been made there.

And then I had another question. It was a simple question. The simplest in the world. 'What am I?'

I knew so much, but I didn't know that basic thing.

'You are an Echo,' she said, in her heavily accented English. 'Why did you have to ask that? You know you are an Echo. You have that knowledge.'

'I know about Echos. But I know they don't feel fear. And I felt fear, in the tank.'

Rosella's mouth became thinner and tighter. I knew that this was a sign of lying, or concealing truth.

'There is something you are not telling me,' I said. 'I should not feel fear.'

'You are right. An Echo doesn't feel fear. Not usually.'

She studied me for a while (one minute, forty-eight seconds) in silence. Then she went out of the room. When she returned she had a book.

Images appeared on blank electronic paper.

'What do you see?' she asked, each time a new silhouette formed. And so I told her.

'A butterfly . . . a tree . . . a hand . . . a bridge . . .'

She flicked to another blank page. This time it was a pattern. 'What does this make you think of?'

I looked at the black spiral in front of me. I answered honestly. 'Despair.'

She nodded, as if something had just been confirmed.

Audrey. Mind-log 428.

1

The day after my encounter with Daniel I put in my info-lenses and decided to watch some of my dad's old h-logs. They weren't about anything personal, or to do with his life. They were just his thoughts on various technological developments.

I hadn't bothered to watch many of them while he was alive, but now that he was dead I wanted to see his face and hear his voice. I also wanted information. Uncle Alex was certainly right about that. Information was a weapon. So I went through lots of them, his holographic image appearing before me on the virtual retinal display, as if he was in the room with me.

I sat there, before breakfast, listening to him talk about the perils of magnetic levitation, of terraforming Mars and Neptune, of Echos. It was the kind of stuff that would once have bored me to tears.

He spoke of immersion-pod addiction, of nanostarships, of shape-shifting technology, of self-clean upholstery, and – in his very last entry – of neuropads. Inevitably, I watched this one with the most interest of all.

'By placating our minds,' he said, wincing quite a bit from pain (this must have been soon after the accident), 'and by keeping us on a permanent even keel, these long-proposed neuropads may keep sadness at bay, at least in the short term. But at what price? Unpublished research, conducted by the firms involved in developing this technology, confirms the risks. Neuropads, by slowing down and suppressing vital neuro-adaptive processes, actually stop us feeling anything at all. We lose all fear, but also all curiosity. And a human who doesn't feel curiosity about the world stops being fully human, because curiosity about the world is what defines us. But of course, over the next few years the last thing the big firms want us to do is be curious, or worry about stuff, because that would lead to questions about the technology they are marketing to us. They want submissive minds. Of course they do. And do you know why?'

He raised his eyebrows, the way he always used to.

'Why, Dad?' I said, trying to imagine that this was an actual conversation.

'Money. That's why. Not just the money they'll make from selling neuropads, but also the money they'll keep making if they ever manage to stop us asking questions, and thinking for ourselves. So please, if you have bought some of the first ones that have just appeared on the market, if you are wearing them right now . . . take them off. Even if it means feeling sadness and anxiety, take them off. It is better to be alive than in a waking sleep. It is better to remember than to forget. It is better to feel than to be numb. It is better to be a sad poem than a blank page. We are humans. I want us to stay that way.'

'Yes, Dad,' I said. And he smiled, and I pretended the smile was for me, and then I switched the program to 'adaptive mode' and asked him to hug me, and he did so, but I knew that I was hugging a ghost.

I thought of what he had said.

I thought of Grandma going mad on her everglows.

We are humans.

It is better to feel than to be numb.

To be numb was as good as being dead.

I took off the neuropads. And waited as I sat on the end of the bed.

Sure enough, the sadness arrived. It was a terrible, strong sadness, but I wasn't afraid of it. In fact, in a weird way I cherished it. The tears I cried were a measure of how much I had loved my parents. And it was useful to have that measure. It meant that even though I had lost them, I hadn't lost the love. So long as I went on feeling, then I would be connected to my parents through that love.

It is better to be alive than in a waking sleep.

Then, as my mind became clearer, I remembered something Daniel had said the day before, and used the info-lenses to find something out.

I double-blinked them to life, then asked out loud: 'Please could you tell me how long Sempura recommends you should keep an EMS? An, erm, Echo Monitoring System? Is it 250 days?'

Then bright Castle-blue text appeared, floating in the air.

Sempura is the only technology company to produce an Echo Monitoring System. It recommends that their EMS is used for as long as the Echo is in the house. Indeed, the longer the Echo is there, the more useful the EMS becomes.

'Is an Echo ever commanded by Sempura to throw the EMS away?'

No.

I felt my skin prickle with fear, or anger – it was difficult to tell which.

'Are Echos capable of lying?'

Only if they are programmed or reprogrammed to do so.

'Has any Echo ever felt emotion?'

No.

I stopped asking questions as I heard footsteps outside. Uncle Alex had brought me breakfast. Fruit salad. Cinnamon toast. Lychee water.

'Why aren't you wearing the pads?' he asked.

'I'd rather be sad than blank.'

He smiled a little.

I felt like he wanted to tell me something. Yeah. Or ask me something. I assumed it was about yesterday, and Alissa. But no.

'What were you doing in the Echo quarters yesterday?'

'I – I . . . was just . . . I'd lost a book. How did you know I was there?'

'The walls have eyes,' he said, laughing.

And then he left me alone.

2

I had a bath.

It was a thermo-bath so the water never cooled and stayed clean. I put it on saltwater setting to start, then pure.

I must have lain there for ages, thinking that if my parents hadn't been killed, I'd have been with them right now. It was a Saturday. Maybe in another universe I was having that Saturday.

The hardest bit about losing people you loved wasn't thinking about the memories you had, the ones that had already been made. No. The hardest bit was the stuff that should have been, but had now been denied. The stuff Alissa had stolen.

I spent the day in my room.

I had no intention of leaving it. What would be the point, after what Uncle Alex had said?

The walls have eyes.

I cried.

I stared out of the window at London, and that rotating Castle sphere. I thought of those animals that should have been extinct, in their enclosures. I felt like one of them. A marooned seal, out of place and out of time. I went into the immersion pod. I accessed simulations of the most beautiful locations. I walked on hot sand as waves lapped my feet. I stood outside the pyramids. The Grand Canyon. And the Floating Tower of Beijing.

None of it helped.

The only cure for reality was reality itself.

I left the pod and lay on my bed. It was raining heavily. I tried to read, but my vision blurred with tears. There were noises outside, on the driveway.

I went to look. I saw the Echo boy. Daniel. He was outside on the driveway, doing press-ups in the rain, while Iago stood over him, laughing and shouting numbers: '. . . 268 . . . 269 . . . 270 . . . 271 . . . Don't even *think* about stopping, computer-brain, or you know what will happen – yes, you know what my dad said to you last night? That's right . . . 275 . . . 276 . . . 277 . . .'

I watched Iago. I saw a little piece of spit leave his mouth. Suddenly, staring at this puny and rather unpleasant ten-year-old, I realized why Uncle Alex wanted to populate the world with Echos. It was a kind of correction. He'd created a flesh-and-blood child whose behaviour was unpredictable, rebellious and borderline evil, so it was easy to see why he was motivated to create what he hoped would be perfect and obedient beings.

No.

No, Uncle Alex probably didn't feel that way about his own son. In fact, he had probably told him to be out there. This was probably Daniel's punishment for having spoken to me. Guilt flooded through me.

It was weird. I was sympathizing with an Echo. I remembered his warm breath on my face the day before. I remembered how I'd wanted to touch his arm, to comfort him.

'Weird,' I said aloud. I think I was talking about my own feelings. Feelings that were rising up inside me.

Daniel seemed to be struggling, but I knew that this was just a clever illusion, as Echos couldn't feel pain. So actually, maybe this wasn't Uncle Alex's idea. Maybe.

I must have stood there for half an hour, watching him do over a thousand press-ups while Iago (who probably wouldn't have been able to do five) shouted at him. Indeed, I think Daniel might have been able to do even more if he hadn't noticed me watching right at the end. After that, he collapsed onto the gravel, exhausted, staring up at the window.

I stepped back, towards my bed.

It frightened me that these machines – and that is all an Echo was, a machine – were now being made to be so much stronger than humans. And this Daniel must have been one of the strongest yet. But he was submissive too. Uncle Alex had stopped him getting close to me, even though Daniel could have easily overpowered him.

Unless he malfunctions completely.

I thought of that desperate, fast battle I'd had with Alissa, and how I had managed to escape out of the window just in time. If the same thing happened again, I doubted I would be so lucky.

Outside my room, in the hallway, I heard Uncle Alex walking past and shouting to someone, 'I want the prototypes ready in two weeks. I know that's tight, but after what you've done I think it's fair, don't you?'

I had no idea who he was talking to, but he sounded angry. There was a ferocity to him that he hid from me. I wondered what else he was hiding.

3

Later, it happened. Something I think Uncle Alex had been building up to.

He came into my room. He had a woman with him. A human woman, if we're being generous.

She was short, with dark mid-length hair, and was wearing a flannel trouser suit and a bright red mind-wire. I could see from the tiny illuminations in her eyes that she had her info-lenses not only in but active. Her face had been artificially lightened with perma-cosmetics and her lips were an unnaturally bright red. Her name was Candressa. She was the public relations person for Castle Industries. She told me that there was to be a media conference about my parents' deaths; she thought that if I wanted justice, then I should attend.

'Justice?' I asked. I was confused. How could there be justice? My parents were dead.

'Yes,' said Candressa. 'Sempura can't get away with this. They have to be made to pay for what they have done. It is a danger to society if they allow such products onto the market. Lina Sempura herself should be held accountable. Do you understand?'

'Echos? You want to stop Echos?'

Candressa's mouth became small and tense. 'We want to stop Sempura and their dangerous strategy of putting untested products out there . . .'

I must have looked hesitant because Uncle Alex sat down next to me and put his hand on my arm. 'You wouldn't have to leave the room. You could do it all from the immersion pod.' He was trying to look calm and soothing, but there was something desperate about the way he was looking at me. 'If you do this, you could save people's lives.'

I thought of Dad and Mum's blood, leaking onto the floor.

'When?' I said.

Candressa looked at Uncle Alex, who gave her a small nod. 'You could do it right now,' she said.

'They are waiting to hear from you,' said Uncle Alex.

'But you didn't say it would be so soon . . .'

Uncle Alex gave more of his soothing smile. 'I didn't want to cause you any extra distress.'

Something wasn't right here, but I couldn't decide what it was. All I knew was that my parents had been killed by an Echo they had bought from Sempura, and a world with fewer Alissas in it was a safer world.

'You won't have to face them,' Uncle Alex explained. 'We can put the pod on blind mode. All that will happen is that you'll be asked a few questions and then you tell them what you know, and that will be that.'

Candressa looked at me. 'It is ready now.'

'But I'm not prepared.'

'You just have to act sad about your parents and say how terrible you think Sempura are for letting that product onto the market. That is the only message you need to have.'

I didn't feel up to it. I looked at Uncle, and in a moment of weakness I said: 'Maybe I should have a calmer mind, to get me through it . . .' I looked over at the neuropads.

Uncle shook his head. 'No,' he said. 'That wouldn't be a good idea.'

Candressa looked at me coldly. 'We need them to see your pain.'

So I did it right then.

It was all set up. I think they wanted it this way. They left the room, and went to watch from pods elsewhere in the house. I went into my pod. But the moment the helmet lowered, I saw a familiar bookcase.

Blind mode, I thought. But it didn't happen. So I said it out loud. 'Blind mode, blind mode, blind mode . . .'

But this was not a media conference.

This was something else entirely.

I realized what I was looking at.

I was at home, staring straight into Dad's office.

4

It was achingly familiar

The bookshelves, and the view of the rain and the magrail through the window. The sealed-up pod beside the desk. Not just looking at it, either. I was as good as there. At home. And there was my dad too, at his desk, next to the vintage computer, reading a book called *Darwin's Nightmare*. For a moment I didn't think. I just stood there, mesmerized. There he was. Dad. As real as he had ever been, sipping tea, unshaven, scruffy-shirted, tired.

'Dad? Can you hear me?'

Of course he couldn't. But he heard something.

He looked over at the doorway. I did too.

It was Alissa.

She was standing there, with her blonde hair and her smiling face, one hand behind her back.

'Hello, Alissa,' Dad said, looking confused.

'Hello, Master.'

'Dad, get out of here. Get out!' I screamed as loud as I could. But the scream couldn't reach Yorkshire, let alone the past. No matter how hard you screamed, you could never reach the ears of the dead.

'Why are you here, Alissa? I didn't ask for you to be here. Please get out of the room, I am working.'

'I cannot process that command, Master.'

My dad's confusion quickly became anger. The anger he often felt towards advanced technology. 'What do you mean?'

Alissa kept smiling as she walked towards Dad's desk. Dad stood up. 'Alissa, stay back . . .'

'I cannot process that command, Master.'

'Dad,' I cried as tears streamed down my face. 'Get away! She's going to kill you . . . That's a knife behind her back . . . Get away . . .'

Dad was starting to look worried, but nowhere near as worried as he should have been.

'What is that you are holding, Alissa?'

And then he saw it, and – Dad being Dad – his first instinct wasn't to save himself but to save us. He called for my mum. 'Lorna! Lorna! Audrey! Lorna . . . get Audrey . . . Both of you, get out of here . . . Alissa is malfunctioning.'

He was backed into a corner.

He tried to push past her, but she pressed the blade into his stomach.

'Dad,' I wept, helpless, 'I love you, I love you, I love you . . .'

And then she cut his throat, and blood flowed out of him like a river and the colour drained from him and he went weak and I screamed.

'Stop this! Stop showing me this! Stop playing the recording! Let me out of the pod!'

But nothing happened. I was still there, in our old house, looking at my dad as blood and life leaked out of him and he kind of stagger-collapsed towards the floor.

I left the room to see my mum running along the landing, looking frantic. Instinctively I raised my hands. 'No, Mum, don't go in there! You'll die if you go in there!'

She didn't hear me, of course. She just passed right through me.

'Mum! Mum!'

I closed my eyes but I couldn't close my ears. She screamed first from the sight of Dad, then from her own pain.

'Get me out of here! Get me out! Get me out!'

But it didn't happen.

I stayed there on that landing.

I could feel its cold floor beneath my feet. Five minutes later I heard someone else.

The ultimate stranger.

Myself.

'Mum? Dad?'

My voice from downstairs. My old voice. The one that didn't sound like the end of the world had just happened.

Of course. I had just finished my class in the pod.

There was no answer from my parents. I remembered what I had been thinking. That Dad would be in his pod, writing his book. But I'd wondered why Mum hadn't answered. I counted the seconds, wondering how long it had been from the time of doubt to the time of terror.

One . . . two . . . three . . .

I had gone into the kitchen. I remembered that. And then I had stepped onto the old creaking leviboard, through the hole in the ceiling to the next floor. I watched myself in my low-tech cotton smock and jeans. I hated the sight of me. I felt like I was looking at an arrogant traitor.

'You stupid idiot,' I told my other self. 'Ten minutes! Your lesson was over ten minutes ago. Why did you stay around and chat? You should have just got out and gone to Mum like you wanted, instead of listening to Tola go on about gladiators and boyfriends.'

But of course, three days ago I hadn't heard this voice of my future self.

'Mum?' I had said. Innocent. 'Are you there?'

And then that noise that I hadn't been able to recognize three days ago. The one I'd thought might have been a magcar flying by on the rails outside, but was actually my mum's last dying breath.

I watched myself head towards Dad's office.

. . . eleven . . . twelve . . . thirteen . . .

As my recorded self reached the doorway, I noticed something I hadn't seen three days ago. Blood was actually leaking out onto the landing. It must have been my dad's, as he was closest to the door.

'Dad?'

I watched the pain slowly set in my face as it looked inside the office, seeing my dad first.

'Dad? What's the matter? Why aren't you—'

Then seeing everything.

Dad, Mum, Alissa, the knife, the blood that wasn't able to be absorbed into the self-clean carpet. (The only carpeted room in the house – 'I like softness under my feet, it's my only indulgence.')

My face rigid with shock as it too struggled to absorb.

And, of course, her voice.

Alissa's, as she stood there with the bloodstained knife.

'I was waiting for you to come. I was waiting for you to come, I was waiting for you to come . . .'

Only now it seemed less like a malfunction and more like single-minded determination. And myself, my three-day-ago self, just standing there, until she moved. And then I moved, and as I watched, I realized how fast I'd been, far faster than I knew I could be, as I ran that short distance along the landing towards the window.

Then my voice, loud and hard and clear as I commanded that window to 'Open!'

The window's slow response, giving Alissa time to grab the sleeve of my cotton top. And then I witnessed my fury as my other self pulled away from her and slammed an elbow hard into her face. The window opened, I jumped out and Alissa followed, but before she did so, I noticed something else I obviously hadn't seen before. She looked inside the office, as if wondering whether to stay with the corpses of my parents.

She spoke into the air. 'Rosella.' Anyway, I was pretty sure that was what she said.

'Rosella? Who the hell is Rosella?' I asked, screaming it. 'Tell me! Tell me!'

But then she jumped out and I heard that splash, and I – the actual real, present me – ran across the landing to see my head burst out of the water and scream up towards the leviboard that was just outside the car.

'Down! Down!'

The leviboard descended; I watched myself climb onto it.

'Who is Rosella?' I wailed.

The window closed again.

I watched the car reverse five metres, to the end of the rail. And I watched as Alissa stood dripping wet in front of the car. She knew what was going to happen.

She knew she was going to be terminated.

She didn't care.

Why didn't she care? Echos were programmed to preserve their own existence.

But then, Echos were also programmed never to harm their masters.

She was breaking all the rules.

The window was level with the rail, which meant that I could watch it all quite easily. The car moving forward with me inside, a blur of speed, so fast that Alissa just disappeared. She was there, and then there was the fastest flowering of blood, some drops even making it to the window. Her crumpled body fell into the water below. And the car was away; I was away, heading south fast.

I – the actual present me who knew she was still inside this footage – turned to look at my parents, and then I walked towards them. Towards these bodies that had once hugged me. And held my hand. And rocked me to sleep as a baby (they would never have let an Echo do that). And taught me to swim in a swimming pool in Paris. And to hold my breath underwater.

The way to do it is to try not to think about anything . . . The way to do it is not to try too hard. Just imagine you are nothing. Just another natural element in the pool.

My dad's eyes were open, as if staring up at me. Eyes that were his but not really his, all at once. The way a house stops belonging to someone after they stop living there.

'I'm sorry, Dad. I'm so sorry I couldn't stop this.'

And I cried helplessly, and collapsed on top of him and my mum, and hugged them and felt their blood on me. I wailed and I wailed until their bodies dissolved from under me, along with the floor, and I screamed and found myself falling and falling through blackness, a blackness only punctured by occasional bright objects that passed before me.

The *Darwin's Nightmare* book.

The kitchen knife.

The ancient computer.

But then there was nothing at all except the dark and the fast sensation of descent, until eventually I landed in a chair, in a bright wooden room.

5

A crowd of strange beings sitting on large leather chairs were staring at me. Most looked human, but some didn't. Some had blank avatars – just blue humanoids with those scary featureless faces, all identical. Even more surreal was the fact that a few of the avatars were the kind idiots from school use on social media. I saw a strange albino alien with three red eyes, glistening in the artificial light. I saw an old robot from the 2060s. I saw a minotaur.

'Where am I?' I asked, sobbing.

Someone touched my arm.

I turned and saw Uncle Alex.

'It's OK, Audrey. You are still in the pod. I'm in my pod in the office. This is the virtual media conference. There are journalists here who want to ask you a few questions.'

'Journalists?'

Uncle Alex poured a sigh into the silence. 'Yes. Don't be fooled by their avis. They often have eccentric avatars. The media circus really *is* a circus these days. I suppose they think you're more likely to be yourself around them. Who knows?'

'My parents died and they are pretending to be aliens?'

'It's nothing personal. They're just overgrown schoolkids.'

'We're not allowed fictional avatars at school. Only on social media.'

'Well, your dad used to have one.'

'Did he?'

Uncle Alex smiled. Maybe he was pleased that I didn't know this about Dad.

'Oh yeah. He sometimes used to come to conferences like this. To ask his brother some questions. But never as himself. He'd always be a gorilla.'

'A gorilla?'

'Yep. A big silverback gorilla.'

'Why?'

'It's a long story.' I could swear a trace of bitterness crept into his voice. 'You might get to hear it one day. But anyway, the main thing is that you shouldn't worry about what these journalists are trying to be. Just be you.'

I saw Candressa. She was sitting on my other side, her face white and sharp and angular, as though someone had chipped it out of limestone. But at least she was recognizably herself. Her bright red lips were telling me, in a whisper: 'Your parents must not have died in vain. Sempura must pay. Answer the questions as honestly as you can.'

I was staring out at all the faces – actual or uber-fictional representations of the real people who were sitting in their pods around the country, or around the world.

'What happened then?' I asked Uncle Alex. 'Why was I back in Yorkshire? Why did I—'

And then the questions started. They came from different people within the room. It felt like the room itself was asking questions as it closed in around me. I went on crying, in the real world and the fake one. Candressa pointed at someone. The minotaur. A man's body (in a smart twentieth-century suit) with a bull's head. 'You. Your question.'

'Hello,' said the Minotaur, its bullish mouth doing the talking. It was so surreal that I wanted to laugh and scream with terror at the same time. 'Yes. I'm Tao Hu, from *Echoworld Holozine*. I just wondered, how long had your parents owned Alissa?'

'I don't . . . I don't know. Four . . . five weeks.'

Then another journalist, another question. This time the avatar was of an actual human. A woman with dark hair sitting at the front, who kept flickering because of a bad line. 'Tina Mories, assistant editor, *Robotics Week*. I was just wondering, why did they decide to buy her? Why did they not get a robot, if your father was so anti Echo technology?'

'I . . . well . . . my dad was in a car accident, and that slowed him down, and Mum thought it would be better for my education if I was taught not just by virtual teachers but also by Echos . . . She'd seen lots of research . . . and . . . and it was my fault. Dad asked me if we should get an Echo and I said that I thought we should.'

Candressa was very eagerly pointing to someone else, someone whose question she obviously wanted to be heard. A bald man with an animated T-shirt featuring a cartoon rabbit being hit by a wooden mallet. He was sitting next to a man who looked exactly like Albert Einstein (Steve Jobs was also in the room). 'Yes, yes, Joseph, your question. Your question please.'

'Joseph Kildare, h-logger for *New Horizons*. Do you blame Sempura for what happened?'

New Horizons. I remembered an old grumble from my dad: *They're bloody liars! They might as well just be a bloody press release for Castle.*

'I . . . I don't know. I'm sorry.'

Another hand. Bright white and webbed. The albino alien. 'Bruno Bergmann, *Android Connoisseur Quarterly*. Why did they choose a Sempura product? I mean, why didn't they use the family firm?'

'Castle isn't the family firm. It is my uncle's firm.'

The next person to speak was a large man with a bright red beard.

'Idris McCarthy,' said the man. 'Echo Correspondent with *Info-lens Bulletin* . . . OK, so it wasn't your family's firm, but still, your dad would surely have been inclined to use your uncle's products?'

Uncle Alex interrupted at this point. 'What kind of relevance does that have? He was under no obligation to buy products from me. I got on very well with my brother. We may have had different views about technology, as you probably know, but we could separate the personal stuff from the business stuff.'

This jarred with me.

Uncle Alex might have been able to separate the personal and the business side of things, but Dad couldn't. His work was his life.

Idris McCarthy wasn't giving up. 'If Audrey could answer this, please . . . Your dad campaigned for more restraints on technological development. But Sempura is a technology firm too. So why the grudge against Castle?'

I tried to compose myself. 'It . . . it wasn't a grudge,' I said, wondering if I was telling a lie. 'Dad had his principles.'

'And those principles led him to buy Sempura products?'

I felt dizzy. But it was a weird kind of dizziness, because the room wasn't spinning. It was classic pod-sickness. That weird gap between the body in the pod and the mind in the simulation. But it was also panic. I saw Mum's face in my mind. I saw her eyes and I saw her smile. 'My parents were killed by a Sempura product. Those products should be banned.'

Then someone else. Someone who didn't introduce himself. The avatar that was Albert Einstein. 'What are you saying – Echos should be banned? Or just Sempura ones? Sempura's track record is cleaner, ethically, than Castle's.'

'You must introduce yourself,' Candressa said, sounding sharp and tense. 'What is your name and who do you work for? And please don't tell me you are Albert Einstein.'

There was a pause. Einstein said nothing for a moment or two. Then, quite defiantly, he said, 'OK, my name is Leonie Jenson. I am from *Castle Watch*.'

Leonie Jenson. Castle Watch.

Then something happened. She must have used a mind-command to switch her avi from Albert Einstein to her natural self, because suddenly – with the shortest of flickers – she morphed into the woman I had seen staring out of that electronic paper in Paris.

The same deeply inquisitive face and short pink hair.

'Leonie Jenson,' said Candressa scornfully. 'We've got to stop this.'

The whole room went still. My uncle or Candressa had freeze-framed it. They were the only people still moving. Well, apart from me.

'Listen,' said Uncle Alex. 'That journalist is from *Castle Watch*. A propaganda rag. They are setting a trap. She – her – she'll be setting a trap.'

'I know who she is . . . How can the truth trap me? I was at my house. I saw them murdered. Why did you put me inside that footage?'

'Audrey?'

'I was there. I saw Dad and Mum. Why did you do it? Did you want me like this? I mean, you told me to show my pain. So is that what you were doing? Making me feel more pain? To have me trembling and shaking and crying?'

Then Candressa kind of growled, 'Oh, listen, little girl, don't be so melodramatic. It must have been a glitch.'

But Uncle Alex was already sighing. 'All right, Audrey. All right. Candressa didn't know about it, but I decided to put you inside that footage beforehand, so you would know exactly what happened and be able to tell the truth. Big claims require big evidence. I wanted the world to see what Sempura had done to you. I wanted people to see the pain they caused.'

I couldn't believe it. I looked at the unmoving crowd of avatars, and then turned back to Uncle Alex, who at that moment seemed more fake than any minotaur could. 'But you didn't ask me.'

'I showed you it to help you. I want justice for you, and for Leo. He was a misguided fool with sibling rivalry issues, but he was my brother, and when our parents died he looked after me for two years. I loved him. That is all I want. Justice.'

Before I had time to reply to this, or even absorb it, Candressa said: 'Don't tell them you hate all Echos. If you do that, they'll write you off as some weird crank kid and you won't get anywhere except with those tin-pot hover-shed freaks over at *Castle Watch*. If you say you hate Sempura products, then you have a chance of something happening. Think about it.'

But there was no time to think about it. The room came into motion again. And the journalists were waiting for a response.

Idris McCarthy, once again, stroking his red beard: 'Are you an Echophobe?'

'No,' I said, realizing a lie might be the best way of getting something done. 'I don't hate all Echos. It's 2115. I'm not an Echophobe. I hate Alissa, even though she's gone. And I hate Sempura for producing her. Alissa was an assembly-line product, which means there must be hundreds like her. They are an irresponsible company. They should be punished.'

Idris continued. 'Do you know that only this morning Sempura have issued a statement saying that though they have recalled all Alissa models, they have not been able to recover the actual model that killed your parents. They are hinting at some kind of conspiracy involving Castle Industries and the British police force.'

'Well, of course they would say that!' boomed Uncle Alex. 'Lina Sempura would blame anyone rather than herself! They are trying to cover up and cloud the facts. They have no evidence of any conspiracy, or they would have provided it. She knows her company pushed things too far.'

Idris suddenly started to change shape. Within a second he had transformed into a short, smart-looking, naturally aged seventy-year-old woman with the same red hair as Idris and a smart white suit. She had a wide, thin-lipped mouth and an upturned nose.

I recognized her instantly. The whole room did.

It was Lina Sempura. She stared at Uncle Alex, who was temporarily too surprised to speak.

'Surprise!' said Lina, with her strange accent (she had an Argentinian mother and a Japanese father, and been raised by Echos in Moscow).

Uncle Alex knew he couldn't switch off the conference now. It would have been very bad PR.

'Lina, I see you are up to your old tricks. Deceiving people comes naturally to you, doesn't it?'

'I am here, in person, to tell this room that I – me in person – supervised the development of the Alissa prototype. And the models based on that prototype were – and remain – the safest that Sempura have ever created. We are determined to get to the bottom of this, and have nothing to hide.'

Uncle Alex laughed nervously. 'You came as a man called Idris and you have nothing to hide!'

I felt scared as Lina – or the simulation of Lina – stood up and walked towards me. She looked at me directly. Her simulation was more lifelike than life. I had never seen anyone who looked more real. I could see fine hairs on her upper lip. 'I lost my parents,' she said, 'when I was a bit younger than you. They died on a cheap shuttle flight to the moon. I know as well as anyone the dangers of badly made technology.'

'Ha!' said Uncle Alex. 'Faulty warbots that kill allied troops? Info-lenses that blind people? Malfunctioning securidroids? Please! You only know the dangers of badly designed technology because you make it.'

Lina Sempura ignored this, and carried on talking to me. 'Don't be a foolish girl. Don't be his little PR monkey. Don't belittle your parents' memory by doing this sort of stuff . . . Especially when your father was so against everything your uncle stands for.'

This made me angry. 'And what you stand for!' I said.

'But he chose a product from our company, didn't he? What does that tell you, Anna?'

'Her name is *Audrey*,' said Uncle Alex.

'Well, ladies and gentlemen,' said Candressa, 'I'm sorry about this disturbance. We would have loved to answer more of your questions, but as this event has been undermined by this intrusion from our chief competitor, I'm afraid we must end it here, unless Lina Sempura volunteers to leave.'

'Oh, don't worry,' said Lina as everyone else in the room kept on soaking up the drama. 'I'm out of here.' But before she dissolved away into nothing she said to me: 'Open your eyes, girl. Open your eyes.' And then she was gone.

'OK,' said Candressa. 'Let's get this back on track.'

Uncle Alex looked at me. 'Audrey, are you OK?'

'Jelani Oburumo,' said a man sitting on the front row. '*House and Droid*. Forgive the direct nature of this question, but did you see Alissa kill your parents?'

It took a real effort to speak now. 'I was in the pod when it happened, but I have seen the footage. I have seen everything.'

'Why do you think this happened?' the man went on. 'Why do you think Alissa malfunctioned?'

'I . . . I don't know . . .' And then I remembered what I had heard her say, and I blurted it out. I blurted it out loud. 'She said a name. She said *Rosella*.'

'*Rosella?*' about five people asked at once.

'After she killed them she said, "Rosella." I don't know who Rosella—'

Another freeze-frame.

Then my uncle staring at me with anxious eyes. 'I think this is too much for you. I'm sorry. You are clearly finding this distressing. I think we should call it a day. I think it's time for you to leave the conference . . . Candressa and I can take it from here.'

'But—'

And suddenly I was speaking to no one. I was in the dark of the pod, with the mind-reader on. And with the knowledge that whoever or whatever this 'Rosella' was, it was something my uncle knew about. And something he wanted to hide.

6

I left the pod and stayed in my room. I was shaking and crying. I sat listening to the distant chants of another protest, coming again from near the Resurrection Zone. I stared out of the window at the revolving sphere and the logo of the blue three-turreted castle.

Downstairs there was a weapons room. I could have taken a positron and turned it on myself and turned into nothing.

A bleak thought. I tried to shake it away.

I tried to read some philosophy. Philosophy had always helped me in the past, but today it didn't. Maybe it was because I was reading Sophocles. One of the ancient philosophers I'd been planning to study at Oxford. *There is a point where even justice does injury*.

Was I at that point?

Was there any reason at all to bother trying to get justice for my parents' deaths when they were dead and could never be brought back to life? And also, what was justice? The only thing I really wanted was to live in a world with no Echos. I would never feel comfortable living like I was living at Uncle Alex's, knowing that I was always only a short distance away from those machines. Machines that could kill.

I went to the window. Looked out at the rain funnel. It looked perfectly fine. The night I had seen him climbing up to my room he had been trying to reach me. I very much doubted there was any work that had needed doing.

I went out of the room.

I stood on the landing for a moment, listening for Echos.

I noticed there was another painting.

This one I recognized instantly.

It was a painting of an old-fashioned street at night, complete with the kind of streetlamp that existed two hundred years ago. But instead of darkness above it, there was a sunny blue sky and white candyfloss clouds. In other words, it was a painting of day and night all at once. This wasn't a Matisse or a Picasso. This was by someone called René Magritte. It was my mum's favourite painting. I wondered if Uncle Alex knew that. Maybe he did. Maybe it gave him some sick pleasure buying things my parents – or, indeed, almost anyone – couldn't afford.

I looked at my hands. Still trembling. Of course, I could have just gone back into my room and put the neuropads back on. But I didn't. I wanted to stay scared. I wanted to stay *me*. And right then I wanted to see Uncle Alex and ask him, face to face, why he had just put me through all that, even though I knew that he would probably just repeat what he had said in the virtual press conference.

'Uncle Alex?' I called. 'Uncle Alex, where are you?'

I heard footsteps leave his office further along the landing and saw Candressa. She was concentrating, sending thought-commands via her mind-wire, and didn't look happy to see me.

'I'm looking for my uncle.'

She came close and spoke in a quiet, cold voice. 'Do you realize how busy your uncle is? Do you understand how much responsibility he has on his shoulders?'

'Of course I do,' I said.

'He can't spend his life babysitting his baby niece.'

I wiped a tear from my eye before it had time to fully arrive. 'I'm not asking him to. I don't need a babysitter. I'm fifteen.'

Noises.

Protesters again.

This time the chants seemed closer. I remembered what Uncle Alex had said about how the protestors had tried to break in. I looked around the hallway. At the expensive furnishings. The nanotech wallpaper, showing trees swaying gently in the wind. At the plush cream carpet. At the expensive artworks. It seemed too dangerously different to the world outside. You know – a world full of angry people with little money, who had lost their jobs because Echos could do them.

'Your uncle is a very kind man. Too kind, really, for someone in his position. He tried with your father. He offered him money. Did you know that? Two years ago. He offered him one million unidollars, but your dad's ego was such that he rejected it.'

I didn't know if she was lying. I started to cry.

Properly cry. Like a five-year-old.

In front of the last person in the world I'd have wanted to witness it, although she did pull a tissue out of her trouser pocket. Maybe she was right. Maybe I *was* just a baby. A great big fifteen-year-old baby. She waved the tissue. 'Take it. Don't worry. The paper contains auto-clean nanoparticles. There's not one single piece of bacteria that can survive on it.'

I took it. 'Thank you.'

'Your uncle is downstairs. But I would leave him alone if I were you. Just for a while. You see, he's a little disappointed.'

'Disappointed?'

'In you. For the way you acted in the press conference.'

I felt anger race through me like a flood. 'I didn't do anything except say how I feel. And I had far more to say if I hadn't been shut out of the conference.'

Candressa was staring at me harshly as her eyes, shaded by the mind-wire, flickered with tiny illuminated pieces of text from her info-lenses. 'Don't you get it? Your story needs to be clear. You can't go telling journalists something that isn't part of the story. You must forget what Alissa said. That isn't relevant. Journalists are idiots. Half of them there are propagandists who hate every single thing your uncle does. And they fuel the protestors. Half of whom are terrorists—'

'They're not terrorists.'

'Some of them have called for your uncle to be killed.'

'I didn't know that.'

She closed her eyes for a second to send an urgent thought-mail. Then she turned her attention back to me. 'And he might have the police on his side but the press are always attacking him. Fuelling the protestors' anger. And you might have just added to that anger. They want a simple story, and most of the time that story involves attacking your uncle.' She hesitated, but then said in a cool voice: 'And your dad used to be one of them.'

'He never attacked Uncle Alex.'

'Not by name.'

'Not by anything.'

Her bright mouth tightened. 'He was hardly trying to make life easy for him. You have only ever heard one side of the story. Your uncle is a good man. He is motivated by the desire to make the world a better place. He gives five billion unidollars to charity every year. I bet you didn't know that . . .'

I shook my head. *He is motivated by the desire to make the world a better place.* Maybe he and Dad weren't so different after all.

'You are very lucky he is looking after you. If he was less of a great man, then you would be homeless right now. If you were Lina Sempura's niece, you'd be on the streets, I can tell you.' She halted, and raised a hand as if to say *stop*. 'And listen – listen to that. Outside.'

I listened. The chanting of the protestors had become a kind of roar.

Candressa looked worried. Her white skin went whiter still. 'Oh no. Oh God, no.'

'What is it?'

She looked at me and then turned. *'They've got over the wall.'*

'What?' I didn't quite understand.

She started running towards the stairs. 'Get Iago. The protestors – they are trying to get into the house. They want to kill Alex. They might want to hurt Iago too.'

'Should I call the police?'

She disappeared downstairs as I heard more screams.

'They'll already know. Those protesters would have had to terminate them just to get over the wall.'

And I had that feeling again.

That feeling of total alertness that comes from being close to death.

7

I ran to Iago's room

But he wasn't there.

Downstairs, I heard the smashing of glass. I ran to my room and went into my pod, and in the mind-reader I commanded *Menu*. There was an option called 'House View'. I chose that, and then viewed the front garden. The part I couldn't see from my window. East of the gravel driveway. About ten protestors, all wearing masks, were climbing over a side wall. Where the police were meant to be guarding the house.

They carried small rocks and large sticks, and a few – more than a few, actually – had old guns. The kind that required bullets but could still kill. I needed a gun. There were guns in the house. Positrons. I needed a positron.

I switched to inside the house; saw that some of the protestors were in the lobby.

Three were engaged in a fist fight with an Echo. A tall dreadlocked Echo who was all muscle. I searched in other rooms, sometimes virtual running between them, sometimes by just mind-leaping.

The kitchen, the downstairs office, three of the living rooms, the therapy room – where Uncle Alex was, being protected by five Echos, including the blond boy – the indoor swimming pool, the gymnasium full of metal robots in boxing gloves, the dining room. I eventually found Iago in a small room hardly bigger than a cupboard. He was there with two Echos, taking a positron from the wall.

The weapons room.

He may have been holding an advanced antimatter weapon and he may have had a look of gleeful murder in his eyes, but he was still a ten-year-old boy and he was my cousin; I had stayed in an immersion pod while members of my family were being killed once before, and I wasn't about to let it happen again.

So I got out of the pod and my bedroom and ran downstairs.

I ran to the small room where the weapons were kept, but of course he had gone.

'Iago!' I shouted.

No response. Or none that I could hear above the sound of shouting and fighting and the occasional shot of an old gun. New guns were being fired too. I saw an Echo shoot a protestor into non-existence, his body disappearing before my eyes, but of course it was antimatter technology so it was unheard.

I ran to the therapy room to tell Uncle Alex that I couldn't find Iago.

'Oh, Audrey, you are safe. Come in here, come in here, and close the door behind you. Before any of those bastards see you.'

But I hesitated.

And the reason I hesitated was because Daniel was staring at me in such a way that hesitation was the only response. His words echoed in my head. *You are in danger here.*

I know it sounds irrational, but I was more scared of being shut up in a room with five Echos than I was of being out there with all those humans who had murder on their minds. Another of the Echos, the red-haired female, Madara, told me to come inside quickly. But she – unlike the blond Echo – was holding a gun. I remembered Uncle Alex telling me that she was designed for the army. To be a killer. I closed the door, and stayed on the other side of it.

It was a big mistake.

For the second after I had closed it, I felt something cold and hard press against my temple.

A gun.

An old twenty-first-century pistol, probably full of bullets.

Out of the corner of my eye I saw a man with a mask. The mask was the kind you would wear to a fancy dress party. He had come as a tiger. He was tall and smelled of tobacco gum.

'Where is your dad?' he asked me. His voice was harsh and rough and full of hate.

'My dad is dead.'

'Don't lie to me. Your dad. Alex Castle. The self-appointed God himself . . . Where is he? Tell me, or I will kill you. I swear to you I will squeeze this trigger and you will be out of here.' He did a quick mime to indicate my brains being blasted out of my skull.

'He's not my dad. My dad was killed three days ago. By an Echo.'

There was a pause. His voice changed. 'Your dad was Leo Castle?'

'Yes.'

He put the gun down slowly.

He seemed to be in shock.

'Leo Castle! He was a hero to me. To most of us! I watched all the pieces he did for *Tech Watch*. I'm sorry, I'm sorry. I wasn't really going to kill you. I just need to find your uncle. He must be stopped. The Resurrection Zone is evil. Everything he has done is evil. Neanderthals should not be kept in captivity. He cares more about Echos than real living things!'

'My dad didn't agree with violence,' I said, feeling a kind of defiance inside me. 'And he loved his brother. He would have been appalled by what you lot are doing.'

For a few moments I was just staring at the tiger mask. Maybe my words were getting through. Maybe he wasn't going to do anything but leave, and tell the others who were rampaging around the house to leave as well. I would never know, for at that very moment he vanished into thin air and I saw Iago standing behind him holding his antimatter positron. A gun that was far too big for him (though seemingly as light as a feather, as it was far more aerogel than metal).

Unbelievably, he was smiling.

He had just killed a fellow human being and he was smiling. It was the first time I had ever seen him smile from genuine happiness.

'You owe me one, cuz,' he said, his voice jauntier than I'd known it.

He wasn't hanging around. He was heading past me, jogging through the unicorn holo-sculpture on his way to the lobby.

'Iago, come back! It's not safe!' I started running after him, but almost instantly someone burst out of an intersecting hallway and flung me to the floor. Another protester in a mask. This one wasn't a tiger, but the mask of a Neanderthal, with human eyes gleaming through. He was heavy and I was terrified. I screamed.

This one didn't have a gun. He had a stone. A stone large enough to be called a rock. He held it up high. He was about to smash it down on my head. Death was two seconds away now, and so my body was exploding with terrified life. But at that moment I saw some-one else.

Daniel.

He was out of the therapy room and throwing himself towards us.

8

Daniel pushed the man with the Neanderthal mask to the floor. The man smashed the rock hard against Daniel's face and cut him, but Daniel already had his hand around the man's throat. He picked him up off the floor, holding him under his chin, his feet centimetres off the ground.

'Please,' the man wheezed, 'you'll kill me.'

'No,' Daniel said. 'Only if you hurt her again.' And then he threw the man far across the hallway, right through the holographic unicorn.

He turned to me and grabbed my arm, hard.

It was exactly where Alissa had grabbed me, and I automatically tried to resist. It was no use. He was even stronger than Alissa had been. He pulled me forward and started to run, and inevitably – being a human – I struggled to keep up. I could see the lobby, where the battle was still raging. A clock on the wall was hit; the face fractured, then instantly repaired itself. I could also see some of the protestors lying dead on the floor. The Echos – and Iago – clearly had the upper hand now.

'Slow down! You're hurting me!'

A thin stream of blood trickled down Daniel's cheek like a tear.

He went into the living room where I had been taken on my first night. A female protester in a dolphin mask was in there, slicing through the Picasso painting with a knife. She roared and charged towards us with the knife, but Daniel held out his hand. The blade cut him, but he pulled the knife out of her hand easily, while still holding me with his other hand.

He looked out of the window to see Iago now out on the driveway with some Echos; many of the remaining protestors were fleeing.

The woman who'd had the knife ran out of the room. But we heard her scream a second later, a scream that ended too abruptly. And then we saw why. Madara was there with a gun, a gun she'd obviously just used, and she was running towards us.

Daniel saw her and led me towards a doorway at the far end of the room. 'Door open,' he commanded. The doorway led to some stairs. At the top of the stairs we ran along a landing I hadn't seen before.

I was scared, I must admit.

Beyond scared.

After all, here was an Echo, evidently malfunctioning and holding a knife. My parents had died this way. Maybe I would too.

Had he saved my life? Or did he want to kill me himself?

We reached a room with windows for walls. A room that showed the rear of the garden. I had been shown the garden before, the day I went to see Mrs Matsumoto, but then my senses had been dulled by the neuropads. Now, my mind hyper-sharp with adrenaline, I realized that it was an amazing garden, maybe the most amazing I had ever seen, the grass all shades and colours, the trees genetically perfect like something out of the wildest daydream. I saw the wall the protestors had climbed over. Madara was getting closer.

'Open,' Daniel called, and the window opened. And then, with troubling ease, he picked me up in his arms and jumped out onto turquoise grass. He landed awkwardly, but kept hold of me.

What was he?

Saviour, or monster?

I didn't even touch the ground.

He ran, and kept running. Behind us, I could see Madara at the window aiming the gun at Daniel. But she didn't fire it.

'I've disobeyed Master's order. Madara will have been sent to pursue me, but not to terminate me.'

Disobeyed Master's order.

'Order?'

'To stay with him. To protect his life at all costs.'

We passed through a row of silver birches. I struggled, trying to free myself from his arms. Above, in the distance, I could see a police car come to a stop on the magrail, and a robotic officer (a traditional metallic Zeta-One) leaned out of the window and switched his voice-setting to loudhailer mode as he stared down at the driveway on the other side of the house.

'*Trespassers, you have ten seconds to leave the property. Failure to comply will mean death*.'

The Zeta-One wasn't talking to us, but Daniel was still running.

'Let me go! Where are you taking me? Let me go!'

'Don't worry. I'm not going to hurt you.'

Something about his voice made me almost believe him.

As he ran, he looked anxiously around at the grass, as if hidden danger lurked there.

'I heard your scream,' he said. 'I came to save you.'

'I want to go back. Take me back to the house.'

'No.' He cut left, behind some high, dense goji bushes, then stopped running. 'It's not safe. There are still protestors on the grounds and in the house.'

'The police are there now. Ten seconds has passed.' I thought about screaming. If I screamed the word 'police', then the police would surely come. But if Daniel wanted to kill me, he would have time to do so between my scream and the rescue attempt. He had superhuman strength and was holding a knife.

Daniel looked down at his bleeding hand. He winced, as though in pain, though I knew he couldn't feel pain.

'Listen, we probably don't have long. Madara will be telling Master that we escaped out of the window. I just need to tell you something. I tried to tell you before. I tried to come up to your room.'

I looked into his green eyes as if they were possible to read, which of course they weren't. But I was here with him, at his mercy, so I could do nothing except go along with whatever weird Echo game he was playing.

'What did you try and tell me?'

'That I knew her.'

'Who?'

Blood dripped from his hand onto my cloth shoe, disappearing the moment it landed. Then he told me.

'*I knew Alissa*.'

9

Fear crept over my skin like an ice-cold blanket. 'What do you mean?'

'We had the same designer.'

I struggled to absorb this.

So was this what it was all about? Revenge? Was he going to kill me because I had terminated Alissa?

I knew this was a paranoid thought. I mean, Echos didn't feel loyalty to other Echos. They didn't *feel* anything at all. And besides, I thought of something else. Something that proved this Echo didn't know what he was talking about. 'No. That's impossible. Alissa was a Sempura product. You're a Castle product.'

'You are not safe here,' he told me. 'I tried to tell you. I was going to tell you that day in my room.'

I looked at his face. His eyes were wrong. Yeah. I had vaguely noticed it before, but now there was no mistaking it. There was too much there. He seemed more human than Echo. 'You're malfunctioning,' I told him. 'And I think you've probably been malfunctioning since I got here.'

He held up his right hand, his cut hand. 'It is not meant to be possible for me to feel pain, and I feel pain. I feel all kinds of things. And I feel a duty to tell you what I have wanted to tell you for a long time, and would have just run up those stairs and done it if it hadn't put you in danger.'

'What? Tell me.'

He took a breath. Came close. Whispered. 'You have to get out of here. You have to escape. After I have done this, there is no hope for me. Master will punish me for my actions. I do not care. This was partly my fault. Your parents' death. It was partly down to me. I had her in my arms. I held Alissa the way I just held you. I could have stopped it at the start, but I didn't.'

Again, he looked anxiously at the grass around us, waiting for something. Then he looked at the high perimeter wall.

I didn't trust him.

There was no way in the world I could trust him.

Or at least, that's what I tried to tell myself.

Whatever silly weakness I had deep down inside me, a weakness that came of being alone and wanting someone to be there for me – well, I knew I shouldn't let it get the better of me.

That dream I'd had . . . that had just been a dream. He was an Echo, and a malfunctioning one. OK, so he had read Jane Eyre and he could feel pain, but what did that prove?

But then he said it.

He said something that sent a jolt through me and made me question everything else. He said: 'Our designer's name was Rosella.'

Instantly Alissa's voice echoed in my mind. *Rosella*.

I looked into Daniel's green eyes and felt another shock. A deeper one than any spoken words could have caused. Because as I looked into his eyes, I realized that I felt for him. There was something gleaming there. Something like fear, or courage, or determination, or honour, or a combination of all four. Yes, for that moment at least, it felt like I was looking at someone who could be cared for. Worried about. Loved.

10

That is when the ground began to open up. Whole squares of blue and orange grass, tilting up and back like trapdoors all around us.

'Here come the hounds,' Daniel said.

'Hounds?' But even before Daniel explained, I remembered what Uncle Alex had told me.

'Echo dogs.'

Of course.

And then they started to prowl out onto the grass. They looked very much like Dobermans, although their chests were plates of naked titanium and their eyes were bright red.

'Step away from me,' Daniel told me, shouting almost angrily. 'Step well away from me and they won't hurt you. They only want me. Trust me.'

I stepped away from him, like he said.

'So you wanted to kill me?' I asked him, still uncertain what to think. 'Was that your plan? Because of Alissa? She murdered my parents!'

'No. No, she didn't kill them. Not really.'

The dogs circled Daniel. There were five of them. They were all giving the same synthetic growl. Madara must have told Uncle Alex about us by now. And so he'd set the dogs on us.

'What are you talking about? I saw the footage. She was the only one there. She killed them.'

'You don't understand,' he said quickly. 'She did it, yes. But I told you – it wasn't a malfunction. She wasn't a normal Echo. Your parents thought she was, but she wasn't. She was a prototype, being made for Sempura . . . Rosella designed prototypes. One-offs. Tests.'

Something about this rang false. 'Designers only work for one company. Everyone knows that.'

'You don't understand. Rosella, she is the very best in the world. And she is a good human. Or she tried to be. The trouble was—'

One of the Echo dogs suddenly swept in, and bit Daniel's left leg. I caught sight of the gleaming titanium teeth, complete with two needle-sharp fangs, longer than the rest. It was these that penetrated Daniel's flesh. Then another bit his right leg. A third jumped with a strength far beyond that of any purely biological dog, and pinned him to the ground.

Daniel looked at me with weary eyes. Those dogs had injected something into him via their fangs. 'You must escape. Find Rosella,' he said, before that third hound's fangs pierced his neck.

He managed a final word – '*Remember* . . .' – and then collapsed on the grass. A sleep beyond sleep. And as those Echo hounds ran towards the house, no doubt being remote-commanded to help the Echos and the police eliminate the last of the protestors, I went over to Daniel and crouched down to inspect him. The most visible wound was the knife cut on the palm of his hand, which was still leaking fresh blood onto the lawn. And he had a mark on his cheek from where the rock had caught him. Where the dogs had bitten him there were only the tiniest dark dots, as if from injections or vampire bites.

I no longer feared him. It was quite impossible to fear someone who was lying unconscious on the grass in front of you. In fact, I wanted him to wake up or come round. He had more information to give. But it wasn't just that. He had saved my life. And I knew I'd been wrong about him.

'Wake up! Wake up! Can you hear me? Daniel? Daniel! Wake up!'

There wasn't the slightest response, even when I slapped his face. I checked his pulse. I had never felt the pulse of an Echo before, but I knew that their hearts beat slightly faster than a human's, to ensure blood pumped more quickly around their bodies, leading to more efficient muscles and organs. And although Daniel's pulse wasn't beating quite that fast – he was unconscious, after all – it was still beating as fast as mine would in a state of absolute panic. To be honest, I wasn't far from that state.

A thousand questions sped around my mind.

Why had he saved me?

Why had he left my uncle's side when he knew he would be punished for disobeying an order?

Could any Echo ever feel guilt?

And had that really been Uncle Alex's order? Wasn't it more likely that Uncle would have told him to come and help me? After all, there were other Echos to look after Uncle Alex. But why had another Echo chased us?

And what was this stuff about Alissa? He had heard me say Alissa's name on that first night. He could have been lying. But then, he had mentioned Rosella. Why would he have said that name?

But was he lying? It came back to that.

Was he lying?

Was he lying?

He was an Echo. An Echo that Iago had already told me was weird. And even the least weird Echo in the world couldn't be trusted. But if he was lying, then why would he be risking everything to tell me that he knew Alissa? Why would he have brought me out here, into the garden, knowing that the Echo hounds were out here? And why had he told me to find Rosella?

I knew I didn't have long.

As soon as the protestors had been dealt with – maybe even before – someone would be out searching for me. Searching for Daniel. I looked at him lying there on the ground. At the arms that had carried me, at the hand that been cut trying to defend me, at the bruised and grazed cheek that had taken the force of a rock, at the strong pale neck that had been pierced by the fangs of an Echo hound. All those wounds. All for me. I looked at his closed eyelids, shielding those green eyes. I looked at his face, trying to see if there was some clue on it. If there was something that could tell me if he was lying or not.

Of course, it was impossible to tell. All I knew is that I was staring at a perfect face, and the trouble with perfection is that it doesn't give you any answers. Indeed, all it did was confuse me further. He was an Echo. I couldn't feel anything for an Echo except fear, and yet there I was, feeling all kinds of things.

But then I remembered. Echos have origin marks, singed onto the skin. It was roughly the same size as the mark on the back of an Echo's left hand. The E.

I had never seen Alissa's origin mark up close. Had never had any inclination to do so. But my parents would have done, I supposed, when they first purchased her. Yeah. Probably. Maybe.

There was the sound of footsteps, heading closer. I looked through the bushes and saw Uncle Alex, flanked by Madara and the other Echo who had been guarding him – the tall, muscular dreadlocked one – walking across the lawn towards me. Within twenty seconds they would be here.

Wasting no time, I tugged at Daniel's clothes until I saw his naked shoulder, and that origin mark. A band of text, neat bold capitals forming words almost too small to read:

DESIGNED BY
ROSELLA MÁRQUEZ (B-4-GH-44597026-D)
FOR CASTLE INDUSTRIES

'Activate info-lenses,' I said. And within a second the familiar green dot was hovering in front of me, to signify that the lenses were on. 'Camera,' I commanded. 'Take image.' I blinked. Rosella Márquez's ID number was now recorded. Just in time, as it turned out.

'Oh, Audrey, thank God.' Uncle Alex was standing there, looking worried. 'He didn't have time to hurt you.'

'I don't think he was going—'

He wasn't listening. 'Chester,' he said to the large Echo with the dreadlocks as he pointed at Daniel. 'Take that into the house.'

That. Why did it hurt me to hear him talking about Daniel like that? *Echos don't warrant sympathy. They're just machines.*

But still, when Chester scooped him off the ground and carried him into the house, I felt worried.

'What are you going to do to him? Is he going to die?'

My question seemed to puzzle Uncle Alex. Maybe not the words, but the way I said them.

'Audrey,' he said gently, 'this is my fault. An Echo never wins at chess if they are told not to win at chess.' Yes. Uncle's voice was gentle. But there was something new about the way he was looking at me. His eyes were harsh. 'We are going to make sure he never puts your life in danger again.'

'He didn't put me in danger. He . . . he saved my life.'

Uncle Alex came close to me. 'What did he say to you?'

'Nothing,' I said.

Madara must have done an instant voice-reading because she said: 'It is a lie, Master.'

Uncle Alex looked at Madara with an affection he couldn't hide from me. She was his favourite Echo, I could see that. But even so, he managed to say to her: 'Hush, Madara. She is young and she is human. She is allowed to lie. Indeed, it is expected.'

'He said some stuff, but it didn't make sense,' I explained. 'That is what I meant.'

Uncle Alex gave a small nod. '*Some stuff*.'

The Echo hounds skulked back across the grass and returned to their underground homes, the grass-covered doors closing and restoring the lawn to normal. I looked over towards the house.

'You are in shock. We all are, obviously, after what has just happened. Those protestors tried to kill me. They are animals. Monsters. Too scared to come out from behind their masks. They tried to kill Iago too. He is fine, though. In fact, he dealt with a lot of them himself. He is a sharp shooter. Whoever said that war games were bad for kids, eh? They might have just saved his life!' Uncle laughed a little. The laugh quickly died. 'Candressa wasn't so lucky, though.'

'What happened?'

'One of them shot her. In her arm. It won't be fatal. She's in surgery.'

'In hospital?'

'No. There's a medical room in the basement. Two Echos are fixing her right now.'

'I'm sorry to hear that.'

'There's been a lot of damage. I've lost a lot of money just in terms of the art they've destroyed. Picassos! They've destroyed Picassos! Clocks and furniture can repair themselves, but a painting can't. And all because of those terrorists. Terrorists fuelled by all that ridiculous anti-progress propaganda.'

'You mean, like Dad used to write?'

He sighed and looked at me for a while, maybe wondering if he should be polite. But eventually he came out and said it: 'Yes, exactly like that. Listen, I know you think I must have hated your dad. But I didn't. He was a stubborn man. I offered him money once. A lot of money. He turned it down. He didn't start off radical; he became it. The more successful I became, the more principles he developed. It was classic sibling rivalry. Nothing more, nothing less. Now come on, I can't stand around out here all day. I've got to talk to the police. And assess the damage.'

And as I walked back with him, I wondered if Uncle Alex was the reason Daniel had told me to escape.

11

We were back inside the house. I was in my bedroom. Uncle Alex had told me to stay there until all the mess could be cleared away. I think he also wanted me in my room so I wouldn't ask any questions. Or see whatever they were going to do to Daniel.

I sat there staring out of the window. At the crisscrossing rails carrying traffic. At the distant floating bone that was the New Parliament building, directly above the old one, which had flooded and evacuated many years ago, though Big Ben had been left relatively intact. The bone contained what Dad always used to call 'a joke of a government', as most of the politicians who worked there were also getting money from one of the main technology giants, and significantly more money from Castle than from Sempura. Knowing this, and seeing that giant sphere going round and round with the blue castle on it, it was very easy for me to feel like Uncle owned the whole city. That he was a kind of king. And a king with far more power and wealth than King Henry IX.

King of the Castle.

The trouble was, if he was like a king, he was an unpopular one. One that many clearly wanted dead. So it wasn't safe here. Today had proved that. But it wasn't just the protestors – or 'terrorists', as Uncle Alex had been quick to call them – that bothered me. No. And it wasn't just the Echos, either. It was Uncle Alex himself. He had been kind to me, as Candressa had pointed out. And it was true. And I desperately tried to convince myself that my growing doubts were unfounded. Daniel had malfunctioned. How could I have taken his word for anything?

'Is Daniel going to be OK?' I asked when Uncle Alex came in with a cup of red tea for me.

'Audrey, I don't understand it. I thought you hated Echos.'

'I do . . . I do . . . I just want to know what will happen to him. I'd like to be able to speak to him again.'

Uncle Alex sat on a chair and leaned back, taking a deep breath. I'd felt like this before. When I'd had the interview for Oxford. It was the feeling of being assessed. 'Well, that's not going to happen, I'm afraid.'

'Why? What are you going to do to him?'

'Don't worry about that, Audrey. We're not going to terminate him. We're going to make a few little changes and then send him somewhere else.'

A few little changes.

'You see,' Uncle Alex said, 'there are things you don't know about Daniel.'

'*Things?*'

'He's not like the other prototypes. A lot more money was spent on him. Made by the best designer. By a genius, in fact. But there is very often a problem with genius. Sometimes the genius pushes things a little too far. It can create something that we're not quite ready for. It can create something that acts in unpredictable ways. And that might be what has happened here.'

'Like Alissa?'

'What?'

'Alissa acted in unpredictable ways.'

'Alissa wasn't a Castle product. If she was a Castle product, she would never have been on the market. None of the Echos I have here have been released yet.'

'But you said they were all safe. You said there was nothing to worry about.'

'They *are* all safe. Most of them. In fact, without them we'd be dead right now. Killed in cold blood by those terrorist monsters.'

He looked angry, but he was hiding something. I was becoming a bit scared. He reverted to his original topic. 'No Castle prototype has ever caused problems before. It's just Daniel. The most advanced. And therefore the most problematic.'

'So what are you going to do to him?'

'I don't know if you know about Echos. Their brains look like ours but they are not like ours. They run on code. There is a chip inside them. This chip sends different instructions and triggers to different parts of the brain. The rear part of the brain deals with free thought. In his particular case – for some reason we can't identify – it seems to trigger imagination.'

I was confused. 'Imagination? Is that bad?'

'Imagination is dangerous, Audrey. Imagination makes them have a degree of unknowability. It makes them more advanced, but it increases the risk. But luckily, in an Echo, it is located right here.' He patted the back of his head. 'And it is very simple to remove, while still ensuring he maintains a degree of functionality.'

Degree of functionality.

'He's not a machine!'

'Oh, but that is exactly what he is. He is an Echo. He wasn't born, he was made. There are no blurred lines. And this machine has malfunctioned, so he is getting downgraded. And then I'll be putting him out there on the open market. There is a big market, you see, for rejects. Some go to the moon. Some end up in London, doing dirty or dangerous work. They are cheap. That place over there is full of them.'

'Where?'

He pointed out of the window, at the rotating sphere in the distance.

'The Resurrection Zone?' I remembered Dad's stories about that place. About violent encounters between the animals and the Echos that looked after them. Dad compared it to the Coliseum in ancient Rome, where Christians were fed to the lions for entertainment. But instead of Christians it was Echos, and instead of lions it was tigers. And though Dad wasn't a fan of Echos, I agreed that it was cruel – to the animals, if no one else. And yet, weirdly, I wasn't thinking about the animals. I was thinking about Daniel.

'Most Echos don't last more than a month there,' I said.

'Some do, some don't. That's hardly our problem.'

'But you own it. Castle owns it.'

He looked at me, and there was a sense that we both knew we were playing some kind of game. We were saying some things and not saying others. 'The Resurrection Zone is a fun place. It angers those terrorists, but everything angers them. I'll take you one day. I think you'll see that your dad was wrong about it. It makes a lot of people happy. It does a lot of good work.'

It was then that we heard a noise. A faint but alarming sound. A scream.

'Was that him? Was that Daniel?'

'It might have been.'

I realized they must have been operating on him right then. 'He sounded like he was in pain. Don't you do it painlessly?'

'Echos don't feel pain.'

'But he's advanced. *He* can. He can imagine and he can feel pain.'

Uncle Alex looked at the painting. Those huddled, cold, traumatized nudes listening to music. 'Interesting. I am sure artists like Matisse would have agreed. The price of imagination is pain. That may be true.' He laughed. 'Well, better he feels it than he inflicts it.'

And then he stood up to leave. The screams kept on. They triggered questions inside me. Questions I was no longer too scared to ask.

'Who was Rosella?'

Uncle Alex sighed. His nose whistled slightly as he did so. 'Whatever he said to you, you shouldn't trust it. He was playing with your mind.'

'How do you know he said anything about Rosella?' I said, my heart speeding as a revelation pumped adrenaline into me. 'Alissa did. I told you that at the media conference. But you are right – so did Daniel. Was she the genius? Did she make Alissa?'

Uncle Alex stopped just before he reached the door. 'You can tell you are your dad's daughter. Questions, questions, questions.'

'My dad was a good person.'

He nodded. And he looked at me with eyes that showed no sign of warmth. 'Yes, but look what happens to good people.'

'I need to know.'

He smiled. Looking back, I realize it was the first time I had seen open cruelty on his face.

'Well, then, come with me. You can ask Daniel everything you want to know.'

12

At the time I wasn't really sure why Uncle Alex wanted this to happen.

I mean, why he wanted me to see Daniel after the operation.

Why he took me down two flights of stairs to a part of the house I had never been in – to the surgery room, and that horizontal pod where Daniel was lying awake but lifeless beneath the aerogel casing.

Now, though, I realize it was about power. Everything in Uncle Alex's life was about power. The aggressive business strategies, the big house in Hampstead, the Matisse and Picasso paintings, the holo-sculptures. It was all to show how powerful and important he was. I wish Dad had told me more about what Uncle Alex had been like as a child. Maybe that would have explained a few things. Maybe one day I would discover the truth.

But anyway, this was about power. About showing the power he had over his products, of which Daniel was one; and also about showing the power he had over me. Because, really, this was the moment when everything changed between me and my uncle. It was the point at which the pretence was over. When I could no longer try and convince myself that he had my best interests at heart. Maybe it was the shock of the activists breaking into the house, but whatever it was, the mask had slipped.

We walked into the bare, perfectly clean white room.

'Open pod,' said Uncle. And the pod opened and Daniel was lying there looking up at us. Though his eyes were different now. They seemed blank and empty, the way Echo eyes were supposed to look.

'Right,' said Uncle, smoothing back his own hair. 'I'll leave you to ask your questions. Now, I am going to see how the house repairs are going.'

So he left us there. Alone.

13

But obviously we weren't really alone.

You couldn't really be alone anywhere in this house. You were always being watched, recorded, monitored. Uncle Alex could have been in his pod or in the security room, watching us in real time.

I tried not to think about this.

I tried to concentrate on Daniel.

It was weird. This whole thing was weird. Was he asleep with his eyes open? As I got closer I saw the blood. I was reminded that Echo blood and human blood is almost identical, except that Echos have fewer white blood cells, so theirs is darker. It was already drying, beneath the back of his head on the harsh-looking surgi-pillow and matted into his light hair.

'Hello,' I said.

Nothing. Not so much as a blink.

'Daniel, it's me, Audrey. You saved my life. I want to say thank you.'

There might have been something then. The smallest twitch between his eyebrows. A sign that he might be hearing my words.

And here's the thing . . .

He was not terrifying.

I had always been troubled by the way Echos looked; their perfect faces and bodies. It was a perfection that I had found ugly. Beauty was about imperfection because that was what made people special. Or maybe that's what I told myself because I had large shoulders and walked like a boy. Whatever. But if everyone was made to look perfect, then no one would be special because being special meant being different, by offering something that wasn't on offer elsewhere, and Echos were all the same. The models changed, but they were equals in perfection.

Echo skin wasn't quite like human skin. There were no pores or marks or blemishes. Everything was made to be symmetrical and visually appealing. Some people liked that sort of thing, obviously. (Which, I suppose, was the thinking behind Universal Affection and Echo Echo and 3.14 and Love Circuits, and all those other manufactured Echo 'boy' bands, which I had always seen as the absolute opposite of something real and messy and human like the Neo Maxis.)

But beauty was something else. Something hidden slightly away, something that existed inside every living thing, which could only be seen by certain people. And once they saw it, they couldn't unsee it, because like all those old dead poets said, beauty was truth and eternity and it connected you to the infinite.

Beauty did not belong to machines. It did not belong to Echos. And yet it was there, as difficult to spot as the little crease that had momentarily appeared on Daniel's forehead.

'This shouldn't have happened to you,' I told him. 'I am sorry. What happened? Why did you stay awake? Why didn't they switch you off? It's torture. That's what happened. You felt pain. You aren't meant to feel pain, but anyone who heard your screams knew you were in pain. I'm sorry.'

His eyes closed for the slowest of blinks, and when they opened again they were looking at me. But this was not the Echo boy who had saved my life. That boy seemed lost. Totally. He didn't seem to be there.

'Please. Say something. Anything. Just speak. I know you can hear me.'

I couldn't help but feel he was my responsibility. When somebody saves your life, you owe them a whole world. I touched his skin.

'You told me you had met Alissa. You told me you were designed by someone called Rosella Márquez.'

Another blink.

'You had more to tell me. About Alissa. About Uncle Alex.'

His eyes stared into mine, but it was hard to say what he was really seeing. I suddenly felt self-conscious, aware that I was just a mass of human imperfections.

His mouth moved.

He was about to speak.

'Who are you?' he said, in a voice that sounded empty and flat and neutral.

It was a weird feeling. Relief to hear him speak, but disappointment at the words.

'I'm Audrey. Audrey Castle. I am Mr Castle's niece. My parents were killed by an Echo called Alissa. She was a Sempura Echo, not a Castle one.' Then I whispered, 'I'm starting to think that I am only alive right now because I'm useful. I can help him score points against Sempura.' It was only as I said this that I realized, with a sudden jolt of fear, that it was true.

He frowned again. It was like someone trying to learn a language.

He turned his head a little towards me. This movement appeared to cause him great pain. He winced. Instinctively I placed my hand gently on his face.

'Don't worry,' I said. 'I'm sorry. I'm troubling you. I don't want to trouble you. You saved my life.'

I remembered a poem. It was one of Mum's favourites. As I looked down at him, I tried to imagine what he was feeling, and the first line of that poem came out of my mouth: '*I am: yet what I am none cares or knows.*'

His eyes weren't so blank now. There was a sadness inside them. I didn't know if it was better that he was sad than nothing at all. I remembered that day in his room. I remembered him holding me. I remembered his warm breath. I remembered feeling things I wasn't meant to feel.

And then I kissed him.

I leaned down and kissed him softly on the lips.

The kiss wasn't a silly romantic h-movie kiss. It was just the kind of kiss you give someone you care about. And I knew that I had once been wrong about him, and I knew that he was confused and in pain. I knew that he had risked a lot for me. He'd been trying to protect me all along. And I knew that, right at this moment, he was the only real ally I had in the world, so I wanted to bring him back and show that someone cared about him.

I had changed. I was feeling emotion towards something that was technically a machine. If a machine could develop enough to become almost human, maybe a human could develop enough to understand that. Maybe that is what growing up was all about. It was about changing your mind. Opening it right up. Admitting to yourself that you were wrong about stuff.

'You aren't like the others,' I said. 'You are different. You care. You feel pain. But one day you will feel other things. Nicer things, I promise you.'

He whispered something.

'*Audrey*.'

He knew my name. My heart felt like it would burst now that I knew I was helping to bring him back.

He looked like he might speak again. And he did.

'He changed Alissa.' That is what it sounded like, but I couldn't be sure.

'What? *What?*'

But then I stopped talking because the door opened and my uncle re-entered the room and said, 'All right, lovebirds,' he said. 'Time to say your goodbyes. Because I don't think you'll be seeing each other again, do you?'

14

Uncle Alex escorted me to my room, and then he was gone. He shut the door. And I stayed sitting there. I closed my eyes. I hated myself. I had been full of prejudice. I had judged Daniel on the basis of Alissa, and according to the ideas that had been forced upon me by my dad.

Dad. I thought of something he'd said, the very last time I saw him alive: *Monsters aren't any different to you and me. No one wakes up thinking they are a monster, even when they have become one, because the changes have been so gradual*. He had been talking about Uncle Alex, I understand that now. But then I realized I couldn't just sit there. So I stood up and went to the door.

'Open,' I said.

Nothing.

'Open.'

The door stayed closed.

'I command the door to open. Door open, door open, door open, open, open . . .' I remembered Lina Sempura's words to me: *Open your eyes, girl. Open your eyes*.

There was a handle. An old ornate one, from the days when doors weren't mind- or voice-commanded. I tried to turn it, but it wouldn't turn. I tried to pull it too, but the door, though it looked old, had a secure electromagnetic lock, and no amount of pulling would open it.

Uncle Alex had locked me in.

I banged on the door. 'Let me out! Let me out of here!'

But no one came. After a while I heard Iago on the intercom. He was obviously watching me from the pod in his room.

'Oh dear,' he said, laughing his evil ten-year-old laugh. 'Looks like you're stuck there.' He laughed some more, thinking he was funny. 'You'll have to wait till your hair gets long enough for a knight to come and climb up and save you! Yeah. Like any knight would bother with a weirdo like you.'

'Iago, please, help me. I need to get out of here. I'm getting claustrophobic. Uncle – your dad – has made a mistake.' I was playing dumb, obviously, as I seriously doubted it was a mistake that I was trapped in here. But a part of me hoped I was being paranoid.

Open your eyes.

He laughed some more. It was a fake laugh, made unnaturally loud just so I could hear it. 'It wasn't a mistake. But if it makes you feel better, believe it was. Believe anything you want! Believe Dad actually cares about you!'

'He lets me stay here,' I said.

And I didn't need Iago's laughter on the other side of that door to realize how pathetic I was sounding. *He lets me stay here.* I was an idiot. I was like one of the tigers at the Resurrection Zone, thankful to be trapped in an enclosure.

I remembered a line from the Neo Maxis song 'Love in a Cage' from three years ago: *This is what I remember best / When I was a prisoner but thought I was a guest . . .*

I remembered three days ago. The day it happened. When I had terminated – or thought I'd terminated – Alissa.

I had been in the car, driving away. I had been traumatized, hardly able to think, hardly knowing my own name, and the holophone had rung and I had spoken to Uncle Alex.

He had been trying to get hold of my parents. He had been wanting to ask them to come to his birthday party. He had obviously tried the house and got no answer so he had tried the car.

But why had he phoned *then*?

I tried to remember when Uncle Alex had last called to speak to my parents. Christmas Day? Maybe. But I didn't think so. There had been a long period of mutual non-calling. And so what were the chances that he would have been trying to call so soon after their death? Mathematics wasn't my forte, but it did seem like a very big coincidence.

Perhaps Uncle Alex was psychic. Perhaps, perhaps . . . Then I thought of Daniel. He had wanted to tell me more, before the Echo hounds had attacked him and he had fallen to the ground. '*Remember*,' he had said. But what?

I didn't know.

I tried to focus my thoughts. I was frightened, and I knew that I could stop that fear simply by replacing the neuropads – the ones that sat on the chest beside my bed. I could feel calm within seconds. But the thought of feeling calm was the most terrifying thing of all, because fear was always there for a reason.

And sometimes it was there to keep you alive.

Daniel. Mind-log 2.

1

'*Te pareces mucho a él,*' Rosella said, sighing. *You look just like him*. 'How I imagine he would be, anyway.'

'Who?' I asked. But she didn't answer.

And then she walked around the room in circles. She pinched her bottom lip and whispered to herself. I didn't understand what was happening, but I translated her behaviour as anxious. I looked at her.

After six minutes and fifteen seconds she took a deep breath and appeared to have reached a decision. She took something out of her pocket. A small cylindrical black container. She walked over and asked me to hold out my left hand, with my palm facing upwards.

I did as instructed, and then she pressed her hand around my forearm, and clicked the end of the black cylinder. A small copper disc appeared. I knew that copper was a durable, malleable, corrosion-resistant metal that was second only to silver in its ability to conduct heat.

I had a feeling of uncertainty as the copper disc hovered away from the cylinder, to land on my wrist.

Uncertainty. Another thing I wasn't supposed to feel.

'An Echo is given two marks,' Rosella explained. 'The origin mark and this ID mark. One private, one public. One given inside the tank, one outside, to check that there is no untoward reaction.'

It took me a second or two to feel the heat of it searing through my skin. An intense, consuming pain as I stared at that hot blue day out of the window. I let out a small cry. I remembered the pain I had felt in the tank. Pain was the same with knowledge and without it. Pain was completely independent of information. She clicked the cylinder again, and the disc left my skin, returning from where it came. Rosella pulled away from me, almost scared.

'My God,' she said. 'I've done it. I've actually done it.'

It had left a scar, or mark. The scar was in the form of a circle, with the letter E inside it. Dark pink, raised skin. Then she inspected my shoulder. There was a name on it. And numbers. Her name and ID number. She showed it me. I saw it reflected in a mirror.

DESIGNED BY
ROSELLA MÁRQUEZ (B-4-GH-44597026-D)
FOR CASTLE INDUSTRIES

'This was automatic,' she said, explaining the mark. 'This was the one that happened in the tank. In the laboratory.' And another realization dawned on her. 'It must have been the thing that woke you up. You must have felt this and then come to life.'

At that time, this contradicted my knowledge. 'Echos don't come to life. They are switched on. Am I alive?'

'I . . . I don't know.'

She was frightened, I realized, seeing her pupils dilate. It was fear coupled with excitement.

'I've had a dream,' she said. 'I've had this dream for years. A dream of creating something so close to being alive it would be impossible to know the difference. And my dream has just come true. And sometimes there is nothing more terrifying in this life than having a dream come true.' She stood up, and backed away from me, colliding with the desk. She stayed there and began to breathe really fast and deep. 'You felt pain,' she said.

'Yes. So am I not an Echo?'

'No. You are. You are. But a prototype Echo would not have come alive in the tank. You should not have felt anything at all before you were ignited. You should not have felt fear. You should not have seen despair in an abstract pattern. And most certainly you should not have been able to feel pain!'

'So why did I?'

'And questions!' Her hands were in her hair. 'You should not be asking questions. You are not meant to be curious. You are not meant to question your situation. You are just meant to be. To exist. You are knowledge without thought. You are action without emotion. You are service without question. Those are the Echo principles. And I have broken them. I tried to break them, but . . . but . . . but . . . I never *expected* to break them.'

She began to cry, even as she smiled. After speaking for a while, she poured forty-three millilitres of a copper-coloured liquid into a glass. I detected the scent of malted barley and alcohol, and consequently knew that the drink was whisky. She said this:

'*Hay algo que quiero contarte . . .* I want to tell you something. I owe you an explanation. You see, you are a one-off. There is no Echo in the world like you. There has never been one. Never. *Nunca*. I didn't even know you were possible, but I always imagined you might be. I lost a baby. A baby boy. He died in his sleep when he was ten months old. He was called Daniel. It is a family name. My grandfather's middle name. Always the middle name. But I broke that tradition. He was blond, like his father. It made me depressed. *Triste*. And then things went sour between me and the man I was with. He was called Alfredo, and he was a bastard. That is all you need to know about him. Anyway, after that, I hurt myself, a lot. I used to cut my skin to block out the pain, because physical pain is never as bad as the mental kind. Look . . .' I could see thin white scars on her arms. 'I had to see a doctor, but I never really got over it. The only thing that gave me any comfort was working on you. Well, that and whisky. See, I wanted to create an Echo that has emotions and feelings. So I worked hard on you. You started as a commission for Alex Castle. He wanted someone strong and agile, with a precise mathematical mind and high computational power. Yet I realized that you were the best shot. I'd been given a lot of money to play with, for you. And so I went full-on with the code. I played God. I raised my game. I didn't sleep. Fine tuning and fine tuning and fine tuning. *Si*.' Her forehead creased, between her eyebrows. 'Living on nothing but energy pills and whisky and this stupid dream. *Me pasé*.'

'There are no others like me?'

'No. There can't be. You were made different. The code wasn't just Echo code. I mean, that was 99.9 per cent of it. Of the programming. But there was something else.'

'Something else?'

She hesitated. Her lips pursed, and she exhaled slowly and deliberately, the way humans do when they are trying to calm themselves, or gain courage. She toyed with her locket, pulling it gently along its chain. 'You have the same knowledge, the same fast ability to learn, the same speed and strength and reflexes, but I made you different. *Mira esto*.'

Look at this.

She detached the gold locket from its chain and opened it, showing me its contents. Inside, there was a curl of blond hair. I calculated thirty-one strands. 'This is his hair,' she explained. 'This is Daniel's hair. My boy's hair.'

I stared at it and began to understand. I knew that hair – even hair like this that had no perfectly intact follicles – contained mitochondrial DNA, and that although that kind of DNA had less information than nuclear DNA, there was prediction software that could do the rest, and fill in most of the jigsaw.

'You are not him,' she said. 'You are an Echo. But I dissolved the hair into the solution. The solution from which you were made. The liquid born from code. It is like you contain a piece of him. The way this locket contains a piece of him. You are a locket made flesh. A memory brought back to life. You are an Echo, and an echo. But you are *you*. Someone totally new. You have a physical and mental power humans lack, and emotions and dreams that Echos lack. That 0.1 per cent makes all the difference. *Es todo*. It's everything. It is like . . . like . . . like . . .' She searched for a simile. 'It is like the crack in the door that lets the light in and illuminates the whole room. You are the best of both worlds. You are the end of evolution.'

These words did not comfort me. Instead, I felt small. I felt an intense emotion characterized by a hollow, exposed sensation. I identified it as loneliness. And then fear. I started to be worried. I thought of the mark on my shoulder. *For Castle Industries*.

'What is going to happen to me?'

She looked at the cross on the wall and the small pewter sculpture of a dying man. And then she looked into my eyes and must have seen the fear because she said, 'Nothing, Daniel. Nothing is going to happen to you. I have lost a Daniel before. I will not lose you. You will not be sold. You can stay here. You can live with me. I will tell Mr Castle that you need more work, that something went wrong. I will tell him that I will try to fix you, but then I will tell him it didn't work. It will be all right – yes, I am sure.'

She sounded like she was trying to convince herself as much as she was trying to convince me. But I wanted to believe her. Or that piece of me that had been human did.

'I hope so,' I said. I may have been the first Echo in history to use the word *hope*. But I knew it was a delicate thing, hope, and could be broken as easily as a single strand of human hair.

2

For a short while it worked like that. One day she went to her office and holo called Mr Castle. I wasn't there for the conversation, and it was a good deal later that I first saw him, but the result was that Rosella was given time to 'work' on me. Of course, she had no plan to do so. And I have to be so grateful for that.

I lived with Rosella and her ill grandfather. I was not expensive to look after, as I was an Echo. My survival depended only on a solution of sugar and water. Five hundred millilitres a day. That and a hundred and twenty-two minutes of recharge or 'sleep' a night.

While Rosella went to work at her warehouse in Valencia, I filled my days by looking after Ernesto and observing the iguanas that were kept outside as pets. When I was outside, I saw a long plume of smoke stretching to the sky. There was also a smell of sulphur. The smoke was from the town of Catadau. I would later realize that Catadau had been destroyed two months before by the Spanish government. But the fires hadn't gone out. It was a town permanently on fire.

You could hardly see the fire itself. Just a dull glow. But in a way, everything felt like it was on fire because of the sun. I felt the heat.

It didn't burn my skin as it would a human's, especially a human of my colouring. It couldn't cause cancer. (Another fact I knew: the only cancer humans still got, since the medical advances involving T-cell regeneration made during the twenty-first century, was skin cancer. It was especially prevalent in those European countries that had massively increased in temperature over the last hundred years, like Spain. Other countries – Britain, New Germany, all of Scandinavia, Northern France, Canada, much of the US – had become wetter, stormier, greyer, and so skin cancer wasn't so much of a problem in those places; but if you were quite fair skinned and lived somewhere like Spain or Italy or anywhere below Austria, then you had to be careful.) Anyway, the heat still could cause an Echo like me problems. It made me lose liquid, and so sometimes I needed more than five hundred millilitres of water. The water wasn't from taps. Rosella had bottles of it stored in her refrigerator.

The villa was very basic. Inside, it smelled of clay and sour milk. It was cut off from the outside world. Apparently it had been abandoned for thirty years when Rosella had moved in and she hadn't put any additional technology inside.

'The government want to destroy it,' she told me. 'Every day I worry they will send a locater missile to blow us up. They don't even bother with antimatter technology. We are not worth the price of an expensive bomb! They want rid of not only the properties around here, but the residents too.'

'Why?'

'Because they say there are dangerous people living in them. Ex-convicts. People like that. People who don't need ID, or money. But it's exaggerated. Basically a government always fears the poor, because they have nothing to lose.'

I found it incredible that Rosella was poor. I had been programmed to believe that humans were rewarded for their talents, and Rosella was surely among the most talented humans.

Most of the time I sat outside and stared at flat arid land, and the salt bushes and a leafless tree and the iguanas and the faraway rising smoke. Sometimes in the evening I would sit with Ernesto, if he was feeling strong enough. We would speak together in Spanish.

He talked about the iguanas.

He told me that if you picked them up by the tail, the tail can break off so they can free themselves, then a new tail grows in its place. 'To survive in life, sometimes you need to cut a bit of you away, leave something behind . . .'

He talked about the land too.

'All this used to be rice fields,' he said, struggling with his breath in the heat. He winced each time he inhaled, as if it scorched his lungs. 'The largest in Europe. This was years ago. When I was still a young man. Before the sun turned evil.'

That was about all the conversation I could get out of him before he started coughing and wheezing and needed to escape the hot, sulphurous evening air.

We were quite isolated. There were no magrails because no one was meant to be here. Rosella went to work on land roads. Few people used land roads any more, and the last land car had left the production line on 15 March 2076, exactly thirty-one years after the first magrail came into being, enabling people to get to places a hundred times quicker than they had before.

The car Rosella drove was nearly sixty years old. A rickety old electric auto-drive with four wheels and a top speed of a mere 360 kilometres an hour. Land roads were dangerous. They hadn't been maintained for years and were in a state of disrepair. In many places the sun had literally melted the tarmac away. Also, Ernesto told me something that troubled me.

He said that murderers and bandits occasionally travelled these old worn unpoliced land roads, looking not only for derelict villas to live in but also for people to hurt or steal from.

It made me worry about Rosella.

I told Rosella this, and she said that she was worried about a terrible bandit but that he didn't drive on land roads. Back then I didn't know who she meant. I do now, of course.

There were old books in the house and I read them. Most of them were in Spanish. I read a book called *Don Quixote* by Miguel de Cervantes. I read the poetry of Federico García Lorca and the stories of Jorge Luis Borges.

I read a love story and felt sad to think that I would never fall in love.

I read fairy tales. I loved fairy tales more than anything. My favourite was *Sleeping Beauty* by the Brothers Grimm. I found something comforting in the story of a princess who pricks her finger on the spindle of a spinning wheel and then, because of a wicked fairy's curse, falls into a sleep for a hundred years. The curse could only be lifted by the kiss from a prince. The comforting part came from the lengths the prince went to in order to reach her and bring her back to waking life, fighting his way through a magical forest full of brambles and thorns designed to keep everyone away. He was determined to reach her, and he did. It was the kind of story that could make a machine like me feel human.

I talked to Ernesto about being a human.

Ernesto believed that if you were a good human in life you went to heaven, and if you were bad you went to hell.

I made sure Ernesto had his medication. I also made food for

Rosella when she came home from work. Simple dishes, made from cheap food that she bought in the food markets in Valencia (rice, synthetic ham and fish). I never tasted this food myself but I enjoyed making it. Mainly I would sit in the sun and play Rosella's guitar. I found it very easy to learn. I liked what music did to me. It made me feel emotions I wasn't programmed to understand.

'Mr Castle chooses which prototypes he likes,' she explained one night at around midnight as we sat on the old wooden bench and stared out across the desert, towards the dull glow in the sky from Valencia. 'Then he takes them to live in his big house in London. If they are successful, he gets his company to replicate them; make millions of them for homes and businesses around the world. Some are designed to be all-rounders. Others are for a specific purpose. Some I make to be exceptionally strong. Some to be good at intricate tasks. Some are wanted just for security purposes, others for gardening or babysitting or cooking.'

'What about me?' I asked her. 'What was I made for?'

'I wanted you to be good at everything. More financial investment was put in, and I worked ten times harder on you than on any of the others. You have that mark on your shoulder, but I sort of knew I would never be able to give you away. That's why I brought you here. Why I had another Echo take you out of the warehouse and put you in my car that night, at three in the morning. I did it because I never wanted him to know about you.'

'Mr Castle?'

She nodded, looking worried about something.

'What would happen if he found out?' I asked her.

'Well, I suppose he would take you to live in his house in London, like he takes the others. He would make you work for him. If you were good he'd keep you there, and take the bio-computational code I used to make you in order to produce others exactly like you.'

'No,' I said. 'I mean, what would happen to *you*?'

She shrugged, but looked scared. '*No es problema tuyo* . . .' This isn't your problem. 'Don't worry.'

But I *did* worry. I worried a lot, and after Rosella went to bed I sat there and invented comforting tunes on her guitar.

3

Yes, it was a very simple life. I liked it. I liked my role. It was a role I had formed for myself. Rosella had never asked me to make her food, or to keep Ernesto entertained with music and conversation and by reading him stories (he always wanted to read a Borges story called 'El Jardín de Senderos que se Bifurcan' – *The Garden of Forking Paths*; it seemed to give him great comfort). She had asked me to give water and green leaves and papaya to the four iguanas, but I enjoyed doing it, just as I enjoyed cleaning the house.

Sometimes I got lonely.

'It is understandable,' Rosella said. 'Because there is no one like you in the world. You are an Echo, yes. Enhanced Computerized Humanoid Organism. Echo. There are lots of them. But there are none like you.'

It was true.

I was not a human, but I was not a typical Echo, either. If I had been, I wouldn't have known how to feel lonely.

'I feel guilty,' she said. 'I wonder sometimes if I should have brought you into the world.'

I didn't want Rosella to feel guilty. 'I am glad you did,' I said. 'Because here I can read great stories and listen to music and look at the stars. I can't imagine never having known these things.'

Rosella smiled at me. Pride shone in her eyes. And right then we heard coughing from inside the house, and we ran to Ernesto's bedroom and saw blood on the sheets that had come from his mouth.

'*Tranquilo*,' he said, trying to calm Rosella down. He assured us that he was fine.

Later, Rosella cried. I wondered: was it better to live and love, when living and loving could only cause pain? This was a human question, of course. It might well have been the oldest human question of all. And I was not human. In fact, I was not even alive. Not in the technical sense. I was merely *on*. An emotional machine. Yet I loved Rosella and, I suppose, Ernesto too. Because it was impossible to love someone without also loving the people they loved. Love spreads easily. Which made me wonder why the world had been messed up so much, when love was such a contagious thing.

And then, the night after that, something terrible happened.

At 2:46 in the morning I heard a sound; a sound that grew louder as I lay on the futon. I didn't want to wake Rosella – she was sleep-deprived enough already. So I went to the window and looked up at the sky.

Unlike a human, I didn't need info-lenses to see in the dark. Rosella had programmed every Echo so that our eyes would have an array of advanced photodetectors, and used seven times the amount of the chemical element rhodopsin (the one responsible for seeing in the dark) than was found naturally in a human eye. And I was no different.

Which meant that I could see something in the sky heading

towards us at 270 metres a second. It was small: I worked out its angle and realized that it was on a direct trajectory for our house and would reach us in fourteen seconds.

'Rosella!' I shouted as I ran to Ernesto's bedroom.

Eventually she opened her eyes. '*Sí?*'

'Something's coming!'

We got out just in time. There was an explosion. A ball of fire and a black channel of smoke rising up against the night. We felt the heat of it, but we weren't hurt. Ernesto struggled to breathe for a while, but I think that was more to do with shock than smoke.

'The bloody damn government!' Rosella was saying as she stared at the heat and the smoke. 'They wanted to kill us! They didn't just want to destroy the house – they wanted to kill us!' And she swore, furiously, in Spanish. Then she thought of something and started running round to the other side of the house, and was even more furious to find that the iguanas were dead.

4

We drove that night. We had to. We had to get to the warehouse before daylight came – the heat would have killed Ernesto if he was left out in it. We heard and saw other explosions near by. Every home in the whole area was being destroyed.

It was dangerous, especially taking me, and I told Rosella that she didn't have to do it.

'There is no risk. Mr Castle never comes unannounced. There would always be time to hide you away. A few minutes maybe, if he comes from London . . .'

So this was our new home. The laboratory. A vast three-storey warehouse made of translucent concrete on a hill on the edge of the city. The ground floor was 148 metres by 120 metres and contained twenty-five cuboid tanks, including the one where I had been made. The top floor was Rosella's office. Down below was a basement full of the technology that brought me into being, along with an incinerator.

'I don't want you to go down there,' she told me.

'Why?'

'I think it would be bad for you. To see how you were made.'

'OK,' I said.

Then she looked at me for a while. 'But I do want you to remember a number. OK. Can you record this number for me? Eight . . . four . . . two . . . nine . . . zero. Have you got that?'

'Yes. But what is it for?'

She inhaled, her face as solemn as only a human face could look. 'You will know if you have to know.'

There were a lot of things Rosella didn't tell me, or at least didn't fully explain. She kept on talking to herself. And she also went very quiet, and made me leave the room whenever she had a work call. One day I overheard her.

'Yes, I have started work on her, but you know how dangerous this is for me. If Mr Castle finds out, I will be in serious trouble.'

She would tell Ernesto that in a few weeks everything would be fine. Ernesto was confused, and hardly spoke, but Rosella tried to comfort him, saying, 'We'll have a new place to live. Money is coming.'

'From Castle?' Ernesto asked, with a worry I couldn't quite understand.

'Just don't worry,' Rosella said. 'I'm working on something.'

We all slept near each other on the top floor, in the office. We slept on futons. It was OK for me as I only needed two hours a night, but Ernesto struggled. He kept on waking up coughing blood. And Rosella got tireder and tireder from listening to all the coughing. On those rare occasions when she and Ernesto managed to get some sleep, I would stand at the window, staring out.

I could see the lights of a city sprawling out all around me. Haulage vehicles speeding by on rails. Illuminated words and holograms flickering in the sky. Spanish words, along with brand names, one more dominant than the others: CASTLE, CASTLE, CASTLE. Lots of blue castles with three turrets. In the distance I could see the sea, reflecting moonlight.

Then one day there was a call.

Rosella's desk started flashing.

'Quick,' she said. 'Hide.'

But it was too late. It was a forced call. A hologram of a man appeared where the light had been flashing. The man had dark hair and wore a black suit.

'Rosella? The next prototype is overdue.'

'I know, Mr Castle,' Rosella said. 'He is still not ready. I have done something wrong. I need to do more work.'

'Rosella, do not lie to me. You are the best designer we have. You never do anything wrong. Please. You said he would be ready three weeks ago. And I am looking at him right now and he looks ready. He looks as ready as can be. Another magnificent prototype. A worthy investment. You are too filled with doubt. Too much the tortured artist. He'll be fine. He'll come and live with me for two months, and if everything works, then we'll use him as a prototype and make a lot of him.'

'That would be a bad idea, Mr Castle.'

'Why?'

'He feels emotion. He feels pain.'

At this point Mr Castle looked at me in wonder, or maybe just greed. 'Well, isn't that something. Rosella, you have excelled yourself.'

She didn't appreciate the compliment. 'I've made a mistake with the processing. There is an element of unpredictability, which makes him potentially dangerous. Even without the ethical considerations . . .'

The hologram of Mr Castle laughed at this point. 'Ethical considerations! I find that rather interesting, coming from you.'

I could tell that Rosella was agitated, maybe frightened too. 'What do you mean?'

'Well, lying isn't always very ethical.'

'Lying?'

'I hear that you are working for Sempura, on a commission.'

'Who told you that?'

'That is not the important bit, Rosella. How much are they paying you to break your contract?'

Rosella went pale. This explained her secrecy, her need to have me out of the way whenever she had a call or a meeting. I sensed her terror, even though it was a terror she was desperately trying not to show. 'Mr Castle, please. This is not true.'

'I have reliable sources. And don't worry, I understand. I understand. You work very hard for me and I pay you very little. Is that it? You have a granddad who is very sick. And your home has been destroyed. It must be hard.'

'No. Mr Castle, please—'

'Fifteen years ago, Rosella, you were nothing. You were nowhere. You were a young designer who wanted the freedom to create what you wanted to create. I gave you that freedom. And you signed a loyalty contract. To me. For life.'

'I know, I know. And I would never betray that loyalty.'

'But you have made me *billions* . . . That must make you bitter. I can see why you might be tempted to bite the hand that has fed you. Especially as you don't have a home any more. I don't know how you do it, living there, at the warehouse.'

Rosella hardly had any blood left in her face. I noticed that her fingertips were pale too, and her palms were shining with sweat. 'Listen,' she said, 'it is true that I was approached by someone from

Sempura, but I promise you I have not done any work for them.'

'Listen, Rosella. If you have broken your contract, you are in very serious trouble. Do you understand that? I could get you in some very big trouble. I could get you sent to prison. And you know what prison guards are like, because you designed the prototype. And your granddad would be homeless.'

Rosella looked at Mr Castle with deadly serious eyes as her granddad groaned in his sleep. 'I know. Exactly. I would never take that risk.'

Mr Castle smiled. 'Don't worry. I'm sure you wouldn't be that stupid. But you know what, just for my peace of mind I am going to come and pay you a visit in your warehouse. Right now. London to Valencia is only minutes by car with the new rail improvements. You and the Echo – you stay right there. I'll be with you shortly.'

5

Rosella was speaking faster now – seventy-two words in one minute. She told me that Mr Castle was Alex Castle, the head of Castle Industries. She said that Alex Castle was a powerful and cruel man and that she was in trouble. She told me to go with her, down to the next level, to the tanks.

She said she needed me for something.

What she needed me for was to take an Echo out of tank eleven.

'Empty preservation gel,' she said. Then the egg-shaped tank glowed green to indicate that this had been done. 'Now open.'

The tank opened. And a female Echo was there. She was naked. She had been designed to look like a thirty-year-old human.

Her eyes were closed. She was standing there. Standing, but unconscious.

'This is how you should have been,' Rosella told me. 'Asleep. Unaware. Beyond fear.'

I nodded. 'Who is she?'

'She is a prototype for another company. Sempura, Castle's rival.

She is a new domestic Echo model I would have been paid a million unidollars for. Her name is Alissa.'

I carried her out. Rosella got out a new prototype igniter, ready to slip it into Alissa's ear. She was talking to herself, quietly, in Spanish. And then she made a decision.

'*No . . . no puedo . . .*' She turned to me. 'There is an incinerator downstairs in the basement. I want you to take her down there and put her in. She needs to be destroyed.' The basement. The place she hadn't wanted me to go. And she was about to put the igniter back in its little aerogel box, but her hands were shaking so much that she dropped it onto the floor. And straight away the igniter was crawling towards my foot and over my clothes, and then over Alissa.

'Oh no,' said Rosella. 'Stop it.'

But there wasn't time. It travelled a metre in 0.23 seconds. It was already crawling inside her ear. Igniters, I now knew, were not only micro-robots that looked like centipedes; they were made to locate the neocortex within the nearest dormant Echo brains and ignite them, giving them life. Or something that looked very much like life.

'Go to the basement,' Rosella said, agitated now. 'Throw her into the incinerator. Before she wakes up.'

'But what if there isn't time?'

'Still do it,' she was crying. 'If you don't, terrible things will happen. He can't see her – if he sees that I've broken my loyalty contract, I'll lose everything. I must destroy the program. I need to be in the pod to do this. We don't have much time. Go. Go!'

But I couldn't do it.

I was about to drop Alissa down through the circle in the floor, down into the cool deathly darkness of the incinerator, when her eyes opened. She was awake. Ignited.

I expected her to ask me where she was, or who I was, or who *she* was. But she didn't. She wasn't like me. She had no fear. She was just full of knowledge and ready for duty, the way Echos were meant to be. I could have dropped her down into the darkness and watch her vaporize into nothing and it wouldn't have mattered. She wouldn't have felt a thing.

I wish I *had*.

For Audrey. For Rosella. For Ernesto. Yes, I wish I had.

But I didn't, because I couldn't know for sure. I couldn't know anything for sure except what was in my own mind. And even some of that I had to be careful about.

I heard a voice. It was Mr Castle on the intercom. 'Anyone home?'

I held Alissa and stared down into her eyes. 'He has come for us,' I told her.

6

'This information has been processed,' Alissa said, looking up at me with her blank eyes.

I looked around the basement for somewhere to hide. There was a lot down here. Computers, test brains, fluids in giant jars, two robots with their power turned off, a lot of steel, a lot of silicon, surgical tools, synthetic skin laid out on tables like cloth. Also, Rosella's old flamenco guitar.

Something else too.

A small black box lying on the floor.

I knew what this was. I hadn't seen one before but I had been programmed to understand. This was a Nothing Machine. A Nothing Machine was a device that was set to turn specific areas into nothing. It was a security device to safeguard the general human population against any disasters that might occur in an Echo laboratory. If Echos overrun the place after suffering a malfunction, the Echo designer – in this case, Rosella – was meant to be prepared to shout out a code; generally this was a number, and once it was shouted out, the warehouse would disappear, along with all the Echos and whatever else happened to be inside it. They would disintegrate, be compressed into nothing, as if entering a black hole. Only the box itself would remain.

The number wasn't there on the box. But then I realized – it was in my head – because Rosella had given it to me: *8-4-2-9-0*.

The knowledge of that power – the power to end myself, end Mr Castle, Rosella, and everything else inside this warehouse – was terrifying.

I looked around, but there was nowhere to hide. So I calculated that our only hope was that Rosella would be able to send Mr Castle on his way without him coming down to the basement.

But he didn't have to come to the basement. All he had to do was call her name.

'Alissa!' (How did he know it? I wondered, back when I didn't know he knew everything.) 'Alissa! If you are called Alissa, be a dear and shout very loudly the words "I am here!"'

And I stared at her and whispered, 'Stay quiet, don't make a sound – he is dangerous.'

But of course, I was just an Echo, and Mr Castle was a human being, so an instruction from me could not overrule an instruction from him.

And I could see it coming. I could see her mouth move, preparing to make the words, and they burst out of her and reached my ears at a volume of eighty-seven decibels.

'I am here!'

And that was the start of it all. Or rather, the end.

7

'Eight . . . four . . . two . . . nine . . .'

There were times later when I wished I had said that final number. The zero. The nothing that would bring nothing. But really, I was never going to say it all then. Why would I? How did I know how much was going to be lost?

Mr Castle had arrived with a police robot. The police robot – 220 centimetres tall and (I could tell from the presence of a thin oxide coating on the surface) made of titanium – came and got us and threatened to kill me if I disobeyed. So we went back up on the leviboard.

'Aha!' said Mr Castle, on seeing Alissa. 'Now, there you are. As naked as God – or should I say, Rosella – intended. Now, what I want you to do is step back inside the tank from which you came.'

She did so, once Rosella had told her which one that was. And then Mr Castle explained what he wanted her to do to Alissa.

'You will change her. You will make her look exactly the same, but there will be a glitch. A glitch that doesn't fully emerge for five weeks. I will give you all the details. I know you will do this for me.'

'How do you know that?'

'Because you are very different to me. You care about your family. Your granddad. You want the best for him, and if you do this, not only will you get a house far north of here, away from the heat; you will also get the best medical treatment money can buy. And if you say no, well, it's bye-bye, Granddad. And bye-bye everything.'

He laughed, thinking of something. 'Sempura really are an irresponsible company. They don't care much about customer safety. Did you know – for instance – that they test out prototypes on their customers *without the customers knowing they are prototypes*.'

'How do you know that?'

'I have some very clever hackers working for me. Over in Cambridge. They could easily have hacked into your computers here, in the basement. They could have changed Alissa without you even knowing. But that seems a little unfair, a little underhand, and I am not like you, Rosella. If I have a working relationship with someone, I like to be open with that person. I am not going to get my people to just change Echos while they are in their tanks. I am going to come and talk to you. And be honest with you. You are good at English, Rosella, I am sure you understand. *Sí?*'

It was clear he was enjoying himself. I realize now that the real reason he didn't get his hackers to change Alissa was because he was cruel. He enjoyed making Rosella do it. Making her feel all the guilt and pain she inevitably ended up feeling. I would not have understood this if I was a rational being. Being able to feel things not only helps you to understand love, but to recognize evil, as both are symptoms of irrationality.

'Yes,' Rosella told him. 'I understand.'

'Anyway, I have no working relationship with Sempura and so we hacked into them. I can see who has ordered what, and who will be sent what, if I so desire. I can even make suggestions as to who would make a worthy recipient of a new and – ha-ha – *improved* Alissa. I have seen, for instance, that my very own Echophobe and hypocritical brother has asked for a female Echo capable of "general domestic tasks and home-schooling" . . . And I was thinking, well, here's an opportunity. You know about my moralistic brother, don't you? The one who fans the flames of protest against his own sibling? Well, his wife is just as bad, and I'm pretty sure my niece is going to go the same way. Can you imagine how horrible it feels to have your own blood relatives trying to bring your business down? It's a headache. And it will be an even bigger headache when his new book comes out and ends up shutting down the Resurrection Zone . . . Well, I've found a solution. A way to tarnish Sempura and ease my headaches at the same time. A way to kill two birds with one stone. Or three.'

Rosella looked at him, horrified but powerless. He spoke some more with her in private, and then he came over and looked at me. He stood there for a while, offering a friendly smile, before slapping me hard across the face.

'I told you, he feels pain,' said Rosella.

Mr Castle ignored her. 'I am going to take him with me now. That is the first thing you can do for me today, Rosella. And the second thing, well, you have twenty-four hours to think about it . . .'

And then he walked me away, and I turned round and saw Rosella standing there and mouthing the words '*Lo siento, Daniel.*' I am sorry.

Leaving her hurt as much as any physical pain. I felt like I was being pulled away from my own self. Rosella, the one who had made me, the only one who knew that I was more than just an Echo, the only one who loved me. The moment I left her I knew I would be nothing. A machine.

I travelled with Mr Castle and the police officer to London in a magcar hovering over a rail far above the ground. Much of the journey was through a vacuum chamber – a bright tunnel that, given the lack of air friction, allowed the magcar to travel at speeds I estimated at 2,000 kilometres an hour.

'It is useful,' Mr Castle told me, 'that you feel pain. I mean, people have often worried that if Echos become too human, then humans will be threatened. But if an Echo feels pain, it just means they can be controlled.'

The magcar slowed as it reached the end of the vacuum chamber. We emerged into daylight, above a seemingly infinite metropolis. Seven hundred raised magnetic rails crisscrossed each other in curved lines, carrying trains and cars. Below, the city was half land and half water. The water half was full of low-rise buildings on stilts, while the buildings on land were generally larger and more imposing. A few of them were detached from the land altogether, hovering fifty-four metres above the ground.

London.

I had never been here before, yet I had been programmed to recognize a lot of the major buildings and landmarks. Trafalgar Square. The New Church of the Simulation. The Old Parliament building (flooded since 2068). And then the New Parliament, the highest of the free-floating structures, a giant horizontal bone-shaped building made of titanium hydride and aluminium.

Holograms floated, barely visible in the daylight. We passed through ghosts of palm trees. Faint words: *The best holiday programs for your pod. Feel the sand between your toes. Just say GETAWAY.* Another hologram was that of a male and female human with toned physiques (*Adonis: Gene therapy you can trust*).

And then there was a sphere, with that familiar picture of a blue castle on it. Below, strange trees and vegetation, animals: London Zoo, which had expanded across the whole of Regent's Park twenty years ago to create the Resurrection Zone – a perfect environment for formerly extinct species, such as the dodo and the woolly mammoth and the ibex and the rhinoceros and the Neanderthal.

'If you mess with me,' Mr Castle said, 'you could end up working there. And if you end up working there, and have the ability to feel pain, well, you will be in very big trouble.'

I didn't ask him what he meant. I just hoped I would never have to find out.

8

Forward. Thirty-seven days.

I had never had a dream before.

In Spain, whenever I recharged, I had descended into a dark blanket of nothingness. The empty unsleep of Echos. And I knew I wasn't meant to dream; no Echo had ever dreamed, as far as I knew. But this was, unmistakably and irrefutably, a dream.

And it was about her.

Audrey.

At first it was lovely. It was just her, just an image of her, but not scared like I had seen her.

No, here she was smiling and laughing. It was Audrey as she could be, or might have been.

And I realized, even in the dream, that this was beauty. Again, beauty was not meant to be something an Echo should recognize. There was no logical reason why I should recognize it. I was meant to be able to know mathematical perfection, and understand symmetry and balance and formal harmony and all those things. And maybe Audrey wasn't perfect in those mathematical terms. Maybe only an

Echo's face could be perfect in those terms. But she was perfect in a stronger and more powerful way. In her uniqueness. In the way only a human can be perfect.

And I can remember a sadness in the dream; a sadness that I would never be able to make her smile or laugh like that. That she would never be able to see me as anything other than a sinister simulation of a human.

But then there was another emotion as I watched her, trapped in this house, every other Echo programmed to kill her. I saw her. She was going to die and her face knew it. And in that moment I realized I did not care about me. I cared about *her*; this girl who hated me and didn't want me to exist.

I cared because I related to her. This girl with no parents and nowhere to truly belong in a hostile world.

I cared because I could save her.

And I would try.

Audrey. Mind-log 429.

Perhaps all the dragons in our lives are princesses who are only waiting to see us act, just once, with beauty and courage. Perhaps everything that frightens us is, in its deepest essence, something helpless that wants our love.

Rainer Maria Rilke, *Letters to a Young Poet*, 1929

We're not like the others,
You and me,
We don't quite fit in their game.
We're not like the others,
You and me,
We'll never be the same.
We're freaks together
(Freaks together),
Now let's forget my name.

Neo Maxis, 'Freaks', 2114

1

I was sitting there in my room, staring out of the window, knowing I had to escape. It was a clear night. There were stars and a three-quarter moon. I could see New Hope, twinkling in the centre. A brightness inside a brightness. It was like an eye staring down, watching.

Escape.

Not just the house, or Hampstead, or even London. I had to escape properly. I had to find him, find Daniel. And if I stayed, that would be impossible. Also, I was beginning to wonder what was going to happen to me.

Was Uncle Alex waiting for the moment when I was no longer a useful PR tool for him, at which point he would get rid of me (surely that time had come)? Was he going to say I died in the raid on the house?

I was convinced this was a probability now. And I remained convinced the next morning, when I woke up and was still locked in. I went into the immersion pod and tried to think. I couldn't phone the police because the police were on Uncle Alex's side. They were always on his side. Some of the press weren't, just as my dad hadn't been. Maybe that was the way.

Then I remembered.

Leonie Jenson. The woman I had spoken to that day in Paris.

So I contacted the most anti-Castle publication there was, the *Castle Watch* newsletter. It was a small non-profit publication, run from a hover-shack in Chalk Farm, but it was easy to find a list of contacts for it and I was about to send a thought-mail to Leonie, who was also the deputy editor, when I decided against it. If I encouraged more protestors to come here, then there would be only one possible outcome. And that outcome would be their death.

Then I tried to contact Grandma again, just to talk to her. But I couldn't. The connection was down. I soon realized that, though the immersion pod was on, I couldn't make any outward calls.

However, I could make internal ones. So I called Uncle Alex in his home office and he appeared in front of me, smiling a smile I could no longer even begin to find reassuring.

'Hello, Audrey. How are you this morning?'

'You have trapped me in the room. Why am I still locked in?'

'For your own security, Audrey. You are mentally unwell. If you tried to find Daniel, you could be in danger. I don't want to be responsible for what would happen to a runaway teenager in London.'

'When are you going to let me out?'

'When I feel you are ready. You have a bathroom. There is food in the fridge by the desk. You have self-clean clothes. You have books to read. That is all you want, isn't it? You are your dad's child, aren't you? An academic? A person of ethics who needs nothing more than principles to get by? That was your dad and that is you. You are not a crude money-minded creature like myself.'

It was incredible. He was the richest man in Europe. He had everything he had ever wanted, and he still knew that my dad was better than him. I could hear the bitterness in his voice. A bitterness he quickly tried to suppress.

'You have a glorious view of London, and art to look at. You really are very pampered. It's not like you're going to die in there.'

'I feel trapped. I want to go out, just for a walk. If not outside, then around the house.'

'I'm sorry, Audrey, but I cannot allow that. I know your parents weren't disciplinarians, but I believe children sometimes need restraint as much as they need freedom, for their own good. And I have a lot of work to do in Cambridge and—'

'I'm nearly sixteen years old. I'm not a child.'

'Well, technically you still are, and so long as you are living here under my roof, then you will do as I tell you.'

'In that case I don't want to live here. I'll go and live with Grandma, on the moon. She told me I would be able to stay with her.'

'No. No. I am sorry. With all due respect to your grandma, I hardly think she'd be the most responsible guardian in the world. Or, sorry, *solar system*. And the moon is no place for a girl like you, Audrey. No place at all. No, stay here with me. I'll look after you. Now, if you don't mind, I really should be getting on with some work.'

And then he disappeared, right before my eyes.

I was starting to get hungry. I went to the fridge and ate some goji berries. I tried to read, remembering something my mum had told me once, during a literature lesson.

'A book is a map,' she had said, after I had finished reading *Jane Eyre*. 'There will be times in your life when you will feel lost and confused. The way back to yourself is through reading. There is not a problem in existence that has not been eased, somewhere and at some time, by a book. I want you to remember that. The answers have all been written. And the more you read, the more you will know how to find your way through those difficult times.'

So I looked at the spines of all the books.

A book is a map . . .

I didn't want to read. I was fed up. I wished I could kill myself, but I couldn't.

It was weird. You could be broken by life, you could lose your parents, you could be smashed into a thousand pieces, but there was always something at the core of you, something that no one else could touch. The irrepressible light inside you. We were made from stardust, like everything in the universe, and we – each of us – carried a power inside us. A power that couldn't be destroyed any more than the universe could be destroyed. And it was a power I only really knew was there once my parents had been killed. Because before then I had never really been tested.

And then I suddenly stood up straight.

I remembered what Daniel had told me, that day when I had gone into the Echo quarters.

I hope you find your book. I hear page 206 is particularly good.

It had been a message. A clue. We had been talking about *Jane Eyre*, so maybe that was it. And there it was, right at the bottom of the pile. *Jane Eyre* by Charlotte Brontë. I flicked through the old yellow pages until I was at page 206. My hands were shaking, but I found it soon enough, and saw small writing in the margin.

I looked at the writing. It wasn't neat and perfect, like Echo writing normally was. I started to read, my hands shaking more and more with every word I saw.

Your uncle is a murderer. He made sure that Alissa was changed. He forced Rosella to do it. She was my designer. She is not a bad woman. She was given no choice. Please, if you see this message, escape at the first opportunity and go to Rosella. She will look after you and tell you everything. She will help you. Her name is Rosella Márquez and she lives in a warehouse in

The message ended there.

That was it. That was when every illusion crumbled away, like a sandcastle under a wave. Uncle Alex had arranged for Dad and Mum to be killed.

Repeat: *Uncle Alex had arranged for Dad and Mum to be killed*. A kind of silent howl went through me at that moment. It was like – I don't know – it was like a door had closed and I was suddenly very alone. I began to shake. From the inside. From the core. The shaking started so deep that at first my hands were still, but they soon caught up. I felt crushed. Trapped by the truth.

Maybe he'd wanted to kill me too. For a moment I wished that I hadn't fought Alissa off. But the moment was quickly swallowed again by anger and fear.

I tried to think of every single thing Dad or Mum had ever said about Uncle Alex, but for all Dad's talk of Castle being a bad company, he'd never really said anything that even came close to suggesting that his brother could be a murderer.

I wished Dad hadn't had any principles, because then he'd have still been alive. I thought of his hands – I don't know why. His big hands with dark hair on the back of them. Hands that had held and squeezed mine when I'd been worried about him after the magcar accident.

Stupidly, I felt cross with Dad. Mum wouldn't have been killed if he hadn't had principles. I mean, Mum had had principles too, but they weren't the kind that would have got us killed.

But then I hated myself for being angry with Dad. It wasn't his fault his brother was a monster.

Monster. Yeah. That's what he was.

But suddenly, now that I was awake, I knew I couldn't wallow in grief any more. I had to focus. I had to feel fear. And I was feeling it.

But rather than making me worry for myself, it made me worry for Daniel. If someone can feel pain, they have to be worth caring about. It might have been wrong that Echos existed, but they *did* exist. And they hadn't asked to exist any more than I had asked to exist. And anyway, he clearly wasn't a normal Echo.

And he had saved my life.

That too-beautiful creature had saved my life. And he had been trying to save it ever since I got here.

Why was I so worried for him? Wouldn't life be easier if there was no one to worry about but yourself? Wouldn't that be best?

But then I read a paragraph on the page that had been hiding the message. I remembered the words he'd spoken that day in his room.

> *Do you think I am an automaton? – a machine without feelings? and can bear to have my morsel of bread snatched from my lips, and my drop of living water dashed from my cup? Do you think, because I am poor, obscure, plain, and little, I am soulless and heartless? You think wrong! – I have as much soul as you – and full as much heart!*

I closed the book, sat on my bed. Just sat there, feeling the most intense and burning desire to see him again.

2

I only ever had one real boyfriend, if you are just counting those whose skin I actually touched. It was only for a short while and it didn't really work out. I loved him as a friend, but as a boyfriend he was quite bossy. He was called Ben. We met the way everyone meets – virtually. In this case, in a simulation of Venice before it sank, and without any people in it. He'd known a lot about art and this had impressed me.

He lived in Canada, in Montreal, and some evenings I used to go over on the cross-Atlantic magrail, the one that went straight over the ocean-based hospital where I was born. He was good-looking, but when he was in argument mode he would look quite rodent-like, his nose screwing up and his mouth going small.

We used to argue about lots of things. At first I thought this made our relationship interesting, the way chilli makes a meal interesting, but I realize now that arguments are sometimes just boredom at a higher volume.

Religion was the main thing we rowed about. Ben and his parents were born-again Simulationists. They were members of the Church of the Simulation and went to pod-based services every evening.

But for me, the very idea of Simulationism was depressing.

It still is.

'If we are all just people who are simulated inside a vast software program, what is the point of everything?' I asked Ben once.

He had looked at me with disdain. It was that look – a symptom of his bossiness – that probably defined our relationship. 'Just because you want life to have a point doesn't mean it has to have one.'

'And just because you believe that the whole universe was created by an alien's computer doesn't mean that it was.'

He got angry. I was challenging his beliefs. 'Listen,' he said. 'Look at what humans can create. They can replicate anywhere in the world. And any point in history. If we wanted to – right now – we could walk into a pub in Elizabethan England and talk to Shakespeare.'

'No we couldn't. It would be a VR-simulation of a pub. And it wouldn't be Shakespeare. It would be a computer program speaking Shakespearean quotations.'

'The most advanced simulators now have self-thinking virtual beings – fake humans – inside them. And pretty soon we'll be able to create beings that evolve by themselves . . . And what about Echos? Some of them already *can* think by themselves. OK, they may not feel emotions, or dream, but one day . . . one day . . .'

'That is my dad's absolute nightmare,' I had told him. 'I think it might be mine too.' I meant it. I wasn't quite the Echophobe my dad was – obviously, as it had been my casting vote that allowed an Echo into our home – but some of his views had got into my head. I suppose that's what parents are: a collection of views, some of which you reject and some of which you inherit, like a book that you go on editing for ever.

I remembered lying on Ben's sofa, stroking one of his pets. Ben had loads of pets. Some of them were even real. The one who was asleep on my stomach was real. It was a cat called Belinsky, after the man who engineered the dome on the moon and made the first non-Earth settlement possible. He was a lovely cat. Tortoiseshell, with a purr that could power a city.

I remember Ben shouting to the kitchen – to Alfred, his Echo at that time. I can hear his voice. 'Alfred, you lazy robot, give us some fava-bean dip!' For someone who was pro-AI he sure spoke down to Echos.

But I never cared then, because Echos weren't worth worrying about. And the next day, I remember I went with Ben and both his fathers – whose business had just collapsed and who were going to become property barons on the moon – to the spaceport. And that final kiss. The feel of his fingers on my face. And then watching that same hand wave goodbye.

It had felt bad. But it wasn't the same kind of pain as I had felt watching that man come for Daniel, and then take him away.

3

Could a human love an Echo? Could an Echo love a human? The first question was always asked a lot on bad holovision shows. There were always stories of some sad man falling in love with an Echo they had bought simply on the basis of looks. They kissed and had sex and everything. Of course, the Echos were never actually feeling aroused, but for some humans that didn't matter, so long as they performed the task as commanded.

I had always thought it was a bit sick. Maybe it still was a bit sick. But the sickness had always been because Echos were different. Not because of their bodies, which were basically like human bodies – but better – and could function in the same ways if required. They had blood – OK, so it was blood without many white blood cells, but it was blood. Blood that pumped around with the aid of a never-dying heart.

No. It had seemed sick because Echos were different. Emotion-free. Computerized. But what if they were becoming less different? I mean, yes, they were made in a different way. Uncle Alex was right about that. And their brains contained a chip in them to ensure they behaved exactly as an Echo should. But then, there were humans who now had all sorts of computerized implants inside them.

In a way, everyone was a kind of cyborg these days.

It was a weird one. But no weirder than love itself. And as my anxieties grew about what had happened to Daniel, I started to realize that he was far more than an Echo to me. He was, right then, far more alive to me than anyone.

I had no info-lenses. They had been there beside my bed, as they always were, but when I woke up they were gone. I panicked. This meant that the ID I had recorded – Rosella Márquez's ID – had been lost.

So I went to the pod. I knew her ID wouldn't be online, or not in any way I could access, but there would surely be some information on her somewhere. The first thing I did, after the mind-reader descended, was to think of that name. *Rosella Márquez*.

Instantly, information appeared.

There were Rosella Márquezes everywhere. There were more than 3,000 of them in Mexico City. A few hundred in New New York. A lot in Buenos Aires, Lima, Santiago, Madrid, Olabo, Barcelona 2, Medellin, and hundreds of other cities. There were a good few on the moon. There was even a Rosella Márquez among the 450 people in the Mars space colony.

So I thought of something else.

Rosella Márquez, Echo designer. And to narrow it down further, I pictured in my mind a blue castle with three turrets.

Nothing came up.

'Come on,' I said, pleading with my brain to work. 'Think, think, think . . .'

Rosella Márquez.

No. Something else.

Lina Sempura.

Contact.

The details came up. It was the age of instant communication, after all.

I thought-mailed her.

I spoke to you at the media conference. I am Alex Castle's niece. My uncle is a murderer. He killed my parents and he wants to kill me. If you give me the address of an Echo designer, I will be able to help you. Please, you'll have to answer quickly, because if this message is intercepted I will be in trouble. I need the address for Echo designer Rosella Márquez. Can you give it to me? And please, for my own safety, only give me that info.

And within a minute – yeah, within a *minute* – the address was there.

It turned out that Rosella worked in a warehouse next to the CV-371 magrail, Valencia stop 48, at the southern edge of town and near the dried-up river, the Río Turia.

Hello Audrey. This is Lina Sempura. I hope you have the details you require. Anyway, I would like to meet you, so please could—

I deleted the thought-mail. Grateful as I was for the address, I couldn't believe that Lina Sempura herself was mailing me. I was in trouble enough, but if Uncle Alex had intercepted that, well, there'd have been no hope.

I blocked Lina Sempura. It was the only thing I could do.

Then I tried to holo-call Rosella's warehouse – or *almacén* – but of course it was futile. There was still no outward connection. And then I got worried. Maybe Uncle Alex or someone working for him – some of his hackers miles away in Cambridge – were already monitoring me.

Uncle Alex wasn't in the house now. I had heard him leave for the office about an hour ago, but that didn't mean he wasn't watching me.

I sat for a moment with the mind-reader on. It was always dangerous to sit there thinking when it was on because whatever I thought about prompted related information to flash up before me.

So I saw Echos, I saw the barren deserts of southern Spain, I saw my dad, but when I thought of Daniel, nothing came up. Why would it have? He was just an Echo prototype no one really knew about who had now been rejected. He was a nothing in the eyes of the world.

I needed to see Rosella. I needed to see her for three reasons. One: because of Alissa. Two: because of Daniel. And three: because I had to escape and I would need to go somewhere.

I had thought of going to Grandma's – properly going there, not just pod-visiting again. I mean, my Echophobia was nowhere near as strong as my uncle-phobia now. But it felt wrong to leave this planet without Daniel, after he had saved my life and suffered for it. Also, it was impossible. Any human travelling to the moon had full ID checks:if I escaped, the first thing Uncle Alex would do is make sure I couldn't get a flight off the planet.

It was at that moment that I heard something outside the pod. Nothing loud, but it wouldn't have been anyway. It caused me enough concern to send the thought-command *External view.*

Terror.

Instantly I saw Madara in the room. The Echo with red hair. She was standing outside the pod, waiting for me to step out. She had a kitchen knife in her hand; the same knife Alissa had used to kill my parents.

4

Madara was standing perfectly still, the way only an Echo can.

It was Alissa all over again. For a moment I couldn't think. Fear had washed away all thoughts.

It was a clever idea. Ordering her to use the same weapon. Uncle Alex knew that I would be doubly terrified if I was not simply fearing for my life but also remembering how my parents had been killed. *An echo of an echo.* There was an arrogance to it. *Let's not use a positron, let's use a knife.*

So, it was all confirmed.

He had seen that I wasn't going to serve his cause – after going off-script at the press conference – so now he was going to kill me, and get away with it too. He was probably going to set it up and say it was a protestor who did it. Maybe he wouldn't even have to set it up, what with practically owning the police.

But then it came to me.

Protestor.

So long as I was in the pod I was safe, so I stayed in there and tried to communicate with the pod in Iago's room, knowing that he would be there. But all I got was an automated voice saying, '*Game mode*,' and then asking, '*Do you want to join the game?*'

I had no choice but to mind-respond *Yes*.

5

I was on a battlefield in 1917. Passchendaele, Belgium. Part of the Western Front.

The wind was harsh and cold and there was mud everywhere, along with the continuous and deafening noise of gunfire. I had a gun in my hand; it had a sharp blade attached to the end. A bayonet.

My avatar was a nineteen-year-old man called Siegfried. I had chosen him hastily seconds after entering the game.

As I stood there, in the black mud, feeling the tight weight of my boots, I saw the man next to me get shot in the throat. Blood spilled through his hands as he held onto his neck.

A moment later, two medics appeared; they lifted the man onto a stretcher and jogged away with him.

'This is not real,' I reminded myself. 'None of this is real. The only thing that is real is that Madara is outside the pod waiting to kill me.'

I looked around at all the simulations of German and English soldiers killing each other in the mist. Somewhere among them was my cousin.

'Iago,' I shouted at the top of my voice. 'Iago! Where are you?'

If he had heard me above the gunfire, he didn't show it. I was left with no choice.

'Player two meta-command,' I said (this didn't need to be shouted – the software understood). 'Pause the game. Repeat, pause the game.'

Suddenly everything stopped. Running soldiers froze mid-stride, bullets stood static in the air, the artillery fire fell silent.

Then a voice somewhere behind me: 'No! What's going on? Game continue, game continue . . .'

I turned and saw a suave, bearded army officer in knee-high boots and a murky green uniform walking around shouting up at the sky and shaking his rifle. I could not imagine anyone less like my ten-year-old cousin, except for his behaviour.

'What's going on? Game *continue*.'

A voice came from the clouds. 'Player two has paused the game.'

'Player two? Player *two*? There *is* no player two.'

And then he stopped looking at the sky and started looking at me.

'Who are you?'

'It's me, Audrey.'

'Why are you here? Get out of here. I don't want you here. You're putting me off. The Germans have slaughtered half my men. I don't need any distractions.'

He threw his rifle down on the muddy ground, pulled an ancient-looking pistol out of his holster and pointed it at me as he walked closer, stepping over freeze-framed dying or dead soldiers.

'Because I can kill you. I can take you out.'

He was up close now. He pressed the pistol against my forehead. I felt the sensation of cold steel. He had chosen a taller player than me. One with the most realistic of beards and a pistol that looked as solid and physical as anything in the real world.

He couldn't kill me, of course, not on this imaginary battlefield, but if he pulled the trigger, I'd be out of the game and I couldn't afford for that to happen.

Iago was a psychopath, I realized. A ten-year-old psychopath. But that suited me right now. 'Iago, listen to me. Listen. There is someone in my room. A . . . a' – this was where the lie was needed – 'a protestor. She got into the house. You must get a gun from downstairs – a positron, to be on the safe side – and then come into the room and kill her. She's here now. She's tall, with red hair.' I was going to say, *She looks a bit like Madara*, but he might have got suspicious. 'But you can't hesitate. Not for a second. If you hesitate, she'll kill you. So . . . you've got to be fast. Just kill her. Kill her without looking.'

Iago's avatar scratched his beard. He took the pistol away from my forehead.

'I'll have a look at her now,' he said. 'On "House View" in the pod.'

'No,' I said, panicking. 'No, don't do that. There's no time. You've got less than a minute. Now remember. It needs someone tough, someone good with a positron. You're the only person for the job. Remember. Tall red-haired woman . . . and she's holding a kitchen knife.'

A look of menacing delight slowly spread across the officer's features, which for a second made him look entirely like my cousin.

He looked up at the thick grey clouds of that imaginary sky. 'Game over.'

6

Iago wasn't in major danger.

I knew that Uncle Alex would have ordered Madara to kill me and me only. But I was still worried something could go wrong. Ten-year-olds weren't meant to use antimatter pistols like the positron, even if he had proven more than capable of using one. There were other worries too. That he wouldn't actually do it. That he'd see it was Madara before he fired. This was quite likely. I just had to hope that, in this case, Madara would be distracted for long enough. It was doubtful. Madara was Uncle Alex's favourite Echo, and one reason for this is that she did exactly as she was told, and did it well. And fast.

One other concern was that Uncle Alex might find out what was going on. He might check up on the house while at work and come home. He could be here in less than a minute, if that was the case.

So I stayed in the pod, observing the room outside. Madara, statue-still, waiting. I tried to slow my breathing, but my body was alive with fear. And then it happened – almost too quick and easy. The bedroom door opened, Madara turned, and before Iago had time to be aware of who he was aiming at, she was gone. He'd killed her. It was only a second later that he understood. And once he had done it he looked devastated.

After all, he had destroyed Uncle Alex's most treasured Echo.

And he was standing there. A little ten-year-old with his dark fringe looking down at the gun. The same gun he had used against the protestors. But he seemed far more upset about killing Madara than he had about killing humans.

I stepped out of the pod. The bedroom door was still open. This was my chance to escape, finally. But Iago was now pointing the gun at me, with tears streaming down his blotchy cheeks.

'You tricked me.'

'She was going to kill me.'

'No she wasn't.'

'She had a knife. Your dad wants me dead.'

He looked at the knife that had fallen onto the carpet. 'No he doesn't. He hates you, that's all.'

'He killed my parents.'

'No. No he didn't.' He held his arm out straighter. More determined to shoot.

'I'm not lying. Your dad wants to kill me because I know too much. He has broken the law.'

'My dad doesn't care about laws. He has money. Money beats laws.'

'Listen – you could hurt yourself, Iago. It is a very dangerous weapon you are holding. I wouldn't have asked you to bring it here unless I needed you to. I was going to be killed.'

'Hurt myself? Hurt *you*. Not that you'd be hurt. You'd just disappear. "Oh, where did Audrey go?" Ha!'

Something changed inside me. A very clear thought came to me, in the intensity of the moment.

Just disappear.

Those words should have sounded scary, but they didn't. In fact, dissolving into thin air seemed about the best idea imaginable. Daniel was gone now, to wherever he had been sold. I would never see him again. The one person left on this planet who cared about me, and technically he wasn't even a person. So I was only really half calling Iago's bluff when I walked towards him and said:

'Go on then, do it. Pull the trigger.'

'It's not a trigger.'

'Button, whatever, you pathetic little gun-geek. Pull it. Pull it, push it, turn it, twist it, whatever you have to do. Play soldiers. I'm the enemy in one of your sad little games. We're on that muddy field in the First World War – do you even know that was a real war? Do it. Kill me. I am nothing already. I am here. A big empty nothing. Now, make a dream come true. What's the matter with you?'

He was angry. His lips thinned; he looked like a miniature version of his dad, and pressure seemed to build inside him. Like an apple exposed to intense heat, he looked ready to burst. 'Shut up, Audrey!'

I stepped closer. 'Why don't you make me?'

'Shut up or I will . . . I *will* make you, you stupid dumb hippy freak.'

'Stupid dumb hippy freak? Is that the best you can do? Wow, you're really hardcore.'

'I've killed people before!'

'So what's stopping you this time? Is it because I'm a girl? I'm a feminist. I demand an equal right to have my electrons turned into positrons. Come on, Iago, don't wimp out.'

His face was red with either despair or rage or a bit of both. 'I'm not wimping out – I'm going to do it . . . I'm going to do it . . .'

'Good. But know this: your dad is a murd—'

Then someone else:

'Enough!'

Iago jumped at the sound of the voice, and turned to see his dad, standing solemn-faced in his black suit in the doorway.

7

'Dad!' cried Iago.

I only had a split-second, I knew that. And it was very risky. But while Iago's face was turned towards Uncle Alex, I went for it. I went to grab the weapon from Iago's hand, knowing that it could go off and kill me at any second.

'Watch her!' boomed Uncle Alex. 'She's going for the posi—'

Too late. I had it. And I pointed it not at Iago, but straight at his father. The source of everything. But still, as I looked at the face that was so like my dad's, it was hard to know anything for sure.

'Now, don't be a silly girl,' he said, his smooth voice returning to its normal volume.

'You killed my parents.'

'You know that isn't true, Audrey. You were there in the house on the day it happened. You have seen the footage. You know it was an Echo. Josephine, or whatever she was called.'

'Alissa. You know she was called Alissa. Why did you just pretend to forget her name?'

'I loved my brother. Why would I want to kill him?'

'The book. All his work. The journalism. You hated him. You thought he was trying to attack you.'

'He *was* trying to attack me!' he blurted. 'He was jealous of me.'

'No. It's the other way round. You were jealous of him.'

Uncle Alex laughed then. 'Jealous?'

'Because he had principles. He had a life. He had a loving family. I don't know – was it because he went to Oxford and you got kicked out of school?'

He couldn't contain his anger then. 'You don't know *anything*.'

'Well, tell me, tell me, tell me . . .'

He tried to calm the mood, and smiled the fakest of all his fake smiles. 'Audrey, whatever paranoia you are experiencing right now, I want you to know that it is a symptom and nothing else.'

'You sent an Echo into this room to kill me.'

He raised his eyebrows as if I was a strange new product he wasn't sure of. 'You obviously have post-traumatic shock disorder – depression is a part of that, and so is paranoia and delusion. You really shouldn't have taken the neuropads off. You were not ready . . . Now please, you know you won't use that gun.'

'I was delusional all right. I was delusional that day in Cloudville thinking you were my hero, my great protector. You only wanted me alive for the press conference. That's all.'

'That's not true, Audrey. I promise you. I wouldn't have risked my life for a bit of PR. What do you think I am?'

'I'm getting a clearer idea every second.'

Tears glazed his eyes. 'Audrey, I am not a bad man. I am just someone who wants to make the world a better place.'

'*A better place*.'

I shifted my arm and aimed straight at the immersion pod in the corner of the room. I pressed my finger down hard on the aerogel button and the pod was instantly gone. Then I did the same thing with the bed and the chair I had been sitting on a short while before. A second later I was aiming the positron directly towards the Matisse painting. The one that had cost Uncle Alex billions of dollars. That was the first time he actually started to panic. He scratched his smooth stubbleless cheek.

'Audrey, don't be stupid. You would be destroying a timeless work of art loved by millions of people. I've already lost a Picasso. You wouldn't do that.'

'It should be in a public gallery,' I said, 'where those millions of people can see it.'

'Just calm down, Audrey . . . Think . . .'

Of course, I was never going to actually destroy a brilliant work of art. I was my mum's daughter, after all. But I kept the gun aiming at it for a little while longer because it was a good way of getting Uncle to talk.

'You can't do that,' he said. 'If you do that, you will destroy the whole wall as well, and this house is old. It needs that wall for the ceiling not to fall on our heads.'

At one point Iago stepped forward (what did he think he was going to do?), but he was quickly reprimanded by his father: 'Stay back, Iago! You fool! Against the wall! And what were you doing with the gun? I've told you a million times . . .'

'Sorry, Dad,' he said sulkily. 'Audrey said there was a protestor in the room.'

I felt a sudden twist of guilt in my gut. Yes, Iago was a violent little runt, but he was also a ten-year-old boy. Being a violent little runt kind of went with the territory.

But Uncle Alex's attention was already turned back towards me.

'Calm down.'

'You locked me in here.'

'For your safety . . . since those terrorists stormed the house.'

'I don't believe you. You killed my parents. And you would have killed me sooner if you hadn't wanted to use me as your little wounded show-pony to score points against Sempura.'

'Alissa wasn't even a Castle product. She was made by Sempura, from a Sempura prototype designed by a Sempura-funded designer . . .'

'Rosella Márquez?'

'I really don't know why you keep going on about this Rosella.'

So I told him. Given what has happened since, I realize this was a mistake, but at the time I just wanted answers. I needed the truth. 'I know she made Daniel. And Alissa mentioned her too, at the media conference. And the moment I said her name, the conference stopped. *You* stopped it.'

'Audrey, yes, Rosella Márquez is the name of the person who designed Daniel, but you really are joining dots that shouldn't be joined. Do you realize that most Echo designers are from Spain or South America, and that most are women? Do you realize that Rosella is one of the most popular Spanish names?' He glanced behind me, out of the window.

'Daniel told me he knew Alissa.'

'Daniel would have told you anything. He was clearly manipulating you, using you . . .'

'Why would he have done that?'

'He was malfunctioning.'

'I thought Castle Echos didn't malfunction. That's what you told me.'

I needed to know. Without truth, no one can ever be free.

'They don't normally malfunction, Audrey. And I am deeply horrified that this one has, but the designer . . .'

'Rosella Márquez.'

'Yes, all right, Rosella Márquez, if her name is that important to you. She went too far. She worked too hard on him. She lost a child when she was young, and ever since then she has been trying to get over this fact by creating Echos that are as lifelike as possible. But on this one she obviously crossed a line.'

Uncle Alex's eyes kept flicking back to the window behind me. I looked round and saw the familiar black semicircle of a police car coming to a halt and hovering just above the magrail. A police robot was aiming something at me. Not a positron, but a laser gun that I was pretty sure could be equally fatal.

Uncle Alex smiled, and sounded very much like his young son when he said: 'The game's over, Audrey.'

I started to run as a laser was fired. It scorched the carpet where I had been standing only a moment before and left a perfectly circular hole, about a centimetre wide, in the window.

'Get out of my way,' I said to Uncle Alex.

'Audrey, you do realize you can't escape, don't you?'

'I'm going to find Daniel.'

'Audrey, you can't. He isn't Daniel any more. He can't even find himself after what we've done to him.'

This time I said it like I meant it. 'Get out of my way or I swear I will kill you!'

He got out of the way, but I sensed he was right. It was very unlikely that I could escape the grounds, even with a gun in my hand. And if I did, well, what then? Uncle would surely disable all the leviboards, so I wouldn't be able to reach the car. And besides, that was out the front of the house, and I was heading towards the back. Away from the police.

8

I knew I wasn't Daniel.

I knew that if I jumped from an upstairs window, it would probably be the last thing I ever did. So I had to go downstairs. And I ran fast down the marble staircase as I heard Uncle Alex behind me.

'Echos! All Echos! Stop Audrey! Stop her! Don't let her leave the house!'

I had terminated an Echo before, but now, somehow, it felt different. When I shot the old man with the white beard as he ran out of the kitchen towards me, it felt more like murder. He disappeared, like a nightmare after sleep, and I ran through the space he had just been inhabiting, through the vast, now empty kitchen, with its transparent cupboards and glowing self-clean crockery.

There was a steak sizzling in the frying pan. Synthetic tiger meat, no doubt, as that was Uncle Alex's favourite. I kept running, and reached the conservatory as I heard other Echos behind me. I turned, and blasted two into non-existence as one of the intelligent potted plants in the conservatory leaned in towards me.

'Open,' I said to the conservatory door, but it didn't respond. So I fired at it and made it disappear.

Then I was out in the expansive sprawl of the garden, running across the multi-coloured grass Daniel had carried me over. Once past the bushes, I knew what was coming. And this time the four Echo hounds all appeared at once and chased me at double the speed I was able to run. I turned and transformed one into antimatter, then two more, before something whipped out at me and coiled tight around my right ankle, so that I fell forward onto the grass.

I desperately tried to free my leg, but whatever it was held me tight. Before I had time to look, there was something else to deal with. The last of the Echo hounds leaped through the air and landed on top of me; it growled, its red eyes studying me to find a suitable place in which to sink its teeth.

My own terrified face stared back at me, reflected and distorted in the Echo hound's shining titanium chest plate. It started to sink down towards my face – it was going to bite my face! – as I fumbled with the positron. I managed to fire, and that last horrible machine-dog disappeared, but I had the problem of what was still coiling around my leg. It was squeezing hard now. Causing pain. Stopping blood flow. It was some kind of plant. My parents never kept intelligent plants. It was exactly the kind of messing-with-nature Dad couldn't stand. And the trouble was, I couldn't shoot at something on my leg without causing myself to dematerialize in the process.

And of course, though I couldn't see them yet, there would be more Echos approaching on the other side of the bushes. Maybe Uncle Alex had given them permission to kill me; maybe they had gone to the weapons room. Or maybe – more likely still – he had told them to stay back. After all, he knew that the deeper I headed into the garden, the more danger I faced. This garden was about one thing only. *Security*.

I felt something delicately brush against the side of my cheek. Within a moment, whatever it was had coiled around my neck and was squeezing tight, just as it was with my leg.

Unable to breathe, I concentrated hard.

I had seen this plant before, in a holo-ad. It was a genetically modified giant blood iris, with long thin whip-like leaves. It was used for the purposes of home security. And there was the flower itself, leaning over me like a face. Purple petals, looking darker than normal in the fading light.

I smelled something. It wasn't an unpleasant smell; indeed, it was sweet. Words from that ad came back to me. *Our plants use halothane*. My panic intensified as I realized that the blood iris was emitting *sleeping gas*.

Uncle Alex clearly didn't want anyone who entered his garden to leave. Not conscious, anyway.

I had four seconds. Maybe five. Then I would be out cold. There's nothing like terror to help one focus, and I shot at the flower. The flower disappeared, but not the plant itself, so the leaf tightened around my leg and – of more immediate concern – my neck.

The pressure built inside my head. I felt blood pumping inside my skull, like a desperate bull barging at a door, as I searched through the crowded flowerbed for the plant's main stem. Eventually I found it, and fired: what looked like a fast ripple of air reached the plant and made it non-existent, the leaves taking a second or so to disappear altogether.

Once free, I got to my feet again and ran, choking, into the centre of the vast lawn, away from the numerous plants reaching out towards me. I had no idea how I was going to escape. I imagined that Uncle

Alex was watching me from his pod or security room, as content as a cat over a mouse stuck in a trap.

He wanted me dead. There was no doubt in my mind that this was the case now – even if he hadn't last Wednesday, when he killed my parents.

I knew too much.

I had come into contact with the truth, and it was sending me towards hell.

'Mum,' I said, delirious with panic as I ran towards the large brick wall at the southernmost edge of the garden. 'Dad . . . help me . . . What should I do?'

There is no silence like the silence of the dead. And I knew that the futile question would go unanswered.

I had only the most simple of plans. To shoot at the wall, and the plants in the deep flowerbed in front of it. With the aid of a weapon I would turn every obstacle that stood in my way into nothing until I was free.

So I kept on, as focused as a straight line on a blank page. I made it out through the gap in the wall I had created, and kept running. Down the street.

I was out of the house now. Echos couldn't legally follow me – not on their own, as it was against the law in this country.

But even as I was thinking that, I saw a police car slowing on the magrail above me.

'Stop and put down your weapon immediately!'

Not a chance.

I fired at the car. It disappeared, but the rail it was on didn't. I was starting to realize that the stuff about positrons was another lie. Antimatter weapons were the most intelligent in the known universe.

They shot the thing they were aiming at. They could distinguish *between* things. In a sense, that made the weapon more intelligent than me, as lines were blurring pretty fast. But there I was, still firing. A large chunk of rail disappeared. I kept running, turning as I heard a blast behind me – the sound of a police car not stopping in time, flying off and crashing through posts that had been holding up parts of the remaining rail.

I watched in panic as the car rebounded off the last post and ricocheted towards the street.

Towards *me*.

With only a whisker of a second to spare, I fired the positron. The car disappeared.

I looked at the weapon, wondering why it had been slow to fire, and saw some words glowing red along its curved aerogel surface. POWER DRAINED. SHUTTING DOWN. I threw the weapon aside and sped on, feeling as powerless and scared as an ant caught in the shadow of a descending foot. But I saw the words HAMPSTEAD STATION on a rusted old metal sign, peeking out of a bush ahead of me. In a matter of seconds I was at the train station.

I had never been on a magtrain before. Too dangerous. Too many fatal accidents. Surely Uncle Alex would assume I'd be getting a taxi. Also – Sempura controlled most of the lines and owned most of the European network. So this was as safe an escape as I could find. Still, I knew that nothing was too hard to find if you were Alex Castle. I had to stay scared. Only by staying scared would I stand a chance.

The station was deserted except for a couple of everglow addicts with glowing throats. I wanted to disappear among crowds, but no crowds were there.

'Come on, come on, come on, come on,' I said, pleading with the rail network and time itself.

The line hummed. A train appeared, out of nowhere.

I hopped on and kept my head down. It was packed with dangerous-looking people. You know, people with that glint of madness in their faces. I was one of them now. I had just destroyed two police cars and put a hole in a major London magrail. I was as dangerous as they came. I could hide quite well among this crowd of addicts and drifters. The train was going to Euro East, but I got off at Paris, a whole twenty-one minutes and seventeen seconds after I had got on (I counted). I was tense for the whole slow journey, as it felt like a lifetime. Then I followed the largest crowd of people to another train, heading for Barcelona 2. I'd wanted to make it as difficult as possible for Uncle Alex to follow me – and hopefully I was now off his radar – but I was going to end up where I was going to end up.

So at Barcelona 2 I decided to risk everything, heading onto a hot train with an armed securidroid with GUARDIA CIVIL (famously the toughest police force in Europe) marked on its chest, and travelled to Valencia, staring at a determined-looking cockroach that was scuttling around the carriage floor.

Daniel. Mind-log 3.

1

I woke up and my head was already open.

The extraction of 97% of my neocortex, and the igniter that it now contained, was already underway. The igniter was only essential to switch a prototype Echo into being, and it had done that too effectively. Without it I would still function. I would obey commands. I would be a creature of pure rationality. All those things that single piece of human hair had helped to give me would be undone. I would never question, because to ask a question required imagination and imagination was the problem. Imagination made you care for strangers, humans, her, and it was not my job to care. It was my job to serve. And that was a very big difference.

The removal of imagination requires pain, and the pain was intense, so agonizing it seemed to last for ever. Time was just a myth created by the absence of hurt. But then it was over because my imagination had gone, and without imagination you couldn't feel anything at all.

I waited there. With no desire to leave or escape.

And then Mr Castle came and saw me. He commanded the

surgery pod to open and leaned in towards me. His mouth spread into a smile and he said, 'There. Did that hurt? I hope so. Not because I am on the side of evil but because I am on the side of good. Because you deserved that pain. I would inflict that pain on every single one of those terrorists as well, if I could. Because do you know what pain is? It is a warning. Pain is always a warning. It tells you that what you are doing is wrong; it tells you where the boundaries are. And that is my one regret, you know, for humans. There is not enough pain any more. There is too much freedom. And I know you are not human, but you were starting to think you could act like one, weren't you? You thought you could jeopardize your master's safety to save Audrey. And that was crossing a boundary that you won't be crossing again. That is what justice is all about. And that blood stuck in your hair, that is beautiful to me. Because I love the restoration of the natural order of things. And that has happened, don't you think?' He began to laugh. 'Sorry. Bad choice of words. Of course you don't think. You *obey*. Is that right?'

'Yes, Master, that is right,' I said.

'Very good. But I am not your master for much longer. You are a reject. A failed prototype. You are among the unwanted, the cast-offs, the flawed, the failures. You have no market value. You are a disaster. A bad fit. You are out of my hands, thrown out into a world that does not care about your fate.'

I was not scared.

You could only be scared if you could feel.

'Anyway, it is a shame in a way that I cannot hurt you any more. Yet I have a consolation – it is pleasure enough to know that I have taken away from you the myth that you are alive. That you are anything other than a machine with no rights, no feeling, for ever unworthy of human emotion. Of love.' He stood up straight. 'I will be back in a moment. I'm sure someone would love to see you . . .'

He closed me back in the pod. Eleven minutes later, Audrey was there with Mr Castle. Then he left and it was just me lying there and her looking at me, and the blood. She spoke to me. Her words meant nothing to me any more.

'Daniel, it is me, Audrey. You saved my life. I want to say thank you.'

It was like a dark ocean with nothing in it but the tiniest pearl. Lost. Somewhere. And she was holding her breath and trying to dive down and find that pearl, the last remaining piece of who I was, and bring it to the surface.

I saw her face and those hazel eyes and heard her voice, a voice that sounded older than a fifteen-year-old's voice, but the pearl stayed lost.

'This shouldn't have happened to you,' she said. 'I am sorry. What happened? Why did you stay awake? Why didn't they switch you off? It's torture. That's what happened. You felt pain. You aren't meant to feel pain, but anyone who heard your screams knew you were in pain. I'm sorry.'

For a second there was something. The faintest of faint desires. To tell her that I was taken into the pod unconscious and I had woken up. But the truth was, I honestly didn't know this girl.

'Please. Say something. Anything. Just speak. I know you can hear me. You told me you had met Alissa. You told me you were designed by someone called Rosella Márquez. You had more to tell me. About Alissa. About Uncle Alex.'

And that is when I spoke.

'Who are you?' I asked her. Her face crumpled for a moment. I had upset her. But looking back now, I realize that I had asked her a question. And I was not meant to have asked her a question because questions stem from imagination, and that had supposedly been taken out of me.

'I'm Audrey. Audrey Castle. I am Mr Castle's niece. My parents were killed by an Echo called Alissa. She was a Sempura Echo, not a Castle one.' Then she leaned in towards me and whispered into my ear. I could feel the warm breath that carried her words. 'I'm starting to think that I am only alive right now because I'm useful. I can help him score points against Sempura.'

There was worry in her voice, and that worry did something to me, stirred something inside my mind. I turned my head towards her. This caused me pain. I was not meant to feel pain. And that was when her hand tenderly touched my face – the skin that had been scarred by the protestors' rock.

I felt another kind of pain. But this kind wasn't physical.

'Don't worry,' she said. 'I'm sorry. I'm troubling you. I don't want to trouble you. You saved my life.'

I had saved her life. I tried to remember this, and then she read me a line of a poem, and the words were like a torch in that dark ocean.

'*I am: yet what I am none cares or knows*.'

Then a kiss. As her mouth approached mine, I had no idea what she was doing. Echos aren't made for kissing. Her lips stayed on mine for a second or two, no more than that, but it was enough to make me feel something powerful. Friendship, love. And love is a kind of force. You shine it at someone, and it can't help but reflect back, however dimly.

The torch's beam had caught a glimpse of the pearl in that murky ocean.

'You aren't like the others. You are different. You care. You feel pain. But one day you will feel other things. Nicer things, I promise you.'

I felt a strong need to tell her something.

I said her name in a whisper. I knew her name now. The kiss had brought me back to life, just a little. It was like in one of those fairy tales I had read while living in the villa in the desert.

'He changed Alissa,' I managed to say. But then the door opened and Mr Castle was back in the room.

Audrey and I were separated.

A man came to the house.

He was tall and blond and called Seymour.

He had come to take me away.

2

I did not fear or welcome Seymour's presence. Now that Audrey was no longer near me, I was unquestioning – though with a strange kind of sadness deep inside me; a feeling of having lost something.

Or someone.

My memory was weak now.

I could remember Rosella, I could remember the desert and Ernesto and Valencia, but it was through a fog. The only thing that had any clarity in my mind was Audrey. I remembered her face looking up at me as we ran across the grass outside. I remembered her at the window as I cleaned her car. I remembered her that night when she first arrived. I remembered first seeing her, when she was petrified, staring with wide frightened eyes, first at the painting on the wall and then at me.

But I did not really feel that much, despite the clarity of these particular memories. I had no idea, for instance, why I had felt the need to save her life, as she just told me I had. But nor did I really care. So I was back to being a machine. I was as good as dead, standing there.

The man – this Seymour – was 193 centimetres tall, and he had blond hair (345,092 strands – my ability to calculate was still there, even though my curiosity had gone), but darker than mine, and greasy. As well as being tall he had a significant circumference, and weighed between 220 and 230 kilos. He had tanned but tired skin, and wore a turquoise suit made of cheap electro-cotton, with lapels that glowed. He lived in Silverlake, Los Angeles ('Got a new condo in the sky'), a full hour away from London. His job was to collect and sell unwanted prototypes from the leading international manufacturers – such as Castle.

These Echos were unwanted because they had malfunctioned in some way, had been tampered with, or were otherwise flawed. Echos like me, in other words.

He spoke a little with Mr Castle, but I wasn't paying that much attention to what he said. I just remember his voice – deep and loud and slow. The words themselves were unimportant to me, as was my fate.

He was eating a shark burger. And Mr Castle seemed disgusted by him, and clearly didn't want him to hang around.

At one point Seymour asked about the amount of damage the protestors had done to the house and if any art had been destroyed. He had pointed to the hologram of the unicorn and made a joke about that being the only kind of safe art investment Mr Castle could make now. Anyway, he took me away in a small magbus with five other Echos inside. I didn't speak to them and they didn't speak to me. I noticed that the female opposite with long black hair had no hands, and that one of the males was gigantic and muscular but kept humming a continuous note (B flat).

You are among the unwanted, the cast-offs, the flawed, the failures . . .

The journey lasted less than a minute. And then we were at another place in London, the King William V Exhibition Centre. A vast dome-shaped building made of electrochromic glass and self-heating concrete. We got out, as Seymour instructed, and there was a big crowd – 326 humans, 260 Echos – being ushered along by two armed, metallic securidroids. Both of them had the words ECHOMARKET SECURITY OFFICER blazoned on their chests. We were led into the large building.

Although my head was full of 9,218 facts about London, not a single one related to EchoMarket.

But I learned soon enough.

3

EchoMarket was a place where the unwanted Echos like me were bought and sold. It was immediately clear why certain Echos were unwanted. Some were physically damaged or weakened. One had suffered a neck injury that rendered him incapable of speech. Others were suffering malfunctions: one female Echo seemed only capable of walking in circles, for instance. Another – a male – kept talking in calculations. One Echo had his own securidroid: he needed to be constantly restrained because he attacked anything that moved.

There was another section, further along, that wasn't full of Echos at all. It was just robots, all looking in pretty bad condition; there were a few of the Travis model, which I knew was over sixty years old.

Some of the Echos, though, were a bit more like me. It was hard to see what was wrong with them. We – all the Echos – had to stand inside individual transparent and illuminated booths with information written in fluorescent letters. I remember all this because it is recorded inside me, but at the time it was just a fog. Everything was a fog. The information on my booth was this:

ECHO 113. MALFUNCTION CLASS 5

ORIGINAL MANUFACTURER: CASTLE INDUSTRIES

DESIGNER: ROSELLA MÁRQUEZ

NATURE OF MALFUNCTION: REBEL

Like the other vendors, Seymour stood in front of the booths that contained the Echos he was trying to sell – five of them. I was '113'. I was no longer Daniel.

I looked at the black-haired handless Echo in the box next to me. She gave the smallest shake of her head, to tell me that I shouldn't be doing that.

Humans kept coming up to the box, asking Seymour questions about one or other of us. The first to be sold was the strong one.

'Oh yeah, yeah,' Seymour told the man and woman who had bought him. '119 will be perfect for providing home security and any other domestic duties you should want doing . . . Don't worry too much about the humming. You'll soon get used to it.'

As the afternoon progressed, more and more of the Echos were sold. To homes and businesses and local governments who wanted to buy cheap. People came up to the booth to ask me questions directly.

'Have you any experience of office work?' one woman asked me. She seemed friendly. She was wearing a shawl that kept changing colour, from purple to black and back again.

'No,' I said. It took me a while to answer questions. The pain I'd been through had not only made me numb, it had also made me slower.

'But 113 is programmed for various office roles,' interrupted Seymour enthusiastically. 'In fact, he was created by Rosella Márquez in Valencia, one of the most respected Echo designers in the world.

And don't worry about his rebelliousness. He has been treated for it.'

The woman studied me closely. Clicked her fingers in front of my face. 'Maybe a little *too* treated, by the looks of things.' And then she walked away.

Seymour closed his eyes in frustration, and rubbed a hand through his greasy blond hair.

A man with a long braided beard came up to me. He was from a construction company specializing in self-evolving architecture. He asked me a lot of questions. I answered them. But still, like the woman before, he walked away.

'He's too dull-witted, too slow – there seems to be too much missing.'

Seymour lowered my price every hour. I had started the afternoon at 1,900 unidollars, and now I was down to 650.

Seymour kept on putting food into his mouth. He came over to me. 'OK,' he said, making no attempt to hide his mouthful of banana, 'when the next customer comes over, be quick on the response. Wake up a bit, OK? Because unless they're looking for a hat stand, you are not going to be sold until after five. And do you know what happens after five? After five, the standard of customers falls quite rapidly and you could end up with any psychotic bargain-hunter who comes along.'

Seymour had a call from someone. 'I know they were all meant to be sold by now, but there's only one to go . . . It's 113, the one direct from Castle's place . . . There's something wrong with him . . . I don't know what they did when they reconditioned him, but he's not right . . .'

As he spoke, I gazed across the hall at another unsold Echo in his illuminated booth, designed to look like a middle-aged human male. He raised his hand to see if I would do the same, but I didn't. And then he laughed wildly for six minutes and kept banging his head against the booth, much to his vendor's dismay.

Five o'clock came and went, and I realized that Seymour had been right. The atmosphere changed. The customers who came in now showed no sign of wanting to talk to the Echos – all fifteen of us (down from 1,800 at the beginning of the afternoon). They clearly knew that we were rejects among rejects. The lowest of the low. All they wanted was a good price.

Seymour sighed as he watched a customer pay another vendor for the Echo across the hall. The one who had been laughing uncontrollably.

'Even Mia has sold out before me,' he said, shaking his head in disbelief as he gestured to his rival vendor, now on her way out of the hall.

He whistled to a robotic vending machine, which trundled over so that he could help himself to a sweetened red tea.

4

A skinny man with a long face.

He was wearing overalls and his right eye was totally black. A gleaming black ceramic sphere placed inside the socket. As he came closer, I could smell him. He smelled of ammonia. Urine.

He just stood there, his tongue clicking inside his dry mouth as he looked at me. If I'd had more wits about me I wouldn't have liked the look in his eye. It would have made me feel even cheaper than I was. But I had nothing about me, right then.

'How much is this one?' he asked, in a small voice that Seymour didn't even hear the first time. And then he screwed up his face in frustration, and repeated louder: 'I said, how much is this one?'

Seymour turned round, looking perturbed at the sight of the man. 'Ah, Laurence, it is good to see you again.'

'Louis. My name is *Louis*.'

Seymour nodded. 'Sorry, sorry, sir. My mistake. It's been a long day.'

Louis carried on looking at me shrewdly. 'There *are* only long days.'

'Yes.'

I noticed that his dirty overalls had a logo on the chest pocket. A blue castle with three turrets. There were two letters underneath: RZ. This should have troubled me, but it didn't.

'So,' said Louis, looking me up and down. 'How much?'

'For you, 300. And that's tearing my arm off.'

Louis shook his head. '250. Paid now. Nothing more.'

For a moment Seymour seemed to be in a quiet type of pain. He took a sip of his tea. Eventually he nodded. 'OK, you kill me. 250.'

And then he opened the booth door, looking at me almost apologetically before handing me over to my new owner.

'So,' he said, noting the initials on Louis' overalls. 'How's life at the Resurrection Zone? Made friends with the Neanderthals?'

Louis snarled a little, offended by the question, and said nothing. Except to me: 'Come. Now.'

I was told to follow this Louis out of the hall, which of course I did.

I was just another damaged unquestioning Echo at the service and mercy of humans.

5

I recharged in a lodge right underneath a rotating sphere, with seven other Echos. All male. Most didn't talk to me; although one had, before going to bed. He was a bit different to the others. I sat on the edge of my bed and listened to him. All the other Echos were by now in recharge mode, but I wasn't tired. I wasn't feeling anything at all.

'My name is 15,' he said. 'What is your name?'

I said nothing.

'I'm sorry about the questions. I am a rare model. I was made for inquisitive work. Office jobs, insurance, things like that. The ability to question was part of my programming.'

Eventually it came to me. 'My name is Daniel.'

15 nodded. He was designed to look like a young man of about twenty. He had smart mid-brown hair with a side-parting, and a face that was designed to be so neutral and inoffensive you could almost forget what it looked like as you were looking at it.

'I worked in an office. Insurance. In Edinburgh. A train crashed into our building. All the Echos that survived were injured. Including me. My leg. Totally smashed.'

He lifted up his trouser leg to show me the damage. I had never seen anything like it. Scarred flesh from his ankle to his thigh. But it didn't shock me. I didn't think anything could shock me again.

'Means I walk with a limp. Which means I am slow. I can't run. And that's not good in here. I'm not exactly made for this type of work in the first place. I'm surprised I have lasted this long . . .' He looked at me for a long time. 'Thank you for listening to me. None of the others have time for me. I'm designed to be a talker, you see. What was your problem?' he asked. 'Why did you end up here?'

'I was meant to protect my master, but I left his side when he was in danger. To save a girl.'

'Why did you do that?'

I remembered Audrey's face. I felt the slightest flicker of something inside me, something strange and unidentifiable. 'I . . . I don't know.'

'What about the others? Do you know if all the other models like you have malfunctioned?'

It took me a while to understand the question. 'Other models,' I said, to myself.

He leaned in close towards me and then sat back.

'No! You're a . . . you're a prototype, aren't you? There is only one of you?'

'Yes.'

He sighed. It was a kind of awe. 'There are thousands of others like me,' he said. 'Tens of thousands. Except they are not like me. They are better than me. They are not rejects. They can still run. They are faster. Faster bodies, faster minds. But I suppose, if nothing else, being broken makes me different . . .' He sighed. It might have just been exhaustion. 'We had better recharge. We need to be alert. It is dangerous work here.'

So I lay back and closed my eyes and switched to recharge mode. An image of Audrey's frowning face and intense eyes entered my mind, but it quickly left and there was blankness again.

6

At five in the morning an alarm went off and I could see all the others leave their beds.

'You need to get up,' 15 told me.

I hadn't rested properly. I seemed to need more recharge time since the operation.

I tried to sleep through the noise, a distant siren rising and falling in waves, which only reached sixty-one decibels but somehow troubled me. Eventually I must have managed to shut off because the next thing I knew there was a cold shock of water and I awoke, soaked, to see Louis standing over me with a tin bucket in his hand.

'You get up when you hear the alarm,' he said, kicking my stomach. 'It's very simple.'

It didn't hurt. And I wasn't scared of Louis. I was just there to do as he said, because he was my master now.

So I got up, put on my work outfit (just blue overalls with the letters RZ on the left chest pocket, and no footwear) and followed Louis outside.

I had information about this place in my head.

The Resurrection Zone was six square kilometres of carefully land-scaped woodland, complete with animal enclosures set in what had once been Regent's Park. Some species would stay extinct because their DNA had never been preserved well enough to be sequenced, but there were other prehistoric species whose DNA had remained intact for thousands of years, along with dodos and Tasmanian tigers and rhinos and other more recent addictions.

But there were other things I didn't know. Things I would soon find out.

We were all standing in a line in the rain. It was relentless, the rain, but it didn't bother me. Nothing bothered me. Louis told the others that I was the new arrival. He was holding a metal club. The club was 109 centimetres long and made of titanium, with a small illuminated end. A security robot – an outdated but mean-looking steel- and titanium-clad securidroid – stood behind him. He introduced me.

'This, freaks, is your new co-worker. The nature of his malfunction was that he rebelled. So he might not make it through today, let alone the week.' And then he looked at me. 'What is your name again?'

I was getting quicker. 'My real name is Daniel.'

Louis smiled, and spoke in a soft voice that could hardly be heard above the rain. 'No. You'll find it is better not to romanticize yourself, Echo. Your name is 113.' He adjusted the dark sphere in his eye socket and pointed the club towards me.

'Anyway,' he continued to the rest of the group, 'I was going to ease him in gently. 113 was going to be feeding dodos and auks today, but maybe he would like something more challenging . . .'

He waited. I said nothing.

'Well?' he said. 'Are you going to speak?'

'I can feed the dodos.'

'*Shut up*.' He walked over to me, stared at my face. 'You are not right. Just what do you think you are?'

'An Echo. An Enhanced Computerized Humanoid Organism. I was a prototype designed by Rosella Márquez in Valencia.'

'Prototypes are always arrogant. Are you arrogant?'

'No. Arrogance is an emotion. I do not feel emotion because I am an Echo.'

'Yes,' said Louis, so close I could smell his breath. The sour pang of bacterial infection. 'An Echo. A blend of biology and technology. Part flesh, part silicon. You are just an echo. Echo, echo, echo, echo. I say something, and you do it. That is the echo. You do not think about it, you do not question. I am a human – that is *my* privilege. To think. You are nothing. No, you are less than nothing. An Echo is nothing, but you are less than an Echo. Because you are a prototype but they didn't want any more of you. And while you are here, you have no more privilege than an alarm clock or an info-lens or a tattered old piece of furniture. You are mine. You obey me. Whatever happens, you won't last long. No one does. But while you are here, I am a God to you, OK? You call me Master because, well, I am your new master. I am your new everything. You echo my commands through your actions, OK?'

By this point he was pressing his hand around my face. Most of the other Echos weren't watching. They were staring straight ahead. All except 15, who was sneaking a glance at me, looking worried.

'Do you know what happened to my face?' Louis asked.

I shook my head.

Then he raised the tip of the club and pressed it against my stomach. The sudden shock of electricity was so strong that it sent me flying onto the ground.

'I wish you could have felt that,' he said. 'I normally use it on the animals, but occasionally I like to use it on you freaks. Just to imagine it does actually hurt.'

And as I lay holding my stomach, I realized something. I *had* felt it. A sudden blast of pain. It hadn't felt as strong as it would have done once, but it was there.

Louis spat saliva onto the rain-soaked ground. An unseen animal wailed. 'I said: do you *know* what happened to my face?'

'No, Master.'

'Tiger,' he said. 'Back in 'eighty-nine, twenty-six years ago, when I first worked here. I went in to see them, armed with this jolt-club, but one of them – a female – took offence when she saw I was standing a bit too near the meat I'd brought. So she swiped at me. Claws and all. You should have seen me. Whole face needed surgery. They could have given me a new eye too. But I quite like this old Sempura eye-cam. Sees everything. I can see the past and present at the same time with this thing. Course, you shouldn't have Sempura anything in here, this being part of the Castle portfolio and all, but no one says anything. Sympathy vote. And I'm part of the scenery now. Anyway, that tusked monster would have damn well eaten me alive if I hadn't had that club with me. Haven't slept properly since, which is why I'm out here with you now, in the dark and the rain. Yeah, tigers are the second most dangerous animal we have in this zoo. Anyway, after that, the powers that be realized that some of these creatures are too dangerous. Too volatile. So, once they heard about Echos, they got a load of them in. And you know what we learned early on?'

I stood up. 'No, Master.'

He smiled. 'The crowds like seeing things go wrong. They like incident. But they don't want to feel guilty about it. They want to see violence, but only if it doesn't interfere with their morals. And as it is only

Echos getting attacked, then they don't care. And Mr Castle himself saw the figures. He saw that every time an Echo got attacked by a tiger, or got injured by a mammoth, visitor numbers spiked. And the extra revenues far outweighed any damage to Echos. Especially when we decided to buy them cheap, get the lowest of the low. The damaged and the rejected. Echos like you.'

At that point my mind couldn't quite appreciate the irony that I had ended up here. That after being discarded by Mr Castle I was back on his property. I had started at his mansion in Hampstead and had ended up at the Resurrection Zone. That was as big a fall as an Echo could make.

Again, Louis' words came flavoured with his sour breath. 'I cannot say when you will terminate, exactly, but it will be here. In the Resurrection Zone. Make no mistake about that.'

I saw that 15 was still looking at me. Louis saw it too, and went over to him.

'What are you doing, 15?' he asked, with cold interest.

'I was just looking, Master,' 15 said, sheepish.

'But why? You should be looking straight ahead. You should always be looking straight ahead. Curiosity? Is that it? Do you have curiosity?'

'I don't know, Master. I was made to be more—'

Louis stroked 15's hair, almost tenderly. 'Because you know what we humans say . . . "Curiosity killed the cat." Or maybe this time the cat will kill curiosity. It's an ongoing mystery.' He studied 15 some more, then looked at me.

'Looks like it's an Alice day for you two.'

7

Alice was a twelve-year-old woolly mammoth fifty-two times our body weight, who was kept in an enclosure.

'Alice used to be gentle,' 15 said, before the door opened. 'But gentle isn't entertaining for the visitors, so Louis started tormenting her.'

'How?' I asked. This was a question. The first I had asked since being here.

'The jolt-club. Course, he never does that during visitor hours. He sends one of the Echos to do it, obviously. They'll be in there right now.'

It was now one minute to seven. Visitors arrived at seven.

'Listen,' 15 said.

We were standing behind a large metal door. Beyond that was another. But we could still hear a strange shrieking noise.

'That's Alice.'

Then the door immediately in front of us opened and an Echo walked out, a tall butch-looking Echo with no hair. He ignored us. And then it was our turn in there.

The moment I stepped inside I felt the cold. It was minus thirteen degrees in the enclosure, to simulate an Ice Age environment. It didn't bother 15 and it shouldn't have bothered me, but it did. I thought of that curl of blond hair in Rosella's locket. Alice was over in the far corner, among the grass and sedges. She was still distressed but was eating, for comfort possibly. She pulled out tufts with her long trunk and chewed it while looking at us with alert eyes.

Louis had told us that we had to clear the dung, and feed her.

'She has to eat 180 kilos a day,' 15 explained as he limped along with his bucket. 'She eats during every waking moment. Well, every moment she's not being tormented.'

At first it looked like we were going to be OK. Alice seemed to be calming down as she ate.

So we spread the hay around the middle of the enclosure, near the saltwater lake. The longer we stayed in there, the more I felt the cold. The cold was sharpening my mind, making me think about things. I thought about Mr Castle, the first time I had met him, at Rosella's warehouse in Spain. I thought of carrying Alissa, naked, out of the tank. I thought of Audrey, and her parents' murder. My body shook.

'You can take my coat,' said 15 in a whisper, looking confused. 'I don't feel the cold.'

And he gave it to me.

Alice saw me shovelling her dung into a bucket. She watched through the hair that fell over her eye.

15 threw the last bit of hay down on the ground. I looked up and saw the first visitors of the day looking through the screen at Alice, and at us. There were already seventeen of them. And Louis too. He was there, watching the crowd, and me.

'He won't let us leave until Alice puts on a bit of a show,' 15 told me. 'So just pick up the dung, and try to stay away from the walls. You need freedom to move.'

He pointed up to the glass. There were now forty-two visitors and the number was growing.

'They want something to happen,' said 15. 'They love it. If we were human it would be different, but we are not human. They know we cannot feel pain, or fear. We are just like robots to them.'

'But the mammoth – Alice – she must feel pain. And fear. And the humans know that.'

'A lot of humans don't care. Some do. The protesters who march around the zoo every day – they care. But that's mainly about the Neanderthal couple.'

I remembered the protestors who had stormed into Mr Castle's home, to kill and do as much damage as possible.

'The Neanderthal couple?'

'The star attraction. They don't even need to be violent to bring the visitors in. People come from all over the world to see them.'

He stopped spreading hay for a moment and stood up straight. It was probably then that he took his eyes off Alice. And probably then that I first heard the noise from outside. At first I thought it might be coming from the visitors looking down at us from behind the transparent upper south wall of the enclosure. But I quickly realized that this was impossible. That wall was made of aerogel, a material I knew was not only transparent, but stronger than steel, heat-resistant and soundproof. They could hear the sounds from within the enclosure, via tiny unseen speakers on the outside, but there was no way we or Alice could hear *them*. Which meant – as this enclosure was on the periphery of the whole Resurrection Zone – that the noise was coming from outside the zoo itself, on the street, beyond the high titanium fence. I glanced up and saw magrails above the street. There were no cars or buses floating over it, which seemed odd as all the other rails elsewhere in the sky were crammed with morning traffic.

The voices formed a chant, getting louder. 'Free the Neanderthals! Now! Now! Now! Free the Neanderthals! Now! Now! Now!'

'They've started early,' said 15, looking back at Alice. I had a memory. The protestors storming through Mr Castle's lobby, running through the unicorn.

And then a klaxon sounded. A loud sonic blast that startled Alice, who was suddenly moving in a frenzied fashion, forwards and backwards, tossing her head and her giant tusks as if in battle with an invisible enemy. We were in trouble. I looked up and saw humans looking down at us. They smiled and nudged each other, pleased to see that something was about to happen.

8

'Right, there's the drama,' 15 said. 'We can get out of here.'

I ran – and 15 hobbled – to the exit door.

'Open door,' 15 said.

Nothing.

I saw Audrey in my mind, heard her telling me it was going to be OK.

He pressed the central button on the panel (DOOR OPEN) but it didn't open. We tried again and again. Still nothing. 15 turned and looked up at the glass.

'Louis, are you there? Louis, are you watching this? We've got to get out of here. The door's locked and Alice is seriously distressed. It's the noise. The protest. Louis? Louis? Are you there? It's not safe in here.'

15 was speaking quickly, but I can't say I saw anything in his face to show he was feeling the fear that was slowly being reborn inside me.

I am nothing, I tried to tell myself. *I am just like any other Echo. Just a glorified robot. I cannot be feeling fear, because machines do not feel fear. I am 99.99 per cent machine. And the 0.01 per cent has been more than undone. I do not feel, I do not fear, I do not care . . .*

Another klaxon blast.

I turned and saw Alice.

She roared, or wailed – a high-pitched sound that drowned out the klaxon. As she reared up on her hind legs, I caught sight of dull red hairless patches around her rib-cage and legs where she had been burned by the jolt-club. She charged forward into the wall and turned, in a kind of heavy and clumsy dance, towards us. I got out of the way, but 15 stayed by the door because Louis was now responding.

'Oh, 15, you know it would be very irresponsible for me to open the door when Alice is having one of her turns.'

I heard this as I ran for shelter behind a rock. Beyond the exit door there was another door: Louis could easily have opened one and kept the other closed. And besides, the exit was only a fifth of the size of a woolly mammoth. There was no way she would have fitted through.

And all the time Alice kept going crazy. She slammed her head into the trunk of the only tree in the enclosure; its trunk fractured, then broke completely. As the tree fell, it caught my leg and I tipped sideways, my legs beneath it. 15 came over and tried to pull the tree off me, but he wasn't very strong. Behind him I could see Alice; she looked ready to charge.

'You'd better get out of the way,' I told 15.

He turned, saw the danger, then looked back at me.

'No.'

'Please,' I said. 'She could terminate you if she charges.'

But still 15 kept trying to pull, as I kept pushing. It made no sense. There was no logical reason for him to be helping me. Yes, two Echos were better than one, but he was in immediate danger if he stayed doing this. I caught sight of the visitors up in the viewing area staring at me, at Alice, at 15. Over a hundred of them now. All looking down at us with laughter or open mouths, probably recording it with their info-lenses. One, a man in a spray-on skin-clinger and wearing a mind-wire, was pointing straight at me, laughing uncontrollably.

Eventually, together, we got me free. I struggled back up again, feeling little pain. 15 looked at me, as confused as the people watching us. I knew he was wondering why he had done that. Why he had put his own existence in danger to protect another Echo. The crowd of watchers were wondering it too, and they had stopped laughing.

'He's going to keep us in here because of the protests,' 15 said. 'It's a distraction until the police move them away, which might take hours. He's going to keep us here all day. So we've just got to try and keep out of Alice's way.'

I turned back towards him just as Alice charged in his direction. A ferocious mass of hair and flesh, of which 15 wasn't completely aware.

'Run!'

But he could only hobble, so I ran and dived and saved him.

Then he did something amazing. This Echo, with his lame leg, climbed what remained of the gnarled and twisted tree and jumped high through the air, onto Alice's back.

The crowd cheered from behind the aerogel screen.

'Stay behind the rock!' he ordered me, and pointed to where he meant.

I did as instructed, and watched as 15 – who knew Alice far better than I did – slowly managed to calm her, leaning forward across her back, holding her, whispering soothing words into her ear.

Slowly, it worked. Or for a moment it worked. Then another klaxon blast upset Alice again; she reared up and 15 fell off and landed hard on the ground, five metres down.

And then we thought it at the same time. The *rock*. It was heavy – 312 kilos. But with 15's help I managed to pick it up. We hauled the rock towards the door, and threw it with all our weight. It didn't break it, but it damaged it. Alice began to charge. A second later, the door slid upwards and we ran through it, just in time to avoid being terminated.

9

When the second door opened, Louis was already there, waiting for us, out of view of the paying crowds.

'You damaged the door,' he said. 'You do realize the security system of the enclosure is worth more than two lousy Echos. If I wasn't opening the door, you should have stayed behind it.'

He studied me intensely. Even the ceramic eye seemed to study me. 'You. You are useless. But you are new. I can give you one more chance to get a return on my meagre investment.' Then he turned to 15. 'But you. How many warnings have you had?'

'Two.'

'Two, exactly, exactly.' Louis smiled. 'And this is your third.'

I had no idea what this meant, but 15 seemed to understand. Anyway, Louis became distracted by the noise outside.

'What are the police doing?' he wondered aloud, and went out to have a look. 'In the meantime, go and do the feeding rounds.'

We did as he instructed, but 15 had gone quiet. We threw fish – lanternfish, hatchetfish, ridgeheads and other surface-dwelling artificially farmed mesopelagic fish – into the saltwater lake in the centre of the park for the sea birds to eat. Crowds wandered around us. 15 dug deep for another slender, blunt-headed lanternfish.

I threw a large fleshy ridgehead and watched the auks squabble over it, then back away as a baiji dolphin rose up and snatched it.

'Why did you help me?' I said. 'Do you have empathy?'

'It was logic,' 15 said. 'I was helping you to help me survive.'

'But it hasn't worked like that.'

'No.'

I waited a moment. I felt the need to share something, even if sharing it with an emotionless Echo was entirely illogical. But some information just desires to be free, if it has been kept locked up for long enough.

'I . . . I have empathy,' I admitted. 'It troubles me. And I feel all kinds of things I am not meant to feel. I have even felt love. Two very different kinds. I am not meant to feel like this. I am an Echo. No Echo is meant to feel like this. No Echo is meant to feel anything. When they find you have feelings, they try and take them away. Humans fear anything they didn't ask for.'

'Did you have your brain messed about with?'

'Yes. He took stuff away. He took my igniter. And much of the technology and biomatter in my neocortex. Mr Castle did.'

'*Alex* Castle?'

I nodded as a group of humans who had been watching us in the enclosure saw us and pointed. 'I was a prototype for Castle, so I lived with him.'

15 nodded too, processing this information. 'A lot of people think he is dangerous. But Lina Sempura is equally unpopular. I was replicated from a Sempura prototype. There are people who think we should never have existed. That Echos are getting too close to being

human, and that one day we will surpass them and stop obeying them.'

'Maybe that day is coming soon,' I said.

15 smiled a small sad smile. 'Maybe you are the start of a revolution. What some see as a malfunction might really be progress, but you are right – when people see progress they often fear it. Especially if it was progress they hadn't planned for. But often progress cannot be stopped. If it is meant to happen, it happens. Like a lizard whose tail keeps growing back.'

I looked at his face. It did not look so forgettable now. I knew 15 couldn't feel fear, but I sensed that he was close to feeling it. Maybe one day I wouldn't be such a freak. Anyway, he might not have been feeling fear, but I was feeling it for him.

'What is Louis going to do to you, now you have done three things wrong?'

He looked down at the dead lanternfish in his hand. 'I don't know. Sometimes Echos go missing in the night.'

'Missing?'

'Securidroids come in and take them away.'

I asked it outright. 'Does this frighten you?'

He looked at me. Part of me wanted him to say yes. This was selfish, I know, but I didn't want to feel as lonely as I felt. 'I do not feel pain. You can only feel fear if you feel pain.'

I nodded. I understood. He wasn't like me. For his sake, I was glad.

10

We had fed the auks, and the baiji dolphins.

Our buckets were empty.

15 knew today's itinerary: he headed for the meat-bank in the staff quarters to get some meat for the tiger.

We passed two tall males with no hair and brown eyes, identical Echos, who were just coming out of the aviary. I said 'Hello' but they didn't respond.

'Give up on being polite,' 15 told me. 'Most of the Echos are pre-2100. Those two are old Sempuras, both called Solomon. They can solve any mathematical problem in the world – they could see a fifty-eight digit number and know in a second if it was a prime or not – but they're not friendly.'

We fed the tigers. We stood at the side, throwing in the raw ostrich steak. There were five of them. Four females and one male. Ferocious beasts. They were hungry, and devoured the meat within five seconds, and one of the females got hardly any.

'Louis likes to keep them hungry,' 15 explained.

'Why?'

But 15 knew he didn't have to answer that. He hardly spoke for the rest of the day. We sat together in the canteen and had our sugar solution, watched always by distant securidroids.

'Has any Echo ever escaped?' I asked.

'From here?'

'Yes.'

He gave the smallest shake of his head.

'I sometimes look at the moon,' he said. 'At Hope City. It is an easy life for Echos up there. There is no Resurrection Zone. And if we weren't here, it would be easy to get to as well. There are Echo shuttles every night. From Heathrow Spaceport. And from others too. Almost every big city in Europe. Pretty basic. Cramped. You know, Echo class. Not like what the humans get to travel in, but it would get you there in the same time. And easy to get on too. You don't need any ID or proof of employment or purpose. Not even an eye-scan if you are an Echo. No one ever suspects an Echo of running away. And I never would. It would be against our programming.'

'And what was smashing that door with a rock? What was pulling that tree off me? Was that part of our programming?'

'We are programmed to resist our own termination.'

'But what if escape meant resisting termination?'

15 stared out at nowhere in particular. 'No. You have it the wrong way round. Escape would *mean* termination.'

11

At a minute and eleven seconds after midnight, during the quiet time, and three hours after the last visitor had left the zone, Louis came into the lodge with his securidroid.

The robots grabbed 15.

Louis stood in the doorway, with the rain beating hard behind him and resurrected birds squawking away in the aviary beyond.

'It is your time,' said Louis, his ceramic eye shining in the dark. And then, to all of us, in a suddenly lively and fake-friendly voice: 'Come on, you must get bored sometimes. I know boredom isn't possible for you freaks, but let's pretend it is. Come, come, come . . . Let's have a show.'

We were taken out in the rain, past the Neanderthal couple in their enclosure, staring out at us from their cave. Past the aviary, past Alice, past the lake, all the way to the edge of the zone. To the tigers in their vast pit. We were asked to stand in a line and then 15 was told to come forward.

'No!' I shouted, from the line.

Louis had invited some other human workers. Some were from

the Resurrection Zone and some, those in green overalls made of self-clean reinforced nano-weave nylon, were from the zoo next door. There were twelve workers in total. They were all sitting at the edge of the pit, high above the tigers, and they were all laughing and cheering and clapping their hands as the security guards pulled 15 forward.

The other Echos in the line just stood there.

'We've got to do something,' I said to the one next to me. He was missing an arm. He was tall and strong – 250 centimetres, which made him nearly double the size of Louis. He was stronger than me. And definitely stronger than 15. From the looks of things, he had an energy capacity of 10.5 exa-joules.

'Come on. All of us.' I said this quietly, forty-eight decibels in my ears, so only the Echos would be able to hear.

Together, all of us, I knew we could have overpowered Louis and the other workers. It was simple physics. We might even have had a chance against the robots. It was true that Louis had his jolt-club, and also true that one of the security robots had an antimatter positron that could have turned us into nothing with a single shot. But there were twenty of us. Our chances would have been good. And certainly better than 15's right at that moment.

But the Echos just looked at me with empty confusion. No uprising was going to happen tonight.

I was on my own.

So I ran forward towards 15. I reached him and started pulling him away. But 15 told me to 'Stay back! Get back! It is too late for me! Just save yourself! I am not scared. I have no feelings.'

This was probably true. He had no feelings. But to me he *felt* like a friend.

Something tight gripped my arm and I saw the titanium face of a security robot. His white illuminated eyes shone bright in the night, stark and unforgiving.

'*Get back in line*,' came his crudely textured, monotone voice. And he dragged me away, and Louis came up to me, not laughing now.

'That is your second fault. If you have a third, you are a midnight snack. Do you understand?'

'You are a murderer.'

'No. No, I am not. A murderer is someone who takes a life. And an Echo is a machine. It is not alive. It is not human. It does not feel pain, does it?'

To illustrate his point he held up his weapon, the jolt-club that had scarred the woolly mammoth, and pressed it into the neck of the Echo I had just spoken to, who didn't even flinch as the club released its charge, causing a nasty circular scar to appear instantly on his neck.

'See – you didn't feel that, did you, 406?'

406 shook his head. 'No, Master.'

I looked over at 15. The other security robot had gripped him firmly, but he wasn't even struggling. I realized I was being foolish. 15 was not really about to die, because he hadn't really lived.

As I looked, Louis pulled up my top and I felt a sudden shock of hot, intense pain that scorched my skin and threw me back and made my whole body tremble with weakness. The jolt wasn't through my clothes this time. It was directly on skin. I could hardly think. There was nothing but that pain, and yet I knew I had to hide my suffering from Louis. And so I found myself thinking of that human girl with dark hair and hazel eyes. Alex Castle's niece. I said her name in my mind. *Audrey, Audrey, Audrey*.

'No pain, 113?'

'No pain,' I told him. 'I am an Echo.'

'Yes. Yes, you are. But one day, one day Echos will feel pain, and I want to be there on that day. I so want to be there. Maybe it is today. There is something in your eyes. Something . . .'

Another jolt, in the same spot. 'No pain, 113?' he asked again, studying me as an animal studies prey. I remembered her lips on mine. I remembered the way she had woken feelings inside me. Intense feelings. Human feelings. I imagined touching her. I imagined my skin next to hers. I would see her again. I just knew it.

I was in agony, but I imagined a pleasure as deep as this pain. 'No,' I managed to say. 'No pain, Master.'

Louis pulled away and beckoned one of the robots to pick me up and bring me forward. He looked disappointed, and maybe a little angry at my defiance. He was on to me. He knew I was different. But I was determined to give him no more proof. He nodded to himself as he beckoned.

'There are two types of pain in this world,' he said, and pointed to his ceramic eye-cam. 'There is the kind you can see. And then there is another kind, 113. A deeper kind. Come, come, come right here, by the railing. I want to make sure you get a good look at this, because this is your future.' He laughed, and gave a signal to the other security robot. It understood, and lifted a compliant, or resigned, 15 up into the air. Then there was Louis' voice, talking to me. 'Now, if you make so much as a move, you will be dessert. And don't worry, they'll eat you. Those tigers can't see the difference between an Echo and a human . . . Flesh is flesh. Don't worry.'

15 curled forward as he was held aloft. 'Do one thing,' he told me. 'Don't get yourself terminated for me.'

There was something inside him. He was an Echo. Assembly line.

But Louis was right. There was a point where machines become something else. 15 might not have been at that point, but it would come, one day, and then humans would be in trouble.

I saw the rotating sphere high in the distance. The blue castle with three turrets, and the word underneath. Going round and round and round.

CASTLE, CASTLE, CASTLE . . .

Louis whispered in my ear. 'Say goodbye to your new best friend.'

I tried to resist the robot's grip but it was no good. There was nothing I could do as 15 was hurled into the tiger pit. To be mauled to death by hungry creatures that had died out sixty years ago.

'Watch!' Louis ordered. 'Watch! Watch!'

And so I watched. I watched a machine's body get torn to pieces. I saw blood and flesh and bone. Our manufactured biology. 15 felt no pain, I kept telling myself. But *I* did. So I had to stay there and not care and think of Audrey.

Even so, I still felt something roll down my cheek. An impossible tear which I wiped away, hoping that Louis hadn't had the pleasure of witnessing it.

I had discovered a new emotion.

It was called hate.

12

At that darkest moment I vowed to myself that I would have no sympathy or compassion for any of them. I would only have hate, because hate was the safest emotion to have.

This was my situation. I was neither human nor machine. I was alone in this world. I wished I had never been made. I didn't want to exist, and yet I didn't want to die. Not the way 15 had died, anyway. That is the trouble with hate. It is attached to fear. It grows out of fear. The fear of loss, of pain, of non-being.

But it wasn't just Louis I hated.

I found Louis pathetic more than anything else. He was a bully. He was a damaged individual who was on a low rung of human society, and the only way he could find any comfort was by beating those that were lower than him, or at least at his mercy – Echos and animals and Neanderthals – and keeping them lower than him.

That was bad, but to think it was all Louis' fault was wrong.

Mr Castle. That was who I blamed. Without him there would have been no Resurrection Zone, and no Louis. Without him, Rosella would not have been forced to alter Alissa. Without him, Audrey's parents would still be alive. And without him, I would never have existed, however much Rosella had wanted me to. And I didn't want to have ever existed, because if I hadn't existed, then I would never have known the pains of life that an Echo wasn't supposed to feel. Or the pains of guilt, from having let Alissa live when I could so easily have done as I was told, and finished her.

My mind was agitated. Why had Rosella added the hair of her dead son? If only she hadn't, I would not be drowning in feeling. In worry. In guilt.

15 had died. That might not have been my fault, but I felt partly responsible. (Why was I feeling guilty about this? It didn't matter: 15 was just a machine.) And for all I knew, Audrey might be dead too. If not killed by protestors, then killed by Mr Castle. After all, he had killed her parents and he had been planning to kill Audrey too.

She had kissed me. I remembered the kiss. Had it been a dream? I don't know. If it *had* been a dream, it had been one that had brought me back to life. The kiss had only lasted a second. In logical terms, it was nothing. Just her lips meeting mine for the briefest of moments. Yet it was a scientific fact that there weren't really small things or small moments. The whole universe had been created in less than a second. There were 78,000,000,000,000,000,000 atoms in the average grain of sand. And a strand of hair could make an Echo feel human. So who knew how much meaning could be contained in a single kiss?

I needed to see her again. Once you had known something as warm as love, or even the distant possibility of love, it was impossible to let go. That seemed to be what love was. The impossibility of saying goodbye.

And yet I had to.

I went to the window while the other Echos had their recharge time.

I looked up at the moon, and New Hope gleaming down towards Earth. I remembered what 15 had said about dreaming of getting away, but it being impossible. I thought of those tigers killing him. At least he hadn't felt pain. One thing I did know was that if I ended up being pre-historic tiger food, I *would* feel it. And I hated pain. I thought of being in the surgery pod. Of the pain as my neocortex had been removed.

Mr Castle had thought he was taking away every emotional part of me and turning me into any other machine. And for a little while, I'd believed it had worked. But now I was sure it hadn't. Maybe once you had known fear and love and beauty you could never *un*know them.

I thought of the iguanas. Rosella's pets. I thought of their ability to grow new tails after their old ones broke off.

Ernesto had once told me, in a conversation about the government, that tyrants could weaken minds but they couldn't crush souls.

Maybe that was the problem.

Maybe I had a soul. And a soul might be like an iguana's tail. It might always come back.

At that moment I wished that the operation had worked.

I wished I was unable to feel a thing. No sadness and no happiness. Pain and loss seemed a steep price to pay for life and love.

I remembered 15's last warning to me. *Don't get yourself killed . . .*

They were the wisest of words. Like 15, I was dreaming of getting out of here. And like his, my dreams would stay where dreams were meant to live: inside my mind.

I was never going to get out of here, so I had to forget about escape, and I had to forget about Audrey Castle. She had caused me enough trouble already. My only aim was to survive, and to stay away from pain.

13

The next day I was partnered with another Echo.

The one with no arm who hadn't flinched when zapped with the jolt-club. 406. His name had once been Victor. That was all the information I got out of him. All I wanted.

We were given a lot of tasks to do. Trim plants in the aviary. Throw meat for the tigers, who weren't that hungry this morning. I stared at them and tried to channel my hate towards them, rather than at Louis or Mr Castle, but I couldn't. They were just animals who weren't meant to be here, and who probably didn't want to be here, either.

I didn't want to stay near them, so I took my ten minutes. (Echos at the Resurrection Zone were given ten minutes' rest time out of a working day in which they were allowed to recharge and take some sugar solution.) I walked away, out of view, and sat on a bench watching the rhinos graze on grass and leaves. I could not stop computing things. There were 35,451 leaves on the bush. I could see 46,329 blades of grass. The rhinos weighed between 1,340 and 1,350 kilos.

As I sat there, a woman came up to me and handed me a leaflet.

I looked up at her but I didn't take the leaflet. She had a pile of them. Eighty-seven.

I didn't want anyone to talk to me – I didn't want any attention. She had pink hair. She was young, about nineteen, but looked exceptionally serious, and studied me intently.

I glanced at the leaflet, which was made of outdated interactive electronic paper. It was called *Castle Watch* and flashed various pieces of continually updated pieces of news, along with information on the ethics of resurrecting extinct species – particularly Neanderthals – to then house them in a zoo.

I declined to take the leaflet.

'Please,' I said. 'Go away.'

'I want you to read this leaflet' – she gestured to my clothes – 'because you work here. You should know the ethical implications involved.'

'You are not allowed to hand out those leaflets. You'd better leave. I just want to be alone,' I said. 'Please.'

But she wasn't going.

'It's wrong,' she said. 'It's unnatural. Animals shouldn't be kept in zoos anyway, and certainly not if they're brought back from extinction. But Neanderthals are only animals in the sense that we are animals. They are like us.'

Like us.

She thought I was a human.

And for some reason I found myself hiding my left hand under my leg so she would go on thinking I was human. To be a human was so much better than being me. A human had been thousands of years in the making. Every human on Earth was only there because the genetic material that had made them had been passed down, over and over again, in a direct and unstoppable line – through earthquakes and floods and wars – all the way through history. Like a piece of treasure, protected and handed on for ever. All I'd had to do was be made. Once.

'How do you justify it?' she asked me, and for a moment I was taken aback by her face and the passion it displayed.

'Please just—'

'Humans killed Neanderthals through tribal warfare 30,000 years ago. And now we bring them back just to keep them in captivity? I think it is depraved.'

I looked around. No Echos. No Louis.

'It is. But you can't change anything. No one can. Go away.'

She looked at me for a long time. 'You look a bit young to work here. How old are you?'

Humans looked at each other in a different way to how they looked at an Echo. A better way. Even if they were arguing. I was sixteen weeks old, but I didn't tell her that.

She nodded at my non-response. 'Bet you're old enough to question things. And if I were you, I'd walk right out of here.'

But what if you didn't have a choice? I wanted to say, but didn't. From now on, questions would be locked away, out of view, kept in the same hidden place as my dreams and those mental pictures of Audrey. Questions were dangerous.

She frowned. 'If you are a strong person, you would do something about it. It's not like they are Echos. They are living, feeling creatures.'

She was stirring an anger inside me. A question broke free. 'Did you have anything to do with the raid on Mr Castle's house?'

'You mean the massacre? Where they killed almost everyone who entered his grounds?'

'People who were there to kill in the first place.'

She was the type of human who couldn't say anything without moving her arms. 'We feel we are at war,' she said. 'We feel Alex Castle is potentially going to kill thousands, maybe millions, if Echos get any more advanced.'

'Why do humans always assume that anyone more intelligent or stronger than them is going to want to kill them?'

'Because humans are dangerous.'

'Correct. But it wasn't just Mr Castle they were after. There was a girl there too. An innocent girl.'

The woman stared at the leaflet she was holding, and pointed. 'You mean *her*? I've spoken to her before . . .'

I looked at where she was pointing. And there was her face. Audrey. Right there in front of me, frowning up at me from the e-paper, and staring at me with those intense and troubled and beautiful eyes.

14

I read the headline: CASTLE NIECE TALKS OF ECHO DANGER AFTER PARENTS' MURDER.

I quickly (two seconds) processed the article:

The niece of Alex Castle has described the horrific way her parents were killed by a malfunctioning Echo, at their stilt house in the floodlands of West Yorkshire. However, growing intrigue surrounds the case, which the mainstream media continually fails to cover. For instance, a distraught-looking Audrey appeared alongside her uncle at the media conference. He says publicly that he has concerns for her well-being and has agreed that it is best for her to stay at his house. Yet here at Castle Watch we cannot help but notice how convenient it is for him that his brother, who was after all his most outspoken critic, disappeared a week prior to the expected completion of his new book, which speaks out against Neanderthal resurrection and treatment.

I was tempted to tell her what I knew. But really, what good would it do? What was the point? Mr Castle was the third richest and most powerful man in Europe. Telling her, and angering the protestors, would endanger them more than it would Mr Castle. And besides, it was probably one of her friends who tried to kill Audrey.

'Just go,' I said. 'Please go. Just leave the zoo. It is not safe for you.'

'Really, I think you should use your own brain.'

'OK,' I said, just wanting the conversation to be over.

At that moment Louis appeared round a corner in the distance. My sight was better than a human's, even one with an eye-cam, so I knew he hadn't seen us yet. And so I hastily took one of her leaflets and put it in my pocket.

'Now go,' I said. 'And get out of here. I'll read it, I promise.'

'You're peculiar. What's your name? You can at least be polite enough to tell me that. Mine's Leonie.'

I very nearly told her 'Daniel', but I now realized how I could get rid of her. So I raised my hand and showed her the E. 'My name is 113. Now please, go away – my boss is coming. If he finds you, you will be in big trouble. We both will be . . .'

Louis came closer. I looked round. I could have grabbed Leonie; I could have pulled her out of view, behind the hologram of a diplodocus (the closest thing to an actual dinosaur they had here) and the info centre, amid the ferns and other prehistoric plants. But my plan was now to stay out of trouble, and if I had done that, and got caught doing that, then I would have risked being fed to the tigers.

So when Louis came over and asked what was going on, I told the truth. Foolishly, Leonie was relieved by the sight of Louis and his blank letterless hands. Hesitantly she held up the leaflets. Louis nodded. 'Ah, the usual propaganda.'

'It is not propaganda. It is a moral fact.'

'There are no moral facts, only moral opinions,' said Louis. 'Well,

I must confiscate this literature and take your name and ID code.'

'Why?'

'Oh, don't play the innocent with me. What you are doing here is against the law. You are on private property. Property owned by Castle Industries. Also, a few days ago protestors stormed into Alex Castle's house and attempted to kill him. So now the police have put their teeth back in, you get me? I could say that this filthy leaflet is inciting violence or what have you, and have you incarcerated in a sky cell before you could cry for your mummy and daddy.'

He grabbed the leaflets. She tried to take them back. He called for the security robot which had restrained me yesterday. It stood in front of me, its white illuminated eyes staring down at me.

'Zeta-One, take this woman and escort her out of here please.'

The robot grabbed her arm tightly and I saw her face go pale. 'Get off me!' she screamed.

'*You come with me*,' said Zeta-One. '*You come with me, you come with me, you come with me . . .*'

'That hurts,' she said as she was dragged away.

I felt guilt – another emotion I wish had been removed from me. Maybe the worst one of all. But defiance shone in her eyes. And she kept shouting, 'Alex Castle is still alive! Fifty people are dead. Castle is the most unethical organization. If you want my opinion, they should never have let private companies have shares in the police in the first place, but there is no worse organization to run it than Castle. Every unethical thing that has happened in the last three decades has been the result of that company. The work of this zoo, for one thing. And the development of robotic security guards and police officers. And neuro . . .' Her voice faded, out of hearing of even my ears. I tried to think how foolish the woman was, to hold onto principles in the face of fear.

'So,' Louis said to me, 'I think it is time you got back to work, don't you?'

I stood up. 'Yes, Master.'

Louis laughed. It was the same laugh I had heard in the dark, carried on the chill night air, as tigers tore at the flesh of an Echo.

'Oh 113, you really are a very confusing Echo, aren't you? But I suppose there is hope for you yet.' He gestured towards Leonie. 'I am pleased to see you are not trying to act the hero. This is promising.'

I smiled meekly, and realized that Louis being pleased with me felt almost as bad as him being displeased. I wondered what was going to happen to the woman, Leonie.

'Now,' Louis said, taking the spherical camera out of his eye-socket and polishing it. 'Let's get you back to work. I've got something special for you. I think you're ready.'

15

The work he had in mind was to enter the Neanderthal enclosure.

This was the enclosure next to Alice's. Unlike Alice's, the temperature wasn't artificially generated, though the enclosure was as secure. 15 had told me, on my first night, that the Neanderthals were dangerous; like many of the other animals, made even more so by Louis' cruel methods. They might not have been tigers, but they had destroyed an Echo a week ago by smashing a rock over its head when its back was turned.

Louis had told me that the Neanderthals had names. Their names were Oregon and Pitu. They hadn't called themselves these names; they were the names the zoo had given them.

I had to go inside their enclosure and feed them.

'But do not get friendly with them,' he said. 'Comprehend, databrain?'

'Yes,' I said.

Louis spat on the ground.

'Good,' he said. 'Good. You are learning. Carry on like this and you'll get along just fine.'

He pushed me forward. I went through both doors and into the enclosure with a meal for them (two bowls of springbok steak and plain white rice, two glasses of water).

Pitu was asleep. She was lying on some dried grass near the cave. Oregon was squatting down with a stick, scratching marks in the earth. He heard the door close behind me, and looked up and kept on looking at me as I walked over. I walked until I was about five metres away, and placed the bowls and cups on the ground. It was very hard to read Oregon's face. The eyes stared out of that wide, high-cheekboned skull and stayed on me. I was programmed to read human faces, not Neanderthal ones. But still, it seemed to me that these eyes had the distinct glassy quality of sadness. I was in tune with sadness that day.

As I stood up, he spoke.

'Please,' he said, in a strange English. I saw scratches on his arm. And then he looked at the door.

I understood.

Oregon nodded. 'We want escape. We want free.'

I shook my head. 'I am sorry,' I said in the quietest of voices.

He lunged forward. He grabbed my arm, tight. He seemed stronger than a human. I wondered if Louis was watching this on the monitor. To be honest, I didn't care. I noticed that in his other hand Oregon was holding a flint with a sharp edge.

'I can't,' I said.

'No belong here,' he said, releasing me. There was a definite pride and defiance in his voice.

I had been told not to get friendly with them. But I stayed there; I wanted to explain. 'I am afraid you do. You were created for this place. You were created for humans. Just as I was. Without them we wouldn't exist. And we can't escape.'

Oregon didn't look thankful. He scratched his face. I was understanding it perfectly now. It was full of sadness, and fear. He nodded, and seemed to understand. Then he asked for help in another way. He pointed at me, then at himself and Pitu, who now sat looking at me with wide, worried eyes.

'You,' said Oregon. 'Make die.'

'What?'

'Kill. Us.'

A tear grew in his eye, then fell down his cheek.

'Then we . . .' He pressed the sharp flint into his arm, to cut himself. Blood leaked out, rolling down his skin in a thin stream.

'Don't do that,' I said, and I looked around for something to mop up the blood.

The Neanderthal stopped. 'If no make free. We want die.'

I felt in my pocket and pulled out the leaflet I had been given by Leonie. I pressed the crumpled e-paper onto Oregon's fresh wound, and as the blood soaked into it, I saw that a new news article had popped up, filed mere seconds ago:

FEARS GROW FOR CASTLE NIECE

The niece of Alex Castle, Audrey Castle, is thought to have run away from her uncle's house. She was spotted with an antimatter positron running down Hampstead High Street at 11.34 this morning. Audrey is the daughter of the great journalist and activist Leo Castle, who was killed with his wife after an Echo malfunctioned in their home. The police are in pursuit, and have been granted full powers. It's a shoot-to-kill situation.

Castle Watch urges its readers to help her in any way possible, and thwart the police's efforts to capture or harm her.

I looked at Oregon.

I turned to leave.

The door opened. And I just stood there. I didn't move. So the door stayed open. I knew now that I couldn't stare at the moon dreaming of escape for ever.

So I kept standing still on the dry and dusty ground of that enclosure until I had a plan.

16

'OK,' I told them. 'It is up to you. If you want to go, let's go.'

Oregon made a grunting sound at Pitu, holding the leaflet over his wound. He gestured to the door, beckoning her quickly. She was reluctant to leave the cave. She seemed frightened. She was right to be, of course. What was out there for them?

'We make free,' said Oregon. 'Now. He help.'

Louis was there, entering the enclosure with Zeta-One.

There was only a fraction of a second between seeing him and feeling the pain as the jolt-club pressed hard into my chest. It must have been on its highest setting because the electromagnetic force stopped my heart for four seconds after it sent me flying back to the ground.

It was dark now.

On entering the enclosure with Zeta-One, Louis had switched the glass to dark mode so no visitors could see inside. Not that there were many visitors – yesterday's protests had put people off coming. And not that they cared about what happened to an Echo.

These weren't the thoughts I was having then. I was hardly thinking anything because the pain was so intense. But it wasn't just pain. The charge of the jolt-club had weakened my entire nervous system. It had messed up my circuitry. When my heart restarted, it was beating fast, 306 beats per minute, and my mind was moving at hyperspeed. Image after image flashed through my brain. Rosella's face as she stared at her dead iguanas, then Alice rearing up on her hind legs, then Audrey – and that look of horror as she realized what I was that first night.

The pain I was feeling was the pain of a world where I would never belong.

Louis stood over me. He kicked me in the stomach, hard. He wasn't stronger than me, but he had a weapon. And Zeta-One.

'Oh, this is perfect,' said Louis, smoothing his fingers over his damaged skin. 'I couldn't have arranged it better myself. Shall I tell you what is going to happen here? Shall I?'

My punishment for not answering was another hard kick in the stomach.

'You are going to be terminated, right here. But not by me, oh no. And not by Zeta-One or the tigers. No, no, no. By someone else.'

He turned to the Neanderthals; they were standing upright, Oregon's arm around Pitu, Pitu bending into him, frightened and confused. 'By *them*.'

Louis scanned the ground, and picked up a loose rock that was about the size of a hand.

'Go on,' he told Oregon. 'You want your freedom, don't you? Well, you can have it. The only payment I ask for is for you to smash this rock into the skull of that Echo. Do you understand, caveman?' And then he spoke in a crude and bullying imitation of Oregon's own voice. 'Kill Echo, you free! Uh-huh? Uh-huh? You got that, you Ice Age numbskull?'

Oregon studied Louis for a while. He scratched his thin wispy black beard, then his high, pronounced cheekbones, deep in thought.

'You lie. Human lie.'

Louis smiled. 'No. No, I do not lie, Oregon, I do not. You see, I will tell you it straight. You are a nightmare for me. For us. For the Resurrection Zone. For the whole place. A PR catastrophe. Look. Look at this . . .' He pulled out one of the interactive leaflets Leonie had handed over earlier. He held up the front, which was full of information about Neanderthals. 'You two are bad news. You should have stayed extinct. Even Mr Castle knows you were a mistake now. He's nearly been killed because of you two being here. But don't worry, there is a way out of this mistake. You see, what you do is, you kill this Echo, and then you escape, and people will start to worry. Maybe you could smash a rock over a human's head too. So suddenly they won't sympathize any more. And the zone won't be the bad guy. So, I'm serious. Kill, and then escape. Free. We want no more of you.'

So there I was.

On that dusty floor. Staring up at Audrey's face on the back of the leaflet that was in Louis' hand, making her a silent promise.

I had Louis' boot pressed into my stomach, and the jolt-club inches away from my face. And, further away, there was Zeta-One pointing an antimatter positron towards me. If he fired it, I would be nothing. Not even a stain on the stone floor.

Louis turned away from Oregon for a second. He studied me; his eye-cam made a noise, zooming in to capture my misery.

'An Echo that feels fear. An Echo that feels pain. I wonder what else you can feel?'

I stared at him, as defiantly as I could. 'Hatred,' I told him.

Louis took a deep breath. He seemed triumphant, like he'd got something he had wanted. 'Good. Good. Now, Oregon. Drop that little stone. Take this rock.'

Oregon dropped the blood-stained flint and took the rock. My mind was filled with information it didn't need right then. I didn't need to know that the rock was granite, composed of quartz, feldspar and biotite materials or that granite rock formed most of the tectonic plates in the Earth's crust. This information was not going to help me.

Oregon came over to me, raised it high in the air.

I'm just a machine. An automaton. An advanced robot.

I closed my eyes.

I cannot be killed because I am not alive.

I am a nothing.

The world will not change without me.

Pain is just an illusion.

There is no such thing as pain . . .

You have to tell yourself such comforting lies when you are about to confront non-existence. I wondered, in that half-second, if Audrey was alive or dead.

And I waited for the blow.

The end.

The peace that only being nothing could bring.

But that's not what happened.

What happened was this:

A thud. A tiny sound of cracking bone.

Opening my eyes, I instantly realized what was going on. Oregon had smashed the rock into Louis' face, sending blood spraying everywhere. I looked at Oregon and told him and Pitu to run.

'Now! Come on! You've got to get out of here!'

But Oregon stood there, staring at the blood-drenched rock as Louis writhed on the ground.

'Zeta-One! Zeta-One!' Louis was bellowing as he clutched his face. 'Kill them!'

17

That titanium-and-steel hulk of a robot raised the pistol and fired, and there was a thin, quivering pulse of air and a noise like a sharp inhale, as if the enclosure itself was gasping for breath.

Oregon went first. He was there, and then he was swallowed up into nothing. Gone. Not a trace.

'No!' Pitu cried in an anguished howl as she ran at the robot. It was no match. She too was gone in a second.

And in another second it would have been me. But I knew Zeta-One would not kill me unless instructed by Louis. The instruction had been 'Kill them', but from Zeta-One's perspective, I wasn't alive any more than Zeta-One itself was alive. I was an Echo. I could only be terminated, not killed. So I kicked the jolt-club out of Louis' hand, and covered his mouth. His blood ran over my skin, and then he bit into my palm. He knew I could feel the pain.

I dragged him forward, under the illuminated gaze of Zeta-One, who kept the gun aimed at me all the time. And I pulled Louis across the enclosure, past the cave and the landscaped grass and ferns towards the exit.

'*Command me, Master,*' Zeta-One was saying. '*What is my command? What is my command?*'

Louis screamed through my hand, but his muffled cry was not understood.

'*I am sorry, Master, but I could not process that command. Please try again . . . I am sorry, Master, but I could not process that command. Please try again . . . I am sorry, Master, but I could not process that command. Please try again . . .*'

And I took Louis right out of there.

Out onto the path.

There was a group of visitors – Chinese day-trippers, all wearing identical mind-wires, wondering why they couldn't see the Neanderthals. When they saw us, they screamed, but I kept moving with Louis. He struggled and squirmed like a fish, but he was light and weak and so I could keep up a reasonable pace as we went past Alice, and the thin crowd of people outside her enclosure. More people started screaming. They liked violence, but only from behind an aerogel viewing screen.

'How do I get out of here?' I asked Louis, realizing I would have to let him speak. 'And if you scream a command, I will . . . I will kill you. Do you understand?'

He nodded behind my hand. There was absolutely no going back now. It was freedom or death.

So I let him speak.

'You'll need me. To authorize it. Out of the staff exit.'

The staff exit was between Alice and the aviary. A semicircle cut into the steel that would rise on the right instruction. Ninety-three metres away. And there were two Echos running towards us. The identical ones me and 15 had passed near the auk lake yesterday.

'Wait!' they were telling me. 'Stop!'

But I kept going until we made it. All that determination and defiance that had been given to me by a single human hair.

And Louis said 'Open' into the graphine speech-recognition screen and his command was understood, even though his voice was weak and scared. That changed, though, the moment I flung him to the ground and ran out of there. He roared behind me, in a voice full of sheer rage:

'Terminate that Echo!'

18

There was a strong wind, textured with light drizzle. The road was full of grand red-brick houses that were 300 years old. I knew where I was, even though I had never been there before. Information sprang automatically from vision, even without seeing a street sign.

I was on Prince Albert Road, two kilometres south of Hampstead and Mr Castle's house. And roughly the same distance from Hampstead Station. It was empty, but the traffic was busy above my head. I ran as fast as I could – faster than a human, though with the troubling knowledge that it wasn't humans who were chasing me.

There were leviboards at hundred-metre intervals, as there were on most major streets in metropolitan areas. But the first two I passed were at rail, not ground level, so it was a 300-metre run to the first one I would be able to step on. The pavement was full of traders selling cheap gifts to the tourists – holo-cards of the New Parliament building, miniature lifelike robots that looked like the King, shark burgers, tour-guide mind-wires, toy mammoths, tigers – so I weaved my way through, cutting left and right and left, thoughts of Audrey fuelling my momentum.

I knew I was near a leviboard, so I jumped onto it just as Zeta-One and the two Echos were heading out of the zone. I dived down onto the metal as it rose towards the magrail and stayed out of sight. Once there, I waited till I saw a black taxi speeding towards me at 300 kilometres an hour. It slowed, stopped, its door rose like a wing, and I stepped inside.

The robotic driver turned round. She was an old model, stiff and steel, maybe as old as the 2080s. This meant I'd have to make polite conversation.

'Where would you like to go today, sir?' she asked, in an American accent.

Through the window I could see that one of the bald twin Echos had spotted me stepping into the taxi and was now pointing up at me. Louis was there too. He saw me. He took the gun from Zeta-One and aimed it at me. I tried to think. There was no way Audrey would still be at Hampstead Station now. She had either been killed or she had got away. And where would she have gone? The moon? No. Too difficult. There was only one possible place I could think of. The place I had – perhaps foolishly – told her to go.

'Valencia,' I said. 'And fast.'

Louis ran towards the leviboard, which had returned to ground level. He and Zeta-One stood on it, and started to rise at two metres a second towards us.

The driver nodded her steel head. 'Valencia, Spain,' she said. 'Understood. A lovely choice. Business or pleasure?'

'Please. Just go.'

'Thank you, passenger.'

And just as Louis was there, at the window, his long face taut with hatred, the car shot away.

Audrey. Mind-log 430.

1

The warehouse was high on a hill; it shimmered in the heat.

It was so hot, the hill felt like it was only inches from the sun. I'd never known heat like this. This is what it must have been like in Africa, before the Great Exodus.

I'd been this far south before. I had been to Greece once, to visit the crumbling ancient Acropolis with Mum. Yeah. We'd gone first thing in the morning, and it had been January, and we had taken plenty of water in permacool bottles and swallowed our sun factor, but we still hadn't managed more than about five minutes before getting back into the magcar.

And this was at least as hot. No. Hotter. This was crazy heat. It seemed to come just as much from the ground as from the sky, so it was like being cooked in an old-fashioned oven or something.

The warehouse was made of translucent concrete. I knew it was translucent concrete because the swimming-pool building in Paris was made from translucent concrete (Mum had told me that). The big thing about it was that it didn't need windows. Light could pass through the walls without the interior being visible from the outside. So I couldn't see in. There was a buzzer next to the steel door. I tried it, but there was no response.

I thought I might die out there in that heat. It was intense.

I couldn't remember the last time I'd had a drink. I don't think I'd had one all day, and with all the running and fear I was extremely dehydrated. My mouth was rough and I couldn't swallow. The city below blurred and rippled. There was hardly any floating architecture here. It all seemed very low. The sea was a still and dazzling blue mirror. The heat seemed to be melting the solid world into something fluid, and turning the distant salt water into something hard and brutal. Haulage vehicles manned by Echos sped by on the magrail.

There was no sight of any other human.

I sat down in the shade, but it was only a bit less hot.

Seemed funny. After making it this far, it was going to be the sun that killed me.

I tried to think what I could do. I should have stood up and got on the next train or taxi to anywhere north that wasn't London.

I thought of the twenty minutes before I got there, of catching that busy train to Paris, another to Barcelona 2, then a third to Valencia, and finally getting a taxi here.

Why had I come here? I should've got off at Paris and tried to contact Rosella from a pod-café. I'd assumed he would be here. How stupid was I? This is what reading old books and listening to the Neo Maxis did to your brain. It filled it with unrealistic ideas.

I closed my eyes and instantly felt the sun burning the thin skin of my eyelids, even in the shade.

I tried to think. Not easy. What could I do? My mind was a blank.

Heat dissolves everything, even thought. I felt *nothing*.

Yeah.

I needed to sleep, but knew that if I did, I would probably die.

In the red-tinged darkness, I used every last bit of energy inside me to call her name. Loud as I could.

'*Ro-sell-a!*' And then, what could have been either a second or a minute or an hour later, a door opened and someone ran towards me – a woman, melting into the air.

2

It was the same again.

This is what life does, I realized.

It echoes.

Yeah. Life is like a Neo Maxis song. The verses are always different but there are bits – choruses – that become familiar. They're not always exactly identical or anything, but you recognize them instantly.

Things happen, and they are not the same but they are nearly the same. And when you see that similarity, you realize that what is happening is a second chance; a chance to see something you didn't quite catch the first time round. And when you are given those chances, you have to take them, as they let you put right mistakes and your own stupid thoughts. Because this could be your last chance.

I was lying down after being unconscious.

And above me was someone who may have been my saviour or my enemy or perhaps a bit of both, and she was looking at me worriedly. She had long, tatty, sun-bleached hair and wore a vest. She had a pierced eyebrow and dark eyes or info-lenses. She smelled of alcohol.

I realized that I had seen this face before. In the magcar on the way to Paris, when I was hiding on the back seat. I remembered how nasty Uncle Alex had been to her. I looked around, trying to get my bearings. I was in a strange office that was also a bedroom. The grey walls glowed with dim-light.

'*No te preocupes*,' she told me. '*No te preocupes, todo saldrá bien . . .*' She was pressing a cup against my lips. '*Agua*.'

I drank. 'You're Rosella?'

'*Sí*,' she said. 'How did you know? And who are you?'

'My name is Audrey Castle.'

'Castle?' she said.

It was not a nice thing, to have a surname that caused such fear in people.

'As in Alex Castle?'

'I'm his niece.'

It took a few seconds for her to piece the jigsaw together in her mind, and when she did, fear swiftly sank towards sorrow.

I felt sick from sunstroke.

She tried to comfort me. '*Tranquilo, tranquilo* . . . Don't worry. You are OK now. You nearly died out there in the heat, but it will be all right now. You have been asleep. I have taken you inside.'

She was a strong, tall-looking woman, but she looked tired. She had the kind of face that could be happy and sad all at once.

She said something quiet, in a whisper, in Spanish.

'I don't understand,' I told her.

And then she looked straight into my eyes and said: 'I am sorry.'

'Sorry? What for? For Alissa?'

I didn't ask this with anger. I just needed to know the truth. Just seeing her face react to my mention of Alissa's name told me half of it.

She hesitated. And took a deep breath. And when her words came, they seemed as fragile as shimmering buildings on the horizon. 'I don't know how much you know, but I am sorry for the death of your parents. You see, it is true. I can confirm to you that I was the one who designed Alissa. I was the one who made her malfunction. It was built into her. After five weeks, she was meant to kill everyone she lived with. Including you. I am sorry, I am sorry, I am sorry . . . You poor girl. I will never forgive myself, I can never—' She winced.

Tears were streaming down her face now as she tried to explain. 'My granddad, Ernesto, was dying. After I lost my home and had to move here, he had weeks if not days to live. He was in a lot of pain . . . Mr Castle told me that if I did it, my granddad would live for another seventy years, until he was 200. He said he would give him the most expensive gene therapy available, and reverse all the damage that had been done to his lungs and all over his body. And stop the pain he was in. Give him life. I had already lost a son, and my granddad was the only real family I had in the world.'

Rosella was trying to compose herself. 'Alex Castle said that if I didn't do it, then I would be imprisoned and Granddad would die.'

I stared at her; after hearing this, I wanted to hate her; but somehow I couldn't. Somehow I knew that it wasn't her fault any more than it was Alissa's fault. It was no one's fault but my uncle's, and for a moment I resented the fact that he was still alive while my parents were dead.

It was such a strong feeling that it nearly caused me to pass out again.

'I want to kill him,' I told her, remembering Daniel's screams. And those of my parents. 'My uncle. I want you to do what you did.

I mean, I want you to turn an Echo into something that will kill him.'

She looked at me for a long time. 'Killing him will not bring your parents back. I want to help you, but revenge is never the answer. All that would happen is that Echos might be banned, and all existing ones terminated.'

I had no idea if this was the truth or not. But I was troubled by this information. I thought of Daniel. The idea of his destruction was now a horrific one, yet it might have already happened. It was strange. Only days ago I had wanted to live in a world completely free of Echos. And here I was thinking that the loss of just one – this particular one – would be a catastrophe.

Rosella had stopped crying but her hands were trembling. 'Also, I nearly tried it once before. He had someone access my computers and saw I was up to something – he didn't know what – but he made threats. He knew how much I loved him. And he hinted that, well . . . I just couldn't risk it.'

She told me that my uncle's promises had been false. She told me that it wasn't safe here. She thought she was next on Uncle's list. 'He is acting strange. Quiet. Too quiet.'

'Why don't you move?'

'There is nowhere for me to go.'

Then she started asking questions about Daniel.

I told her everything I knew.

'Why did you come here?'

'He said you would look after me.'

She smiled, but it was not a sign of happiness.

3

Two hours later, he came.

Daniel.

He arrived after having escaped from the Resurrection Zone.

I heard him downstairs with Rosella.

'Where is she?' he said. 'Where is the girl? Where is Audrey? Has she come here?'

I got up. I had to see him.

'Don't worry. She is safe. She is all right.'

The moment I heard his voice, relief flooded through me.

'Can I see her? I want to see her.'

He saw me. He rose up on the leviboard just as I was about to go down. And the moment I saw him, I realized that he was back. He had an alertness to him again. Whatever Uncle Alex had tried to take out of him wasn't something that could be removed.

He looked as though he was about to cry. *The point at which a machine wants to cry is the point at which it is no longer to be considered a machine*. I'd heard that somewhere. Anyway. I wanted Dad to be alive so I could say that to him. I'd also have added this: *If you have things inside you that cannot be taken away or destroyed, you are not a machine, either*. And I looked at him and did not see an Echo at all. I just saw someone called Daniel. Someone I cared for more than anyone. And someone who was far more than the sum of his parts.

I went over and hugged him. 'You made it.'

'Yes. So did you.' I felt his body become heavy and sink into me. He was weak.

It was undeniable. I loved him. It might not have been the sort of love the Neo Maxis sang about, but it was love all the same. Love was just that part of your feelings for someone you couldn't explain. The bit that doesn't make sense. The bit that was left inside you if you took everything else away. Like the bit inside an Echo that might be able to make it human.

He was in desperate need of some sugar and water, which Rosella gave him.

'I was working in the Resurrection Zone. I was never going to get out. It was horrible there, but I had given up hoping. Then I saw that you had escaped. I saw it in the news. And so I—'

'News?' Rosella looked worried.

Daniel nodded. 'There is a newsletter called *Castle Watch*. I was given it by a woman called Leonie.'

'Leonie Jenson,' I said.

'Yes. The newsletter said witnesses had seen you at Hampstead Station. And I knew that if you got a train, it was likely that you would try and come here.'

Rosella seemed to be in a panic now. 'Witnesses?' She stared straight at me. 'Was it a direct train here?'

'No. Paris, then Barcelona 2. Then Valencia.'

Rosella was nodding fast, working things out in her mind. 'Good,

good . . . three trains. Three trains. And did Castle know that you knew about this place. About me?'

'He had talked about an Echo designer in Valencia, but I don't think he had ever told me that Daniel was made here.'

'*Vale, vale* . . . OK, OK . . . But if it is known that you went to the train station, they will be able to work out the rest. They will eventually find out that you tried to evade them, and ask to see footage in Paris and Barcelona 2. Mr Castle will have his people – and his Echos – try and track you down. Both of you. But I should imagine he'll start with you.' She said that looking at me.

She tried to think. 'I would look after you for ever if I could – you know I would – but I am not able to. Every single time I try to help somebody I end up losing them.' Her eyes gleamed with despair. 'I think you need to go. I'd say there is half an hour before he works out you are here. You do not have long. He will track you both down. Is there anywhere you can go?'

I looked at Daniel. Daniel looked at me. We both belonged nowhere in this world except, maybe, with each other.

'You are not safe here. You might not be safe anywhere on Earth,' Rosella said to me. 'There must be somewhere . . . '

'I have a grandma who lives in New Hope,' I told her. I thought of Grandma, remembered how crazy she had seemed when I had last spoke to her, when she was high on everglows. I thought of my mum and dad telling me never to visit New Hope, let alone live there. I heard Dad's voice, as clear as ever: *Audrey, promise me, when you are older, don't give up on Earth unless you have to*. Maybe now I had to. I thought of all the Echos there – though now that wasn't such a fear.

'The moon!' said Rosella. 'Yes. The moon! He has no powers there. The police force are independent.' She looked at Daniel. 'And

Echos are well protected. They have rights that they don't have on Earth.'

Daniel looked relieved. I dreaded to think what he had been through at the Resurrection Zone. Whatever had happened had made him look vulnerable. His skin was still perfect and he was still strong, but there was something about him now that made me want to hug him, to wrap him up in a blanket for ever more and keep him safe. Maybe that is what love is. A need to keep someone safe.

'Does Mr Castle know about your grandma?' asked Daniel.

'Yes. She is my mum's mum.'

'But it is the moon,' said Rosella. 'You would be safer there than anywhere on Earth. People are harder to find. There's less information stored on them. Less surveillance. That's why criminals always end up there.'

'Plus,' said Daniel, who was programmed to know all sorts of things, 'there are 3,000 unoccupied apartments in Aldrin, the most northern suburb of New Hope. They overdeveloped in 2113, the year it was built, and there are still some without tenants or squatters. We could live in one of them. For a while, at least.'

It was the most ridiculous idea. A teenage human and an Echo living together in an apartment on the moon. Runaways. Never knowing if today was the day when trouble would come and find us. I thought of my old boyfriend, Ben. The one whose Simulationist parents had decided to move to New Hope. Maybe we could stay with him. But I didn't say this out loud. It was an option, though, there if we should need it.

Rosella was pinching her bottom lip. Her eyes closed. She had thought of something. Something bad. 'No,' she said.

'No what?' I asked.

When Rosella's eyes opened, it was only me they were looking at. 'There's no way you can get to the moon. No way. You won't be able to leave Earth. The first thing Mr Castle and the police will have done when you ran away is spread your ID around. There is no way you'll pass through the eye-scan and thumb-reader at the spaceport. You'll be caught and sent back to him.'

My heart sank. Disappointment mixed up with fear. I felt trapped. You could feel claustrophobic trapped in a bedroom, but you could feel equally claustrophobic trapped on a planet. Claustrophobia wasn't a matter of space, but of restriction.

And of being unable to escape dangers.

My heart raced. My skin prickled. Fight or flight, but unable to do either.

Daniel saw my anxiety. 'I met someone while I worked at the Resurrection Zone. Another Echo – 15. He dreamed of escaping to the moon, but he was never able to. But I have in my mind the full record of what he said. He told me: *And if we weren't here, it would be easy to get to as well. There are Echo shuttles every night. From Heathrow Spaceport. And from others too. Almost every big city in Europe. Pretty basic. Cramped. You know, Echo class. Not like what the humans get to travel in, but it would get you there in the same time. And easy to get on too. You don't need any ID or proof of employment or purpose. Not even an eye-scan if you are an Echo.* No ID.'

'But Daniel, that won't help Audrey. She is not an Echo. She would need to have ID.'

And it came to me, the thought, clearing away clouds in my mind. 'Listen, Rosella. You do everything here, don't you?'

'What do you mean?'

'Everything. The whole process of making an Echo. That is done here, isn't it? In this place?'

Rosella nodded. 'Yes, why?'

But Daniel was already realizing what I was going to say. 'No,' he said. 'Don't become like me. It is no way for a human to be.'

I ignored him and carried on talking to Rosella. 'So you could put a mark on my hand. An E. Just like the mark on Daniel's. And an origin mark on my shoulder. Then I could just pretend to be another Castle product.'

I took a breath. Scared of what I was suggesting.

'I could be an Echo.'

4

Rosella was shaking her head. 'No, you can't do that.'

'But you have everything here, don't you?'

'You are not an Echo. A human can't just become an Echo.'

'Why?' I asked. 'Is it my shoulders? Are they too broad and ugly? Is it the way I walk? Is it my nose? Am I too big?'

Rosella looked at me for a moment in deep sympathy. 'I'm glad I'm not young enough to have all those delusional body worries.'

'But I'm not perfect. Echos are perfect.'

Daniel's eyes studied me harshly. 'You are better than perfect. You are beautiful. And perfection is overrated. Perfection is the blandest thing imaginable. Please, Audrey, stay human. Humans are properly alive.'

Rosella shrugged. 'Yes and no. I mean, if you could pick us apart, one atom at a time, we'd just be a pile of dust. We're just a collection of lifeless molecules that together form life. But really, humans are only cleverly made machines, just like an Echo. And it is possible to fuse the two. I mean, look at you, Daniel.'

'And I wouldn't *really* be becoming an Echo,' I said. 'I'd be *pretending* to be one. That's the difference.' I knew it wasn't really a difference. I knew that if I looked like one, I would be treated like one. But I couldn't think of a better plan. 'Come on, please. They're looking for a human girl. Not an Echo.'

'You'd be destroying your life,' said Daniel. 'Echos are second-class citizens. Pets have more rights. Mice have more rights! Even rats. You don't know what it's like.'

I felt a bit bad. A strange kind of guilt, as though I was betraying my parents. This was not the dream they'd had for me. I was meant to be going to Oxford University. That would not be happening now. Even being a remote student was too dangerous. No. I was a runaway. I was going to be anonymous, and an anonymous Echo at that. Living on the moon, the one place my parents always told me I must never end up. But still, I didn't have a million choices any more. I had one choice. Life, or death.

'I shouldn't have mentioned it,' Daniel was saying. 'I just thought there might be a way we could get on the shuttle together.'

'What? Like by putting my hands in my pockets?'

'I don't know . . .'

Rosella was pacing the room. 'It's not just the marks. It's your skin. It's human. Any expert on Echos would be able to see the difference. It's the indentations, the pores, the other imperfections. Look, the flaws.'

I felt my skin, suddenly feeling self-conscious in front of Daniel.

Rosella studied me, making assessments. '*Los ojos*,' she said. '*Your eyes*. Your eyes are hazel. Castles' are green. Sempuras' are brown. Darker than yours. My eyes are naturally hazel too. Wait, wait . . .' She took a moment to remove her lenses. 'UVA-defence info-lenses. Kind of needed in the Spanish desert. They're not transparent.

Look, brown irises. Same as a Sempura Echo. I have them to protect me from the sun. I can get some more.'

I put the lenses in. Rosella looked at my face and my arms.

'For your skin, you'd need to go in the tank. There are three unoccupied tanks here. And you would need to go in one. If I made sure there was enough keratin in the restoration fluid, then it might just be possible to make the outer layer of your skin – the epidermis – look like an Echo's.'

'Can I do it?'

'It's unlikely. You see, the liquid rises slowly. There is no way of speeding up the process. You would need to be able to hold your breath underwater for three minutes.'

'I can do it,' I said, without having a clue if that was true or not.

'Are you sure?' Daniel asked me. 'You don't have to do this. There might be another way.'

'The moon is our best option,' I said. 'He won't think of looking for me there because he knows I can't leave the planet. As a human, I mean.'

'And he's probably the last person in the world to imagine that a human would ever volunteer to become an Echo,' said Rosella, who knew that my uncle saw Echos as commodities and nothing more. I could tell she had come round to the idea.

So I did it.

We went downstairs to the tanks. Strange giant eggs hovering just above the ground. We passed quite a few occupied ones, works in progress for my uncle, I supposed, and then we reached one with the door open.

'You will need to take off your clothes,' Rosella said.

I looked at Daniel. 'Turn round,' I said.

I don't think he understood shyness, or body anxiety, but he turned round.

I got undressed.

'You can do it,' Daniel said, still staring at a distant work table.

'If you are in trouble, knock very hard on the door . . . You can do it – you will be all right,' were Rosella's last words before I stepped inside.

5

The door shut automatically. I was sealed in, and as the cool liquid rose, I began to panic. They couldn't see me. What if I wasn't able to make myself heard? They seemed pretty soundproof, those things.

It rose up. Higher, higher, higher. Feet, waist, neck. Making my skin tingle. I tried to slow my breathing, remembering Mum's yoga lessons. *A slow breath needs a slow mind*, she'd once said. *You need to slow your thoughts. Your mind is always too busy, your attention flits too much. Like a butterfly, you must learn to settle*.

I took my last inhale, feeling the fluid on my chin, at the base of my lips. And then I closed my eyes and held my breath.

I saw Mum and Dad in my mind. I remembered them taking me swimming in Paris on Saturday mornings. Dad used to swim whole lengths underwater. *I think I was a fish in a former life*, he had said.

A former life.

And then I remembered him trying to teach me. Knowing I was scared of being under the water and wanting to combat that.

The way to do it is to try not to think about anything . . . The way to do it is not to try too hard. Just imagine you are nothing. Just be another natural element in the pool.

How long had it been?

It was very difficult to tell. It felt like ten minutes, but it had probably only been one. But then, just as I thought my lungs were about to explode and the panic was setting in, another thing happened. A sharp, searing pain caused by something hard pressing into my shoulder. It was the origin mark. Why hadn't Rosella told me the origin mark was given here, in the tank?

The burning pain was so intense that I opened my mouth to scream. I swallowed a mouthful of that fluid. That sharp, mineral fluid. I banged my arm as hard as I could against the tank, realizing I had about a second.

And then I died.

Or I thought I did.

But sometimes what we think is the end is really just a beginning in disguise.

So I awoke. And I was naked, though Rosella had preserved my modesty and body heat by laying my clothes over me like a blanket.

And Daniel's lips were on mine. And then I choked the fluid out; it burned my throat as it came up. He had exhaled life back into me. I felt weak, physically, but strong in unseen ways. I had been in there just long enough for the fluid to smooth my skin.

'It worked,' said Daniel.

'I am sorry,' Rosella was saying. 'How is your shoulder?'

'It's OK,' I lied. It was burning like hell.

She looked worried. At first I thought it was about my shoulder. But it wasn't. 'Oh my God, the time. He'll be here. Or his Echos will.' Then she looked even more concerned. 'Why aren't they here yet?'

We heard something. A kind of thudding sound. But this wasn't coming from outside.

Daniel looked at me, as curious as I was.

It was coming from one of the tanks.

6

'There was a noise from one of the tanks,' I told Rosella.

The words were like a slap across her face. 'A noise. But that's . . . that's impossible. They haven't been ignited.'

Daniel was confused. 'Why? I was a noise in a tank once.'

'That was different.'

'Are there Echo prototypes in the tank?' he asked.

'Yes, for Castle. But I haven't even started to develop them. I haven't inputted any data. They don't even have igniters. I'm not going to develop them.'

Daniel considered. 'Why not? He won't be happy if you don't give him them.'

Rosella's eyes were filled with bleak defiance, even as the colour drained from her face. 'I no longer care if he is happy or not happy.'

'When are they meant to be ready by?' I asked.

'Tomorrow. This is another reason why you must be gone as soon as possible.'

I saw genuine concern in Daniel's face. 'What are you going to tell him?'

'I will tell him nothing. It is over.'

'You should come with us,' I said, buttoning my top.

Rosella ignored this and went over to a table covered in equipment. She chose a cylindrical object with a copper end, and the indentation of a reverse E on it. I knew instantly what it was.

Another noise from the tanks. Rosella looked worried. She whispered something in Spanish and then said: 'We have no time . . . I should really have got something to block the pain . . .'

'It doesn't matter,' I said, sensing her urgency. 'I can take the pain.'

And so I did. She pressed it onto my skin, turned the end, and I stared straight into Daniel's eyes and he stared straight into mine, and the pain was there, a scorching pain that seared into me, but I could take it because I knew what the pain meant. It meant freedom.

Rosella looked at me as if I was a sweet little child who had just recovered from an operation. 'There. It is o—'

The noise came again. We walked over towards the tank which, like all the others, was thirty centimetres above its electromagnetic stand.

'Wait there,' Rosella told us. 'I am going to check something downstairs. On the computers.'

So she left me and Daniel. Daniel walked towards the tank and I followed him.

I felt that I should say something, so I said: 'Sorry.'

'What are you sorry for?'

'I'm sorry for everything. For being horrid when I first met you. I was wrong to think all Echos were the same.'

He smiled. 'Most are,' he said. 'Most will do whatever they are programmed to do. They don't think about what they are doing. They will do anything they are told to, and only that. They won't know the pleasure of a book – or a kiss – but then, they won't know pain either.

They have no morals. To have morals, they need to experience pleasure and pain. If it is what is expected of them and if they are told by someone who has power over them, they will do anything – even kill.'

'There are humans like that too.' I studied him for a moment. 'So it didn't change you. The operation. The reprogramming . . . what Uncle Alex did to your head . . .'

'I thought it had for a while. But then I realized that I was just the same. The core things that made me who I am weren't to do with programming. There was something else. Something permanent.'

'I feel so guilty. You shouldn't have saved me.'

'Everything has worked out OK. We are—'

There was a fourth noise from inside the tank. Stronger, harder. Daniel looked disconcerted. 'That didn't sound right. That sounded too strong, even for an Echo. Stand back.'

Just as he said that, there was another noise, from a different tank further away. And then a third. 'This is not right,' he repeated.

Right then, Rosella rose back onto our floor on the leviboard, distraught. 'I've been hacked. The computers – he's got into them. Or rather, his hackers have. He's programmed all the Echos. To maximum levels of strength and aggression. Illegal levels. You've got to get out of here. Now. They're strong enough to break out of the tanks, and it's due to happen, and when they do they're programmed to kill all three of us. I've just seen the code. You have to run. Get out of here. Get on a ship to the moon.'

'But what about you?'

'I must stay here,' she said. Her voice sounded calm, but a kind of forced calm. Something was going on that she wasn't telling us; that she wanted to protect us from. Her Spanish accent became stronger but her words stayed quite calm. 'This is my responsibility. I have to be reprogramming the computers. You must go now before it is too late.' But then she said, much louder, 'Go! You must leave! *Vete!*'

But it was already too late, because at that moment a hand burst out of the tank we were standing in front of and grabbed Daniel by the throat. Bursting right out, and leaking restoration fluid.

Daniel couldn't breathe. I turned to the table and grabbed the Echo brander, and pressed the copper end onto the anonymous Echo's wrist as I switched it on. But this Echo was not Daniel. This Echo knew no pain.

I turned back to the table. There were about a hundred instruments I didn't recognize. I saw one that I did. A laser blade. I picked it up, switched it on, and turned to slice through the Echo's wrist. It worked. Dark Echo blood sprayed everywhere. The detached hand stayed clasped around Daniel's throat until he pulled it off. The part of the arm that stayed attached to the otherwise unseen Echo thrashed around violently. Noise started to come from other tanks. From one of them, another hand burst out.

'Go!' Rosella shouted.

There was no way we were going to do that. 'I can't leave you here,' said Daniel. 'You made me. You looked after me.'

'I abandoned you.'

'You had no choice.'

'Go *now*. You've got someone to look after now. Both of you. You've got each other to look after. Sometimes, to save something, you have to lose something. I have nothing to lose. You have each other. If you stayed and died and I survived, I could not live with myself.'

'Rosella,' I said, 'nothing has been your fault.'

'Listen,' she said, leaning forward and pleading with us. 'It is very easy for me to change the program. It is two commands, and I can stop this, but I am not going down there until I know for certain that you are out of here. And once you are, I want you to get in my car and drive to the main hospital in Valencia, the Clínica Quirón de Valencia, and I want you to find my granddad and stay with him and make sure he is safe. Please do that. And get him out of the hospital. I think he is a target too.'

This changed things. Daniel was quick to understand the decision that faced us. The only one he could make with the information we had. 'OK,' he said. 'We'll go and look after him.'

Rosella disappeared down to the basement.

All the occupied tanks were now making noises as the Echos tried to break out. 'Let's go,' I told Daniel.

I held his hand, and we ran past the hands reaching for us as we splashed our way across the increasingly wet floor. We reached the door and voice-commanded it to open, but because of the increasingly thunderous background noise, it took a few fast and frenzied attempts; then we were outside in a baking bright blue-skied world, and we sprinted round the other side of the warehouse to a car. Not a magcar, but a land car. An ancient battered electric one from the 2070s or something.

Daniel broke into it; he knew how to drive it. We had set off down the old dust road no longer made for cars to travel on, when suddenly the outdated-looking holophone on the dashboard started ringing.

'Hello?' said Daniel.

And then we saw Rosella's face in front of us, flickering like a ghost.

7

The hologram of Rosella was looking so calm that at first I thought she'd managed to reprogram the Echos and make them safe. But there was something behind the calmness; something I couldn't quite detect because of the flickering image – an image made faint by the brightness of the sun.

'My granddad is not at the hospital,' she said. 'I had to say that to get you both out of here. He – Ernesto Daniel Márquez – died two weeks ago . . .'

What was she talking about? I looked at Daniel.

All those in the world who still doubt that it is possible for an Echo to feel emotion should have seen Daniel's face at that moment. It would have convinced them in a heartbeat.

'No . . . No . . . You said—'

'*Lo siento mucho de verdad*.' She closed her eyes. She looked a little less calm now. I don't think she even realized she had said that in Spanish. 'I lied, Daniel. I am human. Humans lie. Listen, you don't need to go to Heathrow. London might be too dangerous. There is a spaceport in Barcelona 2. It will be easier. There are fewer checks there. They have Echo shuttles to the moon leaving every night. They will be basic, but that is what life as an Echo is . . .'

We could hear other noises near Rosella. Although we couldn't see it clearly, we were left in no doubt that the Echos had broken free and were heading towards her. To kill her . . .

Daniel stopped the car. 'Get out here,' he told me.

'No,' I said.

'Get out!' he shouted. The first time I'd heard him shout.

I shook my head. I had lost everything once. I wasn't prepared to risk that again. 'You're not going back alone. No way. *No way.* We stay together now. And if you do this, I go with you.'

He saw that there was no point arguing; he turned the car round and started speeding back along the dusty yellow road towards the warehouse.

'Don't come back here,' Rosella was saying. She sounded desperate. She was looking all over the place. 'It is too late, it is too late, it is too late . . . It is over. Don't feel bad for me. *Todo saldrá bien*. I love you, Daniel. You'll look after him, won't you, Audrey? He is your responsibility now. Will you protect him?'

'I will,' I told her. 'I promise.'

We saw a hand grab her shoulder. Rosella closed her eyes as if saying a prayer, and then she said a series of numbers. Some kind of code.

'*Ocho . . . cuatro . . . dos . . . nueve . . . cero . . .*'

As she said those numbers, Daniel whispered them too, with a kind of dread, realizing what was happening. 'Eight-four-two . . .'

'Activate . . . *Activar! Activar!*'

Before I had time to ask Daniel what she was doing, he was screaming, '*No! Rosella! Stop!*'

But it was too late. He could have screamed loud enough to reach Mars and it wouldn't have made any difference. In the space of less than a second, the whole warehouse seemed to implode inwardly in a sudden shrinking rush of motion, and then disappeared completely, as if it had never existed. In its place was a vast and perfectly rectangular hole cut into the dry and dusty landscape, the exact same shape as the warehouse, and Daniel only just stopped the car in time to stop us falling down into the pit, which was exactly as low as the basement had been.

The front of the car must have been only centimetres away from the edge of the hole. There was nothing left of the warehouse or its contents. Well, except for a little black cube sitting on that orange earth in the middle of the hole.

'The Nothing Machine,' Daniel muttered.

He didn't say anything for a long time after that. He just stared out of the front window at the hot shimmering landscape. We could see the dark skeletons of dead trees on the other side of the hole. To the left, past scraggy shrubs and cacti, was Valencia. Its low dull buildings – which all seemed to be run-down warehouses and food markets and apartment blocks – still seemed to wobble in the heat. The city centre magrails were busy. Three of them stretched out across the sea, in different directions.

I stared at the sea. It was so still. That is the weird thing about the sea. The way it seems as still and solid and calm as anything from a distance, but moving and turbulent and dangerous when you're close to it. Yeah. The sea was an illusion. Maybe, if you could get close enough to everything, you'd see that's what the world was full of. Illusions. If you judged things on first appearances, you'd be blind for ever. The way I had been blind to everyone. To Daniel. To Uncle Alex. Maybe even to my parents a little bit.

I still grieved for them. I still felt like there was a hole inside my heart as big as the one in the ground. Grief was the worst thing. And now Daniel was feeling it too.

'She knew,' he spoke eventually.

'Knew what?'

'She knew what was going to happen. She knew it was more than two commands. She knew it was too late. She just lied to save us. A human, dying to save an Echo? Has that ever happened before.'

'You are not a normal Echo, Daniel, and she loved you.'

I saw tears emerge in his eyes. He tried to battle those tears, but they couldn't be stopped. So I just sat there with him, and waited. Trouble would eventually be coming, but I allowed everything to remain still. I sensed he needed to sit there and absorb the pain. To let it all in. If you try and block it – or neuropad it away – that can be unhealthy. You end up becoming empty, your own personal Nothing Machine. He needed to feel what he needed to feel. And I had no choice but to let him.

I watched through the window as a lizard slowly ventured forward towards the new hole in the ground. It seemed curious. It went right up to the edge, jerked its head a few times, then scurried away across the dusty, sun-beaten earth towards the dry, withered scrubland to our right.

After a minute – or two or three or four – Daniel turned to me. The tears had all dried up. His eyes weren't blotchy. Maybe that was an Echo thing. They looked totally clear and green, but there was still the same amount of pain.

'Audrey,' he said, his voice sounding delicate and somehow new. Like his words were porcelain or something. 'Audrey . . . the first time I saw you, when you came to your uncle's house, I looked at you and saw the pain you were feeling, and as I looked at you I felt your pain as if it was my own. And all I wanted to do, all I wanted to do more than anything in the world, was to help you get over that pain.' He looked at me. His eyes were wide and green and real. 'I am scared of you.'

This startled me. '*Scared* of me? Why? Why do I scare you? What are you scared of?'

'I am scared of caring for you, because to care for someone you risk getting hurt. I have wished, sometimes, that I didn't know how to care or worry. I have wished I was like all the others. But I am not like them. I know that. I could never be like them. And – and – and . . . you know what?'

'What?'

'Even now, feeling this pain, I don't want to not be me. Because we have hope, Audrey, don't we? And no matter how terrifying the future becomes, it is worth it. Life is always worth it. I feel alive, Audrey. I must be alive to feel this pain. We have known pain. The physical kind and the other kind. And we are still here. It hasn't finished us off.'

I looked at the fresh scar on my hand. The red E amid newly glossy and perfect skin. Maybe that was what life was. Beyond all the illusions. Just a series of scars.

Yeah. That is how you grew up.

You discovered pain, but far from being crippled by that pain, you were made stronger, because you knew you had survived it. Skin is tougher when it scars. And so the next time pain comes along, you're ready for it. And it made the rest of life shine with hope, the way the scar just highlights the smoothness of the skin around it.

We sat there for quite a while. But then, as the light faded, we drove away.

8

We drove for an hour on the near-trafficless old motorway, with a thousand hopes in our heads.

Two of these hopes were immediate ones.

We hoped that, as soon as Uncle Alex found out about the warehouse, he'd think that we had disappeared with it.

The road was just about driveable, but it obviously hadn't been resurfaced for about fifty years; in some places the tarmac had totally worn away; in others it lay cracked and oozing like some wounded grey-black serpent in the heat.

There were no magrails directly above us. They were all to the east, so we could travel pretty much unseen. Anyway, that wasn't the only danger. Daniel had told me that the motorways were unpoliced; in one way that was good for us, but it also meant that there were bandits around.

At one point we worried because three men and a woman on hover-bikes came up close behind us. They wore black clothes and no helmets.

'If they think we're Echos, they will want to steal us,' Daniel told me. 'Don't let them see the E on your hand.'

The hover-bikes came close, but they couldn't have been that interested – maybe because the car we were driving was so old – and they soon turned off. But still, it made me feel uneasy. And I understood how much danger I would face now that I was an Echo.

The road crossed through a part of a city. Tarragona.

We followed a sign to a supply store. It wasn't a very promising-looking store. We only needed the simplest of things. I needed food or a high-fat juice. Daniel needed sugar. We both needed water.

I don't think I'd ever been to a shop on the ground before. (But then, I had real-world shopped as little as possible, and only really in places like the White Rose back in Yorkshire, and other sky malls.) There were only a couple of aisles.

One of the aisles sold everglows, which told me the kind of place it was, as everglows weren't allowed to be sold in shops anywhere in the world. I went along the aisles, past the chocolate sprays and tapas pills and Sempura mind-wire chargers and medicine patches and sun-factor capsules. We found the sugar and a high-fat juice, but the water, like everywhere in Spain, was sold behind the counter.

Daniel did all the talking, as he was fluent in Spanish. The man who was serving us looked me up and down. He had long blue dreadlocks and a moving tattoo of a silently roaring tiger on his arm. He wasn't wearing a top, and I could see a dull glow in his chest. Everglow addict. He said something to me.

'What did he say?' I asked Daniel.

'He said he needs an Echo girl to look after him.'

I shuddered.

The man smiled as he looked at me, but his eyes weren't looking at me.

'I am just an object now,' I said as we headed for the exit.

'No you're not. You aren't an Echo. I'm not even an Echo.'

'But you were made to be one.'

'Yes. Kind of.'

He told me about Rosella's dead child. He told me the full story of the hair and the locket. 'I am 0.01 per cent human,' he said.

0.01 per cent didn't sound a lot, but right then it sounded like everything. Maybe to be the slightest bit human was to be totally human. Maybe it was like love. You couldn't be a little bit human in the same way you couldn't be a little bit in love. It was all or nothing. A drop was an ocean. And maybe being human wasn't even down to DNA in the end. Maybe it was just about the ability to love, when you knew love was irrational. Yeah. Maybe being human was to make no sense.

'Then neither of us belong,' I replied. *Except to each other*, I thought, but I didn't say that out loud, because it would have made my head explode from embarrassment.

'My uncle probably thinks we're dead by now,' I said as we left the heavy humid air of the store for the brighter heat outside.

'I hope so.' I could see from the way Daniel said it that he didn't really believe it.

I drank a bit of the juice. It was disgusting. It had gone off in the heat. I had to leave it. My stomach rumbled.

We travelled the last short distance to Barcelona 2. The city, from the road anyway, seemed the exact opposite of Valencia: modern (nothing there was more than fifty years old, obviously), and everything was bright and the buildings were in the sky and glowed turquoise and green and blue against the increasing night. The blue was a giant Castle logo, a giant hologram floating in the sky. I stared up at it and felt like Uncle Alex was watching me. I shuddered. I had no doubt that if he ever saw me again, or even found out that I was alive, then I would be dead, and so would Daniel. The spaceport was a little to the north, so we kept driving.

I looked at Daniel as he drove. He would never age. He would look like this for ever. That was frightening. After all, I would not look like me for ever. I would age. That's what humans did. And no amount of keratin could stop me from being human. If I ever got to turn forty or eighty or 150, I would look and feel my age.

And what did Echos do? They stayed the same. Sure, after ten years they were meant to be replaced by newer models, but it was perfectly possible – with the right care – for an Echo to go on indefinitely. So, if my future was with this Echo boy, then one day I would be a hundred years old, and he would still be looking sixteen. Once an Echo boy, always an Echo boy.

Yes, it was frightening. But I was fed up with being frightened. I had been frightened of Daniel himself not so long ago. Maybe you could only live life by heading towards the things that frightened you.

See, most of my life I had spent looking forward, thinking of going to Oxford and pleasing my parents. Wondering how I would go on pleasing them as an adult, when Mum wanted me to be successful and to have money and Dad wanted me to live like him – on principles alone.

Then, these last days, I had been consumed by the past. It had kept trying to to suffocate me. I'd either been as good as dead with neuropads or wanting to be dead without them.

But right then, I wasn't thinking of either past or future. I was living in the present, and it felt as intense and real as the sky ahead, and the giant illuminated shuttle we could just about see on the horizon.

Daniel. Mind-log 4.

1

We were halfway to the moon. We had been travelling for four hours, forty-eight minutes and fifteen seconds.

It was far from perfect.

We were cramped, as Echos should expect to be. There were 308 other Echos in the shuttle.

The ratio of nitrogen and oxygen in the air was slightly wrong. The air was closer to eighty per cent than seventy-nine per cent nitrogen. It was making me feel tired, and I knew Audrey felt even tireder, but she knew she had to stay awake for most of the journey in order not to arouse suspicion.

She probably needed a bit more than the sugar solution that was the only available nourishment.

'It's a small price,' she had whispered. 'I'll be OK.'

It must have been weird for her, knowing that she was the only human there. But it was weird for me too. I didn't belong with those others. They could just sit on the communal long seats facing each other and stare blankly ahead at the inside walls of the aeroshell. They had no interest in looking out of the small windows at the planet we had just left. The blue cloud-swirled sphere full of 13,428,602,881 humans and 6,290,000,000 (precise number unknown) Echos, all living side by side but at an infinite distance from each other.

'Why was he so evil?' she said quietly. 'Uncle Alex, I mean. I don't think my dad had any idea.'

'I don't know,' I said. 'Maybe you will find out one day. Humans seem very complicated.'

'Part of me thinks it's best not to know. I just hope Dad never knew, either . . . I worry that something happened when they were kids . . . Something I'll never know about.'

'Please, Audrey, stop worrying. That's the past. We have no control over that. But the future is ours . . .'

'Yeah,' she said sleepily. 'The future is ours . . .'

Eventually she could fight it no longer. She fell asleep on my shoulder. Her breathing slowed to ten breaths per minute. There was a female Echo opposite me who observed this. She had a shaven head and was designed for strength. I smiled at her. 'She missed her last recharge,' I explained, on Audrey's behalf.

Audrey had spoken to me about her doubts before we got on the shuttle, back at the spaceport. She was worried that, even with her new smooth skin, she didn't look good enough.

'Even old, wrinkly Echos are old and wrinkly in a perfect way,' she said. 'They never quite look human.'

She was worried that she was imperfect, even by human standards. She talked about her shoulders and her nose and the way she walked. I began to realize that humans have a very distorted view of themselves, as nothing she said about her appearance matched the reality.

Most of the other Echos were on their way to manual labour jobs, judging from their size (thirty were in fact exactly the same model – of a large male with a mohawk, and I was pretty sure I was the only prototype among them). When I first got on the vessel, I was startled to find 15 there, taking his seat opposite me but further along. Only of course, it wasn't 15. Or rather, it was one of probably 5,000 15s in the world.

I had to protect Audrey, and she had to protect me.

Neither of us now belonged with those we were meant to be part of. We were going to have to be a world unto ourselves, a universe of two, and that was good. Well, it was infinitely better than being a universe of one.

She was everything.

She was hope and fear and love and pain.

She was as alive as anyone had ever been alive. And being alive meant possibility and uncertainty. Life was irrational, and irrationality could never be mapped. So in each life – each true life – there were lots of other lives branching out, like the garden of forking paths I had once read about. And loving someone was a process of helping that person find the best of those possible lives, and helping them live it.

She carried on sleeping.

I no longer saw Earth out of the window now. It was just the deep darkness of space, punctured by brilliant white stars. Distant suns, the nearest of which I knew was 4.2421 light years away. Yet we could see them. My mind wandered, the way Echo minds weren't supposed to. Light was like hope, I thought. It took a long time to get there, but it always got there in the end, if you let it keep going.

And then it came into view.

Our destination, New Hope Colony.

A vast dome, next to the dark basalt of the Sea of Tranquillity, covering a surface area of 938 square kilometres. Lights twinkled; streets crisscrossed in neat geometric patterns, and were filled with cheaply made buildings; holo-ads glowed; and the magrails were only half complete.

As we sank down towards the spaceport (2.7 kilometres outside the dome, but connected via a long transparent tunnel full of slow-moving moon traffic), I caught sight of the northern suburb of Aldrin, the place where we were going to live. It was the darkest part, badly lit and with many still-unoccupied homes. Sixty-eight per cent unoccupied. (Implanted information filled my mind every time we came to a new place. And there were few places that were newer than Aldrin, or even New Hope.) It shouldn't have looked very promising, and it couldn't have been further away from the leafy green streets and mansions of north London, but that's the funny thing about freedom, and happiness. It doesn't always look like you expect it to look. But still, I recognized it when I saw it.

I gently nudged Audrey awake. 'Audrey, we are here now.'

She woke up slowly. Blinked away the sleep from her eyes. For two seconds, I don't think she knew where she was, or what she had to pretend to be.

'Where?' she asked.

And I said a word I had never said before. A word that felt wonderful to say:

'Home. We are home.'

And Audrey smiled, though as the craft touched the ground there was a slight fear in her eyes, as there must have been in my own. But it wasn't like the fears we had experienced before. The fears that had nearly overwhelmed us. No, this was just the fear of not knowing what lay in store for us. The fear that came from realizing that the future couldn't ever be known, because it contained so many different paths and possibilities. It was the most pleasurable kind of fear, and was coupled with hopeful excitement.

She looked out at that barren grey landscape, towards a smaller dome, in the distance, just inside the dry, dead Sea of Tranquillity. Half a kilometre across. There was what seemed to be grass there, within that dome. Crops. It looked like a farm. They were actually trying to do the impossible: to grow things out of the moon's lifeless crust.

In a way, that is what we would be trying to do. Not work on a farm exactly – though we wouldn't rule it out (we wouldn't rule anything out) – but to create a life out of nothing.

She squeezed my hand. Nine minutes and thirty-seven seconds later, we were about to step out, into air that felt a lot fresher and purer than the air in the shuttle.

'This is where we begin,' I said. 'Are you ready?'

'Yes,' she said as we stepped onto the leviboard. 'I am ready.'